Angel B

"Provocatively intense and hard to put down!"
~ Nikki Urban Author of
Sex Confessions

The Tase
Men Series

THE
LAST
FIRST
Kiss

VOLUME 4
THE TASE MEN SERIES

angel b

THE
LAST
FIRST

Written By

Angel B

ISBN- 13: 9780988736061

The Last First Kiss
Copyright © 2019 Angel B
Written and published in the USA

Printed in U.S.A.

A LETTER FROM THE AUTHOR

February 14, 2019

I want to thank everyone who was patiently waiting for me to drop my next novel. I know it's been a long wait, but life has a way of getting in the way. I'm only happy that I made it through the storm and over all the obstacles in my way. I promise that I have more to come. In the mean time, I hope you enjoy The Last First Kiss: Volume 4 of the Tase Bother's Series, and allow Daniel and Emily to share their story.

Warmest Regards,

angel b

A NOTE TO MY READERS

Dear Reader,

I hope you are enjoying reading about the Tase Men Brothers. I trust you can agree that they are an amazing group of handsome, professional, passionate, and most importantly, honest men. I felt that it was important to lift the stereotype of African American men, which is why I began writing uplifting and powerful stories portraying them in a positive manner.

Each member of the Tase family plays a significant role that binds the family together tightly. Their love and trust in each other comes without question, making them a unbreakable force to reckon with. These brothers have a story to tell and im hoping that you are ready to let me take your mind on a journey as these men capture your heart and soul in The Tase Men series.

I love to hear from readers and I welcome your comments about the Tase family from Pennsylvania. Who do you want to hear about next? Who is your favorite character, and what do you like most about him or her? Send me an email and let me know at angelb@yahoo.com.

Until next time,

angel b

Books By Angel B

The Tase Men Series
Loving Rainy Days: Vol 1
Michael's Heat: Vol 2
Up For The Chase: Vol 3
The Last First Kiss: Vol 4

Child Support: Taken From Me & My Daughter's Invisible Father
Unstable Creature
Accusations

EBOOKS
The 7th Commandment
Birthday Sex: How To Love A Remington (Prequal)
Birthday Sex: The New Hire

I Must Be Crazy Series
My Masked Lover: Episode 1
Teacher's Pet: Episode 2
Daily Dose: Episode 3
Cold Heat: Episode 4

CONTACT INFORMATION:

angel b

Website: freeyormind31.wixsite.com/angelb
Email: angelb@yahoo.com
Author Central: amazon.com/author/angelbearfield

Facebook: www.facebook.com/AngelBearfield
Twitter:@freeyormind31
Instagram: freeyormind31

SYNOPSIS

No more pretending to be someone you're not.
Emily Bawler has only been interested in women since high school.
Then why does she keep having this undeniable yearning for a man?
But not just any man. These yearnings are for someone she considers
a dear friend; a brother even. She believes she should let the feeling
pass and try to move on. Yet, her heart won't let her.

The fear of rejection can cause you to miss out on happiness.
Daniel Tase was stuck between a rock and a hard place. For years
he's been in love with someone he shouldn't. It was a secret he's
kept from his family and from her. But, it's getting harder and harder
to keep his secret, especially when the object of his affection comes
knocking on his front door.

The signs of love are blurred by obsession.
Sherry Woods is on cloud nine. From the first moment she and
Emily lay eyes on each other they were in love. Well, at least in her
mind. Sherry is an erotomanic. She suffers from a delusional belief
that a person is in love with her, despite contrary evidence. Filled
with an uncommon form of paranoid delusion, she will do everything
in her power to make Emily hers, including murder.

Will having Emily close push Daniel to throw caution to the wind
and go for what he wants? Will invading Daniel's comfort zone allow
Emily to see that her feelings are shared? Or will they both run out of
time when an enraged Sherry steps in to claim what's hers.

Definition: Erotomania is a delusional belief that a person is in love
with the affected individual, despite contrary evidence. Erotomania is
an uncommon form of paranoid delusion. The affected person
strongly believes that another individual is in love with him or her.

My Awareness...

"I stood there like an idiot and waited. My back began to tingle as he stepped closer, and when he whispered close to my ear, I believe my heart stopped beating for a full minute."

"Was it Daniel?" asked Rainy.

"What did he say," asked Tara, her attention focused on Emily's every word.

Emily smiled with a far away look in her eyes. She was remembering that moment like it happened last night. It was the night she became aware of men. Of him.

"I can tell you, it definitely felt different. At first we had a respectable distance between us, but before long he drew me in closer, and for the first time I felt real desire. It was so amazing," she said with a giggle.

"We danced all night long. I knew I should leave because of my recital, but I couldn't pull myself away from him. We didn't speak a word. We just danced close. And I mean we were close. It was the first time I felt a man's 'you know what' pressed up against me," she said, and laughed.

"Did he kiss you?" asked Rainy, caught up in her story.

Emily smiled.

The Last First Kiss

Chapter One

The sorrowful sound coming from the violin hid no secrets to the emotions flowing through Emily Bawler as she freed her mind and soul to her music. Her eyes were closed and her posture was straight as she sat perched on the edge of the chair. The studio was completely dark except for a single light above her, gracing the top of her head like a halo.

Nothing and no one could intrude upon the cocoon of wondrous yet, bittersweet melodies flowing around her. She was lost in a cloud. A cloud that bore sadness and confusion. Sadness from a loss of direction and confusion about things she didn't have the answers to. Things she would need help sorting out.

The last note eased across the strings in a miserable hum and Emily sat silently, the violin still tucked beneath her chin. After a while her body began to relax and she let the instrument slide down into her lap. Her head dropped down low and a single tear rolled across her cheek.

"What is wrong with me?" she whispered softly to the empty room.

She swiped at the tear that had rolled under her chin and inhaled deeply. Looking around the darkened room, she felt anger rise inside her. She had come into the studio to practice just like she did every Friday, and just like before, the piece she was supposed to be playing changed from a cheerful love ballet to a sad mournful plea. Sometimes she wouldn't even realize the change until she had completed the last note. This *thing* that she was going through was affecting her music and she didn't like it.

Standing, she moved over to her violin case and carefully placed the violin and bow in the soft red velvet bed. She ran her hands over the rich dark wood lovingly, wishing she could play what was on the music sheets without her emotions taking over and changing it. She was staring down at the violin, almost in a daze when she heard a noise.

She lifted her head abruptly. "Is someone there?" she called out.

"Yeah, it's me Emily," said Laurie turning on the lights. She walked quickly into the room with her always present smile. "We're driving across the bridge to Jersey to Diamondz N DA Ruff Café to grab a bite to eat and perhaps get a little drunk. Who knows, maybe I'll get lucky," she said, wiggling her arched red eyebrows. "You in? It's karaoke night and then dancing afterwards," she said smiling.

Emily had been thinking about going home to mope around her apartment, but the thought really didn't appeal to her. Sipping on a glass of chilled wine and stuffing her face while laughing with her co-workers sounded like something she needed.

"Yeah, I'm in. Let me get my things and lock this place up."

"Okay, cool," said Laurie.

Laurie watched as Emily stacked her music sheets and placed them into a black leather binder. After sliding on her red jacket, she closed the violin case and lifted it from the stool.

"I'm ready," Emily said, walking towards her.

Emily locked the classroom door behind her and they both headed for the exit. She didn't have a car because it was easier to use the subway or Uber. Laurie practically lived out of her car and couldn't think of living without the little silver Acura Hybrid.

"Where is everyone?" asked Emily as she placed her violin in the trunk.

Laurie climbed in behind the wheel and started the car. When Emily slid into the passenger seat she locked the doors.

"They left already in Mark's car. He has Karen, Gail and Bobby with him. We'll meet up with them in a bit," she said, pulling out of the parking lot and into traffic.

By the time they made it across the bridge and to the lounge, the music from inside could be heard outside as a few people were entering. As they followed them inside, a light misty rain began to fall, making Emily glad that she'd worn a jacket with a hood.

Inside, the place was packed. Upstairs, trays of good smelling food were being carried by the staff and drinks were constantly being poured at the bar. There was a woman on stage trying her damndest to be Kelly Rowland singing *Ice*.

"Over there!" Laurie yelled over the music.

She pointed to the table near the back and they began to maneuver their way through the crowded floor. Mark was the first to see them and signaled to the others of their arrival.

"What took you two so long? They're about to close the kitchen and open up the dance floor downstairs," said Mark bobbing his head to the screeching sound of the woman belting out high notes through the microphone.

"Traffic," said Laurie. She and Emily shrugged out of their jackets and hung them on the back of their chairs. "I need a drink," she said, waving down a waiter.

"What can I get you?" asked the woman holding a notepad. She rocked a short hair cut that was slamming. She addressed her question to Laurie, but her attention was focused on Emily.

"I want a rum and coke. Emily, what do you want?"

Emily was laughing at the woman on stage. She turned to face them when she heard her name. She looked up and saw the waitress smiling at her. "Oh, I'll just have a Sangria, easy on the Brandy, please."

The waitress jotted down the name of the drink, hesitating only for a brief second before leaving to place the order.

"Seems like someone has an admirer," said Mark laughing.

"Oh, you peeped that too. She was all up in her grill," said Bobby, joining in with a loud cackle.

Gail leaned back in her chair and shook her head. "You guys are ruthless. Can't you see you're embarrassing her?"

"Yeah, leave her alone," said Karen, joining in the defense of her friend.

"It's cool girls. I'm used to this kind of treatment. They just mad nobody's checking them out," said Emily smiling. She stood abruptly and pulled a few dollars from her jacket pocket.

"Where are you going?" asked Laurie.

"To get my drink and sit at the bar," she said, then disappeared into the crowd.

Laurie watched her go with a slight frown on her face. When she lost sight of her, she turned to face the others. "Have any of you noticed how Emily's been acting different lately?"

"What do you mean, different?" asked Gail. She pushed a strand of her long blonde hair behind her ear and leaned in to make sure she could hear what Laurie was saying.

"You know. Like preoccupied or distracted," said Laurie glancing at each of them.

"Only thing I've noticed is that she hasn't been going out with us lately," said Mark. "I mean, I was totally shocked that she showed up tonight."

"Me too," said Bobby. "The last time she came out she was upset about something. She never did say what it was. I think something's bothering her, but she's keeping it all bottled up."

"Maybe one of us should try and talk to her about it." Karen made the statement, but she was staring right at Laurie.

"Well, I know that look," Laurie said sighing. "Alright, I'll ask her tomorrow to see what she says. I won't push though. Everyone is entitled to their secrets."

"I feel you on that," said Gail.

Just then, the announcer let everyone know the dance floor was open downstairs. It seemed like everyone stood up all at once and started making their way down the narrow steps. The music was bumping louder than before and the club song *Follow Me* was blaring through the surround system. All through the lounge you could hear women and men yelling *'That's my song'* as they danced their way below.

Emily sat on a bar stool nursing her Sangria. It was cold and sweet, and had just enough orange juice and fruit in it. She wasn't much of a drinker, but this little concoction was something she could handle. She sat there bobbing her head to the music with her body swaying side to side. She closed her eyes, letting the familiar song ease away her stress.

Feeling the need for another sip, she looked down to pick up her glass only to realize she had damn near finished it.

"Can I buy you another?"

Emily looked to her left to see a woman leaning against the bar watching her. She was tall and light skinned, with low sexy eyes. She was rocking all black tonight and it made her look mysterious. Usually, Emily would get a pang of interest, but for a long time now she hadn't found anyone interesting enough to date. *Or is it that you're just not into women like you thought?*

Even though Emily never responded, the woman moved closer.

7

"Hey, let me get a light beer and another of whatever she's having," she called out to the barkeep.

The bartender nodded and rushed off to make Emily's drink. He returned, placing the woman's beer on a napkin and then the Sangria in front of Emily. He removed the empty glass and took the cash from the woman before ambling off to help the next customer.

"Thank you," said Emily as she sipped from her straw. *No need to be rude and cheat myself out of a free drink.*

"You're very welcome," the woman said, reaching for her beer.

Emily didn't say a word. She just sat there looking into the mirror that was behind the bar. She could see her friends standing up to make their way downstairs to get their groove on.

"Are you going to make me ask?" asked the woman.

Emily knew what she wanted and smiled, still not looking at her.

"Only if you want to know," she teased.

The woman smiled shyly and looked down. When she looked up, she had a little more confidence in her stare. "What's your name?"

"Emily Bawler," she answered, still looking into the mirror.

"I'm Sherry Woods."

Then nothing.

Emily didn't respond at all. She kept her focus on the crowd behind her. Suddenly, a guy popped up on her right. He was already holding a glass when he moved in towards Emily.

"Hey gorgeous! Let me buy you a drink," he said a little too loud. You could clearly see that he was drunk.

"She already has one," Sherry said, now standing directly behind Emily. Emily didn't even see Sherry move from her side.

"Oh, my bad little Momma. I didn't know she was yours," he said with a slur.

"You should move away now," Sherry said, her tone hard as steel.

"Okay, okay," the guy said with his hands raised in the air. He turned and disappeared into the crowd.

Using the mirror, Emily looked over at Sherry with her eyebrows raised.

"Sorry about that," Sherry said, claiming the seat next to Emily. "Some people don't know their limit and it turns them into disrespectful idiots."

Emily smiled and nodded. "True."

"So, Emily. What do you do?" she asked, jumping right back into getting to know her.

Emily chuckled and shook her head. "I'm a teacher at Julliard. I instruct the advanced violin class. What about you?"

Sherry's smile broadened when Emily asked her a question about herself. The nervous flutter she felt deep in her stomach began to ease and she felt a little more relaxed. When she first approached her sitting at the bar, she was a bit tense. It's been a long time since she's been out trying to mingle and she considered herself lucky to have met such a beautiful woman her first night out. *This is a sign it's meant to be.*

"I'm a Customs Agent Officer at the airport. I handle all the data that comes in and observe the scans on anything they target as a threat."

"Wow, that's interesting," said Emily, genuinely interested. "Is it dangerous?"

Sherry smiled widely seeing she had impressed her. "It's cool. It gets a little hectic every now and then, but I manage."

Taking a few swallows from her bottle, Sherry felt the urge to dig deeper. "Do you have any sisters or brothers?"

What a strange question to ask someone you've just met at the bar, Emily thought. "I have a brother," she answered after taking a sip from her straw.

Sherry smiled even wider. "So do I. He's been away for a while, but he's back now. I guess we have that in common." When Emily looked confused she explained. "That we both have brothers."

"Oh, yeah. That's true," Emily said, getting bored with the conversation.

The music downstairs was blaring loudly and a song came on that Emily liked. She started swaying to the music and nodding her head. Feeling the need to exert some pent up energy and to stop Sherry's list of questions, she hopped up from her stool. With a quick wink she left Sherry at the bar and headed for the stairs.

Emily started dancing as she made her way to the center of the floor. The soothing effect of the two Sangria's began easing the tension in her body and she forced the rest out with every shake and dip she made on the floor. Her eyes were half closed as she allowed the rhythm and base coming from the speakers to increase her heartbeat and help her loosen up.

While dancing, she noticed the same woman from the bar heading in her direction. She kept dancing as Sherry moved up to her and fell in step with her. They danced to several songs moving against each other in a sensual way that had Sherry eyes narrowed and her gaze locked on Emily's body.

Emily didn't see any harm in dancing with the woman. She knew it meant nothing and would be forgotten as soon as she left the lounge. She was enjoying herself until a song came on that caused memories to flash through her mind. Memories of a family cookout and the fun she'd had dancing with Daniel. With those memories came the reminder of her situation and her dance steps begin to falter.

Instantly, her mood turned sour and she decided to leave. She turned quickly and made her way back to the stairs. She pushed through the packed dance floor mumbling a few *'excuse me's'* as she passed by.

Feeling a bit flushed from dancing and the sudden onslaught of emotions brought on by memories of Daniel, Emily headed in the direction of the bathroom. She felt relief in noticing that for once there wasn't a long line of women waiting with impatient expressions. Quickly making her way over to the sink, she turned on the cold water and splashed the cool liquid on her cheeks.

After feeling her body cool down, she turned off the faucet and lifted her head. She was about to turn and grab a paper towel when a generous amount was placed into her hand. She patted her face dry and then looked over to see who she needed to thank.

A woman was standing beside her. Her hair was whipped up in one of those feather cuts that hung to the left leaving the right side shaved close. The zig zag design enhanced the cut and only complimented the woman's beautiful features.

Neither said a word as they sized each other up. Emily's glance did a swift take of the woman and her keen eye took in the designer clothes and the bling of her jewelry. She also took note that she didn't know her, yet the woman was staring like she did.

"Thank you," Emily said, remembering the tissue she now tossed in the trash can.

The woman didn't say anything for a moment. Then, as if she'd made up her mind about something, she nodded her head.

"That woman you had a drink with and was dancing with down stairs... Take my advice and keep away from her. Run the other fucking way, because once she's got her eyes set on you, she will tear your life apart."

Emily frowned. "What do you mean?" she asked out of curiosity.

"Consider yourself warned," said the woman before she turned and left.

Emily was standing there confused and wondering if the woman had been an ex-girlfriend or something. *Well, it doesn't matter one way or the other because im not interested.* Taking one last look at herself in the mirror, Emily decided she was ready to leave.

Not knowing what went wrong, Sherry took off after Emily, but lost her in the crowd. When she finally got back upstairs, she found Emily sliding on her jacket.

"You're leaving already?"

Emily looked up at Sherry surprised to see she'd followed her. *Take my advice and keep away from her.* "Oh, yeah. I need to be somewhere," she said as she zipped her jacket up.

A brief look of disappointment crossed Sherrys' face, but she hid it quickly. "Well, do you think I could have your phone number so I can call you?" Sherry heard a slip of desperation in her voice, but overlooked it. She felt a connection with Emily and wasn't about to let her slip through her fingers.

Emily didn't even break stride as she turned and headed for the door. Sherry was right on her heels.

"I'm sorry Sherry, but no. I didn't come here to meet anyone. I just wanted to unwind a little. You know, loosen up."

"Oh." The dejected look on Sherrys' face was almost comical. Slowly she felt the rejection turning to anger, but Emilys' next words cooled her right down.

"Don't worry," Emily said as she stepped up to the exit. She looked back over her shoulder at Sherry and winked. "There's always tomorrow," she said, smiling before she slipped into the night.

A moment later, Sherry stepped outside to draw in a deep breath of fresh air. She had been upset, but now she was smiling again. Emily had just given her the okay to pursue her. That small sliver of hope was enough to fill her with happiness. She knew in her heart that she and Emily had formed a bond and she wasn't going to let anyone ruin what they now had together.

"You got shut down, huh?" said a voice from the shadows. Sherry turned to see a man leaning against a tree. His drunken slur made it almost hard to understand him. Almost. "It's because you don't have all the right tools," he said grabbing his crotch snickering.

Sherry recognized him as the man that had approached them at the bar being rude. "Mind your business," she replied and turned to watch as Emily slid into a cab.

The man reared back and laughed loudly. "You see, that's the problem with you dyke bitches. You think just because you cut your hair, and dress and talk like a man, that you *are* a man. But you're not. You're still a woman. And without one of these," he said, grabbing his crotch again. "You will never be a man. Never. You'll keep failing just like tonight," he said mockingly, with a hard stare.

Sherry turned to face him. "You think because you have that small flaccid penis between your legs you're a man?" She laughed and shook her head. "You're pathetic. You all are," she said as she approached him, joining him in the shadows.

"If you come over here I'm going to give you something to remind you that you're a woman," he said as he unzipped his pants. He slipped his hand inside and pulled his shaft free. He began stroking it as he watched her continue to move closer.

"That's right. You know you want this dick," he said as he glided his hand over the now hardened flesh.

Sherry didn't even look down as he pleasured himself in front of her. When she was only a few steps away, her hand reached up behind her back and in one smooth, swift movement she yanked the blade from its sheath. There was only a brief shimmer of light from the metal as the sharp blade sliced through its muscled target.

Before the man could scream out in agony, Sherry stepped closer and shoved the blade directly under his chin and twisted. All that could be heard was a soft gurgling sound as the man choked and made bubbles from his own blood.

When she felt the weight of his body begin to lean into her, Sherry yanked out the blade and shoved him backwards away from her. He stumbled backwards and fell further behind the tree. His body was well hidden by the darkened alleyway.

Sherry pulled a wad of tissue from her pocket and cleaned off the knife and the small splatter of blood that she'd gotten on her hand. She returned the knife to its hiding place, shoved the tissue back in her pocket, and stared into the inky darkness where his body now lay.

"I'll never let a man treat me like that again. Never again," she whispered to herself. Then an image of Emily came to mind and she smiled. She looked back down to where she knew the man's body was hidden in the shadows and her smile broadened. "I guess the better man won," she said before she turned and walked back into the lounge.

****

After leaving the lounge Emily hailed the first cab she saw. She slid onto the cracked leather seat and cringed at the heavy smell of air freshener. She eased her window down a little finding relief as she pulled in a clean breath of air. Feeling a slight headache coming on, she leaned back and closed her eyes.

"Where to Miss?" the driver asked as he peeked at her through his rear view mirror.

"Just drive, please. I'll let you know in a minute."

"Okay."

The driver began moving through the traffic at a moderate pace. With the cool breeze left behind from the rain touching her face Emily leaned back trying to gain control of her emotions. She felt confused, agitated, and weighed down by her feelings. Suddenly, a tear slid down her cheek and she reached up to wipe it away.

"What's happening to me?" she whispered the question softly in the back seat not caring if the driver heard her.

Her thoughts settled on the reason for her unsettled nerves and she tightened her hands in her lap. The image of Daniel played with her mind as she imagined his lips pressed against her own. She closed her eyes as she envisioned the kiss deepening while his arms wrapped around her waste closing the gap between them.

A slight moan eased from between her parted lips capturing the driver's attention.

"Are you okay back there, Miss?"

The sound of the driver's voice made Emily's eyes pop open in alarm. She was totally embarrassed that for a moment she had forgotten where she was.

"Yes, I'm fine." Knowing she couldn't ride around in the back of the cab all night, she made up her mind on what to do. She needed to talk to someone before she lost her damn mind.

After checking the time, she pulled out her cell phone to call Stacey. She and Stacey had become really close over the years and she needed a friendly ear to confide in. The phone rung four times and just when she was about to give up, she heard her answer.

"Hello?"

Emily was relieved. "Hey, Stacey."

"Emily! How are you?" Stacey asked with laughter. She lifted her glass of wine and took a little sip.

Emily didn't want to intrude on her night, but she really needed someone to talk to. "Are you busy?"

It was something in Emily's voice that caught Stacey's attention and she stood up to leave the room taking her glass with her. She was with Tara, and they had dropped by unannounced to Rainys' house for a visit. Sabrina had dropped by to pick up Jordan earlier, but had returned for his favorite toy. Now they all were relaxing in the living room working through a bottle of wine.

"Excuse me guys. I'm going to take this in the other room," Stacey said as she made her way to the den. After shutting the door she lifted the phone back to her ear. "What's wrong, Emily?"

Emily started crying again and this time she didn't care if the cab driver noticed. "I don't know. I think I've done something stupid," she said sniffing.

Beginning to get worried that Emily was in some kind of trouble, Stacey started pacing back and forth. "What have you done that you think is stupid?" she asked, trying to speak in a calm voice even though she wanted to blurt it out loud. For a minute she didn't think she was going to answer, but then she heard her reply in a small voice.

"I fell in love."

Stacey let the air out her lungs not even sure when she started holding it in. "Isn't falling in love a good thing?" she asked, taking a large gulp of the wine from her glass.

Emily nodded her head, forgetting that Stacey couldn't see her. "Yes, but I'm in love with a man."

Emily's statement came just as Stacey was trying to swallow the wine. The shock from what she said made her spit the wine from her lips. "What!?" *Oh my goodness. I'm so happy this is white wine and not red,* she thought as she patted the wetness from her shirt.

After gaining her composure Stacey placed the glass on a side table and took a seat in one of the leather chairs. "Emily, did you say you were in love with a man?"

"Mm hmm."

"But I, uh… I thought you were… gay," Stacey said quietly. She didn't want anyone walking by to hear her.

"Me too, but for the past few years I haven't been interested in any women. I don't acknowledge them at all. Instead, my attention has been on…him."

Trying to take it all in and make sense of it, Stacey noticed Emily hadn't said the man's name yet. He was probably someone she'd met at her job. "And who is this guy that you've fallen in love with?"

After a long pause, Emily decided to just get it out. "It's Daniel," she said and smiled, feeling better at finally telling someone else her big secret.

"Daniel!" Stacey sat up straight in her chair smiling. "Oh shit!"

"Yeah, oh shit is right. What am I going to do Stacey? He doesn't even know how I feel about him."

Stacey was still in awe over the news. "Well, first you need to make sure this is what you really want and that you're not just trying to test the waters."

Emily's hand lifted and rested on her chest. She could feel her heartbeat fluttering rapidly against her palm. She got that same feeling every time her thoughts drifted to Daniel. "Yes. I'm sure."

Stacey stood up in excitement. "Okay, then the next thing to do is come up with a plan."

Feeling a bit of comfort from having Stacey's help, Emily began to smile. "Can I come over so we can talk more?"

"Oh shoot. I'm not home. I'm at Rainys' house with Tara."

"Oh."

Hearing the deflated sound of Emily's voice, Stacey came up with a better plan. "You should come here," she blurted out excitedly. "We're all here and you could use the advice and ideas from everyone."

Emily thought for a moment and then hunched her shoulders. *What do I have to lose? I have no idea what to do anyway.* "Okay. I'm on my way."

Stacey picked up her glass and headed for the door. "Good. I'll let everyone know you're coming, but I won't say anything about Daniel until you get here."

Emily felt relief knowing she wouldn't be alone to deal with her torture. "Alright, and thank you Stacey."

"You don't have to thank me Emily. You were there for me when

I was all messed up over Chase, and I intend to be there for you. That's what friends are for, right?"

Smiling, Emily nodded. "Yes, that's right. I'll see you soon then. Bye."

"Bye."

When the call ended, Emily sat smiling out the window. "Excuse me, sir. I know where I want to go now."

"Okay. Where to?" the man asked, thankful she'd finally made up her mind.

Emily gave the man Rainy's address in Pennsylvania and he glanced back at her in the mirror.

"That's a long drive Miss. Are you sure you want to go that far? It'll be expensive."

"Don't worry about the cost. Just get me there as fast as you can without killing me," she said, smiling broadly.

The driver laughed and turned off his *on duty* light. "Don't worry Miss. My wife and I just had a son and I plan to spend every day watching him grow into a man."

"That's good to hear," Emily said with a smile on her lips. "And congratulations"

"Thank you Miss. Thank you," the driver replied with a huge grin.

Emily knew he must be thinking about his family and a warm glow surrounded her when her thoughts drifted back to Daniel. *I wonder what it's like to kiss his lips.*

Chapter Two

"Baby, you hear that?"

Rainy continued to place the vanilla wafer cookies on top of the large dish of banana pudding. She knew it was Miki's favorite so she decided to make it for him. It would be the perfect dessert for tomorrows dinner. *If I can keep him out of it.*

"Hear what?" she replied smiling. *I know that tone.*

"Nothing. Absolutely nothing," he said, moving up behind her and wrapping his arms around her waist. "There's no one here yelling Mommy or Daddy. We…" A kiss on the neck. "Are." A kiss to the shoulder. "All." A nuzzle on the ear. "Alone."

Rainy moaned, wiped her hands on a towel and turned to face her sexy husband. "That's because your mother came and took Jordan home with her for the weekend," she said sliding her hands over his shoulders. "Now I have no one to play with."

Miki smiled down at her. "You can always play with me," he said pressing into her.

"Mmm…" Rainy leaned in further feeling her breast strain against her shirt. "And exactly what will you allow me to play with?" she asked as her lips grazed lightly over his.

The warmth of Rainy's breath fluttered across his lips and he felt his lower region become heavy. Knowing he had just come from working out he eased back from her.

"How about I go take a shower and when I'm done, I'll show you in detail exactly what part I'll let you play with. I mean, if you're up to it?"

Her eyes dropped down low to see his shaft making a rather large attempt at breaking free of his sweats. *Damn, I love a man in sweats.* She reached down and stroked him firmly through his pants, causing him to groan. "Oh, I'm up to it. Just make sure you stay up to it."

Miki smiled sexily and backed away slowly. "I'll need fifteen minutes to shower, but if you're not upstairs by then, I'm coming back down here for you. You got that?" he called over his shoulder as he headed towards the door.

She laughed. "Yeah, I got it."

Rainy shook her head after he left. Her heart felt full with love and she knew she owed it all to him. He never missed a day to tell her he loved her and to thank her for giving him their son Jordan. And then there were the days when he would make love to her and pamper her for hours. Inhaling deeply she let out her breath in a quick whoosh. *He was so good in bed.*

Knowing Miki was a man of his word, she returned to the dish of banana pudding and placed a glass top on it. She then eased it into the refrigerator and cleared the counter of any mess. Figuring she still had some time for a shower of her own, she decided to make sure the doors were locked before heading upstairs.

Rainys' hand was about to turn the lock on the front door when she heard a light tap, and then the sound of the bell. Sliding the curtain to the side, she peeked out the window to see Stacey, Tara and Sabrina waving at her with wide smiles on their faces.

Miki was totally pushed from her mind as she quickly swung open the door. "Ladies! I wasn't expecting to see you guys. What a pleasant surprise," she said, genuinely happy to see them. It had been a few months since she'd been able to set some time aside to make a visit.

She gave Sabrina a hug first even though she had only seen her hours ago. "Mom, what are you doing back over here at this hour?" It was well after nine at night.

Sabrina hugged her quickly and stepped to the side. "I came to get that ugly stuffed animal Sydney gave to Jordan last year. He gave us a hard time getting him into bed without it. Finally, Morgan was able to get him to settle down by promising to take him out for breakfast." She shook her head smiling. "I'm beginning to think we might have another lawyer in the family. You should have seen the way he negotiated."

"I can only imagine," Rainy agreed. She then turned to the others. "And why are you guys out making late night visits? And where is Katrina?"

Stacey smiled when Rainy asked about her daughter. "Mom has

Katrina too. She wanted to give me a night all to myself."

"Yes, but it was Stacey's idea to go out," Tara blurted out. "I don't think she's gotten used to the fact that she can't run the streets all night once you're married."

Laughing, Stacey gave Tara a light shove. "Oh be quiet. You know Chance is in California for four days for some kind of medical convention. He asked me if I wanted to go, but I couldn't see myself sitting there listening to a bunch of doctors go on and on about things I know nothing about," said Stacey as she made her way towards the living room.

"Yeah, instead she gets to drag me out of my warm bed to go to some God awful movie where the audience seemed to want to interact with the actors by blurting out what they would do to them if they ever met them." She immediately followed Stacey and sat next to her on the plush couch.

Rainy closed the door and slid her arm through Sabrina's pulling her along. She was smiling and shaking her head at them. "Are you going to stick around Mom?"

Sabrina thought for a minute and then nodded. "Why not? The children are both sound asleep and Mary is keeping an eye on them right now," she said bringing up the trustworthy maid. "Morgan was engrossed in ESPN when I left. He probably doesn't even know that I've left the house. I guess I can stick around for a bit."

"Good. Have a seat and relax a bit. I'll get us some tea."

Tara looked up and frowned. "Tea?! Girl we didn't come here for no damn tea." She reached into her large bag and pulled out a bottle of white wine. "I took this from Arnez house. He won't even miss it," she said, grinning at pulling a fast one on her brother.

"Shame on you, Tara," Sabrina said, giving her a serious frown. Tara looked away, embarrassed. "Next time bring some red too."

Everyone burst out laughing and that was the start of their tipsy evening. Rainy and Stacey went to the kitchen and returned with four glasses. They each were lounging around sharing how their day had gone and anything important that was going on in their lives.

"Hey, did you guys see the video of Katrina trying to wake Chance up by sticking her fingers in his nose?" asked Stacey.

"Oh wow," said Tara chuckling. "Let us see it."

They all sat quietly hunched over Stacey's phone as she moved through her video folder searching. Seeing that the ladies needed a refill on their glass, Rainy got up and went to the side table where she'd placed the wine and snack tray. She had a feeling she was forgetting something, but couldn't remember what it was.

***

After taking a shower, Miki pulled on a pair of thick socks and was about to reach for his pajama bottoms when a cocky smile came across his face. Instead of his pajamas, he snatched his robe up and left the room naked underneath.

As he reached the top of the staircase he heard a noise downstairs and knew it was Rainy double checking the doors. She just couldn't seem to break that habit after Jordan had learned to turn the door knobs and ended up on the front porch.

Miki made his way down the steps quietly. When he reached the bottom he saw Rainy standing by the table and she looked up and smiled at him. Before she could say anything, he took off running down the hall towards her and slid across the slippery floor in his socks, stopping right in front of her. He then yanked open his robe and began to dance sexily.

"How about you play with this tonight baby?" he said, smiling.

"Miki Alexander Tase!"

Miki's erection instantly went down the moment he heard his mother's voice. His eyes spread wide as he quickly closed his robe and spun around to find his mother, Tara, and Stacey sitting in the living room. Tara and Stacey's mouth was open in a wide grin.

"You should be ashamed of yourself!" Sabrina said, frowning.

"Yes, you should be ashamed of yourself," said Rainy trying to hold in her laughter.

Miki jerk around to look at Rainy and his mouth dropped open when he saw that she was struggling to hold in her laugh. His eyes narrowed with the promise of revenge. He turned back to Sabrina who still looked upset.

"Mom, I didn't know you were here," he said trying to apologize. When she didn't respond, he began to back up from the room. "Excuse me," he mumbled, then turned and fled.

As soon as he left, all four women looked at each other and burst into laughter.

"Well, at least I know my son is happy," Sabrina said, causing Rainy to blush.

Just then, Stacey's cell phone rings and she goes into the other room to have some privacy.

Rainy was still laughing as Tara continued to make jokes about Miki. She knew he would be getting calls about this in the morning from his brothers. They loved teasing each other and this would be the perfect excuse for them to roast him.

When Stacey returned, Rainy walked up and refilled her glass. "Is everything all right?" she asked concerned.

"I think so. That was Emily. She's on her way here and I can't tell you why until she gets here."

"But she's okay though, right?"

Stacey began smiling. "Physically, yes. Emotionally… I believe she will be."

"That's a damn riddle, Stacey," Rainy said confused.

Stacey was still grinning. "Emily is a riddle, but I believe we all will finally understand her better tonight."

Chapter Three

A little over an hour later Emily sat at the main gate waiting for the security guard to let her through. It only took a moment before the gates opened and she was sitting in front of Rainy and Miki's house. Feeling herself about to change her mind, she hurriedly paid the cab driver a hefty sum, including a rather large tip for going so far out his way. She was now standing on the porch watching as he drove away.

"How long are you going to stand out here procrastinating?" asked Stacey.

Emily's head snapped around to find Stacey and Tara staring at her. Tara's bright eyes and wide grin were contagious and Emily found herself smiling back.

"I'm not procrastinating," said Emily. "I was only thinking."

"Mm hmm, well you can think inside the house. Get in here," said Stacey grabbing her by the hand.

Emily shook her head, amused as she allowed herself to be pulled into the house. She followed Stacey down the hall and into the living room where she found Sabrina and Rainy heading in their direction.

"Emily! I didn't know you were coming by," exclaimed Sabrina before pulling her into a hug.

"I only stopped by for a moment," she said, glancing quickly at Stacey.

Sabrina began backing towards the door. "I wish I can stay and visit longer, but I need to check on my grand babies. Ladies enjoy your night."

A black Lincoln town car was waiting out front for Sabrina to drive her back across the lake to her home. She was so glad that Miki had decided on purchasing the neighboring property. Now she and Morgan could get to see at least one of their grandkids as much as possible. And it comes in handy when Miki and Rainy need a night off like tonight.

"Okay, what's going on? Why have you taken a cab all the way from New York when a simple phone call would have done the trick?" asked Rainy.

"Damn Rainy. You can at least let the girl sit down and offer her a drink before you interrogate her," said Tara, ushering Emily to the couch.

Rainy sucked her teeth. "I wasn't interrogating her. I'm just concerned is all," she called over her shoulder as she went to pour another glass of wine.

Emily slid out of her jacket and sat on the couch smiling. The whole drive over she felt confused and distraught over her feelings for Daniel, but now being here with Tara, Stacey and Rainy helped to lift some of her anguish away.

"Here you go Emily. You can tell us when you're ready," Rainy stated after handing her the glass.

"Thank you," she murmured softly before taking a sip. She didn't care too much for white wine, so she quickly sat the glass on the table in front of her.

Her emotions were raw and her patience had run its course. She was there for help and advice and was ready to get it. Sitting forward, she held her hands tightly in her lap as she worked on a way to start the conversation.

Rainy saw that she was struggling with her words. She sat beside her and reached out to touch her hand. "You can tell us Emily. No one here will judge you."

Emily looked up, her eyes bright with tears. "I'm in love," she blurted out and started to cry.

Stacey was sitting in one of the chairs across from Emily looking delighted at her words. Tara and Rainy were not prepared for Emily's outburst and glanced at each other. Emily always seemed to be happy and in a relationship with someone. So what was it about this relationship that had her breaking down in tears.

Tara sat down on the opposite side of Emily and put her arm around her shoulder. "Emily, if you're in love, why are you crying?" she questioned, confused.

"Yeah," said Rainy trying to understand. "You shouldn't be upset if you're in love."

Emily picked up one of the napkins from the table and dabbed her eyes. "You'd be upset too if the person you were in love with doesn't love you back," she said before more tears slid down her face.

Tara pulled Emily tighter in her arms, looking at Rainy and then Stacey with a distressing look on her face. However, she returned her gaze to Stacey when she saw that she was smiling. *Why the hell would she think this is funny?*

Stacey glanced up to see Tara frowning at her, and her smile widened. "Emily, tell them who the person is that you're in love with."

Rainy turned to look at Stacey, who had a silly grin on her face, and then back to Emily. "Who is it?" she asked, hoping it wasn't some tattooed biker chick her parents wouldn't approve of.

Emily took a quick glance at their curious faces. She began to feel self-conscious about the questions she knew would follow her announcement. She sat up a little straighter and used the tissue to dry her nose.

"It's Daniel," she said softly. She felt an instant sense of relief as soon as she said his name out loud.

"Daniel!?" Rainy responded surprised.

"Daniel!?" repeated Tara, looking just as shocked.

Stacey burst out laughing. "Yes, Daniel! Isn't it great?" she shouted sipping from her glass.

Rainy started to grin, but then her smile began to wane. "Wait, I thought you were into women?"

Tara and Stacey's mouth's dropped open before bursting into laughter.

"What?" asked Rainy not understanding why they were laughing. "What did I say?"

Emily smiled with a wide grin. "You didn't say anything wrong, Rainy. You're right. I am into women. I mean I was. I mean, I think I was," she said frowning. Her eyebrows drew close together as she sat there trying to explain things.

Tara leaned over and picked up her glass. "Look, you're confusing the hell out of us. You're either into women or into men. So pick a struggle."

Stacey damn near choked on her wine. "Girl, are you trying to kill me?" she asked, finding it difficult to draw in a deep breath.

"I'm just saying," said Tara, grinning as she sat back and crossed her legs. "Hell, we all want to know. When I first met her, she tried to get my number."

Stacey looked at Tara, then back to Emily. "Really?"

Emily nodded, embarrassed by her behavior back then. "Yes, but honestly, I was only doing it to make her date upset. He looked like Burt Reynolds and I knew she would be miserable her whole life if it went any further than that night."

Tara leaned over holding her side laughing. "Oh no! You're talking about my friend Desmond. Girl, he had hair on his knuckles, on top of his hands and coming out of his ears. That date was strictly business. He is definitely not my type."

"Whew! I am so happy that was the case."

"Wait, didn't she try and push up on Kayla too?" asked Stacey.

Emily started laughing hard. "Oh my goodness. If you guys could have seen Kayla's face when I grabbed her hand under the table. Michael made sure I knew that she belonged to him and was off limits."

Shaking her head Rainy reached for a tissue to dry the tears of laughter from her cheeks. "Man, she looked so spooked when she told me. I was like are you sure?"

"Okay, but damn all that," said Tara. "The question I have is when did it all change? When did it go from I want her, to I want him?"

All the laughter died down and they all turned in Emily's direction waiting to hear her answer.

Emily sat quietly thinking over the question. She already knew the answer to it. She was just soaking in the feeling of relief knowing it would all be out in the open soon.

"I was nine when my parent's transferred me to an all girls school. My dad went berserk one day when he caught me kissing the gardener's son. I tried to explain to him it was because I lost a bet, but he didn't want to hear it. That following week I was shipped off to an all girls boarding school. The only great thing about it was that it had an exceptional music program. So I didn't put up a fuss."

"By the time I was in high school, I noticed a lot of the girls were holding hands. I even saw a few kissing each other. This girl I new name Tabetha told me it was either because they hated boys or because there were none around. The school was isolated and you could only get in or out through secured gates. So if you started to get that loving feeling, you either took care of it yourself or found someone to do it for you."

"I take it that a lot of them found someone else to do it," said Rainy.

Emily nodded.

"Did you?" asked Tara. "Did you find someone to take care of your needs?"

All three women were paused, waiting for her answer.

"Yes and no." She laughed at their confused expressions. "You see, all though I've dated women, and have even been intimate with them, I've never gone all the way with one." When they still looked puzzled she explained further. "I'm saying I've never been penetrated."

"Ohhhh," they all said in unison and burst into laughter.

"Oh shit!" said Stacey, her eyes wide. "Does that mean you're a virgin?"

If Emily had been light skinned she knew her face would be beet red. Luckily, her dark complexion hid her heated cheeks.

Emily licked her dry lips. "Technically, yes."

"What the hell do you mean technically?" asked Stacey.

Emily looked at her and sucked her teeth. *She just won't leave it alone will she?*

"I've never been penetrated, but I have used certain… objects to please myself."

"You mean sex toys?" asked Stacey pretending like she didn't understand. She was getting a kick at having Emily on the hot seat.

"Damn girl, you have a dildo?" asked Tara, rudely.

Emily covered her face with her hands and groaned. *Oh, my Lord.*

Together they all began to laugh at her again. Emily peeked through her fingers and smiled. "I hate you guys. I really do."

Rainy sat back and tucked her feet up under her. "No you don't. You love us just like we love you. Now let's get down to business," she said seriously. "We understand how you started messing with women, but when did you start having feelings for Daniel?"

Again, all eyes were on her. She looked down at her hands holding the tissue and smiled. "I was twenty. Chase had a surprise party for Sydney. I wasn't going to come because I had a recital the next day, but I told myself I could just stop in for an hour and leave early."

"By the time I got there the party was in full swing. There were a lot of people I didn't know so I stood at the door looking for a familiar face. Then I felt someone standing behind me. I wanted to turn around to see who it was, but for some reason I felt strange. Hot. Almost feverish."

"I stood there like an idiot and waited. Then my back began to tingle as he stepped closer, and when he whispered close to my ear, I believe my heart stopped beating for a full minute."

"Was it Daniel?" asked Rainy.

"What did he say," asked Tara, her attention focused on Emily's every word.

Emily smiled with a far away look in her eyes. She was remembering that moment like it happened last night. It was the night she became aware of men. Of him.

"He simply said I looked different. But it was the way he said it, you know. He'd never gotten that close to me before without it being a joke or something. I could tell right off that this was not the same."

"Then what happened?" Stacey asked intrigued.

"The lights were dimmed and the music started. Before I knew it, he was pulling me into the room where everyone was dancing, and took me into his arms." She took a deep breath and let it out slowly. "I can tell you, it definitely felt different. At first we had a respectable distance between us, but before long he drew me in closer, and for the first time I felt real desire. It was so…amazing," she said with a giggle.

"We danced all night long. I knew I should leave because of my recital, but I couldn't pull myself away from him. We didn't speak a word. We just danced close. And I mean we were close. It was the first time I felt a man's 'you know what' pressed up against me," she said and laughed.

"Did he kiss you?" asked Rainy, caught up in her story.

"No. Michael cut in on us and soon after, the lights came back on and people started leaving. I didn't see him any more that night. The next day I thanked the Lord that I was able to keep my eyes open and breeze through my recital. As I was leaving the stage I happened to look out into the crowd and I saw Daniel standing there. He smiled at me and then turned and left."

Stacey cut her eyes over to Tara, then back to Emily.

"Has he ever asked you out?" Stacey asked softly.

"No."

"Have you two ever talked about that night?" asked Rainy.

"I tried to once, but he cut me off saying it was just a party."

Rainy looked at Stacey and smiled. *He's running.*

"Other than the party, how do you know Daniel's interested?" asked Tara.

Emily smiled. "Actually, I don't know for sure, but he's has been popping up at the same parties and events I attend, and he's never done that before. Plus, whenever we are at his parents house he makes it his business to sit next to me when it's time to eat. I also believe that he's been to a lot more of my recitals."

"Why do you think that," asked Rainy.

"There's been more than a few times that someone has left me a huge order of flowers with a card saying Ma Belle Âme."

Tara smiled. "It means my beautiful soul."

"Yeah, I know," Emily said softly, smiling goofily.

"Oh, and remember that day at the pool. These two were playing around in the water splashing each other. Body parts were touching," said Stacey grinning and wiggling her eyebrows.

Emily looked up cheesing. "Yes. I had fun that day."

"Yeah, I bet you did," Tara said, laughing.

"I have a question," said Tara with a serious expression. "How do you know you love him?"

"I've loved him for years and I didn't even see it until now. Over the past few months it's gotten stronger and it's been hammering me left and right. I think about him all the time. I even dream about him. In my dream he's always kissing me and I wake up hot and sweating wishing it was real. I really don't know how else to explain it. I just know that I love him."

"And you're sure you want him and have no more interest in women?" asked Stacey. "Is that truly how you feel?" She needed to know this wasn't some passing fancy she needed to itch and would move on afterwards, leaving Daniel hurt and broken.

"Yes," she said immediately with no hesitation. "I tried not to, but I can't keep lying to myself anymore. It's beginning to affect my music. I can't concentrate on anything but him," she said as tears filled her eyes once more.

They all smiled, looking at each other.

"So for years now, you've been tiptoeing around these feelings you have for him, and the question is why?" asked Rainy.

"You guys don't understand. What I've told you only explains how I feel. I don't truly know how Daniel feels about me," she said as another tear rolled down her face. "What if he doesn't want me?"

"Well, I guess the first thing to do is see how Daniel feels," said Stacey, reaching over and squeezing Emily's hand to reassure her.

"How are we going to do that?" asked Emily.

"Yeah, we can't just walk up to him and ask him outright," said Tara, reaching for her glass.

Rainy smiled. "I have an idea."

"And what's that?" asked Emily, hoping she was prepared to go through with whatever Rainy came up with.

Rainy pulled her legs from up under her and sat up straight on the couch. "You're never going to get Daniel to just come out and say he has feelings for you. He's stubborn and for some reason, if he is attracted to you, he's fighting it."

Stacey leaned forward. "So how does she get him to come clean about his feelings?"

Rainy leaned forward, resting her arms on her knees with a scheming smile on her face.

"She's going to invade his personal space." She turned to look at Emily. "You see, right now, if he does feel the same about you and he's fighting it, he has a safe zone where he can run to and get away from you. You need to intrude on that space and subtly lean into him."

Tara smiled, liking where Rainy's plan was going. "That's right. And popping up at the restaurant will work too."

Stacey sat up wanting to join in. "Yes, but not in the dining hall. Go to the back where his office is. It's private in case you guys decide to sneak in a kiss."

"And make sure you're always wearing something sexy and looking your best," said Rainy. "You want his undivided attention."

"And if he acts like he doesn't want to give you his attention, start smiling and chatting it up with other guys. His jealousy will make the decision for him to stop running," added Stacey.

"Are you sure?" asked Emily. "I don't want to push him away."

"Trust me. Daniel already thinks that you're his. He feels safe knowing you only date women, but if he sees your gaining the attention of men and accepting it, that will drive him nuts."

"That's right. No man wants another man touching what he already has claimed. Remember how Michael reacted when you grabbed Kayla's hand," said Rainy. "He made sure you knew she was his and told you to back off."

Emily smiled as she remembered. Michael had made it clear that Kayla was off limits and to look elsewhere. "My God, you guys could write a book about this stuff," she said, laughing.

"You think so?" asked Stacey, laughing.

"What will the title be?" Tara chimed in with a silly grin.

"How To Catch The Meat Preasure!" blurted out Stacey.

The room fell silent as the women looked at each other with serious faces. Suddenly, laughter tumbled from their lips as they fell over with girlish giggles.

****

Later that night after making love to Miki, Rainy lay relaxed and satisfied as he snuggled up close behind her. His arms were wrapped around her waist as he held her tightly, spooning her backside. She heard the low sound of his breathing and knew she had to act now or she would have to wait until tomorrow.

"Baby?"

"Mm?" The sound he made was barely audible, but it was enough to let her know that he was still awake.

"Is Daniel dating anyone?" she asked softly in the quiet of the room.

No answer.

"Baby?"

"Why do you want to know?" he asked, his words muffled by her hair.

"I was only curious."

Miki lay quietly for a moment and didn't respond. He knew his wife only asked things for a reason. He'd learned that about her a long time ago. If she asked you if you broke it, then it meant she already knew that you did. So with her asking about Daniel meant she had a legitimate reason for it.

"Spit it out Rainy. Why do you want to know?"

She tried rolling over on her back, but he held her still.

"Ask before I fall asleep," he said in a deep tone.

"I just wanted to know if he was dating anyone," she tried to sound nonchalant about it.

"Again, I ask why?"

She sighed loudly and he smiled behind her. Seeing that she wasn't going to get any answers out of him without answering his questions, she relented.

"I want to set him up with someone."

"Who?"

"Is that important?"

"Who, Rainy?"

This time when she tried to roll over he allowed her to. Rainy looked into his face shown to her by the then line of moonlight that had crept through the curtain. It gave her just enough brightness to see his eyes, nose and lips.

"I'm going to tell you, but you have to keep it a secret. I promised not to say anything about it to anyone."

Now she had his full attention. She could tell by how focused his gaze had become. She knew that she was taking a risk by letting him know, but she needed answers. He and Daniel spoke almost daily, which meant that he would be the one to know if he was seeing anyone. Also, since Emily grew up with them, and they looked at her as family, she needed to analyze his response after hearing that she wanted to hook Daniel and Emily up. Would he be offended by the notion of them being together?

"Okay."

 "I want to set him up with Emily."

When he didn't respond, Rainy began to explain as best she could the situation between Daniel and Emily, minus the juicy details. When she was done, he lay there again in silence. She knew he was contemplating on whether or not to get involved. She decided not to say a word. To let him make up his mind on his own without her urging.

The silence stretched on for a few more moments and then…

"He told me about a woman he sees from time to time, if you catch my meaning. Also, he said something about a woman that asked him out that works at some real estate office he's been going to. That's the only time he's mentioned anything about a woman of interest."

Oh, well they have to go. "Are you sure?"

Miki smiled. "Yes, Dr. Ruth. I'm sure."

Rainy smiled back at him. "I think he and Emily will make a good match. Don't you?" *Please say yes.*

"I don't know, but I have caught him staring at her strangely from time to time. Then again, he hasn't made a move on her either. One thing I do know about Daniel is if he isn't ready to make a move and you push him, he's going to run."

He saw the uncertainty in Rainy's eyes and touched her cheek.

"However, I know Emily, and if she goes after him, Daniel doesn't have a chance."

He literally felt her relax again in his arms. "Do you think everyone will be okay with it?"

"What do you mean?" he asked, reaching up to tuck her hair behind her ear.

"Well, I know that she's really close to you guys, like a little sister."

"Sometimes I get the feeling that Daniel doesn't regard her as a little sister anymore," he said laughing. "I don't see anything wrong with it and I don't think anyone else will have a problem with it either."

"Good. Operation Meat Pressure goes into effect as soon as possible."

Miki frowned. "Meat Pressure? Should I even ask?"

"No baby," she said laughing. "I wouldn't ask about that if I were you."

Miki shook his head, smiling. "Now, can a man get some sleep, please?"

Rainy pushed him over on his back and climbed on top of him.

"Not right now. We have a few more hours before Jordan will be home. Let me show you what the Meat Pressure is all about," she said, leaning in for a heated kiss.

Two hours later the last thought that ran through Mikis' mind was, *I really, really love this woman.*

Chapter Four

A few weeks had gone by and the school year had come to an end. Emily usually would take the summer off to spend with her parents, but this year she'd made other plans. After receiving a phone call from Rainy warning her about the two other women vying for Daniel's attention, she knew that she would have to go after Daniel right away, showing him that she was the better choice.

Now she was packing her bags to catch a flight out to Virginia, where she had been given an assignment on scouting out new talent. She would be checking on two violinists. Both students were exceptional, yet, there could only be one chosen for the scholarship.

Talk about perfect timing. This assignment was exactly what she needed. It would give her a reason to impose on Daniel and hopefully make him her man.

A soft panicky giggle slipped past her lips. *Make him my man? I only wish I knew what to do or say.*

Emily left her apartment and stood waiting outside her building for the cab she'd called, when suddenly she felt an uncomfortable shiver pass through her. She looked around for anything out of the normal, but didn't see anyone. A few minutes later the cab pulled up and she quickly climbed into the back seat.

"To the airport, please."

"Not a problem," the driver said as he checked his mirror before pulling away from the curb.

Now that she was on her way, Emily relaxed. Whatever caused her to feel uncomfortable was behind her now and she smiled, thinking about what lay ahead.

***

Sherry watched Emily get into the cab with her bags and

wondered where she was going. She had been sitting across the street in her car waiting for the chance to see her so she could approach her. It hadn't been hard to find out where she lived. All she did was show up at her job at Julliard and then followed her home. Now she sat disappointed as she watched her slide in the back of a cab with two small suitcases.

Is she going on a trip? To see who? It better be family, she thought, her eyes narrowing with jealousy.

She pulled in a deep breath and exhaled loudly. "Relax Sherry. It may only be a business trip. *There's only one way to find out.*

She grabbed her phone.

"Find the number for the Julliard school in New York," she said speaking into the receiver.

The phone quickly found the information she needed. Sherry dialed the number and waited for someone to answer.

"Thank you for calling Julliard. This is Mary speaking, how may I help you?"

The woman that answered the phone had a pleasant voice.

"Hello, my name is, uh… Cynthia Duke, and I wanted to inquire about your violinist program. My organization is looking for a fresh program to sponsor by making a generous donation and we've chosen Julliard's Violinist Program as our final choice."

"Oh, well, I can assure you that you've made the right decision," said Mary, enthusiastically. "Last year our violinist program was a hit at the Verde Concert Hall and this year I'm sure will be much better."

"That sounds promising" said Sherry not knowing what the woman was talking about. "Can you tell me who's heading up that department?" Sherry asked, although she already knew the answer.

"Sure, that will be Emily Bawler."

"Awesome. I've had the pleasure of seeing her perform and she's phenomenal," she lied.

"Isn't she," Mary gushed through the phone. "Her music is played with such grace and elegance. She has a sound that's unique and unlike anything you've ever heard."

Wow, my baby must have mad skills. "Exactly! I would love to speak with her if that's possible," Sherry asked, taking a light tone that matched the woman's.

"I'm sorry, but that won't be possible. You see, Ms. Bawler has already left for summer vacation."

"Oh, well, that's too bad. I would need to speak with her and hear her plans before my organization will make the donation. I guess I'll have to replace Julliard with another private institution." *Come on you old fart. Give up the information I need.*

Sensing that she was about to lose a large donation from the woman's foundation, Mary quickly jumped in with a solution.

"Well, you know, Ms. Bawler is rightfully on vacation, but she's also on a partial assignment in Virginia Beach, Virginia."

"Virginia?" She had Sherry's full attention now. *See, I knew she wasn't cheating on me. She's away on business.*

Mary smiled seeing that the woman was still interested. "Yes. She was asked to go to Virginia to assess a couple of new students and their potential. We only have room for one more entry and there are two students there with exceptional potential. It will be up to Ms. Bawler to choose which one will join us for the next school year."

"You know what? I plan on being in Virgina myself in the next few days. Would it be possible for me to drop in and watch the process. I think my benefactors would like to see just how their donations will be providing others an education. It might even encourage them to make an even larger donation to help out more prospects."

Mary's smile widened and she drew in a deep breath of excitement.

"Oh, that wouldn't be a problem at all Mrs. Duke. She'll be observing the student's at the Sherwood High School. It's an open public performance so you shouldn't have a problem getting in."

"Splendid," said Sherry, trying to hold in her laughter at using the word. She smiled like a cat that swallowed the canary.

After hanging up abruptly on the woman, Sherry called her job claiming to be sick with the flu and put in for some sick time. She then called the airline to book the next flight out to Virginia. After completing her traveling plans she sat back and thought about Emily and all the things they would do together.

I want everything to be perfect, she thought smiling. She knew their second meeting had to be timed perfectly and look coincidental. Nothing could go wrong. This time she would get it right.

This time… Not like all those other times. I won't fail this time. She's my soulmate.

Sherry leaned her head back against the headrest and closed her eyes. She let her thoughts travel back to her childhood where she had her first brush with failure. Her father. His new wife Veronica always would complain to him about something she did or didn't do and he never asked her if it was true.

"All I asked her to do was make up her bed and she wouldn't do it! She's just an ugly, useless waste of space, Johnny. She doesn't listen at all. You need to discipline her."

It was then that her father took her over his knee, lifted her skirt, and yanked down her panties. He spanked her right in front of Veronica and her two stepbrother's, David and Brian.

Sherry tightened her eyes as their shrill laughter resounded in her head as if they both were there now in the car with her. The clear picture of their faces brought back painful memories of the abuse she suffered at their hands. The punches to her back or arms when no one was looking. A shove down the steps or a stinging slap to her face.

"You better not tell either," said Brian.

David caught her with a vicious slap to her lips. *"That's right. Keep your mouth shut or else."*

They were so much bigger than her, yet they didn't hold back on the pain they delivered. They always caught her off guard, but it didn't matter. She had been warned to keep her hands to herself.

"Don't let it bother you," she'd say to herself. *"They're only your step brother's. Not your real brother's. When I get older I'm gonna leave and go far away from here."*

This is the life Sherry had been thrust into after her parents split up and her father remarried. Every other weekend she was packed up and shipped off to her father's house. She was supposed to be spending time with him, but she was always left alone with Veronica, Brian, and David. He stayed away for most of the day putting in long hours at his job. Then when he returned, he would be informed how disobedient she had been and he would punish her or give her a spanking.

Sherry always thought that if she tried harder to do whatever Veronica wanted the right way, then the beatings would stop. But that wasn't the case. She never got it right. Never. And the beatings continued.

Even her own grandfather didn't show any sympathy. He had always been strict, but ever since Veronica started dropping her off spewing lies about her behavior, he would look at her with disdain. Once she left, he would speak to her about her manners followed by drawn out scriptures from the Bible on the subject of honoring thy mother and thy father. Then there were the long lectures about being obedient and efficient with her chores.

"You need to be respectful, Sherry."

"But, I do, Grandpa. I always try to be good."

"Then try harder," he said, squeezing her arm painfully. "Your father works hard and he sends money here to help take care of you. You better not mess this up for me, you hear?"

Sherry's head dropped in misery. "Yes, sir."

And it didn't get better. All through high school, and even after, Sherry found herself feeling like a failure. Her father let her know in many ways that she was useless and a disappointment. And her grandfather made it clear that she was only an asset to keep money in his pocket. At the age of nineteen, after coming to terms that she'd always be a let down to others, she found love. Or so she thought.

Jerry Kemp was a guy she'd drooled over in high school just like all the other girls. So when he approached her to ask her out, she was ecstatic. They dated for almost two months and she couldn't have been happier. For once in her life she wasn't a failure or useless, and the man that she adored wasn't downing or abusing her. Jerry treated her with respect and always told her how beautiful she was.

All that came to a halt right after she gave him her virginity. The moment his sperm left his body, Jerry became a mean and cruel individual.

"You need to go," he said as he crawled from off top of her.

"What?" confused and still sore, Sherry turned to look at him.

"Get up, get your shit, and go. I have to be somewhere?" he said, yanking up his jeans.

"But…We…"

"There is no we. I have a girl and it's not you. So get the hell up before I throw you out."

Sherry sat up in the bed, holding the sheet up to her chest. She was trying to figure out what she had done wrong to upset him. The words of her father and grandfather played like a skipping song in her head. *You're an idiot, Sherry. Why can't you do anything right? You're a useless lump of flesh. Nobody will ever want or have use for you.*

When Jerry saw her sitting there frozen and staring off into space, he reached up and yanked the sheet from her body leaving her open and exposed.

"I said get the fuck up!" he yelled.

Feeling embarrassed and used, Sherry quickly got up from the bed and dressed as fast as she could. She had barely slid on her last shoe before Jerry started shoving her towards the door. The rain was coming down in torrents, but he didn't care. She jumped back when the door slammed in her face. With no umbrella, and no ride, she was instantly soaked.

Embarrassment changed to sadness, and then to anger. Anger like never before built up in her and she didn't try to contain it. It overflowed into her heart and all around her. The revulsion for herself and the fierce hate she now had towards men was almost intolerable. *"Never again,"* she said in a tight whisper. *"Never again."*

The walk back home was long and cold. Yet, it was enough time for Sherry to develop a fierce and unstable complex that would last her entire life.

The feeling of something touching her cheek snapped Sherry out of her thoughts. When she reached up and felt tears on her face, she began to shake with rage. In a furious frenzy, she banged her fist down hard on the steering wheel causing the horn to beep in a crazy tune. And just as suddenly, she stopped. She just sat there in the car alone breathing heavily, staring off into space.

"I will never let a man make me feel like that again. Never."

Chapter Five

The smooth taste of the dark liquor flowing down Daniel's throat helped to calm his frustration. His mood today could only be described as pitiful. Or maybe pathetic. It's the only way he could explain the way he'd been feeling for the past eight years. It's the only way to describe the feelings he had for someone he shouldn't.

He leaned against the railing of the terrace looking out at the bright lights of the city he'd grown to love, Virginia Beach. However, the call to visit New York was becoming unbearable with each passing day. It was the same calling that had him dragging his feet at settling on a property deal with his real estate agent, Kimberley Reed.

Kimberley. He shook his head with regret. He'd made the mistake of sleeping with her. His true error had been thinking that they'd been on the same page about it. She said that she understood that it would be no strings attached. Just consensual sex between two adults. *Yeah, right.* She had become clingy the very next day trying to match her schedule to his, asking him where he was going, and calling him at odd hours of the night to make sure he was alone. She obviously didn't understand the meaning of *one and done.*

He didn't waste any time ending that affair, stating that they should just keep it professional. He could tell that she was upset by his decision, but in the end, she agreed. He figured she felt that the huge commission she would get once he made his mind up on which property he wanted to purchase was more important than sex.

He took another sip from his glass thinking about the property he wanted to buy. For some reason he couldn't make up his mind on which building he wanted. Kimberly had shown him six already and he always came back with some excuse as to why he didn't want it.

Then there was that powerful yearning he had to take another trip to New York and he didn't know why. Hell, who was he kidding. He knew the reason why he wanted to make that trip. It's the same reason why he was undecided about the property sites he'd been shown. He took another gulp of his drink and stared down into his glass. *Emily.*

He had been in denial about his feelings about her for years, yet it was becoming harder to ignore. God knows he'd tried, but there was always this intense ache when he was around her. He couldn't even begin to describe it. It damn near consumed him.

Daniel pulled his phone from his pocket and tapped the screen to bring up his pictures. He went to the folder he had a security lock on, punched in his code, and gazed down at the smiling face of the woman who made it impossible to sleep at night. He had snapped the picture last year during his family's vacation to Virginia Beach. They had used one of his rental homes that was located right near the water, giving him a full week in her company.

He slid through the pictures and stopped at his favorite. He had been shoving large slices of mango into his mouth when suddenly she'd snatched a piece out of his hand and tossed it into her mouth. The reason he loved the picture was because right after she ate the mango she leaned over, grabbed his face, and kissed his cheek playfully. Michael had taken the picture and had caught the surprised look on his face. Had Michael known just how excited he'd gotten he would have kicked his ass.

He closed out the pictures and downed the rest of his drink. Needing a refill, he walked back into his condo over to the bar. He lifted the glass container to pour his drink, but decided against it. There was no use getting drunk when he had a huge night planned tomorrow at his restaurant. He'd called in a favor from a friend and had gotten The Mayfield Brother's to make a guest appearance. Their soulful melodies were rising up the R&B charts and already his guest list was filled completely.

On the way through his condo to his bedroom he began pulling his shirt over his head. He tossed it over a chair in his room and then kicked off his shoes. He reached down and pulled his socks off and then unsnapped his jeans. He was about to strip them off too when his door buzzed.

"Shit. I can't have one damn night without any interruptions," he mumbled moving towards the door. "And how the hell did they get past the front desk to use my private elevator?" He snatched the door open and was damn near knocked on his ass by the woman that jumped in his arms.

"Danny!" Emily squealed as she pulled Daniel into a bear hug. *Oh, good Lord, he's not wearing a shirt and he is fine as hell. Can you say six pack?*

At first Daniel was shocked, but that got pushed aside as he realized that she was holding him tightly and her breast were pressed against his bare chest. His eyes closed briefly enjoying the moment, but then he felt low for taking such liberties with her that weren't given freely. He eased out of her hold and looked down at her.

"Emily!" he said, clearing his throat. "What are you doing here crazy lady?" he said jokingly, trying to play off the fact that he'd been thinking of her only seconds ago. "Shouldn't you be in New York with your student's?" he asked, hoping that she hadn't heard his heartbeat quicken when she rested her head against his chest.

Oh my goodness. He smells so good. Emily released him and walked into the apartment. "No. I have a meeting on Tuesday at Sherwood High School about a couple of student's we're interested in. Both are exceptional violinist, but we can only offer one of them a scholarship at Julliard."

"Okay, but why are you *here* in my apartment?" he asked, closing the door. When he turned to face her, she was smiling.

"Well, I was thinking. Since the school is close by, and you have two extra bedrooms, that I could just stay here with you."

Daniel's eyes widened in alarm. "What! No. You can't stay here."

His voice sounded like a small cornered animal and Emily almost lost her nerve. His outburst wasn't the reaction she'd hoped for and it made her think she might be wrong about his feelings for her.

Stay focused Emily. Don't let him run. She heard Rainys' voice clear as day in her head.

"Why not?" asked Emily, her nose wrinkling in a frown. "You live here alone and you're hardly ever home. I can come down to the restaurant with you and help out and on Tuesday, go to the university. I'll leave right after that. I promise."

Daniel was shaking his head before she even finished. "No. It's not a good idea, Em." His heartbeat kicked up a notch thinking of her sleeping so close to him with only a thin door between them.

"Why not, Danny? I won't be any trouble. Besides, it's been a long time since we spent time together. I haven't seen you at your mother's house in months," she complained.

That's because I can't stop wanting to touch you. "I've been busy," he said instead, stepping around the side of the couch to put distance between them. *She cut her hair shorter. I like it.*

"Doing what?" Her tone sounded as if she didn't believe him. "Your staff is efficient enough to operate without you if need be. What could have you so busy that you can't even come home for a visit?" she asked, pulling off her light blue jacket and tossing it on a nearby chair.

He used the first thing that came to mind as an excuse. "I'm working on opening a second restaurant. I just need to finalize on a location. And stop calling me Danny," he said, noticing how she started to lose her clothing one item at a time. He watched in fascination and horror, as she unwrapped the blue floral scarf from her neck and flung it on top of her jacket. The scent of her perfume drifted towards him. *Mmm.*

"Oh, that's great Danny! I know your family is proud of you," she said while kicking off her flats.

"Yeah, I guess you…"

Before he could finish his sentence the doorbell buzzed.

"You gotta be kidding me," Daniel mumbled as he headed for the door once again.

This time when he opened it, Barry from the front desk was standing there smiling.

"Good evening, Mr. Tase. I have Ms. Bawler's bags."

Daniel opened his mouth to speak, but Emily stepped in front of him.

"Oh, you can bring them in Barry. Just sit them over there," she said, pointing to an area away from the door.

Barry did as he was instructed, all the while smiling. When he completed his short task he turned to face Emily, his eyes taking in her appearance like a starving man.

"Barry?" Daniel's voice was flat, but it held a seriousness to it.

"Yes, sir?" Barry responded hating that he had to take his eyes from the dark beauty that was searching in her purse.

"Get out."

Those two words with its deadly intent was enough to spur him into action. Barry shot out the door as if his shoes were on fire. He stumbled a little as he stepped back onto the elevator causing him to blush in embarrassment.

Daniel slammed the door shut and turned to see Emily frowning at him.

"What?"

"Why did you make him leave? I was trying to find him a tip," she said, holding up the twenty dollar bill in front of her.

"I made him leave because he…" *Damn. I can't say because he was ogling her without looking suspicious.*

"Because what?" she prodded, not realizing that he'd been jealous.

"Because he gets paid a salary so he doesn't need to be tipped," was the lame excuse he came up with.

"What! That's not true."

He knew she would see right through his excuse so he hurried and changed the subject.

"And what's with the luggage? I never agreed that you could stay."

Instantly, he regretted what he said when he saw the sadness in her eyes.

"You don't want me here?" she asked softly. Pain and rejection were evident in her tone.

Hell yeah I want you here! "I didn't say that, Em. I was just about to say that you could stay. I was only saying that I hadn't said it yet." *What the hell did I just say?*

"Oh," she said, releasing her pent up breath. *That was close.*

"Just do me a favor. The next time you want to stop in for a visit, call first."

A few days earlier and she would have popped up while he was entertaining a woman. He and Taylor Mills, a tenant in his building, had been friends with benefits for over a year. She was one of the few that hadn't pressed him into anything more than good sex. Luckily, she was away on a business trip for a few weeks, which was a good thing since Emily was here.

Emily nodded, feeling stupid at how she'd handled the situation.

"You're right and I'm sorry. You know what, I'm just going to get a hotel room," she said heading for her bags. "I shouldn't have barged in on you like this. It was intrusive and rude."

Daniel felt a small pang of panic tighten his chest. *Don't let her go!*

"No. It's all right. I want you to stay," he said, picking up her bags before she could reach them. "Come on. Let me help you to your room."

He headed down the hall and Emily followed close behind him. Her eyes roamed across his muscled back and dropped even lower to his butt. *Nice and firm. I wonder what it would feel like if I squeezed it?*

Daniel set her bags down on the floor inside a room decked out in ivy and green. When he turned, Emily was close enough that he could reach out and touch her. *I wonder how soft her hair is?*

"Well, if you need anything, don't call me," he said, trying to lighten the mood. The sexual tension was beginning to rise and he needed to make an exit quick.

Emily smiled and stepped to the side. Just as Daniel stepped out the door, she stopped him. "Danny."

"Yeah?" Daniel didn't turn to face her fearing he'd want to act on his thoughts of touching her.

"Thank you for letting me stay."

He glanced over his shoulder briefly, his eyes meeting hers. "You're welcome," he said softly. And with that, he disappeared down the hall and into his bedroom.

Emily sat on the side of the bed with her eyes closed. She was drawing in deep breaths, trying to gain control over her emotions. She'd put on a great act of being in control in front of him, but she was actually nervous as hell at being alone with him. All this was new to her and she was basically winging it.

After she calmed down, she opened her eyes and smiled.

But I'm here now.

Chapter Six

The steam from the hot water wafted all around Daniel as he stood in the shower. One hand was braced against the black tiled wall supporting his weight as he stood there with his head bowed down letting the water pour down over his body. His eyes were closed, but he could see the image of Emily clearly. He envisioned her in the next room unpacking her bag and getting settled. He shook his head. *What the hell was I thinking letting her stay here?*

He opened his eyes and looked down at his body and saw that he had a full erection. "Fuck!" he growled out under his breath. *Yeah, fuck. That was a good word. I would like to fu…*

Suddenly, he stopped and angrily reached for the cold water handle and flipped it all the way up. The onslaught of cold water came down with a sharp sting and began to chill his body. He was standing there in the dim light of the shower stall shivering like an idiot. His teeth began to chatter and he looked down. He smiled when he saw that his erection had disappeared. *Nothing like a cold shower to do the trick.*

Done with his shower, he pushed the glass door open and stepped out onto the plush carpet. He grabbed a towel and quickly dried his body. When he entered his bedroom, he snatched up his blue pajama pants and slid them on. He then pulled a white t-shirt from a drawer and eased into it. Then he stopped.

He stood there trying to breathe quietly, listening for any little sound. He knew that Emily was in the house with him, but where? If possible he wanted to avoid any unnecessary contact with her. He figured it would be the best thing to do.

If you remove yourself from temptation, there won't be an opportunity to be tempted, he thought to himself as he eased open the door.

He peeked down the hall and didn't see or hear anything. He looked back over his shoulder at the clock on the wall and saw that it was after ten o'clock. *Maybe she's asleep.*

With that thought in his head, Daniel began walking down the hall barefoot. Not seeing any light coming from under her door, he began to relax. He went in the direction of the kitchen and saw the soft glow of light that came from the night light. Suddenly, the feeling of relaxation immediately disappeared when he entered the kitchen and found Emily sitting at the table eating.

Damn.

Emily looked up when she heard a noise and saw Daniel standing near the doorway. His jeans had been replaced with pajamas and his chest was now covered by a t-shirt. *Pity.* Neither of them said anything. They only stared at each other. She in nervous awe, and he in frustrated torture.

How the hell am I going to get through a few days of this, he thought.

"Hi." Emily didn't see him trying to start a conversation and felt she'd be the first to start.

"Hey." *How can anyone be sexy all the damn time?*

"I was hungry," she stated, shyly. *That's obvious Emily.*

"Yeah, I see," said Daniel looking at all the food she had spread all over the table. It looked like she'd pulled out just about every container that was in the refrigerator.

As much as he knew that he should have turned and walked away, he didn't leave. He couldn't. It was the whole moth to a flame scenario.

Feeling a little thirsty he walked over to the cabinet and pulled down a glass. He filled it with water and downed it quickly. When he looked over to see her watching him, he felt the heat begin to rise in his body again, and he refilled the glass. This time he took his time sipping the cool drink. *I want her so bad.*

Emily was watching Daniel not knowing what to do or what to expect from him. Then, for some reason she remembered something her mother use to always say. *'The way to a man's heart is his stomach.'*

Licking her lips, she smiled. "You want some?"

Daniel choked on his water. He managed to get some air into his lungs. "What?!" *Did she just...*

"Well, it's a lot of food here and I just wanted to know if you wanted some?" She looked at him confused. "Are you okay, Danny?"

No, because I'm an idiot. You really thought she was offering herself to you?

Daniel placed the glass in the sink and slowly walked over to sit at the table with her, but all the way on the other end.

All the way over there, huh? He's still playing it safe. Or he just didn't want to sit next to you, her conscious spit back at her.

"Yes, I'm fine." He reached over and grabbed a piece of the still cold chicken and took a bite. He figured if he kept his hands busy then he wouldn't act on the urge to shift his fingers through her short silky curls.

After popping the last piece of a pickle into her mouth, Emily leaned back trying to relax. She had no idea being alone with him would cause her to feel so many emotions all at once. Fear was one of those emotions. She wasn't afraid of him physically. It was more like the fear of the unknown. Being alone with a man was all new to her. Especially a man that she was attracted to. A man that she loved.

Her eyes dropped down to his lips, watching them as he chewed. *A man that had an incredibly sexy mouth.*

Then there was the warmth. It always moved through her starting in her chest, causing her nipples to harden before it settled in her stomach. Next would be the ache. Emily was no stranger to sex and she knew exactly what that ache meant. She shifted in her chair, and squeezed her thighs together, adding a little pressure to the sensitive nub that lay hidden there. *I wonder how his mouth would feel on me down there.*

Daniel was watching Emily as she popped the last piece of pickle in her mouth before picking up another from the plate. He placed the piece of chicken he was holding down, no longer interested in eating. His eyes were focused on her fingers as they wrapped around the pickle and then... nothing. She just held it. When he looked up, he found her looking at him with a strange expression on her face.

Her head had dropped to the side a little and her mouth had opened slightly. With her eyes half closed and fixed on him, her fingers began to slowly tap the tip of the pickle.

Jesus. Daniel cleared his throat. His imagination was running wild.

"Emily," he croaked out.

When he heard the weak sound of his voice, he cleared his throat and tried it again.

"Emily."

Realizing he had called her name, Emily snapped out of her

fantasy and met his gaze. "Yes?"

Daniel looked down at her hand. "Please put down the pickle."

She was about to do as he'd requested, but stopped when she noticed how heavy he was breathing. *What the hell?* She also noticed that he hadn't met her gaze.

"Why?" she asked, curious. She truly had no idea why eating the pickle was a problem.

Daniel still didn't lift his gaze from the hand holding the pickle. He felt his dick heavy and throbbing in his pants and lowered his hand to it. He pressed down on his shaft and inhaled deeply at the intense ripple of pleasure that moved through him.

"Because you're not eating it," he growled out in a deep tone.

A light sheen of sweat broke out on his forehead when Emilys' fingers wrapped fully around the pickle. His eyes stayed on her hand as she lifted it to her mouth and then… stopped. She was holding the pickle close to her lips with her mouth open wide. Daniel leaned forward in eager anticipation of seeing her shove the pickle between her moist lips. *Go on… do it*, he thought. His eyes narrowing.

Not wanting to give up her food, Emily decided to just eat the pickle. She picked the pickle up and stopped when she suddenly realized what was going on. *Oh my Lord.* She sat frozen with her hand in mid air and the pickle close to her mouth. The first thing that came to her mind was, *what would Rainy or Stacey do?*

A burst of courage shot through her and she forced herself to stay calm. The feeling of fear and uncertainty left and was replaced by a sexy naughtiness that she didn't know existed within her. She knew that he was eager to see what her next move would be. She knew that it could either send him over the edge or backfire in her face and have him sending her on her way. However, if she wanted to know how he felt about her, then she would need to take risks. *Don't be a coward. Do it.*

Emily tightened her hand around the pickle and saw Daniels' eyes darken. She then ran her finger up the side, letting it stop at the top. He leaned in closer. Feeling courageous by his response, she eased the pickle closer and closer until she felt it rest on her bottom lip.

Daniel let a low unintelligent sound slip past his lips. His gaze never wavered.

Here goes nothing. Emily used the tip of her tongue and flicked it across the top of the pickle before taking it into her mouth. She gave it a slow stroke, and watched as Daniels' eyes damn near popped out his head. Not knowing what else to do, she bit down on the pickle and tossed it back on the plate ending the show.

"I'm done," she blurted out and wiped the juice from her chin with her napkin. She hopped up from her chair and hauled ass from the kitchen. Her legs were moving fast as she made her way down the hall to her room.

Daniel sat there in the kitchen alone breathing like a marathon runner. He couldn't believe what he'd just seen. Had she really just teased him sexually with a pickle. Or was that only what his perverted mind had seen. *Get a damn grip man. It's Emily. She's into chicks not men. She doesn't want you like that. And even if she did, it wouldn't be right. Would it?*

With his body feeling like lead, he stood up and began replacing the lids back on the uneaten food. When he got to the pickle, he stared down at it before snatching it up and tossing it into the trash can. *Freaking pickle.*

He cursed himself all the way back down the hall to his room knowing he wouldn't be getting any sleep tonight. He knew the minute that he closed his eyes the image of Emily stroking that pickle and closing her lips around it, would play over and over in his mind.

"Here's to another sleepless night," he mumbled as he threw himself backwards onto the bed.

Chapter Seven

The parking lot at Sinful was packed and the valet drivers were constantly busy. Today was a beautiful day and it seemed like everyone was taking advantage of it. There were people standing around chatting, mostly couples. However, there were a few groups of men as well. *Probably having a meeting or something,* Emily thought as she stepped from her car.

She made the choice of coming down to Daniels' restaurant after scouring through the notes she'd jotted down during her brainstorming with the girls. One of them had said it was a good idea to invade his work space if he began to avoid her at the apartment; and that's exactly what he was doing.

After that little incident in the kitchen, Daniel figured the best way to keep his head clear and not humiliate himself was to keep his distance from her. Upon waking up on Saturday and Sunday, Emily had found that he had already left the apartment to go to the restaurant. He would then stay there well into the night, only coming home when he felt she had gone to bed.

Monday was no different, except this time she wasn't going to stand by and let him avoid her. This time, she wouldn't wait for him to come to her. She would go to him.

After the valet had taken her car, Emily made her way over to the front doors. The men that were standing near the door all stopped to stare at the dark beauty that was making her way inside. Their eyes lowered from her face to her breast. Then, as she walked by, her waist and plump ass completed their perusal.

Emily was unaware of their attention and could care less. She only had eyes for one man and she couldn't wait to see him. This wasn't her first time at the restaurant. She had been there several times with his and her family celebrating, and just like the last time, she found the décor beautiful and the atmosphere relaxing.

"Ms. Bawler, is that you?"

Emily turned around to see one of the waiters approaching her with a huge smile on his face.

"Anthony! How are you? Did you get into that school you wanted to go to?" she asked returning his smile. She leaned forward, giving him a brief hug.

Anthony was one of the few waiters that had been working at Sinful since its grand opening. He was only a teenager when he'd first started. He was honest, reliable, and definitely an asset to Daniel. When she found out he wasn't able to get a scholarship at Hampton University because he'd applied too late, she called in a favor and made it happen.

"I'm fine and yes I got in. They said I got a verbal recommendation and they gave me a full ride," he said looking at her knowingly.

"What?" she said, trying to look innocent, smiling.

Anthony laughed. "*You* know what. I know it was you Ms. Bawler and I want to thank you from the bottom of my heart. Getting my degree in business is going to make such a difference in my life and I owe it all to you. I don't know how I can ever pay you back"

Emily smiled shyly. "Don't worry about paying me back Anthony. When you get on your feet and make something out of yourself, just pay it forward."

Anthony nodded. "I will. I promise," he said with conviction. Then his eyes brightened up. "Oh! I almost forgot. I'm up for a promotion as a night manager. I hope I get it. It will make it easier for me to take morning classes at the university."

"I'm sure you will. No one is more deserving of it than you," said Emily.

They chatted for a few more minutes catching up.

"So I guess you're here to see the boss man, right?" asked Anthony, smiling.

Emily laughed. "Yeah. Where's he hiding?"

"In his office. Follow me and I'll take you to him."

Anthony turned and started towards the back of the restaurant. He took her down a well lit hallway and through a pair of swinging doors. He took a left turn, then stopped at the first door on his right.

"Here we are," he said before lifting his hand to knock. He didn't wait for an answer. He knew Emily was considered family, so he turned the knob and stepped aside to let enter. Once she was inside, Anthony winked, then pulled the door closed.

Daniel didn't even look up. He was used to his employees walking into his office after a quick knock to drop something on his desk before retreating. But when nothing was left on his desk, he looked up and froze. There he found Emily standing there in a cream linen pants suit looking lovely as ever. His eyes roamed her from head to toe and her smooth chocolate skin called to him even from a distance. *Aw man.*

Emily couldn't tell what he was thinking and she didn't know what to say. She only knew what she was feeling. Heat. A burning heat that she felt everywhere his eyes had quickly touched.

"Hi, Danny."

"Emily." The one word sounded hollow and void of emotion. *I can smell her perfume.*

She stared at him waiting for him to speak, but he didn't say anything. He just stared at her.

That's it? Is that all he's going to say after avoiding me for two whole days? Does he regret my being here?

She averted her eyes and began moving around the room. Although she'd been at the restaurant before, she had never been in his office. It was decorated in white with deep tones of dark blue leather furniture. His desk was glass on the top and wood underneath. Sculptural console lamps and mirrors added just the right amount of suave. The design itself was simple, yet luxurious. *I like it.*

Emily moved over to a shelf that held photos and she stopped to examine them. She gazed at them, smiling at the familiar faces. She knew family was everything to the Tase's. Always has been. Always will be. They always stuck together no matter what. She guessed that's why growing up, she was always trying to hang around them. She loved being included. Her parents had shipped her off to school and damn near forgot about her until her music ability started to show. Then her mother was always hovering over her making sure she practiced and didn't get distracted by boys.

Should have been watching out for the girls too, mother.

A glass sculpture of a violin caught her attention and she reached out, letting her hand glide across its surface. The detailing of the design was precise and defined. Every line and curve was accurate.

"This is beautiful," she whispered, leaning closer to the design.

Daniel stood up slowly and made his way over to her. "Yes. It is." Although she was talking about the sculpture, he was referring to her. He looked down at her feet and saw that her toes were painted with white swirls. *Such small feet.*

Emily jerked around not knowing he had moved and was now standing so close. His hands were tucked away in his pockets and he looked sexy, yet uncomfortable. He was dressed in dark slacks and a white shirt. His tie was hanging loosely around his collar. She knew somewhere in the room he had a suit jacket. He always wore a suit to greet his guest.

Emily moved away and stopped at his desk. There was a red stress ball lying there and she picked it up. She tried squeezing it, but couldn't. *Figures. He's the one with all the muscles.* She placed the ball back on the desk and moved further into the corner. A photo on a small table caught her attention and she headed for it.

Daniel saw where she was headed and knew he had to stop her. He couldn't let her see the picture of them together. She was smiling directly into the camera, but he was looking over at her and all the love he felt for her was reflected in his eyes. It's the only photo of them that he'd placed into a frame.

"Why are you here Emily? Did you need something?"

His question reminded her of why she was there and she turned around to face him. He hadn't moved, but his presence made an impact on her anyway. His strong, broad shoulders, slim waist and penetrating eyes just did something to her.

"I was hungry. I thought I'd come down and have a bite to eat." *What's over here?* she wondered, as she moved towards a bar at the other end of the room. She picked up one of the bottles of liquor and read the label. She sat the heavy bottle back down and walked back over to his desk.

She's touching all of my things.

"I'll call Anthony and tell him to set you up a table."

Just as he finished his sentence she eased down into his chair. She felt small sitting there and giggled. On impulse, she twirled the chair around in a circle.

Daniel couldn't help the smile that curved his lips. "Are you having fun?"

Emily's eyes were bright with laughter. "Yes. It's just that it's so big." She twirled the chair around once more.

Daniel was glad that she had or she would have seen the shocked look on his face. He knew that she had meant that in the most innocent way possible, but his dirty mind had come to another conclusion for her words altogether. *She doesn't need to know what I was thinking.*

"I know you're tall Daniel, but this chair is huge. My feet are barely touching the floor," she said smiling.

Watching her twirling around in his chair was driving him crazy. He wanted to lift her up and place her on his lap and give her another kind of ride. One they both would enjoy.

Shaking his head to clear it of the erotic images of Emily riding him in his chair, he stepped over and picked up the phone. After he dialed a few numbers Anthony picked up.

"Yes, sir?"

"Dress a table for Ms. Bawler."

"It's already done, sir," said Anthony.

"Thank you, Anthony."

"You're welcome, sir."

Daniel hung up the phone and smiled. *Anthony is always on top of everything. He never makes a mistake. I hope he will be pleased when I offer him the management position.*

"Is everything all set," asked Emily standing.

"Yes," said Daniel. "Come on. I'll take you to your table."

Emily followed him to the door. After he opened it, he stepped aside to let her step out ahead of him making sure there was enough space for her to move without touching. Emily was aware of what he was doing and felt a little bothered by it. It became one of those moments where she began to doubt what she was doing.

Her mind was distracted as she began to pass by him and she tripped. Daniel swiftly reached out to grab her arm to keep her from falling, except she was closer than he thought. By sheer accident, his hand grazed her breast before she stumbled into his arms. They ended up chest to chest.

"Oh!"

Emily felt something equivalent to a bolt of lightening pass through her. Her nipples hardened immediately at the feel of his firm muscled chest against her sensitive orbs. The feeling hit her with a rush and she became lightheaded. Her hands slid up to his shoulders as she tried to regain her footing.

Daniel's skin was on fire. There was no other way to describe it. With Emily pressed up against him, his body could only react one way. Burn. All kinds of fiery sensations traveled through him starting from where her hands touched him. The softness of her full round breast pushing against him had him fighting a moan.

Suddenly, Emily shifted to the right and lightly grazed her breast on his chest. Arousal like never before slammed him fiercely causing his dick to harden fully. Daniel was shocked by his reaction to such an innocent move. To keep her from feeling his erection he took her by the arms and move her away from him.

"Dammit, be careful, Emily," he growled.

He saw her hurt expression and cursed himself for sounding so harsh. He knew she hadn't meant to stumble into him. He was just being an ass because he couldn't control his body.

"I'm sorry, Danny. I don't know what I tripped over."

When he saw her about to look down and examine the floor, he panicked. If she looked down, there was no way she wouldn't see his erection bulging in his pants.

Grabbing her arm, he pulled her further into the hall and turned her in the direction that would get her back to the restaurants dining floor.

"No, im sorry. I didn't mean to snap at you. I just don't want to see you hurt yourself. Look, im going to go wash my hands. I'll meet you at the table, okay."

Daniel didn't wait for an answer. He walked back inside his office and practically closed the door in her face. Thankful for the privacy, he moved as fast as he could in his condition towards the bathroom.

Emily stood there staring at the door at a loss for words. Daniel was upset with her and she was confused as to why. Granted, tripping in front of him was embarrassing, but it wasn't that big a deal. Especially not for him to snap at her and then abandon her in the hallway. *I guess that's proof enough that he doesn't want me.*

Feeling rejected, Emily started on her way down the hall. As soon as she reached the swinging doors, Anthony stepped out of thin air and took her arm.

"Come on Ms. Bawler. Mr. Tase just called me again and said to make sure you didn't leave."

She looked up at him, shocked. "He did?"

"Yup. Don't worry. I set you up on the second level so you can enjoy the open window view," he said, heading towards the elevator.

"That was nice of you Anthony. Thank you."

"Not a problem," he said, tapping the button to close the doors.

It only took a moment for them to reach the second floor. When the doors swooshed open, Daniel was standing there waiting.

"I'll take it from here Anthony. Thank you."

Anthony smiled. "You're welcome, sir. Enjoy your lunch."

Emily stepped off the elevator surprised to see Daniel already there. *He must have run up the stairs.*

Without touching her, he gestured for her to walk ahead of him. It wasn't hard for her to find their table since it was the only one set with glasses and menus. There were at least another twenty tables up there, but Anthony had closed off the entrance giving them some privacy.

Daniel pulled out her chair and seated her, before taking his own. Neither of them said a word. Daniel was trying to find a way to explain his foolish behavior and she was still fighting the uncertainty of his feelings.

Trying to move past the incident in the hall, Emily picked up her menu and hid behind it. She felt a little uncomfortable and needed a moment to herself. *I guess I should decide on what to order.* Her eyes began to scan the menu items. Everything sounded so good, however, she settled on the Garlic Seared Shrimp with Smoked Paprika. It was served with Parmesan Potatoes and a Crisp Garden Salad.

Now that she knew what she wanted, she took a peek around her menu and connected with a pair of dark eyes staring at her. She stared back. *His eyelashes are really long.*

"Shouldn't you be checking out the menu to see what you want to order?"

"I wrote the menu, Emily. I already know what's on it."

"Oh." *Of course he knows what's on it idiot,* she berated herself.

Feeling uncomfortable with the way he was staring at her, she turned to gaze out the window. The sandy beach lay before her and the vibrant blue of the water stretched out for miles. Seagulls were flying about being a pest to a few people whom decided to take a stroll. The view was beautiful and relaxing, and she was happy that Anthony chose this table.

"Are you ready to order, sir?"

Emily turned to see Anthony had returned. She was so engrossed with her thoughts that she didn't even heard him return.

"Emily."

Emily nodded and rambled off her order.

"And to drink?" asked Anthony.

"Water, please." She wasn't in the mood for alcohol.

"And you, sir?"

"Double the order Anthony, but I'll take a sprite to drink."

"I'll return in a moment," he said as he picked up the menus and disappeared.

Now that Anthony was gone the silence returned and she again turned to the window.

"Are you bored?" he asked softly.

Emily glanced over to find him watching her.

"No. Why? Are you?" she asked, wondering if he was the one that was bored.

He smiled. "On the contrary. I mean, I know I haven't made any great conversation so far, but im happy to see you."

"Are you?" she asked, her head tilted to the side in disbelief.

He frowned. "Yes, I am."

"You sure don't act like it. You've been leaving the apartment before I wake up and coming back after I'm asleep. One would think that you're avoiding me," she said, trying to hide her emotions and failing. "If you didn't want me to stay Danny, you shouldn't have let me. I told you I would have found a hotel to stay at."

You're a damn idiot, man. You've hurt her feelings.

Daniel reached over and took hold of her hand. He ignored the tiny jolt of zing he felt and gave it a reassuring squeeze.

"Em, trust me. I want you to stay. I mean it."

She looked into his eyes, trying to see if he was being honest. "Are you sure?" she asked hesitantly.

"More than anything," he said with sincerity, leaving no doubt in Emily's mind that it was the truth.

"Okay."

All the tension and reluctance slid away and Emily relaxed. A huge smile lit up her face and Daniel's chest tightened knowing he was responsible for it. *If only I can make her smile like that forever.*

It was that small break in their conversation when Anthony

reappeared to serve them their meals. He moved swiftly setting down the food and drinks before making an exit. The delicious aroma of the food drifted towards Emily making her mouth water. Suddenly, a small grumble could be heard and her head shot up mortified.

"Em, was that your stomach growling?" Daniel asked, doing his best to keep a straight face.

"A gentleman would have ignored that," she said sounding annoyed.

Daniel gave in and laughed. "Yeah, I guess a gentleman would, huh?"

Emily rolled her eyes and picked up her fork. "You're such a neanderthal," she said, stabbing a shrimp and placing it into her mouth. A million different flavors assaulted her taste buds all at once and she closed her eyes, enjoying the delicious onslaught of spices. "Mmm... this is so good," she said softly.

Oh, shit.

Daniel's heart almost stopped as he watched Emily close her eyes enjoying her food. She leisurely chewed the shrimp and then he got the pleasure of watching her swallow. He could see when her throat constricted allowing the shrimp to slide down. Then to make the whole situation even more erotic, she eased her tongue at a snail's pace across her lips removing the buttery sauce.

When she opened her eyes, Daniel was looking at her. His gaze had become heated and it took everything in him not to lean across that table and press his mouth to her's so he could sample her flavor. Nothing he'd ever seen or experienced was as raw and seductive as what he'd just witnessed. The thing that was bothering him about it the most was that it wasn't forced. It was innocent. *And it's driving me crazy.*

"You have to try it. Trust me, you'll love it," she said, popping another shrimp into her mouth.

Daniel groaned and reached for his drink taking huge gulps. He could see another sleepless night in his future.

Chapter Eight

Sherwood High School sat on the edge of town near a beautiful public park. Its grounds were filled with tall trees and meticulously trimmed bushes giving it the appearance of an expensive private school. The school had only recently been given a face lift on the inside and outside. However, that was only a façade. The students that attended Sherwood were all from a low income district, which meant a slew of hardships coupled with peer pressure, bullying, fighting, drugs, and weapons. The bottom line is that most of the students are being pushed along just to see them go, while a small percentage of others are fighting for a chance to move on and better their lives.

That's exactly the opportunity that Emily was there to hand out; a fighting chance. Today she would be joining Sherwood's staff and family in attending a mini concert given for the senior citizens of the Alexandria Group Home not far from the school. She will be able to assess each nominated student as they play a solo in the performance. Sadly, she would only be able to choose one student to attend classes at Julliard come September. If it was up to her, she would give them both a full scholarship.

"Ms. Bawler!"

Hearing her name being called, Emily turned to find a tall rail thin woman waving at her ecstatically. Her long bleached blonde hair was pulled up into a high bun exposing her slender neck. The blue knee length dress flowed loosely around her flipping in the warm breeze.

"I'm so happy I caught you before you went inside. I'm Mrs. Fidel, the music teacher. We spoke on the phone several times. I wanted to give you the background sheets on the two students you will be viewing tonight."

Emily smiled politely. "Oh, great. This will give me time to read them before the performance starts."

"Exactly! I'm glad we're on the same page," she said while handing her the dark green folder. "I must ask that you not judge the children on their geographic background, but on their musical skill set and academics. They are more than qualified to attend such a school as Julliard."

Hearing the slight warning in the woman's voice, Emily reassured her.

"Don't worry Mrs. Fidel. I'm here to view their talent only. Besides, it's the things we see and experience that we put into our music that makes it exceptional. Don't you agree?"

Mrs. Fidel's smile widened. "Yes! I absolutely do. Shall we?" she asked, gesturing towards the front door.

Emily nodded and headed inside.

Together they found their seats and just as she'd stated, Emily began reading the information in the folder. The first document was on Donald Jenkins. He was a 18 year old student that had been playing the violin since the age of five. His parents had found an old violin at a thrift store and given it to him as a Christmas gift. They'd hoped it would distract him from realizing he hadn't gotten a bike like he'd wanted. Imagine how shocked they were when he began playing a beautiful melody without any music sheets or lessons.

Donald's parents had moved around a lot and now lived in a low income housing complex. Although Donald has never had any trouble with the law, he'd been suspended twice for fighting. Reading more, Emily found that on both occasions he had been defending himself from older boys.

She turned the page to the next student, Khandace Murphy. A 17 year old student that had only been playing the violin for two years. She had been placed in detention, which on that day was being held in the music room. Knowing she was not allowed to touch the instruments, she picked up a violin and never put it down. Mrs. Fidel was convinced the girl was a prodigy.

Emily continued to read and found that Khandace lived with her mother and little brother. Her mother was on a fixed income and seldom showed up for any of her recitals. On many occasions, Khandace had deliberately interrupted her classes so she could be sent to detention where she could play the violin all day. She didn't own one of her own.

Closing the folder, Emily leaned back in her seat. She had noticed the page numbers on the top of the documents and saw that the last two pages were missing on both assessments. She turned to look at Mrs. Fidel.

As if the woman had read her mind, she leaned over towards Emily. "The last two pages are confidential and will only become available to you for the student that you choose," she said softly. "You have to understand that a lot of kids here have had a hard life Ms. Bawler."

"I understand Mrs. Fidel. I'm not here to judge anyone. At Julliard, we have a wide variety of students and they all come with their own issues and concerns. However, by the time they leave, they'll be a totally new person."

"I hope so. These children need to have something to believe in. Hope is what keeps us all moving forward."

Just then a short, balding man stepped to the center of the large room that had been temporarily turned into a music hall. About sixty chairs were set up in a half circle, leaving a large portion of the room open to the performers. The room was now filled with elderly men and women eager to see the show.

"Ladies and gentlemen, can I have your attention please. This afternoon, a few students from Sherwood High School have come to share with us some of their talents. It's my honor to welcome them here at the Alexandria Group Home and I ask that you join me in extending that welcome," he said as he began clapping, and everyone did the same.

Not long after that, a group of kids came out of a side door dressed in tights and bright yellow shirts. They put on a fantastic dance routine that had everyone standing and applauding at the end. That performance set the table for an afternoon of extraordinary talent. Emily was totally enjoying herself.

When it was time for the first violinist to come out, the room got quiet as a single chair was placed in the middle of the room. Donald came out dressed neatly in a white shirt and dark slacks. He was short for his age and Emily now understood why the older boys kept picking with him. He carried his violin carefully and sat on the edge of the chair, keeping his back straight.

"I'll be playing *Open Sun by Emily Bawler*."

Angel B

His eyes met hers and she smiled. *He's not the first one to try that move on me.*

When the room was completely quiet, he lifted his instrument and began to play.

The tune immediately came across as elegant and whimsical. It all sort of floated around the room in a light dance. The chords tiptoed in a sweet ballet, drawing you in to keep you wanting more. The way Donald exerted his energy into the music left you breathless and upset that it had to end.

The moment the last sound filtered throughout the room an explosion of applause could be heard all the way down the hall. Donald stood up slowly in shock, and smiled. His eyes cut over to the two chairs that were made available to his family and his smile faded. They were empty. Shaking his head, he bowed quickly and left through the side door.

Emily looked over to Mrs. Fidel and the woman shook her head, giving her a sad smile.

The introduction of the next student pulled Emily's attention once again. A young girl dressed in a Sherwood High School t-shirt, blue jeans and sneakers, came prancing out to take her seat. The violin she was using had been borrowed from the school and would be returned afterwards. Unlike Donald, Khandace didn't say what piece she would be playing. She sat patiently waiting for the room to quiet down. Once the room was silent, she lifted the violin and began to play.

Right away, Emily was caught. Although she didn't recognize the solo she was playing, it was obvious that it had been written to be difficult and Emily wondered if the girl would be able to pull it off.

The lush arrangement of notes rushed out at you and then suddenly changed direction becoming teasing and light. Its melody would draw you in closer becoming personal and dangerous, only to soothe you with slow electric balladry. The movement of the music held you hostage until you were afraid to breathe and miss a moment of its beauty.

All too soon the piece ended and Khandace stood to leave. She was headed towards the door when the announcer stopped her.

"Excuse me young lady, but you haven't told us the song title and its composer."

Emily heard a few people laugh, yet the young girl wasn't affected by it at all.

She lifted her head high, with a serious face. "It's called *Captured* and I wrote." She then turned and left.

The shocked sound she heard throughout the room caused Emily to smile. *Well, that shut them up.*

The show had ended and Emily was headed out the door. She now had to do the hard part of choosing which student to attend Julliard with a full scholarship. But right now, all she wanted to do was get home and find something to eat. Remembering that she had walked the few blocks from the school to the group home, she turned and started down the street.

Finally reaching the school, she was making her way around the corner towards the parking lot when she bumped into someone.

"Oh, I'm so sorry," she called out embarrassed. "I wasn't looking where I was going."

"It's alright. I'm just as guilty. I had my head down looking at my phone."

Recognizing the voice, Emily took a step back. *What the hell?*

"Sherry?"

She remembered my name. "Do I know you?" Sherry asked, pretending she didn't recognize her.

"Yes and no."

When Sherry looked confused, Emily laughed.

"We've only met once and it was a while ago at a lounge in New Jersey called Diamonds In The Rough. I'm Emily," she said smiling.

A look of fake recognition shown on Sherry's face. "Emily Bawler. Wow," she said, smiling. "I remember now. I mean, how can I forget? That was some night, right?"

It was?

Emily thought it was weird finding Sherry in Virginia and it sort of made her feel uncomfortable, especially when she remembered her encounter with the woman in the bathroom.

Why was she here? "So what brings you to Virginia?" she asked casually.

"Unfortunately, not a vacation. I'm here for a funeral," she answered, showing her a eulogy she held in her hand of a young woman. "She was a close friend of the family. She and my mom grew up together and became besties. Their friendship lasted until the day she died."

"I'm sorry, Sherry. I shouldn't have pried," Emily said, feeling bad for her. She brushed off her being in Virginia the same time as she was as being coincidental.

Sherry gave her a warm smile. "No, it's alright. People die all the time right?"

What the fuck? "Yeah, I guess. Look, I have to go. I have somewhere to be," she said as she moved around her, heading towards the parking lot. "It was nice seeing you again, though."

"Yeah, likewise," said Sherry, watching her walk away. "Bye!"

Emily looked back over her shoulder and gave a quick wave goodbye, never breaking her stride. She was happy when she made it to her car and slid inside. The Lord was watching out for her today, because as she neared the exit, the light was still green and she made a fast dash down the block.

Sherry hurried to her car and tried to follow Emily, but lost her due to getting stuck at a red light. *Damn, now I'll have to stake out the high school to catch her again. Next time I won't lose her.*

***

When Emily got to the apartment and stepped inside, she stood there at the entrance with her head tilted to the side, listening. When she didn't hear a sound, she smiled knowing Daniel hadn't made it home yet. *Got the place all to myself,* she thought as she made her way down the hall.

She walked into her bedroom and took a shower. She slid into a pink midriff shirt and a pair of short jean shorts. Hearing her stomach growl, she hurried out the room towards the kitchen. She was bending over in his refrigerator searching for a snack when Daniel walked into the kitchen and saw her. All of her.

"Jesus Christ, Emily put some damn clothes on!" he yelled. "You're not a child anymore!"

Startled, Emily jumped and dropped the jar of cherries. It hit the floor and burst open, splashing cherries everywhere. When he looked at the wounded look on her face, he felt like an ass. He knew he had yelled at her because he was loosing his battle at staying away from her and his nerves were on edge because of it. He looked down at the cherries and broken glass, then at her bare feet, and swore. He walked over to her and scooped her up in his arms.

He sat her down on the couch gently. "Don't move," he ordered before going back into the kitchen. He returned with a damp towel. He began wiping the sticky red juice from her legs. At first he was moving quickly trying to hurry and get it done, but soon, his movements slowed and his breathing became shallow. Feeling his resolve slipping, he tossed the towel on her lap and stood. He turned away from her quickly so she wouldn't see his dick straining against his zipper.

"You can finish that yourself. I'll take care of the kitchen," he said, and left.

Emily watched him leave and tears welled up in her eyes. He acted as if he didn't want her around him. He stayed away all day and wouldn't come home until she was asleep. And now he yelled at her about her clothes as if he was repulsed by what he saw. She was starting to feel like she was making a fool of herself being here.

Maybe he wasn't interested in me after all. She eased up from the couch and went back to her room. That night she cried herself to sleep.

Chapter Nine

The next morning when Emily woke up the first thing she realized was that she wasn't alone. She knew this because she could smell coffee brewing. After being embarrassed and hurt about last night, she tried to draw out her need for food, but her stomach growled its disapproval. Deciding to get dressed and leave the safety of her room, she found Daniel in the kitchen sitting at the table with his back to her drinking a cup of coffee. She still felt nervous and embarrassed about yesterday, and was about to turn and leave when he spoke.

"Come sit down Emily." His voice was low, but it still made her jump.

Emily walked further into the kitchen and sat down. She didn't say a word as she tried to look at everything except him.

Daniel saw that she was avoiding his gaze and knew her discomfort was his fault. He missed her laughter and silly jokes, and knew he had to fix things between them.

"Em, I was a jerk yesterday and I'm sorry," he said staring at her.

"It's okay, Danny. You've been working long hours and you probably were tired."

"No. Don't do that."

She finally looked up and met his gaze. "Do what?" she asked confused.

"Don't make excuses for my behavior. I was wrong and I shouldn't have treated you that way. I'm sorry I made you feel uncomfortable. Do you accept my apology," he asked and she realized he really needed to hear her answer.

"Yes. I accept your apology," she said sincerely.

She heard him release a long breath and saw him physically relax in his chair.

Seeing that the awkward moment had passed, she got up to pour herself a cup of coffee. She returned to the table, grabbed a bagel from the plate and began plucking off pieces, dipping it in her coffee. Daniel frowned at her and she smiled.

"What?"

"How the hell can you eat that like that?"

She hunched her shoulders. "It's all going to end up in the same place anyway," she said, smiling broadly.

He shook his head and smiled. He held her eyes for a long moment, wondering... wishing.

"You need to do that more often," he said, staring at her lips as she chewed.

"Do what?" she asked and licked her lips.

He didn't say anything at first getting distracted by her tongue.

"Smile," he responded with a forced calmness. "You should smile every day, all day. It's beautiful. Breathtaking," he finished in a whisper.

Emily stopped chewing and was looking at him with a surprised expression. She watched how his hands were clenching and then relaxing against his legs. How his eyes were boring into hers with such intensity that she had to look away.

Damn... he's gorgeous and I have no idea what I'm doing.

After taking a few deep breaths, she looked up to find him gone. She wasn't upset by it. She was actually happy. He apologized, but the best thing was that he paid her a compliment while looking at her like he wanted to kiss her. Emily smiled widely and then giggled as she popped a large piece of the bagel into her mouth.

Chapter Ten

Emily was happy that she and Daniel had cleared the air between them. Knowing that her assignment for assessing the students during their recital was over, she needed to find another reason to extend her time here in Virginia. The only idea she could come up with was to say she would be giving herself a mini vacation. The only thing is she would need to convince Daniel to let her stick around a few more days.

Technically, she was on her summer vacation and so there wouldn't be anything suspicious about her saying she wanted to take in the sites. However, her real objective was to stay close to him and stay in his personal space. As for the students, she only needed to type up her report and mail it back to Julliard, and then drop off a copy back at the high school. After that, her time was her own.

Since she had yet to hear Daniel moving around in his room, she decided to go for a run.

Emily was stretching in the living room when Daniel came from his office. His gaze took in her gray tights and a red T-shirt that read *Eat My Dust*. Hearing him laugh, she turned to him frowning.

"What's so funny?"

"I was laughing at your shirt."

She looked down, making sure nothing was on it. Seeing nothing she looked up. "And? What about it?"

He walked over to the chair and flopped down in it, his long legs stretched out in front of him. "Nothing. Just trying to picture those short legs, leaving anyone in the dust."

Emily put her hands on her hips and sucked her teeth. She stood as tall as her five foot three body would allow. "Boy, please. I can run circles around you," she said with her lips tooted up.

Daniel laughed. "That's cute," he said, watching her. His gaze taking in the plump outline of her behind.

"Well, show and tell old man. Go throw on some sweats and come with me for a run," she said, moving into another stretch.

Daniel sat there watching the competitive look in her eyes and felt his heart squeeze in his chest when she bent forward letting her chin touch her knees.

When he didn't respond, she stood up straight again and turned to him. A wicked stare met his heated gaze. "Or are you just a scared little boy?"

He wanted nothing more than to pull her on his lap and kiss that smart mouth of hers. *There are plenty of things I can do to show her why she shouldn't be calling me a little anything.*

Daniel stood up and walked past her. "Give me five minutes," he said, heading for his bedroom.

He returned wearing sneakers, basketball shorts, and a shirt with the sleeves cut off. Emily had seen him in nothing but swimming trunks, yet he still managed to make her heart flutter when she scanned over his body.

And what a body it was. She had the pleasure of peeping out his six two, hard, lean chestnut frame. His muscular arms and legs were twitching as he did a few quick stretches.

"You sure you don't want to do some more serious stretches?" she asked in concern.

"To keep up with you," he asked, laughing.

Emily shrugged her shoulders. "Suit yourself."

"You ready?" he asked heading towards the door.

"Right behind you," she answered.

On their way down in the elevator, she got up the nerve to ask him about staying a few days longer.

"Um, Danny, can I ask you something."

Daniel was leaning back against the cushioned leather wall with his eyes closed, listening to the elevator music.

"Sure."

"Well, I know I said that I would be leaving right after I saw the kids at the high school perform, but now that it's all done, I wanted to extend my stay here in Virginia."

"Mm hmm," he responded with his eyes still closed.

"I wanted to continue to stay here with you."

Slowly his eyes opened and he saw her standing close to the doors with a hopeful look on her face as she waited for his answer.

Did she just say she wanted to stay here with me? Then a thought crossed his mind and he felt foolish. All the hotels were booked in the area because of a celebrity wedding. She'll need a place to stay. He knew he should say no, but truth be told, he wanted her there with him for as long as he could have her before she returned to New York.

Well, say yes then, idiot.

"If you can keep up with me around the park you can stay," he said as they emerged from the elevator.

"And if I can't?" Emily asked. *He knows damn well his legs are much longer than mine.*

Daniel smiled and started singing. "Hit the road Jack, and don'tcha come back no more, no more, no more, no more…"

"Ha ha! Very funny."

An hour later they were walking back to his building, laughing and talking.

"You know you only won because I tripped right?" he said, lifting his shirt to wipe the sweat from his face. Daniel had tripped on a stick that was on the path and pulled a muscle, which is what caused him to lose the race. So he claimed, anyway.

Holy Jesus, would you look at his six… wait, eight pack.

"Man up, Danny. Don't be a sore loser," she said, laughing as she teased him about it. "Just know that I'm going to love having a free place to stay while I check out all the sights and beaches. Oh, and I will definitely be doing some shopping," she said as they entered the elevator.

"I'm not a sore loser. Heck, for all I know, you tossed that stick there as a trap."

"What!?" Emily's mouth was open wide as she looked at him in shock.

"You heard me. That's low, even for you, Em."

Emily burst out laughing just as the elevator doors closed.

Chapter Eleven

At the restaurant, Daniel was dealing with all the little problems that kept popping up that day. His head chef Charles Macano had been complaining about needing prep help in the kitchen for quite some time now, so he'd put an ad in the paper to hire someone to train. He was in the middle of his fourth interview when the chef came charging into his office.

"I can't do it!" he yelled as he stomped towards Daniel's desk wielding a long spoon.

Daniel looked up from the resume in front of him and leaned back in his chair exhausted. He tossed the pen he held in his hand on top of the stack of papers, glancing over at the young man sitting across from him.

"Calm down, Charles and tell me what you can't do." He figured the problem wasn't as bad as he was making it. At least he hoped it wasn't.

Charles stopped right in front of his desk and struck a dramatic pose. "If I tell you I can't, then I can't," he said in a strong southern accent.

"Okay, but you're not telling me what you *can't* do," said Daniel, feeling the tension rise up the back of his neck.

Charles spun his spoon in a circle. "I can't complete tonights menu, that's what."

"And why is that?" asked Daniel, knowing he wasn't going to like the answer.

"Because no one did any prep for the stir fry," he stated with an angry glare.

Daniel eyes narrowed. "What do you mean no one prepped for

the stir fry. You said you had the menu completed already."

"Yes, I know. The menu is completed, however, I had no prep chef for the afternoon, so no one prepared the vegetables for the stir fry. Therefore, I can't complete the meal." He stood there with his head held high waiting for Daniel to give him a solution for the problem.

Daniel knew Charles ran the kitchen and cooked most of the main courses, and basically what he was telling him was that he couldn't be everywhere at once. He himself was in the middle of interviews, not to mention he had a shit load of paperwork covering his desk. There was no way he could stop what he was doing and help out in the kitchen.

Then a thought crossed his mind and he looked over at the man sitting across from him. He was feeling pressed for time, and upset that he had to deal with such nonsense instead of finishing his paperwork and going through the property sites his realtor had sent over to him. Desperate times come with desperate measures.

"What did you say your name was again?"

"Derrek Miller, Sir."

"Well Derrek Miller, the job is yours if you can start right now. What do you say?"

Derrek stood up and picked up his bag. "Where can I put my things?"

Daniel smiled. "Charles, meet your new prep chef, Derrek. Get him settled in, properly dressed, and start him immediately on the stir fry."

Charles exhaled relieved. "Thank you Mr. Tase. I was about to quit and you know I will quit," he said heading for the door.

"Yeah, I know Charles," he said smiling. The man had been quitting for the last five years.

After hiring the new guy, the day had gone by without any more problems and Daniel was finally able to get some work done. He noticed the time and wondered what Emily was doing. He shut everything down and left for the day.

When he got home, she was standing at the window in the living room, eating wheat thins from the box. He stood there watching her before going over to join her. He snatched the box from her hands and popped a few into his mouth.

"Hey, those are mine!"

"Didn't your Momma ever tell you to share?" he asked smiling.

She was looking up at him, but he wouldn't meet her gaze. Instead, he was glancing out over the city as the sky darkened, and the lights began to come on almost one by one.

"I love this time of day. When night comes and people start turning on their lights. It's like they're taking turns and one section at a time the city begins to glow. It's beautiful," he said, looking down at her. "Don't you agree?"

Emily was stuck for words so she just nodded her head. *This man is beautiful and I'm so at a loss as to how to make him mine.*

Daniel gave a short laugh and turned to lean his back against the railing. His gaze was caught by something she was twirling around in her hands.

"What's that?" he asked, nodding at her hand.

"Hmm?" she was still trying to get her wits about her.

Daniel smiled, his sexy lips spreading. "In your hand."

Emily lifted her hand. "Oh. It's one of the chess pieces from your game. I picked it up as I walked by," she said, walking back inside to place it back on the board.

"Do you know how to play?" he asked following behind her slowly.

"Some," she said, placing the bishop back on the board.

Daniel pulled out one of the chairs and gestured for her to sit. He then took the other chair. "Let's play a game."

Emily stood by the chair, but didn't sit. She shook her head. "No. I don't think so. I don't want to beat you like I did when we went running," she said smugly.

Daniel looked up from the board frowning. "You didn't beat me. I pulled a muscle when I tripped over that stick you put there."

"Mm hmm," she said laughing.

"What do you mean Mm hmm?"

"Nothing." She eased into the chair slowly.

Feeling like a sore loser, Daniel wanted to get a little revenge. "How about we make a wager."

Oh boy. Here we go. "Like what?"

"The winner gets to make the loser do something."

Emily looked down at the shiny pieces on the board. She knew how Daniel and his brothers were. They played horrible jokes on each other, and once she started coming around, they had even played quite a few on her. She remembered a trick Daniel had played on her by filling her water bottle with the water from the fish tank. She had never gotten any revenge on him for that.

She looked up at him with determination in her eyes. "Okay, but you can't say no to whatever it is, even if you don't like it."

Daniel leaned back, smiling. "Okay. It's a deal," he said, reaching his hand across the board for her to shake.

Emily reached out and took his hand, enjoying the warmth it provided around hers. "Let the games begin."

Thirty minutes later, Daniel was staring at her across the table smiling. He had played chess in high school and had walked away as the State Champion three years in a row. Obviously this was something Emily didn't know about him, because she was chewing on her bottom lip, searching for a place to move that wouldn't allow him to take another one of her men.

"Do you need to take a break?" he asked, chuckling.

Emily lifted her eyes up from the board and looked at his smug smile. *He thinks he's going to win, when he'd actually lost the game four moves ago.* She was biding her time so she could continue spending time with him. But seeing his cocky little smile made her choose to do him in.

Emily sat up straight in her chair and smiled. "Are you tired? I can end this now so that you can go on to bed old man."

The laugh that Daniel let bellow through the house caused Emily to narrow her eyes.

"Are you kidding? I have half of your men resting on this side of the table. Admit it. You're done, little girl. Old man my ass," he said chuckling.

She drew in a deep breath and released it. "You don't know how much I'm going to enjoy this," she said staring at him. She rubbed her hands together, and then reached for the piece that would let her claim the game. "Checkmate."

Emily watched as Daniel's smile dropped and a frown took its place. "What the hell!" he said, leaning closer to scan the board.

Emily stood up and left the room. When she returned, Daniel was still checking the board for his mistake.

"Four moves back," she said, standing next to him.

"What?" he asked, looking up at her, his eyebrows drawn together.

She pointed to a few of his pieces. "After you moved here and I took your bishop, you left your queen vulnerable. You never blocked me on this side because I drew your attention to the other side by only moving the pieces on that side. It was over a long time ago," she said smiling. "Now," she said, placing a white bag on the table. "Are you ready for your makeover?"

Daniel's eyes widened. "My makeover!?"

He watched in horror as Emily started pulling makeup from the bag. "Yes, but we need to get you prepared first," she said untwisting a tube of lipstick.

Daniel stared at the lipstick like it was a snake. "You're kidding, right? I'm not wearing any lipstick Emily."

Emily stopped pulling out makeup. "We had a deal, Danny. We even shook on it. Are you going back on your word?"

Knowing that he wouldn't live this one down, he shook his head.

"No. Go ahead and get it over with," he said, leaning back in his chair and sighing loudly.

Emily giggled as she walked up close to him holding the lipstick. She reached up and placed her hand on his chin to lift his head. Daniel felt a shiver run down the side of his neck and his eyes watched her as she leaned in close to him. The smell of her perfume wafted up to his nose with a light stimulating scent and he groaned.

Emily heard the sound, but chose to ignore it. She stepped closer and her leg bumped his and he jerked it away as if she'd burned him. Not letting his behavior bother her, she began to lightly slide the lipstick over his lips. Once she was done, she reached for the blush and started to apply it to his cheeks.

Daniel knew that she was making him look like a damn fool, but he didn't care. He was too consumed by the feel of her body brushing up against his. How her soft fingers moved against his neck and face.

"Close your eyes," she whispered.

Daniel didn't hesitate. He closed his eyes and damn near jumped out of his chair when she lifted her leg to place between his. He swallowed hard knowing that all she had to do was look down to see his dick was hard and ready.

Emily was trying to concentrate on what she was doing, but couldn't restrain from enjoying her brief moment of freedom to touch him. Her hand glided around his ear and rested on the side of his smooth wavy hair. She glided the velvet stick coated with blue powder over his eyelids gently and then leaned down to softly blow the excess off.

Feeling her warm breath blow across his face was the most erotic thing ever. His hands gripped the arms of the chair and he shifted, trying to relieve the tension he felt in his groin area. The air around them thickened and his breathing quickened.

Emily slid her hand down his neck, letting it rest on his shoulder. She flexed her fingers over the strong muscle under her fingers. When Daniel sighed softly, she squeezed again, and his head leaned to the side enjoying the massage.

Knowing if she took it any further, he would put a stop to it, so she decided to finish what she'd started. Emily turned and grabbed her cell phone from the bag. Making sure the flash was off, she snapped off several pictures while his eyes were still closed.

Stepping away from him, she moved to the other side of the table. She readied the cell phone camera and pointed it towards him. She was damn near in tears trying to hold in her laughter. Gaining control, she called his name.

"Danny."

"Mmmm?" he responded, still under her spell.

"Say cheese."

It took Daniel a moment to comprehend what she'd said. When it finally registered, his eyes popped open and she snapped away. His eyes were confused and then opened wide when he saw the cell phone in her hand. He stared at her with a horrified expression. Still smiling, Emily reached over and slid the mirror over to him.

"Dammit, Emily," he said, standing up so quickly that the chair almost toppled over. When he looked up at her, she was backing up from the room laughing.

Seeing the warning in his eyes, she turned and took off running. She just made it to her room, locking the door when she heard his heavy hand knocking.

"Emily, I just want the phone," he said, trying to sound mad, but she could hear the laughter in his voice.

"Why do you want my phone," she asked as her fingers were moving over the keys in swift movements sending the pictures to his brother's and their wives.

"I just want to see it for a second," he said shaking the doorknob.

"I don't think so, old man. I'm in the middle of something," she said laughing.

Daniel stopped laughing, and then a look of dread crossed his face. "Emily, please tell me you didn't post those pictures on Facebook."

"Of course not. I would never do that, Danny."

Daniel sighed in relief.

"However, I can't speak for everyone else."

Daniel rested his forehead against the door. "Everyone else?" he mumbled.

Laughing, Emily walked closer to the door and placed her hand against the smooth wood. "Yeah, you know. Everyone else," she said, smiling.

When he didn't respond, she stood there holding her breath. "Danny?"

"Yes?"

"Remember when you made me drink the fish tank water?"

Daniel frowned and then smiled. "Yes." When she didn't say anything else he stepped away from the door and laughed. "Are you kidding me? We were like sixteen."

"I know, and you told everybody about it too. I was embarrassed for the whole summer," she said, trying to sound angry. "Every time I came outside, they would call me flipper."

He burst out laughing remembering that summer and how happy he was that she'd gotten to stay home instead of going off to music camp. They had spent almost every day together making a nuisance of themselves.

"Hey, Danny?"

"Yeah?" he responded, laughter still filled in his tone.

"If you had won, what would you have asked me to do?" Curiosity spurred her to ask him.

Almost instantly Daniel became serious. The image of him pulling her into his arms and tasting her full lips as he held her tightly against his body had him shutting his eyes in beautiful pain.

"Does it really matter now," he asked softly while looking at the door as if he could see her through it.

"Yes."

For a minute she thought he had walked away, but then she heard his deep reply.

"I would have asked you to play for me," he lied, knowing a kiss was what he truly desired. "Good night, Em."

"G'night, Danny," she called out softly before backing away from the door. She turned, then ran an jumped onto the bed with a huge smile on her face.

Chapter Twelve

The rain was coming down in a harsh downpour giving the humid morning a much needed cooling down. The raindrops were huge as they pummeled the cars windshields causing traffic to slow down to a snails pace. Some drivers decided to pull over to wait for the storm to lighten up, feeling it was a little too dangerous to keep driving.

However, the storm didn't stop Emily. She was on her way back to Sherwood High School to have a sit down with each of the students privately. During that time, she would have the chance to get to know them on a personal level. It was the last step before she made her choice and emailed her decision back to Mary at the office.

Finding a parking space close to the door was easy since the school was closed for summer recess. Grabbing her bag and securing it on her shoulder, she reached into the passenger seat beside her and picked up her umbrella. Opening the car door, she shoved the umbrella up, and slid from the car.

Happy that she hadn't gotten all that wet, Emily made a fast dash to the front of the building where a security guard stood holding a door open for her.

"Oh my goodness. Thank you so much for opening the door for me. If I had to stop to ring the bell I would have gotten soaked to the bone," she said as she closed the umbrella and stepped inside.

"It's not a problem Ms. Bawler," said the young woman. "Mrs. Fidel already told me you were coming and since the weather was so nasty today, I thought I'd come up to keep a look out for you."

"Well, I thank you anyway," said Emily, sliding out of her jacket. "Is Mrs. Fidel in her office?"

"Yeah. She told me to send you right in. The kids are there too," said the guard nodding towards an open door to her left.

"Great," said Emily, heading down the hall in the direction the guard had nodded. "And thank you again."

"Not a problem," the woman said, smiling before taking her seat behind the front desk.

Emily checked the time on the clock she saw on the wall and smiled at being a few minutes early. She hated being late. It always made her feel inadequate or unreliable.

Reaching the open door, she lifted her hand and tapped on the glass door.

"Mrs. Fidel?"

Mrs. Fidel looked up from her work and smiled. "Ms. Bawler, please come in," she said standing.

Stepping inside, the first thing that Emily noticed was all the achievement plaques, ribbons and trophies in the showcase cabinet that dominated the whole right side of the room. It was decorated with a beautiful brass design with bright lights beaming down on the awards. Obviously, it was Mrs. Fidel's pride and joy.

"I hope I didn't keep you waiting long," Emily said, knowing darn well she wasn't late.

"No, no, no. I'm always here early, but you're right on time. The kids are over there in the conference room waiting. I gave them some breakfast and they just finished up."

Mrs. Fidel came around her desk and handed Emily two folders. These were larger than the ones she gave her during the recital at the group home. Right away, Emily knew she had their full files and was eager to read them.

"You can leave your jacket here," she said, pointing to a coat hook on the wall. "This shouldn't take long at all. I know you have a short list of questions to ask the children and from there you'll make your decision. But, before you go in, I must warn you that Khandace is in a bit of a funk this morning. She won't tell me what's wrong with her and she's being difficult. If for any reason you feel you can't deal with her, let me know and I'll pull her."

"I understand. How about I start with Donald. Maybe that will give her a little more time to cool down," said Emily.

Smiling, Mrs. Fidel touched Emilys shoulder, thankful for her understanding.

"I think that's a great idea."

Together they entered the brightly lit room. Donald was sitting on one side of the table skimming through one of the music books. When Emily searched the room for Khandace, she found the girl practically hidden behind a stack of chairs playing a game on her cell phone.

"Alright guys. Ms. Bawler is here and Donald she's going to start with you. So Khandace you come with me."

Khandace looked up with a frown. "How come you're starting with him and not me?"

Mrs. Fidel opened her mouth to say something, but Emily beat her to it.

"Because D comes before K in the alphabet."

That was the only explanation Emily gave her as she stared at her. Slowly Khandace stood up and picked up her book bag. She remained staring at her as she walked in her direction. When she saw Emily wasn't going to back down, she looked away.

Mrs. Fidel exhaled in relief. She didn't want to have a big blow out with the girl and cause Ms. Bawler to never want to come back. If this went well, they may possibly gain the attention of other schools to start recruiting some of their students academically.

Emily watched as Khandace and Mrs. Fidel left the room before turning to Donald. She sat across from him laying the folders and her satchel on the table. After pulling out everything she needed from her bag, she sat back and smiled.

"Are you ready to begin Donald?"

"Yeah," he said in a flat tone.

Okayyy.

Twenty minutes later, Emily sat her pen down and excused Donald.

"That's all Donald. You can go. Can you send in Khandace on your way out, please?"

"Yeah."

Emily almost laughed when he again answered her with a flat, yeah. She watched him pick his fitted hat up and slap it backwards on his head. He then grabbed a bent up umbrella and headed for the door.

Moments after he left, Khandace came into the office. She walked over and claimed the seat that Donald had just vacated. Tossing her bag onto the floor next to her, she slouched back in her seat displaying a bored look.

Emily opened the folder on her and headed straight for her academics sheet. Just as she thought. Every teacher said she was bright or held potential, but her behavior was what was holding her back. *Well, there was an easy way to get past that barrier. Find out the center of the problem.*

Closing the folder, Emily picked up a blank questionnaire sheet and her pen. Glancing over at Khandace, she had a thought. She was about to say something when the girl spoke first.

"Is that folder about me," she asked, eyeing the folder.

"Yes."

She stared at the folder with piercing eyes. "What's in it?"

"Just about everything that you've done since first grade."

Khandace met her eyes.

"Does it have my personal business in there?"

Emily glanced at the folder and then back at her.

"Some."

She shook her head and looked away.

Emily didn't say anything. She wanted to wait her out. It was obvious that she'd had a bad morning, and Emily didn't want to push her and make it worse.

"Don't you got some questions on that paper to ask me or something?" she asked, staring out the window at the rain.

"Yes, I do. But let me ask you something first."

Khandace didn't even look her way.

"Do you even want this? Because if you don't, we can stop this right now and you can leave." *Come on Khandace. Make me believe you want this.*

Khandace abruptly stood up and kicked her chair to the side. She tried snatching up her bag, but it had become tangled with the legs of the chair. She struggled with the bag for a few seconds and yelled out in frustration because she couldn't get it loose.

Mrs. Fidel opened the door, and without looking, Emily spoke to her. "Mrs. Fidel, we're still in an interview. Please don't return until I call you. Thank you," she said, trying to soften the blow of her words.

Mrs. Fidel, closed the door just as Khandace finally freed her bag. She made her way around the table and Emily just sat there watching her.

Come on Khandace. Say something!

Khandace spent around angrily. "You know what! That crap you got in that folder, that don't define me!" she yelled. Her chest heaving with anger.

"It doesn't?"

"No! Not by a long shot. These snotty ass teachers pretend to listen to what you have to say, but they don't. They twist your words and write bullshit in there that ain't even true. All they care about is getting that check."

"So what's the truth?" asked Emily calmly.

"What?" She wasn't prepared for that question.

Emily stood up and approached her. They now stood face to face with only a small space between them.

"Tell me the truth about Khandace Murphy."

Khandace stood there quietly. Her body stiff with pent up aggravation.

"You want to know the truth?" she asked angrily as a tear slid down her cheek.

"Yes," Emily said seriously. "I want the real truth. Not that bullshit they have in that folder. Tell me about you."

"Okay," she said, nodding. "Fine. I need it, alright."

"What do you need?"

More tears came.

"It! Music! I need it. I don't know why, but I just do. It helps, you know."

"Helps with what?"

Khandace closed her eyes tightly and held her head down. Her small hands gripped the strap of her bag tightly.

"Everything," she whispered. "All of it. It drives away the noise. It kills the pain. It blinds me to the depression and hopelessness of my life." She looked up and Emily could see a young soul tormented by the life she was forced to endure, because of poverty and the lack of positive influence.

"Why did you choose music?" Emily asked.

Khandace threw her bag onto a chair near the door.

"Why did I choose music?" she asked walking away. She let out a hollow laugh and wiped her wet face. "Man, I didn't choose music. It chose me."

"What do you mean?" asked Emily, walking back up to her.

"I mean, I was put in detention for kicking over the trash can in the cafeteria and was sent to the music room. I saw the violin sitting there and wanted to break it. But when I picked it up I accidentally strummed the strings. That sound made me pause, you know. I felt... funny."

"I saw the bow sitting there and picked it up. I remember seeing people on TV playing and lifted it to my shoulder." She looked over at Emily. "At first I felt stupid. I had to look around and make sure nobody was watching me. Then I started to play. I mean, really play."

She laughed, but it sounded strained. Hollow.

"You see, I never took no lessons or read any music sheets. Hell, I always skipped music class thinking it was lame. So how did I do that? I still don't understand to this day how I did it. How come I was able to learn how to read music so easily?"

"Khandace, you can..."

"No, you don't understand, Ms. Bawler." She moved closer to her. "I said I would tell you the truth about me. And the truth is it's not just the violin, it's everything."

When Emily stood there looking confused, she went on to explain.

"I can play the piano, flute, saxophone and guitar, and I don't know how. I think I'm some sort of freak or something," she said as the tears began to flow freely.

Emily smiled and reached over to take her in her arms. *Yes!*

She held her for a few minutes until she felt her relax in her arms. She then took her by the hand and pulled her to a chair. They sat down next to each other, both content with the silence.

"Listen to me Khandace. You're not a freak." When she didn't respond, Emily took her hand and lifted her chin. "Did you hear me? You're not a freak. But I do know what you are?"

Khandace looked nervous. "There's something wrong with me, right?"

Smiling, Emily shook her head. "No, you're just special. They have a name for what you are. Prodigy."

"What's a prodigy?"

"It's a person, especially someone young, that's gifted with exceptional qualities or abilities. In your case, it's music. It's why you're able to play just about any instrument you put your hands on. It's why learning to read music is so easy for you. It's also why you feel you need it so much. It's become a part of your life. Khandace, you're not a freak. You're extraordinary."

Khandace looked down at her hands as if seeing them for the first time. When she looked up, Emily was blown away. It was the first time she'd seen the girl smile and she was absolutely adorable.

"I hope that smile means you won't be kicking over anymore chairs," said Emily, smiling back.

Khandace chuckled. "Yeah, I'm sorry about that. I was so upset and confused about things, because I didn't understand what was happening to me."

"You'll learn to channel all that energy and emotion into your music. It gets easier."

"Yeah, I guess so."

"Oh, darn. Look at the time. We've been chatting for almost thirty five minutes now. I didn't mean to keep you so long," said Emily standing.

"It's alright," said Khandace. "At least it stopped raining."

"Yes, that's true," said Emily, glancing out the window.

Emily went back over to the table and got her things together while Khandace collected her book bag. They both met up at the door.

"Ms. Bawler, thank you for everything. For explaining things to me and most of all, for listening. I know I won't get the scholarship, but I'm okay with that. Donald deserves it. He's been playing since he was a kid. Anyway, thanks a lot."

"You're welcome," said Emily and watched as Khandace slid out the doorway.

Mrs. Fidel came rushing into the room as Emily was coming out, almost bumping into her.

"Oh! I'm sorry. I didn't know you were at the door," she said looking around. "Is everything alright?"

"Yes, everything is fine." Emily walked passed her to retrieve her jacket from the hook and the umbrella from the floor. "I'll be in contact with you about my decision soon. I know you might not be here, so I'll come by personally to deliver the scholarship papers to Principal Vox."

Mrs. Fidel began to smile. "I'm so happy that everything went according to plan. Maybe next year we'll have more students for you to assess."

Emily smiled. "Maybe." With that she picked up her satchel and left the office.

Stepping from the building Emily shook her head at Virginia's crazy weather. This morning it looked like hurricane season outside, and now the sun was shinning, the birds were chirping, and the humidity was trying to ruin her hair. There was no more need for an umbrella or a jacket.

"Good Lord, this heat is something awful," she said, descending the school's stairs.

"Hey, Emily."

Startled, Emily turned to see Sherry at the bottom of the steps.

What the hell? "Sherry? What are you doing here?"

Since losing Emily in traffic, Sherry had sat for days in her car where she could still see the school entrance, waiting to see Emily again. As soon as she saw her step from the building she rushed over to greet her.

"Oh, I was in the neighborhood," she said, slowly easing up one step.

"The neighborhood?" Emily moved to her right, feeling uneasy. "Do you know someone that goes here at this school?" she asked skeptically.

As if Emily never even asked her a question, Sherry changed the subject. "Since you're here, I was wondering if you would like to have lunch with me? Maybe something Italian. I know you like Italian food," she said, smiling.

How the hell does she know that? "Sorry, but no. I have somewhere I need to be." She began making her way down the steps making sure to keep her distance from her.

Hearing Emily decline her offer yet again, Sherry's smile disappeared. "You like playing games with me, don't you?" she asked, watching Emily walking away from her.

Emily stopped and spun around irritated. "Excuse me? Playing games. How the hell am I playing games with you? We're not dating. I don't want to date you. As a matter of fact, you need to stay away from me, Sherry. Whatever you think is going to happen between us is not going to happen. So the next time you just happen to see me, don't bother to speak to me. Pretend you don't fucking know me."

With that Emily turned and headed towards her car. She looked back over her shoulder once to find Sherry nowhere to be found.

Upset at having to set her straight, she continued to her car and slid behind the wheel. She was so mad that Sherry had the nerve to say she was playing games as if they were seeing each other. She was so pissed that she never thought to look in the rear view mirror behind her, because she would have seen Sherry following her.

Chapter Thirteen

Emily was trying to shake off the uncomfortable feeling she experienced after running into Sherry. She knew there was no way her being there for the second time was a coincidence. Needing to clear her mind and not wanting to be home alone, she made the decision to go see Daniel at the restaurant.

The lunch crowd had recently cleared out and there were only a few patrons taking their time eating. A few staff members who remembered her from her last visit smiled at her as they continued with their duties. She was standing off to the side near a huge mirror when she saw Anthony come out the kitchen carrying a stack of menus. Not wanting to yell out across the restaurant, he pointed in the direction of Daniel's office with a smile. Emily returned the smile and headed down the hall.

She tapped lightly on the door before reaching for the doorknob.

"You looking for someone?"

Startled, Emily turned to see Daniel standing in the hall behind her.

"Don't be sneaking up on me, Danny," she said with fake irritation.

Daniel chuckled. "Then stop trying to break into my office," he said walking towards her. He was wearing gray dress pants, a white shirt unbuttoned at the neck. His sleeves were rolled up to his elbows and she took note of the fine hair that dusted his arms.

I wonder if its soft.

"Were you busy?" she asked, hoping he wasn't.

"Not anymore. What are you doing in my neck of the woods?"

He noticed how sexy she looked in her blue slacks and gray top. A wide silver belt was fitted around her waist and his palms began to itch with the need to replace it with his hands.

"I just came from the high school having a sit down with the kids. I was feeling a little hungry, so I decided to let you feed me," she said smiling.

"What did you have in mind?" he asked, trying to keep his eyes off the way her shirt fit firmly over her breast. *I wonder if her bra is lace. Maybe black.*

"I don't know," she said, tilting her head to the side. "How about some sea food. Do you have scallops?" she asked, looking excited over her choice.

Daniel laughed and nodded his head. "Yeah. I believe I do. Come on," he said, heading towards the kitchen.

"In the kitchen?" *He's actually inviting me into his personal domain?*

"Yes, the kitchen woman. How else am I supposed to cook for you?"

Emily followed Daniel through the double doors and was amazed at what she saw. Everyone was wearing white from head to toe and were moving around the kitchen while calling out times, items, or dishes that were either needed or completed. Although there was a lot of talking all at the same time, there still seemed to be a semblance of order to the chaos.

The dining area with its low lighting, smooth music and soft conversation, always gave her the impression that the kitchen would be the same. However, back here, everything moved quickly, yet efficiently. It was like a well tuned machine and if any part got broken, the whole system would crash.

Daniel watched her look around with an amazed looked on her face. It wasn't the first time he saw that look. His family faces were the same when he brought them back here to see how things worked. As much as his mother loved to cook, she said it all seemed too overwhelming to her. He agreed that it could become tiresome, but he loved it, and he was happy to be sharing it with Emily.

"Come on," he said, grabbing her hand.

Emily saw the grin on his face and returned it while letting him pull her along. He was in his element and he was enjoying himself. She was enjoying it because she was with him.

"Hey, Lewis. Tell Anthony to take over with the seating for me. I'm going to be busy for a while."

Lewis turned around and was clearly shocked to see Emily

standing there. He was even more shocked when he saw Daniel holding her hand. A wide smile lit up his face and he grabbed a clean towel and began wiping his hands.

"Yes, sir. Right away, sir." His hurried movements carried him from the kitchen into the hall.

Daniel continued through the kitchen until he ended up in a section that was cut off from the rest. It was set up like the other stations filled with stainless steel utensils and appliances. However, this section was much larger. It was filled with cookbooks, note cards and a shelf with several red binders.

"Is this your station?" she asked curiously.

Nodding, he reached for an apron and wrapped it around his waist. "Yeah. No one cooks in here but me." He took down another apron and held it out to her.

She eyed the apron and then looked up at him.

"I thought you said you were going to cook me something to eat?"

"Damn, woman. You can at least chop up an onion or two," he said smiling.

Pretending to be annoyed, she snatched the apron and wrapped it around her waist. "My goodness. I should have just sat in the dining area and ordered something. At least I wouldn't have to slave over a hot stove."

Danniel started to laugh. "You are something else, you know that?"

Emily laughed and folded her arms. "Whatever. What now boss?"

Wanting to see how far he could push her he turned and pulled a hair net from a box.

"Here," he said, holding it in front of her.

Emily stared at the hair net like it had the plague.

"And what am I supposed to do with that?" she asked, knowing full well what it was for.

"It's a hair net. You have to put it on," he stated with a straight face.

She looked down at his hand as if she was considering putting it on. Then, after a moment she shook her head.

"No. I can't do it."

"You can't do it?"

"I won't do it," she said with conviction. "There is no way I'm putting that thing on my head."

"Well, it was worth a try," Daniel said before he tossed it in the trash can. A huge grin was on his face.

She sucked her teeth. "You're such a jerk, you know that?" she said, playfully pushing him.

"What I do?" he asked innocently.

Emily crossed her arms again, however, she smiled back at him.

"Okay, okay. Here put this on." He was now holding a white hat.

"Oh great. Now I'm going to have hat hair."

"Everyone wears a hat, Em." And to prove it, he pulled one down over his own head. "It's regulations."

"Yeah, yeah," she mumbled while trying to straighten the hat on her head without messing up her hair.

Daniel pulled one of the binders from the shelf and started flipping through the pages.

"What's in there?" asked Emily.

"Recipes," he answered, his head still down.

"What kind of recipes?"

"Seafood recipes. They're all new and I'm thinking about adding a few to my new cookbook. I wanted to try one and have you sample it."

"Oh," she said, easing closer to him. Her arm brushed up against his and she smiled. *Mmmm, it's soft*, she thought when she felt the hair on his arm touch her skin.

Daniel felt when her arm brushed against his and a tiny static shock zapped him and traveled up his arm. *Damn it.*

"So I get to be your guinea pig today, huh?" she asked, scanning the other books on the shelf. Some were sporting white labels with his neat handwriting.

"Yup! A guinea pig with a free meal," he said smiling. Finally, he found the recipe he was searching for and pulled it from the binder. "Here we go. This is a simple spicy lemon and Jalapeño scallop dish. I'm going to make it with thinly sliced red potatoes seasoned with garlic and thyme. I'm also going to do a fresh spinach and cherry tomato salad splashed with my home made lemon zest salad dressing. What do you think?" he asked, looking down at her.

Emily looked down at the picture of the dish that was paper clipped to the recipe card. "I think it looks delicious, and I might end up messing it up. But..." She picked up one of the onions that was sitting in a bowl off to the side. "I'll just chop this onion and leave you to it." She started looking for a knife.

"Woman, this is a simple wash, season, and cook recipe. There's nothing hard about it. It's basically *Emily* proof," he said and laughed.

"Ha, ha. Laugh it up. I'm not like your brother who burned up the kitchen. I can cook when I want to."

The look of determination on her face made Daniel laugh again.

"First of all, don't take jabs at Miki, because he's not here to defend himself. Secondly, heating up TV dinners and dumping it on a plate is not cooking," he said taking the onion from her.

Emily's mouth fell open. "I only did that once! I had finals and didn't have time to cook, or the time to stop and run to the cafeteria."

"Doesn't matter. You still did it," he said, laughing at her.

"Yeah, well at least I didn't get my tongue stuck on a frozen spoon," she countered.

"Maybe not, but I won that bet, so you can't use that as a comeback."

Emily looked at him standing there with a silly grin and couldn't think of a damn thing to say. He was absolutely gorgeous.

"Look man, just make me something to eat. I'm dying here." She frowned and placed both hands on her stomach.

"That's what I thought," he said laughing. "Okay, I'll get the scallops. You get the potatoes, tomatoes, and the spinach from over there," he said, pointing to a large silver door marked *Frigidaire*.

"I can do that," said Emily. She playfully slapped his arm before moving off in that direction.

Daniel smiled, watching her head towards the walk in refrigerator. He shook his head when he saw her detour over to another work station asking questions. He watched as the chef there gave her a sample. Based off her smile she must have liked what he'd given her.

At that moment she looked over at him and waved. Their eyes held for a moment and something fluttered in his stomach. He watched her lips move as she made conversation with the chef and was captivated. She placed the last of the sample in her mouth and Daniel stared, held in place by the sight of her tongue sliding slowly across her top lip. *I wonder what her lips taste like.*

"Excuse me, sir, but did you need me to prep the stations for tomorrow's menu?"

Daniel's attention was drawn by the new prep worker Darrek he'd hired on the spot. He was a little annoyed at being interrupted from his gazing at Emily, but turned to answer his question. Derrek had already been given a list of duties for the day and shouldn't be asking him what to do.

"Derrek, you were given a duty sheet this morning when you came in. I advise you to refer back to that to see exactly what your responsibilities are for the day," said Daniel in a tight voice.

This wasn't the first time the young man had messed up. A lot of things had been broken, misplaced, or missing all together. Daniel was beginning to second guess hiring him.

Derrek's jaw tightened in resentment. He hated being talked to like he was a moron. It was one of the things that bothered him the most. However, he let it slide and gave his boss a fake smile. *You're fucking lucky im just here for a payday.*

"You're right, sir. Sorry to bother you," he said, before cutting his eyes over to the woman that held Daniel's attention. *Damn, she fine*, he thought before ambling off down the hall.

Emily returned to Daniel's workstation with all the ingredients he'd asked for. She watched as he began chopping the vegetables needed for the salad.

"Are you going to help or just stand there watching?" he asked, as his hands continued to move swiftly with the knife.

Before Emily could reply, an older chef walked over and placed a stool beside her. He was the only one wearing a colorful apron. Everyone else's was white.

"Oh, thank you," she said, smiling.

"You're very welcome," Jeffrey said, smiling from ear to ear.

Daniel turned and gave Jeffrey a heated stare. "Don't you have some soup to make?"

Jeffrey was his Second Chef who worked directly under Charles, the Head Chef. The two of them together, using Daniel's recipes and a few of their own, has put Sinful on the map.

"Quiet kiddo, my soup is already done and it's amazing as usual," he said, frowning at Daniel. He turned his attention back to Emily now sitting quietly on the stool. "Would you like a sample?" he asked, smiling.

Emily nodded. "I would love some."

Jeffrey ambled off quickly heading for his station. He returned in no time with a small soup cup filled with a soup that made her mouth water.

"Here you go, my dear. Careful, don't burn yourself," he said, handing her the cup.

She lifted the cup to her nose and inhaled deeply. She closed her eyes, letting the delicious aroma relax her.

"Wow, it smells amazing."

Daniel licked his lips, and it wasn't because of the soup.

"Yes. It's my Greek Chicken soup." He leaned closer to whisper near her ear. "The trick is in the cheese. I use crumbled Feta in mine," he said before standing up straight.

"It's my recipe," Daniel mumbled under his breath, feeling left out.

"You need to cut those onions smaller," Jeffrey said, peeking around Daniel. "Are you trying to choke her?"

"I know that," Daniel said with a huff. He looked down at the pile of onions and noticed that they weren't diced at all, but were huge chunks. *Dammit.* He swiped the onions in the trash can and grabbed another to start over. This time he'd pay attention before he did something stupid like chop a finger off.

Shaking her head, Emily took a sip of the soup and fell in love. "Oh my Lord. This is downright illegal." She took another sip, then another. "Daniel, have you tasted this? It's so good."

"I've had it before," he said, sounding like a jealous lover.

Jeffrey chuckled and clasped his hands together. "Good! Then my job is done. I've made sure you have at least one proper meal for the day," he said before returning to his work station.

What the hell was that supposed to mean, thought Daniel. He glanced over at Emily just as she was finishing off her soup.

"I'm done," she said, shoving the cup in his direction. She sat there with an innocent look on her face, knowing damn well he was upset.

Daniel took the cup from her hand, tossed it in the trash, and slowly turned back to his own recipe. He was finally able to concentrate, and in no time, had all of the ingredients prepared. Taking out his favorite pan, he began preparing the scallops. Emily sat there fascinated as she watched him move around the kitchen. Soon the smell of his spicy scallops had the kitchen smelling wonderful.

Once it was complete, Daniel plated the food and carried both of their plates back to his office. He had a small eating area there and thanks to Anthony, it was already set for two. *I'm going to give that guy a bonus.*

During their lunch, Emily asked Daniel a lot of questions. Secretly she was trying to get on his nerves. She did this a lot with her brother Alexander and it drove him crazy. She couldn't wait to see how far Daniel would take it.

"Did you decorate your office?"

Daniel was placing his glass back on the table when she asked her twenty third question. He knew what she was doing and wanted to laugh. But he didn't care. He wanted to spend as much time with her as possible. This was probably the closest he would ever get to having a real date with her. Besides, he wasn't her type anyway. He and his brothers all knew what Emily's sexual preference was, and he wasn't it.

"Yeah. I didn't want an interior decorator to touch it. I like simplicity more than I like flashy."

Emily nodded. She already knew that about him and she liked it. She took another fork full of her salad.

"Do you work out at a gym?" she asked, eyeing him across the table.

"No. Why? You think I need to?" he asked, pausing with his fork halfway to his lips.

Emily let her eyes roam over his broad shoulder, tight muscled arms and firm chest. A bout of heat took form in her stomach before settling between her legs. *What the hell?*

"No, I guess you're okay. You might want to try running on the treadmill though, so you won't be tripping over sticks that aren't there,"she said smiling.

"There was a—"

Emily held her hand up cutting him off. "Yes, I know. There was a stick lying on the ground and you tripped over it. I get it," she said laughing.

Daniel popped the last bite of scallop from his plate into his mouth. He lifted his glass for a drink, but before he took a sip, he mumbled, "There *was* a stick on the ground."

Emily heard him and looked at him. When their eyes met, they both burst into laughter.

***

Sherry pulled up outside the restaurant and watched Emily give her car to the valet. She parked away from the entrance and then entered the restaurant only a few minutes after her. She noticed that the staff actually knew her by name and became curious. As she followed her past the hostess booth, and over near the restrooms, they came to a long hallway. That's when she saw her greet Daniel and burning flames of jealousy and hate filled her eyes and mind.

She could tell by the way he was looking at her that he wanted her. Sherry could do nothing but watch as they walked beyond a door marked staff only, out of her view. Gritting her teeth to keep from calling out and charging behind them, she turned and left. She sat there in her car, without the AC running letting the heat engulf her. Sweat was pouring down her face and back, but it did nothing to distract her from her purpose. To find out more about the bastard that was gawking her woman.

Hours had passed before Emily exited the establishment. From afar, Sherry watched her accept her car from the valet and leave. Sherry pulled out behind her, careful not to be seen. Thiry-five minutes later, she watched as Emily pulled into an underground parking lot and never returned.

Wanting to take a peek inside, Sherry climbed from her car and made her way towards the all glass building. When she stepped inside, she knew from the way the security guards at the front desk looked at her that she wouldn't be given any information.

"Can I help you miss?"one of the guards asked.

Sherry glanced around the foyer, narrowed her eyes, and left.

"Did you get that?" asked the other guard sitting near the cameras.

"I sure did," said his partner. He then walked over to retrieve the photo print out he had captured of the woman on their security camera and placed it in a folder.

Sherry went back to her car and sat there waiting until she saw the man from the restaurant. All types of things were running through her mind. Why is she here instead of a hotel? Who was the guy? What if he doesn't show up? *He'll show up. I saw the way he was watching her. He wants her.*

Her anger continued to build by the minute and her thoughts weren't helping matters. She was outside staring at the front entrance for hours in the heat. She was about to give up when Daniel pulled up. She looked down at her watch and saw that it was almost two in the morning. Sherry watched as Daniel gave his car to a man that appeared out of nowhere and then entered the building. After a quick nod to the men at the front desk, he disappeared into the elevator.

Sherry had only one thought. *He had to go.*

Chapter Fourteen

The next few days played out the same with Daniel working until the wee hours of the morning to avoid running into Emily at the apartment. It was the only way that he could guarantee that he would keep his distance from her. However, his resolve had declined and he now found himself riding the elevator up to the top floor in hopes of seeing her.

He couldn't stay away from her another day, and not from lack of trying. Whether he was asleep or awake he was always fighting his attraction to her. His body was constantly craving her touch, her smile, and her laughter. Yet, at that very moment, it was his mind that was in need of her attention.

Today he had a meeting with Kimberly, his real estate agent, that he'd foolishly slept with. The meeting turned sour when Kimberly started asking if they could have one more night together. It was a conversation they'd had before, and quite frankly, Daniel wasn't interested in having again. Once he'd made that clear, the meeting was focused once again on his new building site. However, the conversation became tense. Her answers to his questions were short and clipped. Basically nothing got done and she left with an attitude, which left him upset because nothing was resolved.

Daniel reached up and rubbed the back of his neck trying to relieve the stress that he felt as he stepped from the elevator. When he walked inside the apartment, he found Emily going through his music collection. She was down on her knees on the floor in front of the entertainment center pulling out CD's and stacking them in front of her. Just the sight of her put him in a better mood.

He headed in her direction and flopped down on the couch. "What are you doing woman?" he asked, giving her a lazy smile.

Emily looked up and smiled. This was the first time in a while that he'd come home earlier enough for her to see him. Usually she would already be in bed, but this time he'd caught her rummaging through his music.

"I'm sorting through these old CD's you have in this cabinet. Don't you buy anything new?" she asked, tossing aside another CD.

Daniel shook his head. His eyes were checking out her gray lounge pants and gray spaghetti strap shirt. The top of her shirt had a thin strip of lace and he kept dropping his gaze down hoping to get a peek.

"Nope. I have most of the new stuff on my phone. Whatever you find down there was copied and then uploaded to everything I have that's digital. Besides, most of that stuff is old school and you don't know nothing about that," he said teasingly.

"What! Boy, stop! I sampled a lot of these old songs for practice and for my recitals when I first started to play. Now if we're talking about you and those lame dance skills you think you possess… " she said trailing off.

Daniel sat up and leaned his arms on his knees. "See, now you definitely don't know what you're talking about. I invented the word smooth when it comes to my moves, woman."

Emily tooted and twisted her lips.

"Danny, you always looked as if you had hot rocks in your pockets when you danced," she said, laughing. "When we were little even your mother cringed when you danced at parties."

He laughed, remembering how his mother would always seem to make her way over to him to tell him to calm down.

"Yeah, well, maybe I wasn't too good at all that fast crap, but I got skills when it comes to those slow jams" he said, giving her a knowing look.

Instantly, she was taken back to the day when they had danced together at the party at his mother's house.

"I guess you were alright," she said, reaching for the remote to try another disk.

"I'm much better now," he stated, smiling. He reached over and plucked the remote from her fingers.

"Good for you," said Emily, keeping her head down. She was pretending to read the song list on the back of a CD case she'd picked up.

Daniel used the remote to switch through the twelve disk CD changer until he found what he was looking for. The sound of *Blue*

Magic's, Teach Me How To Love came through the Boss surround system clear and crisp. He turned up the volume and stood up. Moving closer to her, he reached his hand down.

"Care to give it a try?"

Emily looked up at him and at his hand, and swallowed nervously. She remembered the feelings she felt when he last held her in his arms and felt a shiver slide down her spine. Danniel saw her hesitation and let his next words push her to accept.

"If you can," he said, his gaze narrowing with his dare.

Emily met his stare and her chin raised boldly.

Come on, Em. Say yes, he thought. His gaze never wavering.

Placing the CD on the floor, she touched her hand to his allowing him to assist her in standing. As soon as she was on her feet, he pulled her in his arms. Holding one hand up close to his shoulder, he slid the other around her waist. Feeling her body tense up, he leaned down near her ear and whispered softly.

"Relax, Em. I got you."

Hearing his words, Emily nodded, and Daniel felt her relax against him. They swayed together to the music, letting the slow rhythm twirl around them. He knew this was new to her, so he didn't press her to do more. He only closed his eyes and tried to enjoy this moment of her letting him get this close.

After the first song went off another began to play and Emily began to relax more and more. Daniel felt the exact moment when she let down her guard. She eased closer to him, resting her cheek on his chest. Her head fit perfectly under his chin and a light, fruity fragrance drifted up to him and he inhaled deeply. The softness of her breast pressing against him was sending all kinds of naughty thoughts through his mind, but he ignored them. Right now, tonight, he just wanted to hold her. He might never get her to do this again, and he wanted to revel in it for a long as he could.

Emily was in heaven. Finally, the man she wanted more than anything held her in his arms. There was no one to interfere, no one to scrutinize them, and no reason to stop. It was just him and her all alone.

With those thoughts Emily took a step and moved in closer. She pulled her hand from his and slid both up his sides, across his chest, and over his shoulders. The change caused her to move even closer, pressing her body fully against his. The moment the contact was made she felt his hardened erection pressing snugly against her and a low moan escaped her lips.

Daniel heard the sound, but wasn't sure if it was him or her. The feel of her body sliding and shifting against his was driving him nuts. His heart was beating rapidly and his lower region was throbbing, begging to get released.

How the hell did I let things go this far, he thought as his arms tightened around her. He dipped his hips and applied a little pressure and felt her arms tighten even more around him. *Just a little longer and I'll stop.*

Emily gyrated her hips and gave him a nudge with her pelvis. Hot heat shot through him and he returned the gesture. *Just a little longer,* he repeated to himself, not wanting to pull away from her just yet. *Only a few moments more.*

Never in her life had Emily experienced such desire and ravenous cravings. This was different from anything she'd ever felt while with a woman. The softness was replaced with firmness and hard muscle. The gentleness was exchanged for strength and power. He exuded it. It was magnifying, and it drew her to him. She was lost in a cloud of hunger and only he could satisfy her appetite.

I want this. I want him. She buried her nose in his shirt, breathing in his scent. *I need him.*

This dance of longing and pent up frustration went on and on until the last song on the CD began to play. The *Isley Brother's Living For The Love Of You* would be the song that would bring this dream to an end. But even knowing this, Daniel still wasn't prepared to let go. The sexual charge that was drifting around them held him in it's grasp. He knew this was all in his head. That Emily was only here in his arms for the moment. That once the song ended, things would go back to normal and she would never be his.

They moved slowly like a gentle breeze sailing through the trees. The sway was synchronized as if it had been practiced. The tension was slowly building and Daniel was panicking as he heard the song coming to an end. *No, not yet. Please.*

Emily was literally trembling. The energy between them was unbelievable. Her body was on fire and the only relief came from grinding against the thick length caught between them. Feeling the pressure intensifying, her lips parted and she lifted her head to see the face of the man she wanted.

It was at that very moment the song was in its final stages and Daniel looked down. When their eyes met, he knew he had to have one taste. Deliberately, he rescinded his head until their lips met.

Sweet. Soft. Moist. Hot. All these things rushed through his mind as he devoured Emily's lips. He was left shaken and dazed by the potency of her kiss and amazed that she returned the kiss in equal measure. *Damn.*

Emily had long ago lost any coherent thoughts or words to say. She was operating solely on responsiveness, touch and sound. Once the touch of his lips met hers, she was gone. Her mind went blank, but her body was still aware. She rotated her aching mound on his shaft, releasing a greedy whimper right against his mouth.

Just as the song ended, he pulled back reluctantly. Now that the music had stopped all that could be heard in the room was their loud breathing. Emily was in awe of the difference and felt the need to push closer. She couldn't understand why she felt like she couldn't get enough. She knew it would be different kissing a man, but she hadn't known it would be like this.

Daniel saw the look on Emily's face and took it as her being shocked or upset by his forwardness. He quickly released her and stepped back. He was thankful of his shirt covering his crotch or she would have seen his dick straining against his pants.

"I'm sorry, Em. I don't know what I was thinking," he said as he loudly cleared his throat and reached for the remote. "Must of been the music, huh?" he said with a nervous laugh, trying to downplay the kiss.

Emily was standing there staring at him. She was still trying to gain her equilibrium back. Honestly, she wouldn't be able to hold a decent conversation if she wanted to.

Looking at her and only getting silence, Daniel felt that he really had messed up. He wouldn't hold it against her if she slapped the crap out of him. *What was I thinking kissing her like that?*

Not knowing what else to do, he turned her slightly, giving her a gentle push. "Go to bed, Em," he said softly.

Emily began to walk sluggishly from the room. She turned to look back and stopped. Daniel was standing right where she left him, his eyes were closed, and he was breathing heavily. She smiled, knowing that she had affected him just as much as he had affected her. She wouldn't become offended by him sending her away because she had experienced the desire he felt for her. And although she was ecstatic about it, she had no idea how to handle it.

After taking a much needed shower, she felt more like herself again. She climbed into bed onto the cool sheets and played out the last couple of hours. When she got to the kiss her body responded by getting hot all over again. *That was our first kiss,* she thought smiling. *Actually, that was my first time kissing a man. So technically that was my first kiss.*

Emily was lying in the dark, grinning from ear to ear. She curled up under the cover holding her pillow tightly pretending it was him. She was feeling giddy at knowing she had been right. Daniel does have feelings for her. Those were her last thoughts before drifting off to sleep.

In the next bedroom Daniel is not so lucky. He was in a state of torture, tossing and turning. His body wouldn't let him forget how it felt to hold her in his arms and kiss her. Now his lower region was paying the price for it. He also couldn't get passed the shocked and surprised look on her face. *Or maybe that was disgust,* he thought. Was she disgusted by being kissed by him, by a man? *Of course she was, idiot. She only wants her lips touching another woman's, not yours.*

Angry at his conclusion to Emily's expression, Daniel rolled over, punched his pillow, and prepared for a long restless night.

Chapter Fifteen

The early morning sun crept up on Daniel and he still hadn't slept a wink. It was barely seven o'clock and he was already dressed in a white Polo shirt and a pair of jeans, heading down in the elevator. He knew Emily would be getting up soon, so staying at the apartment was a mistake. No, he would head down to the deli a few blocks away and have a cup of coffee or two.

That was Daniel's intentions when he slid behind the wheel of his all black Hummer, however, he was so distracted by the memories from yesterday that he drove right by the deli. He didn't realize that he'd driven too far until he was on the highway speeding, and dodging between cars. Cursing his irresponsible behavior, he eased off the gas letting the truck slow down to the required speed limit.

Dammit man, you could have caused an accident and killed someone, or yourself, he thought trying to relax. It was futile, because all he could think about was Emily and how good it felt to hold her in his arms. How her hips had pressed into him, sending an intense throb straight to his shaft. The way her lips met his and opened to his demand.

Daniel shook his head slightly, trying to clear his head while still concentrating on the road. The way his heart was beating and the slight rise in his temperature, told him one thing... he was in trouble.

"I can't have her, though," he said feeling agitated. "She's like family. Besides, she doesn't date men, right?" he said, speaking out loud to himself.

Then why was she feeling you up while dancing with you last night. Why did she allow you to kiss her? Why did she kiss you back?

"She did kiss me back," he said frowning. That admission only made him more confused and conflicted about his feelings for her.

On one hand, he knew she was off limits. He and his brother's were raised right along side her and her brother Alexander. Throughout his life she portrayed the figure of being their little sister. But somewhere along the way all that changed for him. The love he had for her was not the same as you would have for a sibling. It was so much more.

Seeing the exit that would take him back to the city, he quickly signaled to change lanes and take the off ramp. Moments later he pulled into his private parking area and killed the engine. He sat there playing tug-of-war with his emotions and what to do about them.

"To hell with this."

Daniel reached into his pocket and pulled out his cell phone. He pressed the button for speed dial and waited.

"What?" The voice came across gruff and muffled.

"You busy?" asked Daniel.

"Hell yeah I'm busy, man. I'm sleeping," said Miki. "What do you want?"

Daniel didn't care about waking him up. He needed someone to talk to before he went crazy. "I need to talk to you about something. Can you meet me somewhere?"

Miki had a good idea about what, or should he say who, he wanted to talk about. He rolled over on his back and yawned loudly. "When?"

"Now." This couldn't wait another day.

"Now? Are you kidding? This is the first day I have the house all to myself and you want me to get up so I can spend time with you."

Feeling rejected, Daniel exhaled noisily. "You know what? You're right. I'm sorry for waking you up. Go back to sleep," he said and disconnected the call.

Deep down Miki wanted to roll over and go back to sleep, but he knew he couldn't leave his brother hanging like that. He pressed the button to call him back.

"Hello?" Daniel answered the phone still sounding miserable.

"The jet is on its way to pick you up, so be at the airstrip in an hour. I'm supposed to meet Arnez at eleven in New Jersey, so I'll pick you up from the airport and we'll head over there together."

Instantly Daniel's stomach began to relax. "Thanks, bro."

"Yeah, whatever. Just have your ass there on time or you're going to get left," said Miki, trying to sound demanding. He hung up the phone and swung the sheet off his body, mad that his sleep had been interrupted.

It was a forty-five minute drive to the airstrip and Daniel made it there with only a few minutes to spare. He locked his truck in a parking garage and hurried to the private gate that was routinely used by his family. After boarding the jet, he secured his seat belt and waited for take off. The drive from VA to NJ would have taken him six hours. He was glad that Miki had sent the jet for him because the flight would only be a little over an hour.

"Good morning, Mr. Tase. We've just got the go ahead for take off and we'll be landing at Teterboro Airport in one hour twenty five minutes. Please buckle up, sit back, and relax."

The voice of the pilot came over the loud speaker and Daniel checked his seat belt once more. He leaned back in the comfortable leather and closed his eyes to rest. Almost instantly visions of Emily and the kiss they shared flooded his mind, but he didn't fight it. He let the memories run freely as he exhaled and relaxed. The image of her was so clear and vivid that he felt he could actually feel her body and smell her scent.

She smelled so good, he thought smiling. *And she felt good too.*

Daniel continued to drift through lasts night's dance reliving each moment slowly and to its fullest. Soon his breathing slowed and he drifted off to sleep. He awoke to a gentle shake and he opened his eyes to find the jets only flight attendant Gail, standing in front of him.

"We've arrived, Mr. Tase. You're free to disembark," said Gail smiling. *Damn, the Tase brother's know they are fine.*

Daniel glanced out the window and saw that they had indeed landed. He shook his head, knowing he had slept the whole way because he'd been exhausted.

"Thank you, Gail," he said unhooking his seat belt and standing.

"You're welcome. If you need anything else just let me know," she said, licking her lips before ambling away.

He shook his head knowing exactly what that was about. It only took him a few minutes to leave the plane and head to the small building that served as a terminal. When he stepped inside, the smell of floor wax hit his nose and he frowned. Whomever had waxed the floors had overdone it with the liquid and it wafted strong and pungent in the air.

"It smells like turpentine doesn't it?"

Daniel turned around to find Miki standing behind him holding a paper towel that covered his nose and mouth.

"Yeah, and it's making my eyes burn. What the hell happened?" he asked heading for the door.

Miki fell in step beside him. "Kevin said one of the maintenance workers dropped a case of cleaners and he obviously didn't clean it up properly," he said stepping outside. "Come on, I'm parked over here."

Daniel followed him down the ramp and across the lot to a red two door BMW. "Is this new?"

Miki opened the doors with the remote and he slid behind the wheel. "No, its Rainy's. She took my car because I said I would sleep in. She said she would be back before I left to hook up with Arnez." He made sure he gave him a side look when he mentioned sleeping in.

"I see the look man, and I appreciate you giving up your day to hear what I have to say."

Now on the highway shifting lanes, Miki gave him a quick glance before returning his attention back to the road.

"Is this something serious?" asked Miki. From the sound of Daniel's voice he figured he might have been wrong thinking he wanted to talk about Emily. Maybe this was a different situation all together.

Daniel didn't say anything for a minute. He glanced out his window watching the scenery fly by in a blur.

"Yeah, it's serious," he finally answered.

"Well, if you don't mind, I'd like to wait until we get to Arnez house before we discuss it. From the look on your face I'm thinking this will require my full attention."

"Indeed, it just might."

***

The traffic from Teterboro to Old Tappan, NJ was unbelievably light so early in the day. Miki had made it to their destination in less than half an hour. When he pulled up to the house at the address Arnez had given him, there were three cars already parked in the long driveway.

"Is that Sydney's car?" asked Daniel. He knew he wanted to talk to Miki, but he sure didn't want a whole room full of people there to listen in.

"I think so, and the white Lexus is Arnez's car. I don't know who the black Lexus belongs to, but that baby is sweet."

"Guess we'll see when we get inside," said Daniel, reaching for the door handle.

He and Miki made their way up to the large house tucked back between two large lion statues. The house was white and almost all glass. The double front doors were dark red and adorned with large silver handles.

Miki pressed the bell and a woman opened the door with a smile.

"Good morning, Miki. Haven't seen you in a while," said Rosie. She stepped aside, allowing them to walk in. "The same goes for you, Daniel. I haven't seen you in almost a year. Where have you been hiding," she asked, pulling him in for a brief hug.

Both men were smiling widely. Rosie had been the caretaker of Arnez's home for over eleven years. She was more like a mother to him than anything. Where ever he goes, she goes. No questions asked.

"I just saw you a few months ago, Mrs. Rosie. Remember, you made me the brownies without the nuts?" asked Miki.

She smiled sweetly at him. "Yes, I remember. I made them just like you like them." She turned to look at Daniel. "What about you young man? What's your excuse for staying away so long?"

"Work," Daniel said simply.

"Psh!" Rosie sucked her teeth. "That's not good enough. How are you ever going to find a wife and give me some babies to bake my famous cookies for if all you do is work?"

Daniel was saved from responding when Arnez entered the foyer.

"Mrs. Rosie, are you holding my boys hostage out here," he asked before giving Miki, and then Daniel, a handshake.

"No, I was trying to find out why Daniel hasn't settled down yet. The both of you aren't getting any younger."

"Well, I would have asked you Mrs. Rosie, but you be playing hard to get," said Daniel, smiling.

She laughed, giving him a gentle swat to his arm. "You better stop teasing, boy. In my younger days I would've had you bringing me flowers and sweets," she said before she walked away, heading towards the kitchen, their laughter loud in her ears.

"Damn man. How old is Mrs. Rosie now?" Miki asked, smiling.

Arnez rubbed his chin in thought. "I don't really know. Every year on her birthday, she keeps claiming to be fifty-four. Why do you want to know anyway?"

"Because she just might be your last chance at marriage," Miki said and laughed.

Arnez stared back at him with a straight face. "Yeah, well, you're lucky you married Rainy when you did, because I would have made a move and Jordan would be calling me daddy."

All humor erased from Miki face. "That shit's not funny," he said seriously.

Daniel and Arnez burst out laughing.

He walked over and slapped Miki hard on the back. "Then stay out of my personal affairs, punk." He then walked back into the living room. They both followed him, but Miki followed at a slower pace. He was trying to figure out if Arnez had been serious or just joking.

Arnez went to the bar and opened the small fridge below it. "You guys want anything?"

"Not me," said Miki. "I have to drive this idiot back to the airstrip and then drive home. Besides, isn't it a little early to be drinking?"

"It's apple juice, smart ass. What about you Daniel?"

"No, I'm good," said Daniel. He caught movement to his left and saw Sydney walking into the room from the patio. "Sydney," he said in a way of greeting.

Sydney smiled widely at seeing his two brother's. He reached out and shook first, Daniel's hand, and then Miki's. "I didn't know you guys were going to be here."

"I was invited," said Miki. "This guy is a stowaway," he said jokingly, nodding in Daniel's direction.

They all hooted with laughter at Daniel's blank face.

"Then what the hell does that make me?"

Everyone turned to see who else had ended up at Arnez's front door. Standing in the doorway was a tall man dressed in white from head to toe. He wore designer shades to cover his bright blue eyes. Even from where they were standing you could see that his clothes were expensive, maybe even tailor made. His hair was brown with blond highlights, and his skin was a dark tan signaling that he'd been spending time outdoors.

"Don't everyone say I love you all at once," he said before breaking into a wide grin.

"Well, I'll be damned. If it isn't Mr. Money Man himself. Jerome Hawthorne, how the hell are you?" bellowed Miki. He met Jerome halfway across the room before grabbing him in a brotherly hug.

Jerome was pleased to see Miki and Daniel. He hadn't seen his longtime friends in over eight years. To him, this was as close to having siblings as it gets. His birth mother left him in the hospital as a baby, and soon after he was adopted by the Hawthorne's. His adoptive mother couldn't have children, and that left Jerome an only child and constantly ringing the Tase family doorbell.

"Life's been treating me well, but from what I hear, you've been doing pretty well your damn self. Heard you latched on to a beautiful woman and got yourself a little mini me running around."

Miki puffed up with pride. "Hell yeah, she's beautiful and Jordan is my heart. I can't wait for you to meet them both."

"And what's up with you, Daniel," Jerome asked, giving him the same tight hug. "How's life by the beach?"

Daniel stepped back, grinning. "Same ole, same ole," said Daniel.

"Don't be modest," said Sydney. "Daniel's about to expand. He's been searching locations all over. My brother's about to turn Sinful into a five star restaurant chain." He walked over to Daniel and threw his arm around his shoulder. "Daniel, I wanna be like you when I grow up."

"Get the hell out of here," Daniel said, laughing.

Laughter rang out throughout the room.

"Wow. When was the last time all of us were together?" asked Arnez easing down onto the plush green sofa. The whole room was decorated in forest green, cream and white. It was something straight out of a magazine.

"Man, I can't even remember," said Jerome, taking a seat at the other end of the couch. "I think it was that time Sydney was running from Tonya Miller. She said she was pregnant and he'd gotten her pregnant in her dream."

They all laughed at Sydney.

"Come on man, that was back in college. I swear, that girl was on medication. All I did was kiss her good night after one date. I already had no intention of seeing her again. She called me for weeks."

"Oh, I remember that," chimed in Daniel. "Mom nearly flipped out her chair when Tonya told her that she was about to be a grandmother."

Sydney flopped down hard on one of the white leather chairs.

"I'm glad you guys still find it all so amusing. I'm not the only one that's had a few stalkers," he said looking at Arnez.

"Carol wasn't a stalker. She was only a little misguided," he said, sipping from his glass.

"Hmm. That's not how I remember it," blurted out Daniel. "She had proof that you told her you loved her. I believe it was a letter."

"That's right. I read it too. It was in your hand writing man. You have to stop saying it wasn't you," said Miki.

"Alright, damn. I wrote the letter. It was the only way she would let me get to the cookie," said Arnez, laughing.

Jerome shook his head. "That's just fowl man."

"I'll admit it was wrong, but I was only nineteen. Back then my mind was set on one thing only... cookie."

They all burst out laughing, nodding their heads in agreement.

The catching up went on for hours. It had been a long time since they'd seen Jerome, and Miki was quick to set up a date for them to all hang out. He knew Chance, Myka and Michael would make the time to come up. His parents would also be happy to see him again. His small lunch date soon turned into a full dinner party.

"I'll tell you one thing, it's good to be home. My mother damn near tackled me when I walked through the door and my dad was almost in tears. It made me see how my being gone all the time was affecting them. From now on I'm going to spend more time at home. That shit hurt my heart to see them like that."

"Where were you anyway. The last I heard, you were in Moscow rubbing elbows with politicians," said Miki.

"Yeah, and that crap got old quick. I found myself surrounded by a bunch of stuck up snobs that only cared about how to make the next dollar. Even at concerts and ski resorts the main topic was money. I mean damn, give it a break. The room was filled with beautiful women and all they saw was money. I got low quick."

Daniel shook his head. "I guess when you become a billionaire talking about money becomes taboo, huh?"

Jerome gave Daniel the side eye. "Who you playing the fool for. Remember, I know how much you're worth too. All of you," he said, glancing at each of them. "And what are you doing here anyway? Shouldn't you be at the restaurant cheffing up a new recipe or something?"

Miki looked over at Daniel with a smirk. "Yeah, why are you here, Daniel? Didn't you want to talk to me about something?"

Daniel gave Miki a sharp stare which made everyone curious.

"We can talk about that later," he said stiffly.

"Come on now man. We're all family here. Hell, there's not a secret among us," Sydney said, glancing briefly at everyone. He gave Jerome a knowing look before quickly glancing away. "You can talk freely here. It's like being in Vegas. Whatever happens here, stays here."

Daniel looked at them trying to come to grips with what to say. He was tired of keeping all of this bottled inside, but he still wasn't sure how they would react to him having feelings for Emily. He decided to keep that part to himself.

"This is serious. It's not a joking matter. I don't want to break up the mood," he said, hoping they would let it slide.

"I think this is the perfect time for you to say it. You'll get more than just my opinion on it now," Miki said, backing him into a corner.

Daniel nodded and turned towards the patio window. He stood there looking out onto the landscape and the ridiculously huge pool. He was trying to find a way to begin when Sydey gave him the perfect start.

"You look like you're having woman trouble," said Sydney, shaking his head. "Only a woman can make a man look like that."

Jerome hid a chuckle behind his hand. "Okay, cool. You're having woman trouble. Who's the lucky woman?"

Daniel glanced over his shoulder to find them all staring at him waiting for an answer.

"Who she is isn't important right now. I only need to hear your opinion about something," he said, walking over and going behind the bar. He opened the small refrigerator and pulled out a bottle of orange juice.

"About what," asked Arnez. He had finished his drink and was now reclining back in a slouched position.

"About this situation I find myself in. It's more of a 'what would you do' situation. It's complicated," he said, gulping down his juice.

Sydney was tired of Daniel procrastinating. "How about you just tell us what's going on."

Daniel nodded. "Alright." He took a deep breath and let it out slowly. *Here goes nothing.* "I'm interested in asking out a woman I've known for years, but the problem is I've been put in the friend zone. Actually, it's more like the family zone and I have no idea how to get out of it without making a mess of the situation."

"So you want to know if you should ask her out or leave things like they are?" asked Sydney.

"I can't leave things like they are," he said in a desolate tone.

"Why the hell not," asked Jerome, looking confused.

Miki smiled and answered the question for him. "Because he's in love with her."

Daniel met Miki's gaze and he saw the truth in his eyes. *Does he already know? Or is he guessing?*

"Wait. What? Did I miss something?" asked Sydney, staring at Daniel frowning. "You just said you haven't even asked her out yet. How is it that you're in love?"

Arnez laughed and crossed his legs at the ankle. "You of all people should know the answer to that, Syd."

Sydney knew exactly what, and who, Arnez was referring to and gave him a hard stare. "This isn't about me."

Arnez only laughed. "Mmm hmm."

"Okay," said Jerome pacing back and forth slowly near the patio windows. "You're in love with this woman and it's obvious she doesn't know this," he said and looked at Daniel to confirm it. When Daniel nodded, he kept going. "Maybe the best thing to do is to make a move and see what happens. I mean, you're never going to know if you don't at least try. If you get shot down, then you can either do two things; try again with a new approach or tuck your tail and drink away that loving feeling. You will at least know that you tried and where you stand."

When Jerome was finished giving his opinion, he noticed that everyone in the room was quiet and looking at him.

"What?" he said, throwing his hands up confused. "Is that bad advice or something?"

"No," said Miki. "It's actually excellent advice and I would have said the same thing. It's just that we didn't see that coming from your womanizing ass," he said, chuckling.

"Womanizing!? Man, I'm offended by that accusation," he said with a serious expression. "I am not a womanizer."

Arnez sat up and leaned forward laughing. "Rome, you took

naked pictures of yourself and slipped them into the girls locker room."

"Oh, hell yeah! I remember that," said Sydney. "He had chicks popping up at his house for months."

"His mother played tag on his ass too, if I remember correctly," Miki chimed in laughing.

Jerome slid his hands in his pockets smiling. "All that may be true, but I can tell you one thing, I got a lot of cookie that year. Shit, I had dates lined up for the next year too," he said grinning widely.

"I don't know why," Sydney said jokingly. "I saw those pictures and I wasn't impressed. Looked like it might have been cold that day."

They all burst into laughter.

"Yeah, whatever," said Jerome tugging at his belt. "Y'all know the Hawthorne's are my adoptive parents. When I look down in the shower, I know my real daddy is a black man. Plus, how many white boys you know named Jerome?" he asked. "Don't worry, I'll wait?"

"You a fool, you know that," Daniel said, trying to gain control of his laughter.

"I'm just trying to help my brother's from another mother understand that I'm blessed below the chest." Jerome lifted his shirt and tightened his six pack.

"Aw damn. This is turning ugly," Miki said standing. He walked away from Jerome shaking his head.

Jerome was smiling while trying to look innocent. "What I do?"

Miki cut him a side look.

"Look, it all boils down to this," he said looking at Daniel. "If you really care about this woman and you believe she's what you truly want, then I say go for it. Tomorrow's not promised to anyone, and if I were you, I'd be trying to get as many *today's* in with her as much as possible."

Arnez stood up and stood by Miki. "In other words, stop being a little punk and push up on her before she meets Jerome and he shows her his nude photos."

Jerome approached them holding his cell phone.

"Bruh, I keep a copy in my phone, and if I show her those pictures, it's over for you."

"You really have a copy of those pictures?" asked Arnez, shocked.

"Sure do. Here, let me show you," he said, opening his phone.

Arnez, Daniel and Miki all moved away from Jerome at the same time and headed into the hallway towards the smell of food. Sydney was right on their heels.

"Wait guys. I found them," Jerome called out laughing, trying to catch up.

Chapter Sixteen

With her body all tangled up in the sheets, Emily awakened to a quiet house. Nothing could be heard from inside or outside the apartment and it was totally peaceful. The super softness of her bed added to the peacefulness that she was feeling, and she pulled the sheet over her head and snuggled deeper.

Suddenly, a thought crossed her mind and she began to smile. Her first kiss with Daniel had been only a day ago. Although he had already left the apartment before she woke up, she'd still been in a great mood. Even when he text her, letting her know he would be working late and not to wait up, it hadn't ruined her day.

He'd never text me before to tell me he would be late, she thought smiling sleepily.

Like today, she knew he would already be gone and at the restaurant, yet she was still happy. The reason for that rushed through her with a cheerful tingle and her smile widened. She fought to get the sheets from off her head and around her legs and ended up being out of breath and cheesing.

"It's my birthday," she shouted loudly in the room, happy no one was there with her to look at her like she was crazy. She began to swing her arms and legs open and wide, back and forth, as if she was making a snow angel. She giggled to herself at her silliness.

Rolling over, she sat on the side of the bed and reached for her 'To Do List' she'd created last night. She had mapped out a plan for the whole day starting with cooking dinner and setting up a romantic evening for her and Daniel. Ironically, sitting there thinking of him, her cell phone vibrated in her purse. She hurriedly searched for it and pulled it out. A sudden heat wave claimed her middle and her nipples hardened when she saw it was a text from Daniel.

Happy Birthday, Em.

If her smile widened anymore her face would crack. A weird screeching giggle escaped her and she fell back on the bed, rolling over onto her stomach.

Thank you, Danny baby, with that sexy body. Okay, she didn't write that. She wasn't that brave.

Thank you, Danny.

I would have called you, but I have a few of my venders in my office. I hope you slept well.

Like a baby, she responded. *How about you?*

Some.

Emily stared down at the phone. *Should I say something nasty or sexy,* she wondered biting her lip. Her nervousness shut that thought down. Instead, she came back with something less nerve racking.

I'm making dinner tonight.

Is that right? I guess I can stomach a microwave meal for one day, he joked.

Ha, ha, very funny. Just make sure you're home by seven or else.

Will there be a cake? I love cake.

Emily shook her head. *Yes, greedy boy. I'm making a cake.*

Will it be chocolate?

Do you like chocolate, she asked, feeling like the conversation was about to get naughty.

I love chocolate. Especially if it's sweet.

Knowing she could get a little freaky at times, she decided to see if he was the same.

I think my complexion resembles dark chocolate. Her eyes were glued to the phone waiting for his response.

I agree, said Daniel. *And I can't wait to see just how sweet you taste.*

Oh, shit.

Emily's mouth dropped open, literally. She hadn't been sure how Daniel felt about the kiss they'd shared because she hadn't seen him since it happened, but this clearly let her know exactly where his mind was on that subject.

"Wait. Oh, no! I didn't mean to type that!"

Looking at the screen, she saw that she had indeed typed the words 'Oh shit!' in the box and had somehow touched the send button.

I didn't mean that, she wrote trying to fix her blunder. *I meant that last part, not the first part,* she typed quickly. She was about to type

117

something else when her phone rung. It was Daniel.

"Hello?"

"You okay over there?" he asked softly as if he was trying to talk quietly. He hoped he hadn't pressed her too hard and made her uneasy.

"Oh, umm... Yes, I'm fine. I was trying to say I didn't mean to say that last part to you."

Daniel looked up and saw Kimberley enter his office. He hated the fact that she never knocked. She just barged in like she had the right to. That would be something he would need to rectify.

"Well, I meant the last part that I said to you," said Daniel. He knew he was putting her on the spot, but he wanted to make sure they were heading in the same direction.

She laughed. "You wouldn't be the first," she said flirting. "Just make sure you're here for dinner or there won't be anything sweet waiting for you."

Daniel laughed. He was about to say something to Emily when Kimberly leaned down and tried to kiss him on his lips. He frowned up at her and immediately pulled away. He then twirled his chair around turning his back on her.

"Don't worry. I won't be late for dinner."

"You promise?" she asked, sounding hopeful.

"I promise."

Emily sat back up on the bed smiling. "Alright. I guess I'll grant you permission to get back to work then."

Daniel found himself grinning goofily at their teasing. "I appreciate that. Thank you."

"You're welcome. Bye."

"Bye."

The moment the phone hung up Emily wanted to call him back, but knew she couldn't. He had work to do and so did she. Standing up, she opened her purse to drop the cell back inside and that's when she saw it. It was B.O.B., her battery operated boyfriend. The flexible vibrating silicone universal massager was bright neon pink and winking at her. The shiny silver button on the top beckoned her to pick it up and press it.

Slowly, Emily reached in and pulled B.O.B. out. She'd bought this little device last year. It was small enough to fit in all her bags and she never left home without it. The smoothness of the silicone is what drew her attention to it after seeing it on a commercial. It was soft, pliable, it bent with ease, and she loved it.

Crawling back on the bed, she eased back onto the pillows and got comfortable. She closed her eyes and began to relive the kiss she'd shared with Daniel. It didn't take long for her body to react and her peach began to juice up quickly. One hand was tweaking her nipples while she used the other to massage her wetness. Her fingers were rotating and sliding all across her folds until she built up a fiery tension inside her.

Grabbing B.O.B., she pressed the button twice for more speed, ready for the orgasm she knew would come. She began moving it slowly over her center, loving the vibrations shooting across and through her. Her breathing became erratic and she pressed the pink gadget harder to her clit enjoying the electric trimmers.

Her eyes were squeezed shut and all she could see was Daniel, his head exactly where her hands now were. This wasn't the first time she'd masturbated with Daniel on her mind, but after their shared kiss, her body was reacting crazily. She was on fire.

In her mind, Daniel's mouth was wreaking havoc on her clitty and she was meeting each stroke of his tongue by lifting and rotating her hips. The juices created by her slickness allowed B.O.B.'s smoothness to move like a moist tongue against her. Her arousal became overpowering as she began to moan in pleasure. Her pussy was throbbing with longing as if her own touch wasn't enough.

Emily began to buck her hips harder, her body desperately searching for relief. She continued to gasp and buck, moving the pink gadget's magic directly where she needed it. Then it happened. Her body tensed and Daniel's name slid effortlessly from her lips as the first onslaught of spasms rocked her foundation. She rode the orgasm out, pressing her head back into the pillow as tiny flashes of light fluttered behind her eyelids.

The sweet nectar of her orgasm poured from her peach giving her fingers a slippery treat. As the shocking quivers began to recede, Emily rolled over onto her side, the vibrator still tucked snugly between her thighs. Soft whimpers slid from her lips as she lay there in awe of her love session. Trying to catch her breath, she pressed the button on B.O.B. twice turning it off.

I wonder if Daniel is good with his tongue, was her last thought before she drifted off to sleep, exhausted and satiated.

***

The irritating sound of Emily's phone ringing interrupted her sleep. She rolled over and pulled her phone from her purse. She didn't bother to see who the caller was, because she could barely open her eyes.

"Hello," she answered groggily.

"Happy Birthday!!!" her mother and father, both yelled into the phone.

And that's how the rest of her morning went. After her parents called, her phone was ringing like crazy. Alexander called from China. He was stationed there for some training camp or something. He was trying to explain it as best he could, but she had no idea what he was talking about. She was happy when he told her he would be coming home in a month or so.

Then all the Tase brothers called one right after the other. She also got to speak to Rainy, Stacey and Kayla briefly before they left on an errand. She made plans to give them a call later to touch base on her progress with Daniel. She couldn't wait to tell them about the kiss.

Her friends from Julliard called, and right after that, Tara. They chatted for a while before Emily ended the call knowing she needed to get things ready for tonight. Looking at the clock she saw that it was a little after one. She still had plenty of time to get things done. She got up, took a long hot shower, then got to work on dinner.

***

Kimberley had returned from her business trip with an extra pep in her step. She had closed a deal in New York, selling a bar to two young men from Chicago way over the market value. She had pulled in a mighty, healthy commission and her boss was now looking at her as a prospect for a higher position in the company. She knew if she got Daniel to purchase one of the old warehouses near the docks for the new location of his restaurant, she would snatch the promotion from everyone else. She didn't understand why he was dragging his feet.

She looked over at him and smiled wickedly. In the meantime, until he made up his mind, she would try to get another sample of that huge joystick he carried around. *Hell, I could barely take it*, she thought letting her eyes drop to his crotch. *And he damn sure knew how to use it.*

Kimberley was all in her thoughts, reminiscing about the one night they shared when something Daniel said drew her attention. He was on the phone with his back to her talking in a low tone, but as clear as the morning sky, she heard him tell someone he'd be on time for dinner.

Dinner! Who the hell is he talking to? The way he was trying to keep his voice low let her know it was a woman.

Daniel ended the call with Emily and turned around to find Kimberly staring at him with a frown. He knew that she'd been away on business and that she had returned, but he hadn't expected her to show up today without an appointment.

"Did we have an appointment today, Kimberley," he asked even though he already knew the answer.

He glanced over in the direction of the last two vendors filling out paperwork that he would need to sign. It seemed they all showed up around the same time with deliveries and his staff was hard at work trying to sort out the orders so they could be stocked. He knew he should be back there helping them, but Kimberly was there. He would rush whatever she had to say and see her on her way.

Kimberly recovered quickly from the sting she felt about Daniel making plans with another woman.

"No, we didn't, but you know I've been gone for quite a few days and I was hoping that you've made a decision on the locations I showed you."

Daniel stood up and moved towards the door, hoping that she would follow. No such luck.

"I've been extremely busy these past few days. I haven't gotten to it."

Because you were chasing that whore on the phone. "Oh, that's not good," she said, pulling out her tablet.

Daniel stopped short, and gave her a concerned look. "What do you mean not good?"

"Well, I believe there are two new clients that are interested in the same locations."

Daniel moved back over to his desk and sat down. Anger showed in the tenseness of his shoulders. "I thought you said I was the only one interested in those locations."

"Yes, a few weeks back, but things have changed. With the weather changing and more tourist showing up in Virginia Beach because of that new hotel, real estate is picking up. The people are looking for fresh places to explore their nightlife. And I told you, I can't hold the property forever. I have a boss Daniel."

"Yeah, I know that Kimberly, but why am I just hearing about this now? When we spoke on the phone three days ago, you never mentioned this."

"I only learned today about the new buyers. It's why I came right over," she lied. *And to suck that joystick of yours*, she said to herself.

Daniel sighed in frustration. He knew he couldn't blame Kimberly for his slow decision making. He had been dragging his feet about the whole ordeal. Now his plans to open up a new restaurant might have to be pushed back. *Damn.*

"Okay, tell me what are my options."

"I looked into the file of the new clients and they come from old money and already have the bank's approval on whatever they choose. So, in response to that, I went through my listing and found several other sites that fit your criteria." When she saw Daniel frown, she quickly added, "It's just in case they make an offer within the next few days. This would only be your backup plan."

Begrudgingly, he nodded.

Kimberly pulled a USB cord from her suitcase and walked around his desk. She connected her tablet to his computer and opened the company's site. She leaned in close to type in her password on his keyboard and he eased backwards.

"Oh, I'm sorry. Let me get a chair." She pulled a smaller chair like his from a table and moved it closer to him. She took her seat and the smell of his cologne triggered her kitty. *Mmmm.*

"Let's get to work," she said, and started showing him the properties she thought would fit his needs.
***

Hours had gone by as they worked together to put together a new list for him to inspect. They ate lunch together in his office and continued working until Anthony tapped on his office door.

"Yeah?" Daniel called out, his head still bent down looking at the papers Kimberly had handed him.

Anthony opened the door and peaked inside. When he saw Kimberly sitting a little too close, he grimaced. There was something about her he didn't like and he liked most people.

"Just letting you know everyone is gone. The last of us are heading out."

"What? Wait, what time is it?" he said, looking up at the clock and seeing it was after eleven. "Oh, damn," he said, letting his hand drag down across his face. *Emily.* With all this property searching business going on, their dinner date slipped his mind. *Way to fuck up your first date idiot.*

Daniel hopped up out of his chair. "Get your things Kimberly, we're leaving."

"But, you haven't settled on any of these yet," she said as she stood up slowly.

"Leave them and I'll fax you my decision tomorrow," he said grabbing his car keys. He turned to Anthony. "Wait for us. We can all leave out together."

Anthony glanced over at Kimberly and smiled at her sour face. *Thought you were going to make a move once we were all gone, huh? Not tonight Thot. Not tonight.*

Once Kimberly finally retrieved all her things, Daniel moved them quickly down the hall and out the door. He didn't even wait to see if Kimberly made it to her car before he tore out of the parking lot.

The drive home was slow due to an accident. It wasn't even a bad one, more like a fender bender, yet the traffic was moving slowly because everyone was rubber necking to see what was going on. He ended up stepping off the elevator a few minutes to twelve.

When he opened the door and stepped inside, he stopped. There weren't any lights on and the apartment was pitch black. He smelled something delicious and knew that Emily had indeed cooked, and it made him feel even worse.

He left the lights off and moved down the hall. He knew where everything was, so nothing got knocked over. He saw the table was set beautifully and the food was now cold.

Daniel felt like an ass. He knew that after this, the flowers and the necklace with the diamond heart pendant wouldn't be enough to gain her forgiveness. Every year she had always spent her birthday with her friends at work. This year she was going to spend it with him and he'd messed up. She ended up spending it alone.

He walked pitifully into the living room and found her asleep on the couch. He reached over and turned on a lamp giving the room a soft golden glow. She was still dressed in a short white skirt showing off her smooth legs and a white peasant blouse that was covered in splashes of colors. Her sandals had fallen off her feet and Daniel moved them to the side.

Not really wanting to, but knowing he had to, he reached down and shook her shoulder lightly.

Emily began to stir and opened her eyes, trying to focus. When she looked up and saw Daniel standing there, she sat up. The first thing she did was glance at the time on the stereo.

Daniel saw a brief show of anger cross her face before she hid it. She was definitely upset with him, but chose not to show it. Any other woman would have let him have it, but not Emily. She was too much of a lady to act out of character.

"I'm sorry, Em. I had to stay late at the office. Kimberly came by and we had to sort some things out about the property I'm trying to buy. Before I knew it the time had flown by and the restaurant was closed."

Emily was already disappointed because she'd really been looking forward to spending her birthday with him. However, she became really upset when he said that he was with that real estate woman all this time. All kinds of sordid images flew through her mind of what they had been doing.

All day long she had been thinking about the kiss they'd shared, but obviously he hadn't thought it was a big deal. He was too busy getting his body groped and pawed on by that floozy. And just like a good little woman, she was here cooking his dinner and waiting for him to remember that she even existed. *Well, it won't happen again,* she thought standing.

With hurt feelings, she turned away, not looking at him. " It's alright, Daniel. I'll clean that up in the morning," she said, nodding towards the table. She then walked to her room, disappointed.

Daniel felt like shit. Even though she'd spoken calmly, he knew she was mad at him. *And she called me Daniel, not Danny.*

Chapter Seventeen

It was seven in the morning and his cell phone was ringing excessively like a dog constantly barking. There was no escaping it, so he reached over and snatched it from the nightstand.

"What!" he barked into the receiver.

The sound of Miki's irritated voice didn't deter Daniel at all.

"I need your help."

When Miki heard Daniel's voice he groaned loudly into his pillow.

"Did I do something to you?" asked Miki. "Did someone tell you to do this. Am I being PUNKED."

"No, you're not being punked. I just need your help with something."

Miki sighed wearily. "What do you need help with?"

Without giving up Emily's identity, Daniel proceeded in telling him what happened. "I mean, I missed the whole day. I swear, it slipped my mind and I don't know what to do to make it up to her, or if she even still wants to see me."

"Look, you just need to make it up to her, but in a big way. Do something special for her."

Daniel's face was a blank stare. He had no idea what to do. "Something like what?"

"Come on man, think. Remember what I did for Rainy the first time I got to spend her birthday with her? I flew her out to your restaurant and had Maxwell sing to her. I mean, I wasn't in the dog house, but I still wanted to do it big and out-do any guy before me."

"Yeah, I remember that. Okay, now I see what you mean."

"Cool. Oh, and don't forget to give her a gift. You did get her something, right?" Miki asked.

"Yes, I got her something. It's a chain with a heart on it."

Miki sat up like the wrestler, *The Undertaker.* "What? What are you a teenager. You got her a freaking chain with a heart on it? That's it?"

Daniel was feeling like a loser. He never had to purchase gifts for other women. He never stuck around long enough to have a relationship, so no gifts were given.

"Well, what should I get her then?"

"Man, I don't know, but not that!" Miki stopped and took a deep breath. "Look, how well do you know this woman?"

Daniel thought about it and smiled. "Pretty well."

"Then take what you know about her and go from there. I'm talking about her dreams about tomorrow. The things she daydreams about. What she thinks about the most. Take that and turn it into a gift. You got it?"

That's when Daniel got an idea and he began to smile.

"Hey, do you think I can borrow your jet again?" he asked, already making plans in his head.

Miki flopped back on the bed. "You know, it's not a cup of sugar. You don't call people up asking to borrow a jet."

"Come on, bro. I'll owe you one."

"No, you'll owe me two. This is the second time I've helped you out, and trust me, I will collect."

"So is that a yes?"

"Yes. I'll send it to you. Now get off my phone," he said before hanging up.

Daniel began to feel a little better. He grabbed his phone and called up a friend he knew who moved to Italy. After a few more calls everything was ready. He'd made a deal with a well known violin shop, Amici della Musica, for a rare violin. Although the merchant was willing to part with the violin for an obscene price, he wouldn't be able to have it shipped no sooner than next week. That was going to be a problem.

That's when Daniel came up with the idea to go get it himself. He was thankful for asking Miki to use his jet. Now all he had to do was go pick it up and hope for the best.

Moving to his desk, he quickly scribbled out a note to Emily saying he was going away on business and would return shortly.

After packing a few things, Daniel headed out the door. Thankfully, Emily was still asleep and he was able to slip away without seeing the hurt expression on her face again. The drive to the airport was fast enough, but the flight to Italy would take nineteen hours with two layovers. He would then give the pilot a whole day of rest and head back home that night. The whole setup should only take four days.

***

"Are you still feeling miserable or do you feel better now," asked Tara.

She was sitting across from Emily and Rainy at The Lakeside Club waiting for their waitress to return with their order. The three of them had spent the day getting pampered at The House Of Life, a hair salon and spa. Together, Tara and Rainy had treated Emily for her birthday. Mainly, they just wanted to cheer her up after Daniel's no show.

Feeling like she didn't want to be alone, Emily accepted the gift, and Tara flew her to New York in the company jet. From there, they swooped her up in a stretch limo and headed into the city for some fun and relaxation.

Emily leaned back in her chair and smiled. "I must say, after two hours of shopping, a massage, manicure, pedicure, and then getting my hair done in this fly ass style, I feel like a brand new woman," she said patting her newly curled hair. Her curly mohawk was a replica of Rihanna's and fit her perfectly. The way the men kept glancing at their table, and smiling their way, let them all know that their hairstylist had done her thing.

Leaning back and crossing her legs, Rainy smiled. "I'm glad you're feeling better. I know you were down in the dumps earlier and I'm glad to see a smile on your face."

"Me too," agreed Tara. "Besides, even though Daniel dropped the ball this one time, I don't think you should give up on him. I mean, you did say he lost track of time while working, right?"

Emily nodded her head. "Yeah, but it just bothered me that he was with that Kimberly woman all locked up and alone in his office. All I kept imaging was what they could have been doing together."

"You have to trust him, Emily. If he said he lost track of time working, then that's what you have to believe. Don't let your imagination steer you into seeing what isn't there."

"I know," Emily said, sighing loudly. "I just hate the fact that she's still in his life, even if it's only for business. At one time it had been more and he never mentioned if she was still in the picture. We haven't had the chance to talk or spend any time together."

"Then give him the chance to. Don't jump to conclusions. Besides, you have the upper hand right now," said Tara before taking a sip of her water.

Emily looked at her confused. "What do you mean?"

Tara sat forward, narrowed her eyes, and smiled devilishly. "Technically, he's in the dog house. That means he'll have to do something really spectacular to get out of it."

Rainy burst out laughing. "Tara, you are something else."

Tara laughed. "I'm serious. He'll have to treat you extra special just to get back in your good graces. Shoot, I would have him serving me breakfast in bed and massaging my feet."

The three of them laughed a little too loud and most of the men turned in their direction again. One of the men sitting at a table by himself raised his glass to them, smiling.

"I hate to say it, but Tara's right. He'll definitely need to work hard at fixing things between you. Then maybe you can give him some tongue action as a reward."

Rainy and Tara looked at each other and snickered behind their hands.

Emily glanced at them, shaking her head.

"Um, I need to tell you guys something."

Wanting to hear a little gossip, Tara and Rainy settled down.

Emily was glad for her dark complexion, because she felt her cheeks warm up with a blush before she could even get it out.

"Daniel and I kissed the other night," she blurted out.

"What!?"

"Heifer, you holding out!" bellowed Tara.

Again, all eyes turned on them. Most of the men were staring with smiles at the three beautiful women sitting alone. Others openly ogled them with lustful eyes.

Emily smiled widely. "No, I wasn't trying to hold out. I was so upset about my birthday that I didn't even want to discuss it. But since I feel better now…" she said, letting her sentence fade out.

"You are too much. Give up the details woman," Tara said, leaning in closer not wanting to miss anything.

Emily laid out the details about that night when she and Daniel danced together in his living room. She didn't leave out anything, because she truly needed to get it out and see what they thought.

Tara leaned back once Emily was done with a fat smile on her face. She glanced over at Rainy and saw her grinning as well.

"He's a goner," said Rainy.

"I know," said Tara, responding giddily.

Emily looked at them both with a confused look on her face. "Okay, what do I do now. I have no clue what to do next."

"Nothing," they said in unison, then laughed.

"Nothing?"

"Yes, do nothing. The ball is in his hands. Let him bring it down the court to you. Remember, you're in control, so play it slow. He won't do anything until you let him."

Emily sat back and sighed. "This is much more complicated than being with a woman."

Tara was about to take another sip of her water but stopped. She placed the chilled glass back onto the table and gave Emily her undivided attention. Naturally curious, she felt the need for an explanation.

"Really? How so?"

Emily saw that they were looking at her like she held the golden rule of dating in her hands.

"Well, for starters, women are obviously more emotional, and I say that in a good way. We love to share our feelings, whereas men more or less don't. The way I see it, you have to damn near pull their feelings and thoughts from them physically. It's like playing guess what number I'm thinking. There's no damn way I can do that without a bit of luck. Every relationship I'v been in with women, we sat down and put all of our feelings out in the open. Of course it all boils down to the individual you're with. However, for the most part, when you have two emotional creatures willing to be open about their feelings, it makes things much easier."

Rainy and Tara both were looking at Emily like she was Dr. Phil. Tara's mouth was open and Rainy looked surprised. Before either of them could say anything else, their waitress showed up with their meals.

For the next hour, Tara, Rainy and Emily had fun on their girl's day out. They chatted about relationships, movies and business. They laughed when several of the men finally got up the nerve to approach their table, only to be sent away embarrassed or let down. It was the perfect distraction that Emily needed.

Angel B

Chapter Eighteen

The sun was quickly going down and Emily decided to take a pit stop on her way back to Daniel's apartment from the airport. The woman that styled her hair told her the name of the products that she used and Emily stopped at a beauty supply store to buy them. She loved the way they made her hair look and feel, and she wanted to continue using them.

She found a large store in a mini shopping mall and pulled inside. She grabbed a basket and headed down the aisle, picking up items and placing them back on the shelf. When she saw what she was looking for, she grabbed them and tossed the items in her basket. Heading for the register she stopped short when someone stepped in front of her. Startled, Emily looked up to apologize.

"Oh my goodness. I'm so sorry. I should…" The words fell from her lips when she saw Sherry standing there smiling.

"It's alright, sweetheart. I don't mind you bumping into me."

Sherry was pleased that she'd caught up with Emily in the store. She had returned to the airport parking lot every day checking to see if her car was still there. It had been pure luck that she pulled up just as Emily was sliding behind the wheel. Keeping a safe distance away, she was able to follow her here to the store. Now she stood there gazing down at her with lust in her eyes.

"You look beautiful," she said, reaching out to touch Emilys' hair.

Emily smacked her hand away in displeasure. Disbelief showed on her face at Sherry's audacity. "Are you freaking kidding me!? Are you insane or something?"

Sherry looked around noticing a few customers had turned to see what the skirmish was. "Baby, calm down. People are starting to stare."

Eyes wide, Emily stepped up in Sherry's face. "Listen to me Sherry, and listen well, because this will be the last time I say this to you. I don't want you. I will never want you. So please stop following me or I'll slap a restraining order on your ass with the quickness. You got that?" Her anger caused her to breathe heavily and her breast rose and fell with each breath.

Sherry became very still. "You don't mean that," she said flatly.

"Try me," said Emily before walking off. When she got up front she was happy to see one of the cashiers coming back from a break and rushed to his line.

"Hello," the young man said, smiling brightly.

Emily was so stressed and upset all she could do was nod.

The man sensed something was amiss and leaned closer to Emily. "Are you alright?" he whispered. He knew the signs of a scared woman after witnessing his mother in an abusive relationship growing up.

Emily shook her head slowly and glanced over to Sherry, who was standing by a tall display of shampoo. The man caught her meaning and nodded. He hurried with Emilys' order and quickly handed her the bag and receipt.

"Walk fast," the man whispered as he handed Emily her change.

Not wasting any time, Emily speed walked towards the automatic doors. Just as she passed through them, Sherry began to follow. The doors closed in her face and she was pissed that she had to wait for them to open again. But they never did.

The cashier saw Sherry make a quick dash for the door and reached down to press the door-lock button. He continued to serve his next customer, pretending he hadn't noticed.

"Hey, these doors is stuck! Somebody come open them!" Sherry yelled. When no one came over, she turned to the cashier. "Hey, open these doors. I need to go."

"I'm sorry, Miss, but I don't have a key. Let me call the manager. Sometimes they get stuck."

Sherry watched the man continue to take money from the woman in his line. He seemed to be moving too slow and was chatting with the customer taking his time.

"I'm in a hurry," said Sherry, impatiently.

"I have to serve my customers first. Store policy," the man said, smiling smugly.

Sherry realized the man was being a smart ass and frowned at him. *You think you're helping her. She doesn't need a fucking man's help. She has me,* Sherry thought, while she continued to stare hatefully at the cashier.

After a few long minutes passed, the man reached down and

pushed the button unlocking the doors. Sherry had been watching him and knew he had deliberately locked the doors allowing Emily to leave first. It didn't matter because she already knew where she was staying. *With that animal*, she groaned under her breath, feeling her skin crawl.

In Sherry's eyes Emily would be more accepting towards her if Daniel wasn't in the picture. *It's time ole boy got lost.* She gave the cashier a hard look before she turned and left the store.

"But I'll deal with you first," she mumbled as she headed for her car.

***

The run in with Sherry had Emily on edge and she decided to take a long hot bath to relax her nerves. She poured her coconut oil bubble bath into the tub as steaming hot water filled it. Letting the water run, she returned to the bedroom and made fast work of unpacking her bags. Thankful for her short curls, she wrapped a netted band around her edges and then pulled a white silk bonnet over her head.

After getting undressed, she ambled back into the bathroom and eased into the hot water. Instantly, the tension that was caused by Sherry evaporated into the steam. Emily closed her eyes and sighed contentedly. Her muscles relaxed and the sweet smell of the coconut oil put her in a scented high.

Now this is what I'm talking about. Mmmmm.

Emily stayed in the tub until the water cooled and her fingers began to wrinkle. She dried off and slipped into a pair of rose colored silk shorts with a matching silk spaghetti strap top. Not wanting to risk running into Daniel, she decided to lounge out on her small balcony. Grabbing her robe, she stepped out into the now dark balmy night.

***

The house was quiet when Daniel entered the apartment carrying a large wrapped box and a huge arrangement of red tulips. He tilted his head, listening for a sound from down the hall. Although he didn't hear anything he knew she was home because the guard at the front desk let him know.

Looking around, he decided to give her the gift in the dining room. He placed the box on the table, sat the tulips on top, and headed towards the kitchen. Once there, he opened the small wine fridge built into the wall, and pulled out a bottle of red wine. Then he frowned. *Does she even drink red wine?* Not knowing the answer, he decided he'd find out in a minute. Grabbing two large wine glasses, he placed everything on the table.

Returning to the kitchen, he pulled a dish of strawberries and chocolate from the fridge. He opened the chocolate, placed it in a small bowl, and warmed it up in the microwave careful not to let it burn. Feeling confident about his plans, he took his sweet treat into the dining room and placed it by the wine.

Looking at the clock, Daniel saw that it was close to almost 9 P.M. He went to the bathroom and washed his face and hands. When he came out, he grabbed the stereo remote and searched for his favorite CD. After looking around to make sure everything was ready, he went in search of Emily.

Emily sat up when she heard a light tap on her door. Knowing it could only be Daniel, her heartbeat went into overdrive. She licked her lips in nervous anticipation and headed towards the door. When she opened it, he wasn't there.

I know I heard something, she thought while peeking down corridor. She began making her way down the hall at a snails pace. When she stepped into the living room, she heard a noise and looked to her right. There she saw Daniel standing there looking handsome as ever in a blue short sleeve shirt and a pair of jeans that rode low on his hips.

"Hi," he said in a deep timbre. His eyes took in the robe she was wearing, wondering what was beneath it.

"Hey." *He looks so good.* The smell of his cologne floated towards her teasing her senses.

Daniel walked over and took one of her hands in his. That's when she noticed his other hand was hidden behind his back.

"Em, I want to apologize again for missing your birthday. I would do anything to go back and fix it, but it's not possible. The only thing I can do is try and make it up to you." He pulled the flowers from behind his back. "And I'm going to start by giving you these."

When Emily saw the long stem red tulips, a huge smile lit up her face. "Oh, my Goodness, Danny. They're beautiful." She took the flowers from him and lifted them to her nose. The perfumed petals tickled her chin and she laughed.

Daniel looked at her, his eyes full of love. All she had to do was look closely and she would see it. "Do you like them?"

"Yes, thank you. I love them." *And you.*

"Okay, give me these," he said, taking the flower from her hands. He placed the huge bouquet on the table and then stepped aside. "This is for you too."

Emily grinned as she looked at the huge white box with a white bow. Stepping closer, she picked up the small card that was attached.

I can't stress how sorry I am.

Daniel

Emily sent him a quick glance and a smile, before placing the card on the table, eager to tear into the paper. It only took a moment or two for her to remove the paper. Now she stood there looking at a long black leather box.

"Open it," he urged, ready to see her reaction.

After releasing the clamps, Emily lifted the box and stopped. She drew in a sharp breath, surprised at what was in front of her. Her hands shook slightly as she lightly ran them across the dark polished wood. She acted as if she was almost afraid to touch it.

When she didn't say anything, Daniel began thinking he'd made the wrong decision. "I thought you would like it."

She turned to him, her eyes bright with unshed tears.

"Danny, this is the Vieuxtemps Guarneri. It's one of the most expensive violins in the world. It's older than the United States," she blurted out in awe. "The last time I read about it some antique music owner held it in Italy and was asking an obnoxious price for it."

"Yeah, I know. It was a long ride, but it was worth it."

Her mouth dropped open. "You flew all the way to Italy to get this for me?"

Daniel nodded, feeling like no words were needed.

It was in that moment when Emily saw a flicker of her own affection reflecting back at her from his eyes. But just as fast, the fleeting moment was gone.

Slowly she stepped closer to him, and on tiptoe, placed a kiss near the corner of his lips. The softness of his skin enticed her and she pressed a second kiss on his lips. She then slid her arms around his waist and pressed her ear to his heart.

"Thank you, Danny. No one has ever given me anything so beautiful."

Daniel's heart was beating hard against his chest. The sweet smell of coconut fanned around him and he nuzzled his nose into her soft hair. Thankful that she had removed her wrap and bonnet, Emily experienced a slight shiver tickle her scalp when his fingers slid across the back of her neck. The sensation warmed her and she pressed closer.

Feeling his body began to react to her being so close, Daniel pulled back. "Come on. Let's have a glass of this wine. I've been saving it for years. It was a gift from my Dad." He took her hand and pulled her with him to the table. Emily stood there watching as he poured each of them a glass of wine.

"You do drink wine, don't you?"

"Yes. I had some really good white wine at Rainy's house not too long ago," she said, taking her glass. She took a sip and closed her eyes, letting the cool liquid float over her tongue. "Wow, this is really good. It's delicious," she said, taking another drink.

Daniel smiled. "I'm glad you like it. It's a 1811 Chateau d'Yguem. It costs a little over a hundred thousand."

Emily's eyes widened and she struggled not to cough. She barely was able to get the wine down before drawing in a much needed breath.

"Are you alright?" Daniel was watching her closely, making sure she was okay.

Nodding, she continued to draw in deep breaths until she calmed down. "Did you say this cost over a hundred thousand dollars?"

Daniel chuckled lightly. "Yeah, that's right."

"Oh, my goodness. I didn't even know they had wine that cost that much. Why would you open it? You should have saved it for something more important."

Daniel lightly touched her chin. "What could be more important than you, Em?"

That stopped any thoughts concerning the wine.

"Besides, why are you worried about the price of the wine when the violin cost more?" Daniel saw when the logic of his statement hit her and she smiled.

"That doesn't make sense, does it?" she asked sheepishly.

Daniel took her hand again. "No, it doesn't. Now come here and taste this." He picked up one of the strawberries and dipped it into the now cool chocolate. When he lifted it to her lips, she didn't waste any time leaning over and biting the huge treat.

Daniel watched as Emily's plump lips wrapped around the fruit, letting her teeth sink into its heart shaped sweetness. A little of the juice from the strawberry escaped her tongue and ran down her chin. On impulse, Daniel caught it with his thumb and went directly to his mouth. Their eyes met and held for a moment and he slowly placed the uneaten berry back in the bowl. Moving closer, he released her fingers only to ease his hand up her arm, and across her shoulder to the soft curls at the nape of her neck.

"Em?"

"Yes?"

"Do you remember that kiss we shared the other day?"

"Mmm hmm." *How can I forget.*

"I'm going to do that again, okay," he said, trying to feel her out. *Please, say yes. Please, say yes.*

Emily licked her lips in anticipation.

"Okay."

That was all the encouragement he needed and what happened next was amazing.

With an almost hesitant motion, Daniel's head drifted down until his lips met the softness he was searching for. On impact, the inferno that had been gradually building inside him began to seep from his lips into her. Emily parted her lips and eagerly accepted his exploring tongue. He sighed in satisfaction from the chocolate essence of her kiss.

The space between them vanished as they both stepped forward at the same time. Hands began to travel and soft sighs mingled with deep moans as they fought to get even closer. Emily let her hands rise up over his shoulders and up further to run her fingers over his wavy hair. She loved the feeling of being pressed against him and flexed her hips in search of that incredible sensation she'd experienced from the very noticeable bulge sandwiched between them.

A deep guttural moan vibrated in Daniel's chest when Emily raked her nails lightly across the back of his head. Wanting to give as good as he got, he sucked her bottom lip into his mouth with a gentle tug right before deepening the kiss. He was hell bent on exploring her lips and tongue to the fullest by using three of the senses; taste, touch and smell. His skill level with each of them had Emily panting, sighing, and gripping him tighter. The response he received was phenomenal and he wanted to push her further.

He slid his hands lower on her back and over her plump, shapely bottom. When she didn't stop him, he gripped both cheeks firmly and gyrated his throbbing shaft directly on her center. Emily broke the kiss and her head fell back with her eyes closed tightly and a needy whimper escaped her lips.

"Ahhhh…"

Seeing more flesh for the taking, Daniel quickly opened his mouth and sucked her neck, leaving a gentle nip. He pressed into her over and over sending a riot of sensations shooting through her core.

Emily felt the passion inside her building up quickly into a roaring fire. She'd never felt such an intense awareness of her body. The more Daniel kissed and touched her, the more she craved.

Desperate for more, Emily came back for another kiss. She lifted her leg and Daniel's hand caught it, allowing him to gain better access to her heat. He continued to ravish her lips while his lower region thrust unrelentingly against her. The thin silk of her pajamas made it feel as if there was nothing between them.

Incredible sensations heightened her pleasure levels pushing her closer to the edge. The power of his slow gyrating hips made a strong yearning settle directly on her clit, causing it to throb almost painfully.

"Danny, please…"

The sound of her voice pulled him back a little from the fog that had muddled his brain. However, Daniel wanted to at least give her what she wanted, and he knew exactly what she was asking for. The way she was clinging to him and rotating the heat between her thighs against him, left little to the imagination.

He increased the pressure and the motion of his movements with a rhythm that was so powerful that it began to build the anticipation within her and increase the level of her desire. He softly nibbled on her lips, gently licking and biting the curves while firmly sucking and releasing her tongue. Their breathing was heavy and heightened from desire and their heartbeats were beating erratically.

Suddenly, an amazing burst of pleasure shot through Emily, triggering her release, sparking an all over glowing fire. It coursed through her with such pleasurable stimulation that her whole body tensed and then shuddered. Her breathless moans were fed directly into his mouth as he held her lips captured in an intoxicating kiss.

Emily rode the orgasm out to the very end, flexing and releasing her fingers into his shoulders. Daniel didn't stop. He only slowed his pace, allowing her pleasure to linger. The connection between them was both, physical and emotional, allowing him to give her a remarkable and life altering orgasm.

Daniel broke the kiss and they both inhaled deeply. As their breathing began to return to normal he realized that their passionate kissing session had gotten way out of hand. The only consolation was that he now knew that she wanted him just as much as he wanted her. The real question is if it was going to be just for now, or forever. He needed to be sure before letting things go any further.

Standing there holding on to Daniel for support, Emily focused on calming her heart and her breathing. She had never encountered such a mind blowing orgasm before and they hadn't even taken off their clothes. When he released her leg, she tried unsuccessfully to steady herself.

"I got you," he whispered close to her ear, his breath fanning her cheek. He wrapped his arms around her holding her firmly against him.

They stood there in the center of the dining room trying to gain control of their senses. Their breathing was fast and loud in the room and they held on to each other tightly. Daniel wanted to take her lips in another deep kiss, but something kept popping up in his mind nagging him.

How do you know she really wants this? How do you know she wants you and only you? Is she only being curious? Will she get bored and go back to dating women? Where will that leave you?

These were the thoughts filtering through his mind over and over making him skeptical about moving forward. As much as he wanted to be with her and make love to her, he knew he would need to be careful not to get hurt in the long run. He was already head over heels for her and he hadn't even made love to her yet. He knew that once he crossed that line, for him, there would be no turning back. She would own his heart and his body.

That's when he came up with the notion to not let it go any further until he was absolutely certain that she truly wanted him for him, and that this wasn't some passing fancy. The only way to find out was to spend as much time with her as possible. To insert himself into her life and consume as much of her time as possible. If she tired of him she would tell him to get lost, but if she accepted his advances, then maybe she wanted what he wanted after all.

Daniel nuzzled her neck once more before backing away. Taking her hand in his, he walked her slowly back to her room, dreading every step. He pushed open her door and let her step inside. Leaning down, he kissed her briefly on the lips, but even that slight touch of skin gave him a shiver.

"Good night, Em. I'll see you in the morning."

Emily could tell by the deep raspiness of his voice that he'd been affected by the kiss just as much as she had and if that wasn't enough, the bulge in his jeans said it all. *So why is he saying good night instead of joining me?*

"G'night, Danny," she said softly, as he closed the door. She stood there confused and so turned on that she turned and headed straight for her purse.

Chapter Nineteen

The bright light beaming in her face is what woke Emily up the next morning. She pulled the pillow over her head and rolled over, turning away from the window and its annoying sunshine. She lay there trying to nod back out when the smell of fresh croissants teased her nose and made her stomach growl. The growl was insistent and she gave up letting hunger win.

Throwing back the covers she sat up, feeling utterly relaxed. The memory of the intoxicating orgasmic kiss she'd shared with Daniel made her smile broadly. *Damn that man can kiss. And that huge package he was carrying around felt amazing.* She closed her legs tightly remember how she had pleased herself with her toy while pretending it was him. *I can't wait to experience the real thing.*

Hearing her alarm go off, Emily remembered why she had set it and smiled. Although she would love to spend some time with Daniel, she'd made plans to pick up a birthday gift for Jordan. Miki and Rainy were giving him a birthday party for his fifth birthday and she had no clue what to get him. Her stomach gave another unladylike growl and she rolled out of bed to shower, dress, and then go in search of food.

Emily chose an adorable oatmeal colored crochet one-piece romper. It was strapless with a decorative tassel on the front and had an elastic waist, drawing attention to her small midriff. The lace trim around the legs and front halter neckline gave it a vintage look, all the while allowing for a cool and casual fit. To top it off, she added a pair of sexy strappy dress sandals with a short heel. The dangly tassel that hung in the back of the sandal brought your attention to her smooth toned legs. A few sprays of her favorite perfume and she was done. In the bathroom, she removed the sleep bonnet from her head to run her fingers through her mohawk fluffing her tufts of curls. She smiled at her result.

Looking good, Emily. Looking good. A last minute addition of lip gloss, and she was ready. *Perfection!* She posed in the mirror, then laughed at herself before heading for the kitchen.

As she drew closer to the kitchen the sweet smell of the croissants became stronger making her mouth water. Thinking that Daniel had made the pastry and left some for her for breakfast, she wasn't prepared to find him leaning against the counter drinking coffee. He held a magazine in his hand and seemed to be totally engrossed in what he was reading. That gave Emily a little time to check him out.

Allowing her gaze to do what her hands couldn't at the moment, she started with his lips. *Mmm, those lips. Yes, he knew how to use them,* she thought, remembering how he used them to nibble on her neck and suck on her lips. Her eyes then slid down to his shoulders and arms. The outline of his muscles could plainly be seen and she'd enjoyed being held by them. Next was his chest. *Oh Lord, his chest.* Hard and warm is how she remembered it, with the steady thud of his heartbeat. It was almost hypnotic.

Her eyes moved down further and stopped at his zipper. She could clearly see the bulge of his dick print and she felt a little throb in her peach. Moving even lower, she took in his long legs all the way down to his bare feet. She watched as he crossed his legs at the ankle and wiggled his toes.

Daniel heard Emily moving around in her room and knew the exact moment when she made her way down the hall. He smelled her before he saw her. The smell of the croissants did nothing to defuse her essence mixed with whatever perfume she was wearing. Even now, with his head bent down over the magazine, his attention was focused fully on her.

"If you look closer you'll see that I can levitate," he joked, then smiled.

Emily's head snapped up so fast her vision became bleary for a second. After gaining her composure, she stepped into the kitchen, heading for the refrigerator. "Well, good, maybe you can catch up to that big head of yours," she said, taking the orange juice out and pouring herself a glass.

Chuckling, Daniel tossed the magazine on the table and crossed his arms over his chest. He knew she had been checking him out and he was thrilled about it, but he just couldn't shake the feeling that she was still off limits. He drank in the sight of her in her romper and felt his heart slam against his ribs. *Fuck it. I'll deal with the family later. I need this. I need her,* he thought, staring at her.

Emily eyed the plate of croissants and eased over to the plate. Just as she reached for one he stopped her.

"What are you doing?"

She cut her eyes over at him, her hand hovering above the plate.

"I'm getting a croissant."

Daniel licked his lips, and smiled. "Those are mine," he stated with conviction.

Looking around, Emily saw there wasn't anymore croissants put away anywhere. She glanced back at him, her hand still hovering over the plate. "There's three croissants here. It's more than enough here for the both of us."

Daniel straightened up and moved towards her. He pushed her hand to the side and took a croissant off the plate. He dipped it into the small bowl of honey he'd warmed up, shoved half of the croissant into his mouth, and took a huge bite. He chewed a few times before shoving the last piece into his mouth. When he was done, he looked down at the plate.

Two left.

Emily again reached for a croissant and he slid the plate out of her reach.

"Danny! Don't be stingy," she said, laughing. "Let me have one."

"What are you willing to do for one?" he asked, grinning.

"What!?" Emily laughed so hard her sides hurt. "Boy don't make me call your mother and tell her how you're treating me," she threatened, smiling.

Laughing, Daniel picked up the plate. "My mother taught me that you have to give to receive. So what'cha got to give?"

Knowing how to beat him at his game, Emily dipped her finger in the honey and slowly brought it to her mouth. She slid the sticky sweetness between her lips slowly. Dropping her eyelids down to smolder, she made a loud slurping sound while sucking on her finger.

All humor left Daniel instantly. His mind turned to mush as he zeroed in on the finger easing in and out of Emily's mouth. The plate he was holding was forgotten and it slowly began to lean to the side. Right before the croissants slid off the plate, Emily snatched her finger out her mouth with a pop, and grabbed one. The other croissant hit the floor with a soft plop.

"Shit!" Daniel scrambled to grab the plate and sat it on the table. His hands were shaking slightly and his dick was pressing noticeably against his jeans. He quickly turned away before Emily could see how she had affected him. Stepping up to the sink, he turned on the cold water and filled a glass. He downed the cool liquid and drew in several deep breaths.

Emily stepped up beside him holding the croissant. "Here, I'm willing to share with you," she said seductively, lifting it to his lips.

Daniel looked down at her looking up at him with her soft brown eyes. Without hesitating, he bent down and took a bite of the croissant. Emily waited for him to finish chewing before she stepped back and burst into laughter.

Confused, Daniel stared at her and then looked around for what made her laugh. When she looked down at the floor, he did the same. That's when he noticed the croissant wasn't there. Then he remembered biting her's. Shaking his head, a wide grin spread across his face.

"You fed me the croissant from the floor didn't you?"

Laughing louder, Emily bent over trying to control herself.

"That's so messed up," he said, laughing with her.

Finally gaining control, Emily wiped the tears from her eyes.

"That's what you get. Damn, I wish I had recorded that," she said still smiling.

"Yeah, well, I'm glad you didn't." He leaned back against the counter and looked at her. *She's adorable. Gorgeous.* "What are your plans for today?"

"I have a little shopping to do. Jordan's birthday is coming up and Rainy told me I can drop his gift off when I was ready. However, I still haven't picked him out anything."

"Neither have I. Maybe I can tag along with you. That is, if you don't mind."

Emily smiled. "No, I don't mind, Danny. I'd like like."

Daniel walked up to her slowly until only a short space was left between them. He reached up and touched her soft hair loving the mohawk style she was rocking. "I'd like that too, Em."

The sexual tension between them was cracking and sending warm shimmers through them both. He wanted to kiss her, but he knew that once his lips touched hers, he would want to stay on them for a while. Instead, he leaned down and nuzzled his nose to her ear, loving the smell of her perfume. His lips grazed the side of her neck and he sighed heavily wanting more. But he needed to stick to his plan to spend time with her.

Stepping back, he slid his hand across her chin. "Give me a minute to put on my shoes."

"Okay. I have to get my phone anyway. I thought I had it, but I left it in my other bag."

"Don't worry. I'll get it for you."

Nodding, Emily watched him leave the kitchen. Once he was gone, she closed her eyes and drew in a deep breath, trying to calm her raging hormones. *Damn, he's so fine. Even his feet are sexy.* She giggled at her joke and then her smile faded.

"Oh shit," she whispered. Daniel had to go inside her bag to get her phone. "He's going to see B.O.B." Feeling warm from embarrassment, she crossed her fingers and prayed to God that he overlooked it and didn't see it.

Moments later Daniel came down the hall to find Emily waiting for him in the living room. She had a weird, anxious look on her face.

"You okay?"

She nodded, but kept looking at him funny.

"Did you change your mind or something?"

Maybe he didn't see it. "Oh, no. I'm alright. Are you ready?"

"Yup. Come on woman." He took her hand and pulled her behind him.

***

The mall was about forty-five minutes away and with Daniel driving, Emily was assigned to music duty. She was searching through his CD's when she found one labeled *Old Grooves.* Curious, Emily loaded it. *Whatever, by Ideal* came on and she threw her hands up snapping her fingers.

"Oh, I love this song. This use to be my jam." Her hands were up above her head, shoulders bumping, and her hips rocking. She looked over to Daniel with a contagious grin on her face. "Come on, old man. Let's get it."

Daniel reached over and turned up the volume. As soon as the chorus came on they both started belting out the lyrics. Daniel was bopping his head right along with her, grooving to the music.

That was the beginning of a great day spent together. From the car, to the crowded halls of the mall, Emily and Daniel enjoyed themselves. She laughed at his silliness and he teased her about the slippers she purchased with the owl heads. There were a lot of accidental touches with a few deliberate ones. Neither of them were thinking about the questions that constantly nagged them. The only thing on their minds were each other.

After leaving the toy store, Emily see's a lingerie shop and wanted to take a look inside, but she didn't want Daniel watching her shop for her intimate things. Seeing the pretzel booth across from them, she found her way out.

"Mmm, you smell that?" she asked, sniffing the air.

"What are you smelling, Beagle?"

Emily laughed, and threw an elbow to his ribs. "Ha ha, funny. I'm talking about the pretzels. They smell so good."

Daniel leaned in close to her. "Would you like a pretzel Ms. Bawler?"

"Yes, Mr. Tase, thank you," she said, beaming.

"And what kind would you like?"

"Cinnamon, please."

"One cinnamon pretzel coming right up." He turned to walk away, but stopped. He spun back around, leaned over, and snatched a quick kiss catching her off guard. Without a word, he smiled and left to purchase her pretzel.

Emily watched him go, feeling excited to finally be spending some time with him. Shaking off her eagerness, she hurried into the lingerie shop. She knew exactly what she wanted and headed straight for a sales clerk. It took her only a few minutes to make her purchase, and since she didn't want Daniel to know she had bought anything, she shoved the bag inside one of the ones she already had. She returned back to where he'd left her just as he walked up smiling.

He was taller than most of the people in the mall and he easily saw her over their heads when she came out of the lingerie shop. When he was close enough, he scanned the bags she carried, but didn't see one from the shop. *Pitty*.

"Here you go. One hot cinnamon pretzel." He presented the sweet treat and bowed.

"Thank you, kind sir," she said in a horrible England accent. They both laughed at her attempt.

Emily held the pretzel up to him. "Would you like a bite?"

"Nah, I'm still full from the croissants I had this morning."

"You mean the one you ate off the floor?" Emily smiled deviously.

"Hey, baby. I've been trying to call you."

Emily closed her eyes tight and shook her head. *This can't be happening.* She opened her eyes and turned around slowly to find Sherry standing there smiling.

Sherry had been trailing behind them since they left the condo. She watched them laughing and shopping together, and felt the jealousy in her steam roll into outrage. Then the touching started and it was hard to keep from wanting to vomit. But soon the sick feeling in the pit of her stomach fluttered away and an uncontrollable fury planted itself there, feeding her courage. It was all she could do not to run up on him and shove her knife deep into his side. Instead, she boldly approached them.

Exasperated, Emily could only sigh heavily as she turned to face her. "What the hell are you doing here?"

Instantly, Daniel became jealous. It was a foreign feeling and he didn't like it. Emily was his and he'd be damned if he was going to stand by and lose her to this woman. He needed answers.

"Do you know this woman, Em?"

"Mind your damn business," Sherry blurted out viciously.

Before Daniel could respond, Emily placed her hand on his arm to stop him. Her body became still, her eyes narrowed and outrage radiated through her with a piercing heat.

"Have you lost your damn mind? How dare you talk to him like that!"

Sherry took a step forward and reached for her hand. "Baby, listen I…"

"Don't touch me! And why are you still following me?" Emily blurted out, her voice rose an octave and a few customer's were beginning to look their way.

When Sherry reached out again, Daniel stepped around Emily and moved in front of her. "I wouldn't do that if I were you," he said in a deadly voice.

"Sherry, you need to leave and for the last time, please stay the hell away from me." Upset and embarrassed, Emily stormed off needing to get away from all the curious stares.

Sherry stood there silently, watching while Emily walked away. All she wanted was for her to just hear her out, but she knew that wasn't going to happen while this jerk was hovering around. She took a step in the direction Emily had gone only to be cut off by Daniel stepping in front of her.

"Get out of my way," she sneered. Her face showed her disgust for him.

"You need to stay away." He leaned over slightly in her direction. "Stay out of my way," he warned, driving home his meaning.

She frowned screwing her face into an angry sneer. Although she wasn't as tall as him, she was close to it, and wasn't intimidated by him in the least.

"I haven't begun to get in your way," said Sherry, standing her ground.

Daniel shook his head at the woman. He didn't know who she was, but what he did know was that she'd irritated Emily, and that was enough to make him intervene.

He smiled and gave a short laugh at her trying to look formidable. "Consider yourself warned." With that said, he left and headed for the door. He needed to find Emily and get some answers about this woman and her comment about her following her.

Sherry was so mad that she continued to stand there fuming. She was upset that Emily had left her standing there looking stupid. She didn't care that some of the customers were still watching her. She only cared about Emily. *I just have to get her to listen. She needs to know that I love her and that this asshole is no good for her.*

Chapter Twenty

The sun beamed straight into Emily's eyes as soon as she stepped from the mall doors. Immediately the heat from its rays warmed her bare shoulders, making her wish she'd stayed inside with the air conditioner. She was about to go back inside when she felt a rather large hand slide around hers. Without looking up, she knew it was Daniel. The small spark of awareness shooting up her arm spoke volumes.

As they made their way to the truck he started the engine using the automatic key in order to get the cool air going. After helping Emily inside, Daniel loaded their bags in the trunk. He then slid behind the wheel and pulled out into the slow moving traffic. Minutes had gone by without either of them speaking until he was unable to hold it in any longer.

"Is she someone you were seeing? An ex-girlfriend?" *If so, I hope its permanently over.*

Emily's head spun around swiftly. "What!? No. Never. I don't even know her."

"But you said her name," he said, confused.

She shook her head and averted her gaze to look out the window. "You misunderstood me. I don't know her on a personal level. I met her a while ago in New Jersey. She said her name was Sherry Woods."

"Wait, you two met in New Jersey? How the hell did she know you were here in Virginia?"

"I don't know."

Daniel lips tightened in aggravation. "Start at the beginning, Em." He wanted to know everything she knew about this woman so he could do a better job at protecting her.

"I met her at a lounge."

"What lounge?" he asked, cutting her off.

"Diamonds In The Rough. It's in Newark."

He swore under his breath. He knew about the lounge. It catered to both crowds, gay and straight. *Why was she there? Was she looking to take a woman back home with her. If so, what the hell does she want with me?*

"Go on," he coaxed.

"I was out with some friends from work. I got invited, and since I needed to unwind, I accepted. Sherry approached me at the bar. She bought me a couple of drinks and we made small talk for a while. Some guy approached me and she sent him away. After that, the dancing started and since I was there to blow off some steam, I headed downstairs to the dance floor."

"Did she follow you?" He listened closely as he maneuvered the truck through the streets.

"Yes," she answered, giving him a quick glance. "We danced together for a few songs. Then…"

"Then what?" *Please don't say you took her home with you.*

Emily couldn't say a song came on that reminded her of him, so she skipped that part and rushed on.

"Then I felt like leaving, but I stopped in the ladies room first. Some woman approached me about Sherry and then I hopped in a cab and left."

Since they were sitting at a red light, he had the opportunity to look at her. She was leaning back with her eyes focused on the street.

"What did the woman say to you?"

Emily thought for a moment, then turned towards him with a frown. "She warned me not to get involved with Sherry. She said that it was a mistake and something else I can't remember. I don't know," she sighed and turned away. "I really didn't think nothing of it since I had no intention of dating her. I just wanted to get out of there."

They sat in silence for a while, both in their own thoughts. That is until Daniel spoke up.

"I think you should get a restraining order on her. I mean, it's not much as far as protection, but if she comes around again, at least you can have her locked up."

Emily looked at him, shocked. "Do you really think that's necessary?"

"Yes, I do. I mean, think about it, Em. Where did she first approach you?"

"At the school when I first went to meet the kids for the scholarship."

"That means she's been here the whole time," he said as he pulled up to the condo. Once the valet came to take the car, Daniel grabbed the bags from the truck, then ushered her into the building. "How did she even know you were here? Has she been watching you in New York as well?"

Inside the elevator, he felt her slide her hand in his and he gave it a reassuring squeeze.

"Don't worry. I won't let anything happen to you." *I'd die first.*

Looking up, she smiled at him wanly. "Thanks, Danny."

Seeing the alarm in her eyes made him clam up about his predictions. When the elevator doors opened, Emily entered the apartment feeling the stress of the situation bearing down on her.

Daniel didn't want to keep pushing her, but he needed her to see the importance of what was going on. It was obvious the woman had been following her and it made him angry as hell. For her to show up at the mall today meant she'd also been here, which meant she'd followed Emily to his house. A new wave of outrage, coupled with a touch of fear for Emily's safety, caused his body to tense up.

He watched Emily walk over to the sliding doors and opened one half way. She didn't step outside, she just stood there with a weird sort of look on her face as she gazed out at the city.

He sat their bags on the couch and slowly approached her. He stood close enough to feel the warmth of her body, yet he didn't reach out to touch her. Somehow he knew she needed a moment to collect herself. Finding out that someone was literally stalking her, had delivered a shocking blow. And even though she was saying all the right words, he could tell she was physically shaken. *I have to take her mind off this, but first the restraining order.*

"Tomorrow I'm going to take you to the police department so you can fill out the paperwork for the restraining order." When she looked at him as if to refuse, he cut her off. "I wasn't asking you Emily. You need to do this if only to make her aware that she's crossed the line with her behavior. Hopefully, it will be enough to make her back off."

Emily turned away and once again faced the shimmering glass of the other buildings in the area. "And if it isn't enough?" she asked, her voice held a slight tremble.

"Then I'll make her wish like hell she had backed off."

Emily heard the hard steel that laced his words and knew if anything, that she could count on Daniel to protect her. That in itself was enough to make her relax a little. Abruptly, she turned and wrapped her arms around his waist. She rested her head on his chest and the constant thud of his heart against her cheek calmed her stressed nerves.

He held her gently, his arms securely locked around her. There was no way in hell that he would let anyone hurt her. No. He had to put an end to this threat and fast. But right now, he needed to lift her spirits, and to do that he needed to change the subject.

Drawing in a calming breath he inhaled her scent deeply and closed his eyes knowing it was the same smell that had haunted him for years. *I can get used to this*, he thought smiling. All of a sudden, he heard a little rumbling sound and he pulled back a little to look down at her.

"You didn't hear that," she said, with her face buried in his chest.

Daniel chuckled. "I believe everyone in a ten block radius heard that roar."

Emily laughed. She was totally embarrassed. Her hunger had caused her stomach to growl and of course it would happen while she was wrapped tightly in Daniels' arms.

"I'm sorry. I'm still hungry. We never ate anything after the croissants, remember?"

"Yeah, I know," he said, remembering that she'd only taken one bite of the pretzel before Sherry showed up. "I guess I better feed that monster before it breaks loose."

"Ha, ha. Very funny."

Grabbing her hand, he pulled her behind him as he made his way to the kitchen. He pulled a chair from the table and waved his hand towards it in a grand gesture.

"A seat for the lady."

Emily sat down and smiled in his direction. "What are you going to make."

Daniel pulled a half apron from a draw and tied it behind his waist. "Anything the lady desires."

Emily lifted her hand and tapped her finger lightly against her lips. "Hmmm... What I want may be too complicated for you to prepare."

"Trust me. I'm up for the challenge," he said, leaning against the counter with his arms crossed.

The muscles in his arms and chest caught Emily's attention and her hands itched to touch him.

"Well, for a real chef this wouldn't be so hard to make, but I guess

I'll give you a chance at it," she replied, humor evident in her voice.

"A real chef, huh?" said Daniel, as he stood up straight and moved closer to her. He placed both hands on the table and leaned down towards her. "Tell me what you want woman before I give you a bowl of cereal."

Emily laughed. "Okay, fine. I want a peanut butter and jelly sandwich with the crust cut off. I would also like a cold glass of milk with that, and I would like it served in the living room please. And don't be all day with it," she belted out quickly. She then stood abruptly, causing Daniel to step back.

"Are you kidding? A peanut butter and jelly sandwich?" he asked as she turned to leave the kitchen.

"And remember, no crust," she called out as she disappeared into the living room.

Daniel watched her go with a smile on his face. *This is going to be the best damn sandwich she's ever tasted.*

In the other room Emily picked up their bags and headed down the hallway. Before going to her room, she decided to leave Daniels' bag in his own room. She opened the door to his bedroom and just stood there. It was his private space and she'd never been inside. The curtains were drawn closed and it was almost totally dark. She slowly walked in and instantly her eyes were glued to the large bed that dominated the room. Her imagination clicked on and she could see herself spread eagle with Daniel's head nestled between her thighs. Feeling shocked by the intensity of her vision, she hastily sat the bag on the bed and left in a hurry.

In the kitchen Daniel was snatching up ingredients and mixing them together with swift strokes. He mixed together the makings for some fresh bread and placed it in his bread maker. It should be ready in about twenty minutes.

He found a large bag of peanuts and decided to make the peanut butter from scratch. He didn't have any jelly, so he improvised by using the strawberry preserve and added a dash of sweet rum to enhance the taste. He took a taste and smiled. *Damn, that's good.*

Remembering the milk, he grabbed two glasses from the cabinet and reached for a bag of powder sugar. He briefly stuck the top of each glass in the sugar and then placed them in the freezer to chill. Moments later there was a low buzzing sound, letting him know the bread was ready. He removed it from the machine and its pan before placing it on a wire rack to cool.

He stepped back and grinned when he suddenly had an idea. Rushing to the closet in the hall, he snatched up one of the white table cloths and proceeded to set up the small table near the balcony. He set up two place settings using the crystal dishes he received from his mother one year for Christmas.

Now that the table was set, he returned to the kitchen. He sliced the bread and remembered to cut off the edges. He then smoothed out the homemade peanut butter, praying that it didn't tear up the bread. He smiled in victory once he had several slices completely covered.

Next came the jelly. Its sweet aroma lit up the kitchen and Daniel smiled, knowing she was going to love it. He placed the peanut butter slice on top and made sure the ends met perfectly. He then cut them in half, making two triangles.

Now it's time to plate these bad boys. He placed each half on a plate and decorated the plate with a few strawberries and drizzled a design with honey. With a dash of powdered sugar, the dish was complete.

The last of the sandwiches were placed on another plated and placed on the table to the side. He returned one last time to the kitchen to retrieve the pitcher of milk and the two glasses that were left in the freezer to chill. After making sure everything was ready, he stood back and waited.

***

Emily had to take a moment to calm her nerves after letting her naughty mind get her all riled up. Lord knows she loved Daniels' kisses and his touch, but in all honesty, she had no idea what to do pass that. Of course she knew what sex was all about. Well, with a woman anyway. However, her curiosity had gotten the best of her one day and she had watched a few movie clips with men and women. *'Oh my'* was all she could muster to say as she watched scene after scene of hot, wet, intensifying sex between each couple.

Although the clips had turned her on, they had also scared her like crazy. Now all she could think about was doing something wrong or not being sexy or experienced enough to satisfy Daniel. *What if he doesn't like it and decides not see me anymore? What do I do then?*

A sound in the other room drew her attention and she smiled, remembering he was preparing her lunch. She returned to the living room and found him standing near a table set up beautifully. She began to grin broadly as she approached.

Daniel pulled out her chair. "Your lunch, Miss."

Emily laughed at his fake British accent.

"Thank you, kind sir. I hope everything is how I requested," said Emily after taking her seat.

He sat beside her and lifted the silver top covering her plate. "I believe it meets all of your requests and then some."

Emily's mouth dropped open when she saw the beautiful arrangement on her plate. "Oh my goodness, Danny!"

"I'll take that as a yes," he said, smiling.

Grinning, she picked up one half of the sandwich and bit into it. She closed her eyes and began to chew slowly as the flavors meshed together and played a delicious dance in her mouth. After swallowing, she picked up her glass and took a sip.

Emily turned to him and took his hand in hers. "Will you marry me?"

Daniel burst into laughter.

"Why are you laughing," she asked, smiling broadly. "If you can make this for me every day, I will marry you. OMG, Danny. This is the best peanut butter and jelly sandwich I've ever tasted in my life. What the hell did you put in this?" she asked in awe, taking another bite.

Embarrassed by her comments, he leaned back trying to control his reaction. Although he knew she had been joking, her asking him to marry her had caused his breath to catch, but he regained his composure without her noticing.

"I don't give away my secrets woman. You have to earn the right to those."

Emily took another bite of her sandwich. "Just tell me what to do. I need to know how to make this," she said over another mouth full.

He picked up his sandwich and took a huge bite. "Stop talking with your mouth full," he said with his cheek packed with food.

Emily sucked her teeth. "Boy, bye. Your mouth is full right now."

They both laughed and enjoyed the rest of their lunch.

Angel B

Chapter Twenty One

"What are you doing?"

Emily jumped. "Nothing!" she said nervously.

She turned around quickly and held one hand behind her back. She was in her room, searching through the top drawer when she came across Hoot, her childhood stuffed animal. She hadn't meant to bring it with her. She found it tucked into the suitcase where she had stuck it months ago. Her dad had found it in a storage container in the garage and asked her if she still wanted it. Remembering all the good memories she'd had with it wasn't the reason why she wanted to keep it. Daniel had given it to her one day after he'd won it while on a school trip. For years it never left her side. That is until she got older. However, she'd never wanted to get rid of it.

Daniel leaned against the door. "Doesn't look like nothing. What do you have behind your back?" he asked with a smile.

There was no way in hell she was going to show him what she was holding. "I didn't hear you knock," she said, trying to change the subject.

Laughing, Daniel took a step in her direction. "The door was wide open, smarty pants. And stop trying to dodge the question. What do you have back there?"

Her eyes scanned the room trying to come up with something that would make him go away.

"It's not a trivia question, Em," he said, moving closer.

"And I said it's nothing. Did you need something?" she asked, backing away from him.

He stopped and leaned to the right trying to get a peek behind her. Emily turned slightly blocking his view. When he leaned the other way, she shifted to the left. He laughed.

"I wanted to know if you had plans tonight?" He knew his question would get her attention and she instantly fell into his ploy.

"Plans? Um...no. I was only going to watch a movie."

"Well, since you're not busy, I wanted to know if you would like to join me for dinner?"

"Dinner?" *Oh my goodness, will this be a date? Like a real date out in public?*

"Mm hmm. I know a place I think you'd enjoy. That is, if you want to go out with me?" he said, moving even closer.

Only a small space was left between them and Emily was looking up into his eyes. She never noticed how he had moved to her right.

Hell yes, I want to go! "Sure. I would love to go out with you. Should I change," she asked, looking down at the clothes she'd worn earlier that day at the mall.

Daniel's eyes scanned over the jumper and he licked his lips "No, you look perfect," he said, taking a step closer. "But I do have one question?"

He was now close enough for a kiss and she hoped he would use this opportunity to claim one.

"What's that?" she said, licking her lips in anticipation.

"Is that Hoot you're hiding behind your back?" he asked, before reaching behind her and snatching it out of her hand.

Emily had thought he was leaning in for a kiss, so she was unprepared when he pulled the stuffed owl from her hand.

"Hey! It is old Hoot. I didn't know you still had him," said Daniel, checking out the owl.

"Give him back!" cried Emily, reaching for the owl only to have Daniel hold it out of her reach.

"Hold up, now. I just want to check him out."

She reached in again to grab it, but he lifted his arm up above his head.

"You're going to rip him. He's old and needs to be handled with care."

He laughed at her serious expression. She had always beat him and his brothers down whenever they touched the old grey owl. Hell, he thought he was doing something great by giving it to her. Maybe even back then he knew she was the one for him. *Go figure.*

"Okay, but I just want to see him. I promise to give him back once I get a look at him."

Emily took a small step back, making sure to stay close enough to Hoot. When Daniel saw that she wasn't going to back up any further, he brought his arm down slowly. He looked at the owl and smiled remembering all the times she had thrown him out her room for knocking it off the bed, or tossing it back and forth with her brother Alexander, keeping it away from her.

"Okay, Danny. Give it back," she said, with her hand out. When he didn't hand it over she tried again. "Please."

He heard the emotion in her voice and decided to stop teasing her. He knew how much the owl meant to her. It was her only solace through many tearful nights and upsetting moments in her life. It was a chick thing and he understood.

"Here you go," he said, gently passing it back to her.

Emily grabbed Hoot and sighed once she held him safely in her hands. She turned him over making sure the stitching her mother had provided years ago hadn't come undone. Satisfied that he wasn't injured, she walked back over to the drawer and placed him back inside. After she closed the drawer she just stood there with her head down, too embarrassed to face him.

He must think I'm silly getting all fired up over a stupid stuffed animal. Great Emily. Real mature.

"So, how long will it take for you to get ready?"

Slowly, Emily turned around to see him still standing there, smiling.

"You still want to go, right?"

An easy smile replaced her forlorn look. "Yes."

He released a sigh, happy that she still wanted to spend time with him. "Good. I'll call down to have the car brought around."

"Okay."

He smiled, shook his head, and left to make the call. *She's so damn adorable.*

Chapter Twenty Two

Nervous was an understatement compared to what Emily was feeling right now. As much time that she'd spent there with Daniel, this would officially be their first date.

Wait, is this a date or are we merely two friends going out to grab a bite? She lowered her hand slowly after applying her lip gloss and stared at her reflection in the mirror. *Of course it's a date. Right?*

She stood there trying to remember his exact words. *'Well, since you're not busy, I wanted to know if you would like to join me for dinner.'*

Hell, that could mean, let's grab a bite as friends and let's go on a date. Emily sighed loudly as she was no longer sure what to think. When she heard a light knock on her door, she realized she was taking too long. Daniel had already made the call to the front desk for the car and was ready to leave. After going into the living room and not seeing Emily, he backtracked to her room to make sure she hadn't changed her mind.

"You ready to go, Em?"

Emily opened the door with a wide smile on her face. "Yes, I'm ready," she said as she stepped out into the hall.

They made their way to the elevator, her giving him shy glances and him trying not to stare. Once they were in the car it didn't take long for him to drive across town to Vera's. It's a classy, chic buffet style restaurant owned by a good friend of his. Vera was one of his mentors and he loved her like a second mother.

"So where are we going?"

"It's right around this corner," he responded just as he made a right turn.

Emilys' eyes opened wide at the huge three story restaurant that took up the whole block. The structure was enormous, but that's not what caused her mouth to pop open like a fish. It was the beauty of the place. Almost the entire building was made of glass and you could see the guest enjoying their meal as the server's saw to their every need.

"Oh wow! This place is amazing!"

He chuckled at how her face was almost plastered to the window like a child.

"You better not lick my window," he said, joking.

"Oh, stop!" Emily said, swatting at his arm smiling. "I just can't believe how beautiful it is. Have you eaten here before?" she asked still smiling. Her eyes were bright with excitement.

"Yes, on several occasions. The owner and I are really good friends."

An alien feeling of jealousy ran hot through her body and she turned around to look at the name of the fancy restaurant. *Vera's. That definitely was a woman's name. Is this someone he's had a relationship with?*

"Oh."

Daniel heard the deflated sound of her voice and knew exactly what she was thinking. *Is she jealous? Hell, that means I'm making progress.*

The second he pulled up to the front entrance their doors were opened by valets dressed in all white. Vera prided herself on the fact that she never made a customer wait. Not for the valet. Not for the hostess to seat you, and definitely not for your waiter to show up and serve you.

"I see you're back again."

Emily was taken back by the rudeness of the greeter at the hostess stand.

Daniel took it in stride. He's known Samuel for over nine years. He was Vera's husband and he looked at him as the son he'd never had.

"I see you're still having a hard time tying a proper tie," said Daniel in retaliation.

Samuel didn't even waste his time looking in the super large mirror on the wall. He knew before he left his office upstairs that his tie was fitted perfectly.

"At least I'm wearing one. Even I know that when you escort a beautiful lady to the best restaurant in the state that you should wear a tie."

"It's only Vera's," said Daniel with a tone that hinted at boredom.

Samuel's brown eyes opened wide. "It's only Ver—" He stopped in mid sentence and turned away from Daniel with a loud tsk. Completely ignoring him, he gave his full attention to Emily.

"Hello, and welcome to Vera's. Is this your first time dining with us?"

Emily smiled at the older man's regal stance. His chin was lifted high and his chest was poked out giving him the air of an aristocrat. She liked him instantly.

"Yes, it is," she answered softly.

"Wonderful. Then let me be the first to tell you that you will enjoy every morsel that you put in your mouth. Do you have any favorites?"

"She love's seafood," Daniel said, trying to include himself in their conversation. Samuel continued to look at Emily as if he'd never heard Daniel speak.

Emily laughed and shook her head. "I truly do love seafood."

"Really?" beamed Samuel as if he hadn't heard Daniel say it only seconds ago. He heard him mumble something under his breath, but chose to ignore him. "Well, we have the best chef. He's way better than that other place. It's called Sinbad or Sucker... something silly like that."

"Sinful." Daniel blurted out the name of his restaurant even though he knew damn well Samuel didn't need reminding.

He was ignored again.

"So, are you single, dear?" Samuel asked, taking Emilys' hand in his.

"Okay, that's enough or I'll tell your wife how you're out here flirting." Even though he knew Samuel wasn't the slightest bit interested in Emily, he still felt a little twinge of jealousy.

"Little boy, you know that I'm the King of my castle," stated Samuel, tapping his chest in a moncho style.

"Is that so," asked Daniel, when he noticed Vera approaching from behind him.

"Absolutely! So don't get it twisted," he said, causing Emily to laugh.

"And exactly where is this castle that you're the King of?" asked Vera, stepping up beside her husband.

Emily watched as the once tall and regal man shrunk down and began groveling.

"Vera! Baby! I was just telling Daniel that he should always put his Queen first and never proclaim ownership of their castle that he was blessed to share with her."

Daniel's mouth dropped open and Emily burst into laughter.

"You, stand here and be quiet. And you get over here and give me some sugar," she said to Daniel.

He moved in and gave Vera a warm hug. Not a quick pat of the back hug, but one of those hugs where you hold on for a few seconds rocking side to side.

"Boy, I haven't seen you in months. Where have you been and why haven't you come to see me?" she asked after she let him go. That's when she noticed Emily standing there. "Oh! Is this the reason why you've been hiding away?"

He shook his head, smiling. "Vera, this is Emily. Em this is Vera, the owner of the restaurant," he said with a knowing smile.

Emily narrowed her eyes at him briefly, then turned to greet Vera. "Hello, Mrs. Vera," she said politely.

Vera looked at Emily and sucked her teeth. "Away with all that Mrs. Vera nonsense. Vera will do just fine. You two here on a date?"

Before Emily could respond, Daniel stepped closer to her and took her hand in his. "Yes, Mam. We are."

Emily looked up at him with a shy smile.

Vera caught the shyness in Emily and the heated stare from Daniel, and knew there was much more to this woman and situation, and she couldn't wait to get the details.

"Well, at least you brought her to a place where she could get an excellent meal," chimed in Samuel.

"Oh, be quiet Samuel and leave him alone. You're always poking at him."

Daniel smirked over at Samuel. Samuel's eyes narrowed as he smiled with a silent warning of revenge.

Suddenly, Vera lifted her hand quickly, and from out of nowhere, a young man dressed in all white appeared.

"Mrs. Vera."

"Yuri, seat Mr. Tase and his guest on the top level in the R.I.P. room please. And see to their privacy as well."

"Right away, Mrs. Vera. Mr. Tase, would you please follow me?"

"Thank you, Vera. It was good seeing you again." He leaned over to hug her briefly.

"Yes, it was. And don't let months go by without me at least hearing from you again. I *will* call your mother!" she said with a side look before turning to Emily. "And you my dear are now family. You're welcome to come see me anytime," Vera said, pulling Emily into a tight hug.

Smiling, Emily returned the hug, feeling the sincerity behind it. "Thank you, Vera. It was nice meeting the both of you."

"Yuri." Vera said the young man's name and he snapped to attention.

"Right this way, Mr. Tase."

Daniel and Emily followed the man to the far end of the restaurant and into a private elevator. Up they went to the third floor where the man stopped to punch in a code on a set of large black doors. When the door unlocked, he pushed both doors open in a wide arch allowing them to proceed ahead of him.

Emily's eyes lit up and a wide grin brightened her already beautiful face. The room was exquisite. It was brightly lit with chandeliers and candles. A single table sat directly in the center demanding their attention with its crystal place setting for two. All around the room, set in a wide arch, was a humongous table set with a wide assortment of food from all over the country. Some she had never seen before, yet, couldn't wait to try.

Waiter's materialized from a well hidden door and stood in different areas ready to serve them. Yuri pulled out Emily's chair and stood by waiting for her to sit. Once she and Daniel was seated, he nodded to one of the waiter's who pushed a button on a small remote. The darkness of the tented windows lightened giving them a wide cinematic view of Virginia as the sun set and the city lights began to glow.

"Wowwww." Emily had never seen anything so beautiful. It was like watching a symphony of lights perform just for them. "It's beautiful."

"Yes. Vera aims to wow and please her guest." He enjoyed watching the excitement on her face.

"Mmmm. Everything looks and smells so delicious. I can't wait to try the shrimp."

"Greedy."

Emily laughed. "Whatever. You know you want some too."

Yes, I do. "Not tonight. I plan on making my way through that table with all the spicy meats."

"Haven't you had them before?"

"Some, but Vera makes sure to always have something new to try. Trust me, you're going to love everything."

"That's what Samuel said," she whispered smiling.

"Who?" Daniel asked, frowning, purposely acting like he didn't know who she was talking about.

Emily laughed and reached for her glass of water. Just then, Yuri appeared like a genie and took their wine order.

"You ready to fill that growling monster in your belly?" Daniel asked laughing.

Emily leaned over slightly towards him. "Did you hear it again downstairs. I was hoping no one did."

"No. I'm pretty sure you got away with it that time. I was hoping you wouldn't snatch a piece of chicken from anyone's plate as we walked through the dining area to the elevators."

She sucked her teeth. "You're such an..."

"Uh oh," he said, cutting her off. "Here comes the potty mouth."

"I don't have a potty mouth," she said, giggling.

No you have a hot mouth. "Yeah, right. Come on woman. Let's eat."

Daniel and Emily enjoyed their time together, eating food from different countries they couldn't even pronounce. They laughed reminiscing about the good times they had growing up together and all the silly things he and his brother's done to her.

Emily got him to talk about his new restaurant and the ideas he had for it. It wasn't something he shared with many, however, he felt comfortable about sharing it with her.

"I'm not sure what I want to do really. At first, I had a plan all mapped out, but I wiped the slate clean and decided to start over again."

"Why?"

You. "I don't know really. I guess I need to get a few more things in line before I make a final decision."

"Well, I'm sure whatever direction you decide to go in, it will be as great as Sinful. I mean, even though this place is grand and has an enormous menu, I love the vibe I get when I'm at Sinful. Personally, I think your place is better. I don't know if I've ever said it, but I'm proud of you Danny. You took your dream and made it a reality. Most people only get to dream. You're living yours."

Emily had no idea how that made him feel. Talk about a boost to your pride. He felt his chest tighten and his eyes watered a little causing him to look away briefly. There's nothing like having the woman you love, support you and tell you they're proud of your accomplishments. *Damn she's amazing.*

"Thank you for that, Em."

"No thanks necessary." A short yawn escaped her lips and she covered her mouth quickly. "Sorry about that."

"Am I boring you?" he asked with a chuckle.

"Of course not. I'm enjoying myself. I guess I ate too much." She smiled, looking down at her second plate that was half cleared.

"So now I get to take you home and put you in bed."

Instantly, things heated up between them. Their eyes connected and he felt the tightness in his groin grow heavy. When she licked her lips, he glanced down following the movement of her tongue and sighed heavily. He was still hungry, but it wasn't for anything that was on Vera's menu.

"Are you ready to go home?"

Emily couldn't even form the words. She nodded her head slowly, hoping that tonight would be the night he would love her senseless.

Since he knew Vera wasn't going to allow him to pay for their meal, he took Emily's hand and escorted her to the exit where his car was already waiting. He sat patiently waiting for Emily to snap in her seatbelt, when something caught his eye to his left.

Sherry. The woman from the mall, was standing across the street staring right at him. For a long moment they stared at each other. Neither wanting to back down. *This chick is nuts.*

Even though he wanted to move things forward with Emily, he knew he needed to take care of this problem first.

"Is everything alright?"

He blinked a few times and noticed that Sherry had left. He turned to Emily and smiled. "Yeah, everything is fine," he said and pulled out of the lot into traffic.

The ride back to his place was without incident which he was grateful for. For the whole ride, he expected Sherry to try and cause them to have an accident or something, which had him tense and watchful. Basically, her appearance had put him on alert and killed his mood.

Yes, he still wanted to make love to Emily, but Sherry would be at the back of his mind and he wouldn't be able to give her his full attention. *And I want her to have my full attention.*

The elevator ride up was quick and they stepped off together. Daniel saw how she was walking slowly trying to give him a chance to make a move and he wanted to so damn bad. But not right now.

Not until he settled this problem with Sherry. He needed to get her out of the picture and make sure Emily would be safe. He knew she would be disappointed, but he had to do what was necessary.

Taking her hand, he walked her to her bedroom door. Drawing in a deep breath, he pulled her close to him and lowered his head. Daniel gave her a toe curling kiss that had them both panting and shaking. Their bodies were pressed snugly together from chest o thigh and he wanted nothing more than to strip the clothes from her body and see just how beautiful she was beneath them.

But not tonight. He gave her one last chaste kiss, then stepped away. He reached around her to open her door and gently pushed her inside. Without a word he pulled it closed cutting her from his hungry gaze. He stood there a moment telling himself it's the right thing to do. When he felt his resolve leaving, he hurried to his own room, hoping for the strength to stay away.

Emily stood there confused and feeling bereft.

What the hell just happened?

***

Later that night after he was sure Emily was asleep, Daniel picked up his cell to call Myka.

"What do you want?"

Daniel laughed. "It's nice to hear from you too brother."

"I was in the middle of something," said Myka shoveling another spoon of cereal in his mouth.

"Yeah, well, it can wait. I need a favor."

"What kind of favor?"

"It's serious," said Daniel.

Myka sat up and placed his bowl on the table. He opened his drawer and pulled out his laptop. Instantly, he was all business.

"Go ahead."

Daniel told him about Emily being stalked by the woman and gave him her name and the work description that Emily had given him. "That's all the information I have on her."

"Where did she see the woman?"

"She said she met her in New York at some club. Then she followed her here to my place." *Damn it! I didn't mean to let that slip.* He decided to keep talking, hoping Myka would overlook it. "Then she showed up at the school she was visiting and also at some hair store. I saw her again tonight outside of Vera's restaurant."

"Okay, I'll check into it."

"Let me know what you find out."

"Yeah, but one more thing," said Myka.

"What's that?"

"What the hell is Emily doing in your apartment? And did you guys go on a date at Vera's?"

"Why don't you use all that energy to find out who the crazy woman is and stay out of my business," said Daniel in an irritated tone before hanging up.

Myka laughed. *My work is done. Now to get to the real issue. Who the hell is stalking little Emily?*

Chapter Twenty Three

After having a great time with Daniel last night, Emily was completely confused about his behavior. She had been sure that they both wanted the same thing, but now she wasn't anymore. Even though they had kissed on several occasions didn't mean that he wanted something more. Maybe he was only curious about kissing a lesbian. *Great Emily. Look what you've gotten yourself into now. You're crazy about him and he's just having fun with you. Idiot!*

Feeling unsure of herself, she decided to avoid him by staying in her room all day. Well, someone should have given Daniel the memo, because he was all up in her personal space.

Tap. Tap. Tap.

Emily was lying across the bed in some grey short-shorts and a white tank top typing away on her laptop. Music sheets, notebooks and pencils, were spread out all around her. When she heard the tap on her door, she glanced back over her shoulder and paused. *He'll go away.*

Tap. Tap. Tap.

"I know you're awake, Em. I heard you moving around earlier."

She turned back to her laptop. "I'm busy."

"Can I come in?"

Nothing. Not a sound.

"I'm coming in, Em."

She didn't say a word.

He jiggled the door knob before turning it. As he pushed it open, he was lifting a bottle of water up to his lips for a drink and stopped short at what he saw. Emily was lying across the bed in a pair of skimpy shorts showing off her round plump ass. *Oh damn.* Suddenly, the water he was drinking went down the wrong way and he ended up choking and struggling for air.

"Oh my God!"

Seeing him struggling to draw in air, Emily hopped off the bed and went to his aid. She immediately snatched the water from his hand and placed it on the dresser. She then lifted his arms up shoving them high in the air. When he tried to pull them down, she shoved them up again.

"Keep them up!"

Emily stepped around him and began rubbing his back while he continued to fight to clear his airway. Finally, he was able to draw in some air and the tension eased in his chest. Seeing him calm down a bit, she stepped in front of him and rubbed his chest in the same manner she had his back.

Daniel couldn't believe he'd just embarrassed himself that way. But damn did she look good all sprawled out on the white comforter, ass up, and looking edible. He was thinking of several things he could do to her in that position when the water decided to knock some sense into him.

Slowly he lowered his arms and looked down at her as she continued to rub his chest in wide circles. She had no idea that it was turning him on. If he let her continue, all she would need to do is look down and she would know.

He doesn't know what made him look, but his eyes lowered to her tank top and his breath caught again, and this time not from choking. It was pure lust. Her shirt was soaked from when she snatched the water from his hand and was now a useless piece of material. It was almost as if she wore nothing at all. He could clearly see the full outline of her breast and the taunt bud of her nipple through the thin layer of cotton.

Before Emily could open her mouth to ask if he was alright, his resolve broke and he pulled her to him tightly. His lips captured hers in a kiss that was strong and demanding. The feel of her breast pressed up against him drove him a little more insane with need. He released her lips only to capture them again seconds later.

Emily was at a lost for words. She didn't know what had come over him, but he was kissing her like a starving man. His hands were holding her tightly around her waist, making sure she couldn't escape. Liking the feeling he was arousing in her, she stepped closer and moaned against his lips. Her hands slid up over his shoulders, holding on for dear life, as she gave him a little nudge below with her pelvis.

Daniel's whole body was on fire. Everything left his mind except

Emily and the feel of her in his arms. The sound of her soft moans was music to his ears. When he felt her hand come down and slide under his shirt, he was thrilled at having her warm hand touching his skin.

Mama. Mama, you know I love you. Oh, you know I love you, Mama.

Hearing the ring tone he had stored for his mother of the *Boyz II Men* song playing from his cell phone in his back pocket was just as bad as having a bucket of cold water tossed on him. He and Emily both jerked apart. Their breathing was heavy and loud in the room, creating an erotic haven.

His eyes instantly dropped down to her breast. It took him a minute to find his voice and he cleared his throat.

"Em, you need to change your shirt." His voice sounded deep and scratchy.

"What?" Technically, he had just kissed her powerfully enough that it had turned her mind to mush. She was having a hard time comprehending what he was saying.

He nodded down towards her shirt. His eyes taking in as much as he could. Emily looked down and once she saw her breast exposed, her arms came up to cover herself.

"Oh my God! Danny!" she yelled and swatted his arm.

Daniel chuckled. "Ow! What did you hit me for?"

"Because now I know why you got all hot and crazy a moment ago," she said turning away from him. She rushed over to the bed and snatched up a pillow and shielded herself behind it. When she turned back to face him she was smiling.

"Yeah, I'm sorry about that."

Emily's smile dropped. "You are?"

He searched her eyes looking for a clue as to how she truly felt. Was this a fluke or was she really into him? A kiss could sometimes be only a kiss, but he was sure that the kisses they'd shared meant more.

"No. I'm not sorry at all." When he saw her smile return, he knew he'd said the right thing. *Progress. One step at time.*

Emily sat on the edge of the bed. "What did you need?" She left the question vague on purpose.

Daniel's head tilted to the side. *Now that can be answered a thousand ways.* However, he knew she was asking why he came knocking.

He smiled, knowing that if he said what he truly wanted to say, she'd probably smack his face. "I wanted to know if you'd come ride with me?" *How about that for subliminal's.*

Emilys' eyes lowered seductively. "Yes, I'll ride." *Ha! Take that.*

He looked away and laughed. "All you have to do is let me know when you're ready." He took a step in her direction, testing her. "Are you ready, Em?"

Okay, this just went way past her skill level. All her teasing stopped and Emily's courage slid through the floor. She stood up, still holding the pillow, and backed all the way up to the bathroom door. "No. I have to get dressed."

Coward. "Alright then. I'll give you some time to get ready. I'll be in the living room."

"Okay," she mumbled.

He gave a short laugh and left, pulling the door closed behind him.

***

Emily and Daniel were driving down Alamo Drive, just past the Naval base near Virginia Beach. It was late in the afternoon and the sun was beginning to set giving off a bright set of reds and oranges. The soft sound of music playing, coupled with the cool air condition, had Emily nodding out.

"Wake up sleepy head."

Emily opened her eyes to see a huge building. When she looked all around her, she saw nothing but buildings. "Where are we?"

Pulling over in front of a two story building with large windows, Daniel killed the engine and hopped out. He walked over to Emily's side and tried to open her door, but it was locked.

"Open the door woman," he said, smiling

Emily frowned and cracked her window. "Is this where you plan to hide my body?"

"Trust me, Em. I don't intend to do harm to that body." Then he gave her a sexy grin.

Emily laughed and unlocked her door and he helped her step out. He took her hand in his and pulled her towards the building entrance. She watched as he pulled out a key to the huge lock and opened the door. Letting him go in first, she stood back and waited until she saw the lights come on.

"Okay, you can come in now."

Emily walked inside the building and began looking around. It was a large open floor plan office building that had a lot of potential for anyone looking to start from scratch and bring their own ideas to life.

"What do you think?" He waited patiently, knowing he really wanted her opinion. Or was it her approval?

"Is this the building you intend to buy?" She continued to move around peeking in one room and then another.

He watched her every move. "It was one of many that was shown to me."

She glanced back at him over her shoulder before peeking down a dark hall. She made no move to go forward. "And you want my opinion?"

You have no idea how much. "Yes. I do."

She was about to ask him why, but decided not to. "I guess it's okay."

Daniel frowned. "Just okay?"

Emily moved back in his direction. "Yes. I mean, I don't exactly know what your plans are or how things will look once they're completed. So I can only go based off of what I see."

When she got close enough, he took her hand in his. "And what do you see?"

She smiled and then looked around again. "Honestly, I don't like it."

He burst out laughing. "How come you don't like it?"

Emily was grinning widely. "I don't know. It looks spooky."

He laughed again. "Em, it's not going to look this way when it's finished."

"I know," she said, laughing. "Look, you asked, and that's my opinion. It's spooky."

Daniel smiled down at her and touched her cheek. He shook his head slowly.

"What?" she asked curiously.

"Nothing. It's just that... I think you're amazing," he said, looking into her eyes.

"You do, huh?"

He moved closer. "Yeah, I do."

Emily took his other hand. "You better be careful how you say those words," she said, referring to his *'I do'* phrase.

The smile left his face and he gazed down at her, letting her see that he was serious about his next words. "I don't have a problem with saying I do, Em."

Emily was staring at him in disbelief when she heard a noise behind her. When she turned around, she saw a woman dressed in a dark grey pantsuit and heels coming towards them. She wore a loose bun on top of her head with huge loop earrings that caught the light and sparkled. Bright red lipstick stood out against her light skin and her long eyelashes gave her a sultry look. She could easily be called beautiful.

"Daniel, darling. I didn't know you were coming down today. You should have given me a call. I would have met you here." She had been showing someone an industrial property nearby and saw his car and decided to stop by.

"This wasn't a planned visit, Kimberely. I wanted to show the building to a friend of mine," he said, smiling over at Emily.

Kimberly glanced over at Emily and gave her a quick once over, and immediately dismissed her. *No competition there.*

"So does this mean you're ready to meet the seller's asking price and close the deal?"

He shook his head. "Not quite yet. I have a few more things to work out before I settle on it." He glanced over at Emily and smiled.

Kimberly saw how he looked at the woman and realized her mistake in dismissing her so quickly. *Could this be the woman that was on the phone? The one he was making dinner plans with?* She looked at Emily again and this time noticed how beautiful she was. She saw her short stylish hair, smooth dark skin, her shapely body, and the air in which she carried herself would attract any man's attention. Right away, she summed her up as being a problem. Out came the claws.

"You know Daniel, you really shouldn't bring people in here. If they get hurt, they could sue, and that won't go over easy with my boss."

He frowned over at Kimberly. "No one's going to get hurt. We never left the first level. Besides, Emily isn't like that."

"You never know how a person can be when they're destitute,' she said, lifting her head high and looking down her nose at Emily.

"What!? Destitute?" Emily snapped. "Do I look impoverished?" she asked Daniel.

Daniel couldn't believe Kimberly was behaving like this. She had to see that it was bad business to insult a client and their guest. But Kimberly didn't care about that. All she saw was a woman standing there with the man she wanted and she was lashing out.

"No, you don't. And she damn well knows it," he responded angrily. He turned to Kimberly. "I don't know what's going on with you today, but I think you owe Emily an apology. There is no excuse for you being rude to her."

Kimberly saw how angry she had made Daniel and knew she had gone too far. She was now at risk of losing her chances with him and losing him as a client.

"Oh no. I do apologize, Daniel. That came out all wrong. I didn't mean to imply that your little friend was poor or anything. I was speaking in general."

Little friend? Poor? Granted, I'm far from being rich, but I'm not hungry either. Emily took notice of the woman still throwing out subtle rude remarks. However, before she could respond, Daniel spoke up again.

Taking a protective step in front of her, he shielded her with his body. "I said you owed Emily an apology. Not me. And I believe your comment was implied exactly the way I took it. If this is the way you conduct business, then maybe I should take mine elsewhere," he said, handing her back the key.

In a panic, Kimberly began to plead. "No. No. No. Darling, I'm so terribly sorry. I don't understand why my words won't come out right." She begrudgingly looked over at Emily. "I hope you can forgive my impulsiveness. I never intended to offend you." She gave her attention back to Daniel. "Now you hold on to that key and let me know when you've made up your mind," she said backing away, before hastily making an exit.

Emily burst into laughter when she stomped off. Daniel was still upset, but when he heard Emily start laughing his anger slipped away and he smiled.

"You found that funny, huh?"

She placed her hand over her mouth to muffle her giggles. "No… I just couldn't hold it in any longer. Your ex-girlfriend just called me poor," she said, still smiling.

"She's not my ex-girlfriend, Nancy Drew," he said with a half smile. "You think I didn't notice how you just threw that in there?"

Emily looked around sheepishly. "No, I didn't. What are you talking about?"

He shook his head, smiling. "Mm hmm. Come on Drew," he said, pulling her behind him.

"Where are you taking me now?"

"To the movies," he said, opening her door.

"The movies?" *A second date!*

"Mm hmm."

She watched him walk around the car and slide in.

"What are we going to see?"

"I don't know what's playing, so we'll pick something when we get there. Okay?"

She smiled broadly. "Sounds like a plan to me."

The movie theatre was packed which killed Daniel's plan of sneaking in a few kisses before, during, and after the movie. The comedy that they watched with Kevin Hart had them both laughing from beginning to the end. However, the two hour movie had passed by fast, and now it was late in the evening.

"You hungry?"

Emily looked up at him and smiled.

"Of course you're hungry. What was I thinking?" he said and laughed.

"It sounds like you're trying to call me greedy or something," she said, teasing.

Daniel held up his hands. "I plead the fifth."

She swatted his arm playfully. "You sir, are no gentlemen."

"Never claimed to be. Now what do you have a taste for?"

You. "Um, how about over there," she asked, nodding at a diner across the street.

Daniel looked at the place and frowned. "You sure? It doesn't look like they scored an A on inspection."

Sucking her teeth, Emily grabbed his arm and started walking. "Come on, I'm starving. And since its packed in there, I'm sure the food is good."

"Fine. But don't say I didn't warn you."

They entered the diner and was given a table immediately. The red tables and benches gave it an old school appeal, and the R&B music gave it a calming atmosphere. Emily liked it right away.

"How y'all doing. Y'all ready to order?" asked the young girl standing next to their table in a red t-shirt, blue jeans, and black non-slip shoes.

"We never received any menu's," said Daniel, puzzled.

"You don't get separate menu's. Just order from the board," she said, pointing to the wall over the counter. The menu stretched across the whole wall covering drinks, sides, hot and cold sandwiches and deserts. All of the sandwiches had celebrity names.

"Oh," they both said at the same time, and laughed.

"Okay, I'll take the Usher Raymond with an ice tea and a slice of chocolate cake, please," said Emily. She couldn't wait to taste her R&B burger.

"And you?" asked the waiter after jotting down Emily's order.

"Yeah. Umm, give me the Michael Jackson classic with my pickles on the side and a large Sprite."

"Be back with your drinks," said the waiter and disappeared.

Daniel looked around the place and at the people wolfing down their food. Either that meant that the food here was great, or they felt since they paid for it, they better eat it. Nobody was going to waste their hard earned money.

"Scared?" she asked, a look of amusement on her face.

"I know that this will be an experience worth documenting."

She burst out laughing.

Over their food that turned out to be quite good, they chatted about the movie they'd just watched, Jordan's upcoming birthday party, and his plans for the restaurant.

"Will it be a replica of Sinful?" she asked as she watched the waiter coming towards them with her slice of chocolate cake.

"In name only. I think wherever you open a business it should reflect the ambiance of the neighborhood and the clientele that you will be servicing. I know I'm going to have the restaurant on one floor and I was thinking of a dance area on the second. This way I'll draw in further revenue by serving alcohol. But it will be in a tasteful manner."

Daniel watched as Emily picked up her fork and took a bite of the huge slice of cake. He watched her chew for a moment and then close her eyes. A heavy sigh escaped her moist lips and she opened her eyes to find him staring at her.

"I take it the cake is good?" he asked, smiling, although her little sigh had him adjusting the way he was sitting.

"Mmmm, you have no idea. This is absolutely delicious. It's moist and full of flavor. Here try some," she said, scooping up a piece on the fork and holding it out for him.

Looking straight into her eyes, he leaned over and closed his mouth over the treat. Emily's eyes were glued to his lips as it closed over the fork. She watched him slowly pull away, all the while staring at his full lips.

"What do you think," she asked in a soft tone.

Their eyes met across the table. "I'll admit that it's good. But, just yesterday, I tasted something much better. Something I can't wait to taste again."

Emily sat there with the fork still in the air, staring at him. She felt the room heat up and her mouth go dry. Remembering she was still holding the fork, she brought her hand down slowly and placed the fork on the side of her plate. She then picked up her glass and took a long drink.

She stared down at the table for a moment, feeling his gaze on her. "Danny."

He was fixated on her and felt his body reacting to her without being touched.

"Yes?"

Finally, she lifted her gaze to meet his. "Can we go home now?"

Pulling out his wallet, he left a stack of twenties on the table, leaving the waitress a huge tip.

"Let's get out of here."

The drive home would have been fast, but Daniel decided to drive down by the coast, so Emily could enjoy the lights and the nightlife. There were people everywhere milling about and some made a few fire pits on the beach. People were dancing, laughing and having a good time.

When they finally got home, he was eager to say goodnight. He was going to stick to his plan of waiting to fix the issue of Sherry before moving forward with anything else. But that didn't mean he couldn't enjoy a few kisses and soft touches.

"I think I'm going to turn in," he said, watching her from across the room.

Feeling a sense of rejection, Emily nodded. "Yeah, me too."

When he didn't move, she decided to be the first, and started down the hallway. He was right behind her. The view of her bottom captured his attention and he groaned. *She has a sexy walk.*

Emily was reaching out for the doorknob when he stopped her.

"Em."

She looked up at him, hoping he was going to kiss her.

"Yes?"

"Do you mind if I kiss you goodnight?"

"I'd be upset if you didn't," she said, taking a step in his direction.

"Well, I don't want to upset you," he said, before pulling her in his arms.

The moment their lips touch an intense burning swelled all around them. Daniel played with her tongue with a hunger he'd never experienced before. Her body pressing against his, soft and inviting, had him all worked up and ready to forget his plan of waiting. Right now all he wanted was to pick her up, take her into his room, and strip her naked so he could make love to her all night.

Emily was having a hard time breathing. Her body was craving for something only he could deliver and she was ready to receive it. A maddening ache had settled between her thighs and she wanted him to reach down and ease her misery. She wanted him to fulfill her fantasy of seeing his head nestled between her thighs pleasing her with his wicked tongue.

"Danny, please," she whimpered, straining to get closer to the large budge that was nudging at her center.

The sound of her moaning his name almost pushed him over the edge and he knew he needed to stop before he wouldn't be able to. Gently, he stepped back breaking the kiss and the contact between their bodies. Their heavy breathing filled the silence of the hallway as Emily protested with a groan at the irritation of missing his touch.

When she reached out to touch him again, he grabbed both of her hands in his and brought them up to his lips. Knowing he was close to losing control, he reached around her and opened her door. At the moment, he couldn't even bring himself to speak, so he gently pushed her into the room once again, and shut the door.

Emily stood there with her head resting against the door. She could hear him breathing heavily on the other side of it. Feeling the cold pain of his dismissal again, her eyes filled with tears. *How come he doesn't want me?*

"Good night, Em," he whispered, his hand still holding the doorknob.

"Good night, Danny," she said softly before moving away.

She stood there hoping he'd change his mind and come barging into her room to claim her, but he never did. He left her alone, saddened and confused.

Angel B

What am I doing wrong? How come he flirts with me, kisses me senseless, and then leaves me yearning for his touch.

Slowly, she backed up until the back of her legs touched the bed and she sat down. A blue glow of light on the bed caught her attention and she saw that she had left her cell phone and it was blinking signaling a missed call. Picking up the phone, she checked her message. As she scrolled down her missed calls, she saw Stacey's name.

I need to talk to her. I need answers, because this is frustrating the hell out of me.

Stacey had just finished applying her face cream when her cell phone rang. She was going to let it go to voice mail until she saw that it was Emily.

"Hey girl, what's up?"

Emily was relieved when Stacey picked up. "Hi Stacey. Do you have a minute to talk?" She tried to make her voice sound normal, but Stacey heard the pain behind her words.

"Yes, but make it quick. I was about to go rape my husband. But, tell me what's wrong?"

Emily explained everything to her about what was going on and the mixed signals she was getting from Daniel.

"Since I'm about to go have a sexcapade with my boo, I'm going to cut to the chase and get right down to the nitty gritty. First off, if he's flirting with you, touching you, and kissing you like a starving man, then he definitely wants you. So that's not the problem. The problem is he's probably trying to be all noble and show you that he want's more than sex. Now you can either go two ways with this. One, let him continue down the long drawn out road he's on, in which case you won't be having sex for about another month. Or, you can go into his bedroom and take what you want. It's up to you."

"Take what I want?" Emily's eyes widened.

"That's right," Stacey said, while watching Chase kick off his slippers, drop his PJ bottoms, and climb into bed. "Sometimes you have to take control and go get what you want. In the end, it's a win – win situation. Understand?"

"Yeah, I get it," said Emily, contemplating her next move.

"Good. Now take all that sexual frustration you got going on over there and go attach his ass in his bed. He won't have anywhere to run," she said laughing. "Good night!"

Stacey hung up the phone and placed it on the dresser. She crawled on the bed on her knees and leaned over Chase.

"What are you doing," she asked quietly.

Chase opened one eye. "I'm going to sleep," he said and closed his eye back.

Stacey sat back and yanked the covers, exposing his beautiful naked body. "But I haven't tired you out yet baby."

Chase looked up at her and smiled.

Chapter Twenty Four

Emily's body was a raging inferno and she was tired of the yearning her body felt whenever she was around Daniel. She'd never felt this way with anyone else. Only him. Although she's been with women sexually, she never let them penetrate her. She wouldn't allow it. She couldn't explain why. She only knew that she didn't feel heightened sexually enough to want it... until now. And right now, she wanted Daniel.

No more hot kisses and lonely nights. I can either let him continue doing it his way, or I can go into his bedroom and take what I want. Now what should I do? Emily felt her clit jump answering the question for her.

Now that she knew what to do, she jumped into action. First, she filled the tub up with hot warm water. She didn't want to make it too hot, because it would ruin her hair. Digging through her care bag, she pulled out a cocoa oil, milk bath mixture and poured it into the water. She used her hand to mix it thoroughly.

Once her mixture was set, she stripped down quickly and slid into the bath tub. She closed her eyes and leaned back in the huge tub, letting the warmth of the water soothe her nerves and loosen her muscles. Twenty minutes later, she eased out of the water and released the pump. She then stepped into the shower to wash away the milk.

Now that her shower was complete, Emily went to the dresser and pulled out the short, waist length white lace nightgown and panty set she'd purchased from the mall when she was with Daniel. She placed it on the bed and then grabbed her coconut cream. Even though her body was already smooth from the milk bath, the cream would enhance the smoothness and the fragrance.

After dressing in the nightgown and panty set, she stood in front of the full mirror and looked at her reflection. The night gown stopped a little past her waist, showing off the lace panties. Her hair had been brushed down and then feathered back into a Mohawk. Satisfied with how she looked, she drew in a deep breath and let it out slowly.

You can do this. If you want him, then go claim him.

Daniel was standing on the balcony in the living room in his pajama bottoms trying to cool his ardor when he turned to see Emily walk from her room down the hall to his. His body responded instantly at seeing her in the lacy short gown. He groaned when he saw that it allowed him a peek at the curve of her bottom. *Dear Lord, help me.*

"Em?" he called her name, his voice husky with need. When she turned around he drew in a quick breath. He could see her nipples straining against the lace and then his gaze dropped down to the lace covering the plump mound of her pussy. *Aw, fuck.*

He cleared his throat. "Did you need something?"

Mustering up her courage, she nodded her head. *Here goes nothing.* "Yes."

He moved off the balcony and began walking towards her. "What do you need?"

She didn't answer until he was close enough for her to touch. She reached up slowly, one hand touching his face, the other sliding up his chest. "You."

His heart was pounding in his chest as his blood rushed through his veins. She was standing before him, offering him everything he'd ever wanted and needed, and he knew that he didn't possess the strength to walk away from her again. Nor did he want to.

Throwing caution to the wind, he pulled her to him, thirsty to drink from her lips. Their tongues played and teased in a familiar dance that had them both breathing deeply. They stood there in the hall feasting on each other's mouth's with a desire that was constantly building.

Wanting more, he scooped her up and hurried the few steps to his room. When he placed her on her feet he could feel her body shaking and knew with all the courage it took to come to him, she was still nervous. At that moment, he had a deep need to make this special for her, because even though she had been with women, he was pretty sure that she'd never been with any men.

He sat her on the side of the bed and kneeled down between her legs. He then took her hands in his and placed them on his shoulders. While looking up at her, he placed his hands on her knees.

"Whatever you do, don't let go."

Emily nodded and eagerly waited to see what would come next.

Praying that he would be able to take it slow, he began to take the tour of her velvety soft body. First, he leaned forward and buried his face right between her full breast and inhaled. The smell of cocoa butter filled his senses and he groaned in approval. His hands followed his nose and he cupped her breast before letting his thumbs shift over the lace causing her nipples to pucker even harder.

Emily pulled in air sharply through her teeth and swayed towards him. She loved having her breast sucked and couldn't wait for him to do so.

Seeing that she liked that, Daniel pulled down one of the spaghetti straps of the gown and exposed her nipple. The little orb popped free and he quickly drew it into his mouth. She gasped at the heat from his tongue and sighed when he began sucking. Both hands cradled his face, loving the feel of his tongue twirling around her areola. When he felt that he'd given that one enough attention, he moved over to the other.

Emily's head fell back and Daniel saw that as an opportunity. He zeroed in on her neck, kissing his way back to her breast. With the nightgown bunched at her waist, he stood and eased her back further on the bed. He then lifted the gown up over her head and paused when she tensed up. Knowing that it would leave her almost totally bare, she became nervous and covered her breast with her arms.

Daniel leaned down and whispered near her ear. "Do you trust me?"

"Yes," she answered without hesitating.

"Then relax and let me love you."

Knowing she wanted this more than anything, she relaxed and let her arms fall down to her sides.

"No. Touch me, Em. Always touch me," he murmured before claiming her mouth again. While he kissed away her fear, his hips rotated his swollen shaft against her sensitive nub and pleasure like she never felt before moved through her.

Emily's arms slid around his neck and she returned the kiss with passion. Feeling the weight of his body on top of her's was new and arousing, and she began to squirm beneath him. She lifted her leg and wrapped it tightly around his waist and gyrated her mound against the bulge she felt pressing into her. Little beams of lights flashed beneath her eyelids and she dug her nails into his shoulders.

"Ahhhh," she cried out in a frenzy.

"That's it, baby. Let your mind go and enjoy how I'm making you feel," said Daniel, as he rained hot kisses down on her nipples and then lower across her stomach.

He eased to his side so he could see how she looked in the lace panties and damn near lost his mind. His hand moved across her stomach, then lightly across the top of the lace. As much as he wanted to take her now, he wanted to see her bare. He wanted to know how she looked naked and thrashing with need under him. Moving to his knees between her thighs, he lowered his head and opened his mouth over her pussy, right through the lace.

Feeling the heat of his tongue stroking her through the lace, had Emily moaning loudly into the night. The sweet ache of his tongue was torture, and was driving her wild. When he pulled back and blew cool air where his mouth had been seconds ago, only to cover it again with his hot tongue, she reached down and slid her hand beneath the lace and stroked her clit.

"No baby. That's my job," he said, and moved her hand.

"Danny, pleaseeee…"

Daniel sat up and pulled her panties off, then spread her legs wide.

"I know baby. I got you."

Diving in was an understatement. He used his tongue and lips to push her to such a state of hunger that she began to whimper incoherent phrases.

"You… I can't… Yes… Oh, damn!"

He devoured her, delving his tongue deep inside her, and then twirling it back up to her clit. He then would draw it fully into his mouth and suck on it with soft pulls. Her cries of passion drove him to want even more. He lifted her lower body off the bed, leaving only her shoulders to support her weight. In this position she was able to watch him worship her kitty, all the while admiring his tongue skill.

Feeling the sexual tension in her quickly building, she started bucking wildly and Daniel gripped her thighs holding her steady. Suddenly, a tingly warmth shot though her clit and all through her body. She cried out as the first wave of an orgasm rocked her to the core.

"Oh shitttt. Danny, yes. Fuckkkkk, yes."

He continued to suck and lick her until the orgasm passed, and her cries turned to low moans. After easing her back down to the bed, he quickly removed his PJ bottoms. Emily only got to see his shaft briefly, but it was enough to make her feel a little apprehensive.

Seeing her worried expression, he moved on top of her and kissed her fears away. His hands were moving all over her and she was taking in jolts of sensation from every part of her body. When his hand slid between their bodies, she felt him rubbing her swollen clit gently.

Then she felt it. Daniel held his shaft in his hand and was now using it to rub on her clit. Strangely, the feel of his dick was smooth and hard, and felt way better than his fingers. Her kitty must have loved it too, because she was wetter than she'd ever been.

Spreading her legs wide, Emily gyrated forward, yearning for something more. Something deep inside her was longing to be stroked and she needed him to handle it. She wanted it now.

Reaching down, she wrapped her hands around his shaft, causing him to jump. "Now, Danny. I need to have you inside me now," she purred against his neck.

Having her hand wrapped around his engorged flesh sent him over the edge. He teased her entrance one last time before entering her slowly. For a brief moment Emily tensed up and closed her eyes tightly. She felt him inside her, thick and hard, and was trying to get used to the way he stretched her tunnel.

"Don't move, Em. Relax until there's no pain." He sounded strained trying to stay still when he really wanted to shove deeply inside her, filling her to the max.

Emily lay still beneath him, waiting for the pain to ease. When the pain subsided, she began to flex her muscles around his length and he moaned in pleasure.

Her hands slid around his waist and down further to grip his firm butt. She flexed her muscles around him again and smiled when she heard him groan under his breath.

"You like when I do that, don't you?"

Looking down at her, he saw that she had a wicked look in her eyes. When she tightened her walls again, he tried to hold in his moan, but it slipped pass his lips.

Her eyes narrowed seductively. "Yeah, you like it," she said naughtily.

That's when it hit him. Emily was a freak. *Thank you, Lord.*

Happy about his discovery, he sat up and looked down at their bodies connected. When he glanced up, she was looking at him with half closed lids. He leaned forwards letting his hands glide down her neck, between her breast, over her stomach to rest on her diamond shaped, shaved pussy. His thumb made tiny circles on her clit.

"You ready for this ride, baby?" he asked, quietly.

Biting her lip, she nodded. "You made me wait a long time for it," she said with a pout.

"Don't worry. You don't have to wait another second."

He gripped her hips and pressed further into her. Despite the tightness, she was slick, hot, and perfectly ready for his sensual torment.

"Ahhh, damn, baby." Seeing that she didn't recoil from his thrust, he pressed in as far as he could go and gave her a little nudge.

"Mmm." She whimpered in pleasure and that was enough to assure him that it was game time.

Daniel fell forward and began stroking and grinding her pussy with slow thrust. There was no break in his motion as he immersed himself deeper while she gripped the back of his neck. Relentlessly, he filled her only to retreat, and then thrust into her again and again.

Her legs were wrapped around his back, holding him trapped inside her clenching walls. The tightness all around him was unbelievable and had him rocking into her unmercifully. The deeper his penetration, the tighter she clenched. She loved the way he felt inside her, thick, hard and heavy. He was inflicting all kinds of new feelings within her by his lovemaking and she was soaking it in like a ravenous woman.

When he lifted her leg, she actually felt him slide in deeper, touching her most inner parts. Gripping his neck and the sheets, she bit down on his shoulder trying to handle him.

"Yes! Like that, Danny. Uhhhh… Oh, damn, Danny!"

Emily was riding the wave of a sexy symphony filled with sighs, groans, panting breaths, and greedy touches. The intenseness of their lovemaking was blazing hot and neither of them wanted it to end. There was nothing that could separate them while wrapped in the throes of passion. Their attraction was magnetic and frenzied, like a treacherous storm. Hot, wet and primal.

With every movement, it brought them closer and closer to what they both craved. When their target was reached, they spiraled into a fiery depth that had them soaring through the stars holding on to each other tightly.

Hearts pounding and drenched in sweat, they lay intertwined, content and satiated. Their sensual exchange was nothing less than a masterpiece. A delicious recipe of love.

Chapter Twenty Five

It was a little past noon and sleeping in his bed was the reason for his smile, Emily. She lay there on her stomach facing away from him, the covers shoved down at her waist. One foot had escaped the blanket and he grinned at how small her feet were compared to his size thirteen.

He had been up for at least an hour and had closed the drapes so the sunlight wouldn't disturb her. Now he had the pleasure of watching her sleep. He let his eyes roam over her shoulder's and across her spine to the two small dimples on her lower back. Each breath she inhaled and released, gave him peace. *She's beautiful.*

Emily stirred and rolled over onto her back. With her eyes still shut, she raised her hands above her head and stretched, a wide smile plastered on her face. Relaxing her arms, she kept them above her head and opened her eyes. Peeking through her bent arm, she saw a pair of dark eyes staring at her.

"What are you looking at?" she asked, her voice sounding soft and husky from just waking up.

His eyes lower to the swell of her breast, her smooth, flat stomach, and then to the edge of the blanket that had slipped even lower when she changed positions.

Daniel met her gaze. "If you let that blanket slip any further I'll be looking at you gripping my sheets and biting my pillow again."

With a devilish grin, she used her foot to inch the cover down a little more. "Is there something under here that you want?" she asked, licking her lips slowly.

He watched her tongue glide over her lips and groaned.

"If there's something under here that you want, then maybe you should come and get it."

The cover inched down again revealing more of her dark skin. There was only about an inch more to go to reveal to him her shaved mound.

189

"Danny." Emily called to him sounding naughty. She lifted her leg, bending it at the knee and the cover fell between her thighs giving him a small peek at her kitty. He glanced up at her, ready to take what she offered.

"Yeah?"

"I think you missed breakfast," she said, pulling the covers to the side. When her hand traveled between her cleavage, over her stomach, and then slid between her moist folds, he sat up slowly. "Aren't you hungry?" she asked as she slid her fingers deep inside her.

He got to his knees and crawled to her. He grabbed her legs and spread them wide, all the while watching her slip her fingers in and out of her juices. He was focused on her movements and his dick hardened and stretched.

"A man's gotta eat," he said, before lowering his head.

Two hours later…

Emily sat back nice and full after popping the last piece of bacon into her mouth. She glanced over at Daniel who was sitting across from her scanning through the email on his phone. He was focused on what he was reading and she sighed at the feeling of contentment that came over her.

He knew that she was watching him. He could feel her eyes on him checking him out. Undetected, he raised his phone up a little higher, making sure he got a decent angle. The sound was off on his phone, so she didn't hear him click off several photos.

When she stuck her finger in her mouth to suck the syrup off, he snapped the picture. With her eyes half closed and looking directly at him, it was the most erotic scene he'd ever seen. Well, that is except for this morning when she lay naked on the bed, spread eagle. He groaned, remembering how she had allowed him to taste every inch of her.

When Emily heard him moan, she looked up and saw that he was gawking her.

"What are you staring at?" she asked, smiling. She stood and picked up both of their plates and rinsed them off before placing them into the dishwasher.

He leaned back and grinned. He had snapped off a few more pictures without her seeing.

"You." He was still staring.

She turned and leaned against the counter. "Well cut it out," she said, amused. "You're making me nervous."

He placed his phone on the table and laughed. "Do you know we made love last night?"

Smiling, Emily nodded. "And this morning too."

"You were very verbal about what you wanted."

She looked away, embarrassed.

He leaned over taking her hand and pulled her down onto his lap.

"Don't be embarrassed. I liked it," he said, turning her head so she could look at him. "I enjoyed every minute of it," he said quietly, then nuzzled the side of her neck.

She leaned back and wrapped her arms around his waist. "So did I, old man."

Daniel smiled. "I think I proved to you last night, and this morning, that you shouldn't be calling me an old man. Plus, I'm only three years older than you are," he said as his hand rounded her bottom.

She placed a hot kiss behind his ear and whispered softly. "Yes, three very long years," she said with a giggle.

He tightened his hold and shifted so she could feel him hard and ready. "You're lucky we have something important to do today, or I'd take you back into the bedroom and prove my case over and over again."

She slid her hand up his chest, stopping when she felt his heart beating beneath her palm. "And what do we have to do that's so important?"

"We need to go down to the station and put in the restraining order." He felt her body tense up in his arms. "It needs to be done, Em. And once it's done, you can move on from this."

She sighed in resignation.

"Don't worry. I'll be by your side the whole time."

"Promise."

"Yes. I promise."

***

It was early in the evening and the dinner crowd was already pouring in to dine at Sinful. As usual the ambience was serene and the service was impeccable. She and Daniel had already enjoyed their meal and she was now in his office waiting as he made a few calls.

Just as he completed his last call, the phone rang again and he sighed in frustrated. All he wanted to do was take Emily back to his place and spend some time with her alone. Seeing that would have to be put on hold at least for another few minutes, he picked up the phone.

"Sinful."

"Hello, I'd like to place an order for delivery," said Rainy with a smile.

"Yeah, right. Very funny," he said, recognizing her voice. "What do you want?" he said, laughing.

Rainy sat back comfortably on the couch as she watched Jordan through the patio doors playing with Miki.

"Like I said. I need to place an order for delivery."

"And what do you want delivered crazy lady."

"A Teenage Mutant Ninja Turtle birthday cake for your nephew. I want it huge with all of the characters faces on it."

"Ninja Turtles?" asked Daniel, smiling.

"It's his new interest. Everything has to be turtles. His book bag, his sheets, his sneakers, and even his clothes. I can't wait until he grows out of it. Do you know how hard it is to find anything to match with green?" she asked exasperated.

"No I don't and I don't care to. Do you have a picture for me to go by or do you want me to wing it?"

"I sure do. I took a picture of his new poster and I'm sending it to you now."

"Hold on. Let me check." Daniel grabbed his cell phone. When he got the text and saw the photo, he zoomed in on it to see how complex it would be to create the cake. "This seems easy enough. Consider it done."

"Awesome. Let me know how much it— "

"I know you don't think I'm charging you for this?" he asked, sounding insulted.

"Well, I wasn't going to just assume that it was for fr—"

"Get off my phone, Rainy."

"Thank you, Daniel," she said, smiling. "I know he's going to love it."

"You're welcome, and I'll do my best."

Once Daniel hung up the phone he looked up to see that Emily was gone. While he was on the phone, she decided to take a peek in the kitchen to say hello to everyone, and slipped out of the room undetected. After a quick visit, she decided to head back to see if he was ready to go. She was anxious to be near him again.

As she headed down the long hallway, she saw one of his workers coming her way, and stepped to the side to pass him, but he stepped directly in front of her and they almost collided.

"Oh! Excuse me," she said, and took a step to the side to move out of his way.

Derrek moved with her, blocking her path. "Looks to me like you want me in your way," he said with a crooked smile.

Emily leaned back and frowned. "What?"

He took a step closer. "Yeah, you don't gotta play it off. Ain't nobody here but me and you. So what's up?"

I know this little ass boy is not trying to throw game at me. "I'm sorry, but you're mistaken. I'm not interested in you like that," she said, trying to go around him.

"Oh, so I'm not good enough for you. I'm not caking it, so I can't get no play?"

Caking it? What the hell does that mean? "Look, I have no idea what you're talking about. So let's just forget about it, okay. You go your way and I'll go mine."

Emily started to move again, and Derrek moved with her. It was as if they were doing some strange dance together.

"Is there a problem?" The deep sound of Daniel's voice broke through the tension and Emily sighed gratefully.

He approached them quickly feeling the tension surrounding them. His large frame stood over the much shorter Derrek, and Emily hopped the boy was smart enough not to provoke him. He glanced briefly at her and saw that she was uncomfortable. Instantly, he knew what was taking place, and he became angry.

"I believe you owe Ms. Bawler an apology," he said, his voice marked with steel. He had only heard the end of their conversation, but it was enough to make him want to fire the kid on the spot.

For a long moment Derrek stared at Daniel, then at Emily before nodding. He needed this job so he made himself calm down. "I'm sorry I offended you, Ms. Bawler. I saw a fine woman and thought I'd holla is all. I didn't mean nothing by it." Nothing in his tone said that his apology was sincere.

Daniel knew the boy was being an ass and was about to say as much, but Emily spoke first.

"I accept your apology, uh…"

"Derrek," he said, holding out his hand. "My name's Derrek." Again he plastered on his crooked smile.

He wasn't going to let this fool touch Emily's shoe, let alone her hand. "All that's not necessary," he said, stepping in front of her. "Get back to whatever you were doing and refrain from speaking to anyone that isn't an employee. Do we have an understanding?"

Derrek nodded. "Yeah, I understand," he said and continued down the hall to the kitchen.

He watched him until he disappeared, making a mental note to find someone to replace him.

Chapter Twenty Six

The airport was busy as usual as Sherry made her way through Terminal A. She was heading in the direction of a white unmarked door that lead to the many offices that was run by the Customs Department. After punching in the security code, the door buzzed and then unlocked, allowing her to enter.

In no time she had maneuvered through the bright white halls until she came upon her department. When she entered, it seemed to her like the conversation had quieted down some. Looking around suspiciously, she didn't notice anything out of the ordinary, so she walked over to her desk and claimed her seat. She proceeded to boot up her computer and began the long process of typing up the mound of paperwork that was on her desk.

Hours had gone by with her doing exactly what every other guard in the office was doing, putting in paperwork while hoping something exciting would happen. She hated that she had to come back knowing Emily was still in Virginia with that brain washing coward. She vowed to go back as soon as she could.

Every time she thought of their last encounter at the mall, she became angry all over again.

Who the hell did he think he was threatening me?

Ring! Ring!

The interruption of the phone on her desk ringing made her frown. She snatched it up, sounding irritated by the intrusion.

"Yeah."

"Woods, get in my office, now!" Click.

Sherry looked at the receiver confused. Captain O'donald, had summoned her to his office and he sounded upset. The reason for her confusion was because she had only been back for a few hours. What could she had possibly done wrong?

Hanging up the phone, she stood and started towards the stairs. As she walked through the office, a lot of her coworkers were eyeing her sideways. Some sneered or shook their heads in contempt. *What's their problem?*

When she reached her Captain's office, she tapped on the glass door.

"Come in." His voice boomed through the door.

She entered the office and pulled up short when she saw a police officer standing near the door, along with two security guards. She turned to O'donald.

"You wanted to see me, sir?"

"Officer Williams needs to address you first," he said, nodding towards the officer.

The police officer stepped around her putting himself closer to the doors exit. He handed her a large manilla envelope. "You've been served," he said, and dashed out the door.

"Wait! What?" she called after him, but the man was already gone. She turned to look at O'donald. "What's this about? What's going on?"

"Have a seat, Woods." She took a seat in front of his desk and glanced over at the two guards again. She knew them, Joseph Banks and Mark Griffon. Two of the agencies best. *Why are they here and not at their posts?*

Forgetting all about the envelope she held, her attention was focused on her Captain.

O'donald sat behind his desk and tapped a few keys on his computer. Once he found what he was looking for, he hit the print button and soon several sheets of paper shot from his printer. He grabbed them up and tossed them in front of her.

"You've been with this company going on seven years now Woods and it pains me to know that the accusations that are being brought up on you are actually true."

"Accusations?"

"Effective immediately, you are hereby terminated from this company. You will turn over your badge and gun immediately. You are to be escorted from the premises, all the way out to the terminal's main gate."

"Terminated!? Sir, what did I do?" she yelled in a pleading tone.

"You used the company's software and mainframe for your personal use. You searched and found information on a civilian, and then used that information to pursue and harassed them. It's all in the documents that I provided for you. Please be advised that your actions have cause for an investigation."

Sherry sat there in shock as O'donald droned on about her rights as a former employee. She couldn't believe she'd just lost her job. Her career had evaporated right before her eyes. She looked down at the papers he'd handed her and saw that they had everything on them that she'd typed in to search for Emily and Daniel, including the times and dates.

There was nothing she could say or do to fix this. She could only try to leave with her head up and hold on to any dignity she had left.

"Your gun and badge," he said pointedly.

Sherry stood up and unsnapped her gun holster and slowly pulled it from its resting place on her hip. She released the clip and placed them both on the desk. Next, she pulled out the folded badge from her pocket and tossed it on top of the gun.

"These two officers will see you out." When she turned to leave, he stopped her. "Don't forget your paperwork," he said sternly.

O'donald was pissed because he'd had such high hopes for her. She was an excellent customs agent and knew she had the grit to move up in the company. He didn't know what temporary weakness came over her to do what she did. But it wasn't anything he could do for her. This call had come from the corporate office and was way out of his pay grade. Whomever the person was that she'd searched for had friends in some very high places.

Sherry was escorted through the office, down the long hall and right out to the terminal's front doors. It was like the long walk of shame. Even though she lost her job, she felt that it was worth it. She now had all the information she needed on Emily and Daniel. In her mind, it had all been for love.

As she sat in her car, she looked through the printed papers O'donald had given her trying to see where she'd made a mistake to tip them off. She was sure that she'd erased her search history from the browser and the mainframe of the computer. She was confused as to how they found out.

Not seeing anything wrong, she sighed in frustration and tossed the papers on the passenger seat. That's when she saw the manilla envelope. *You've been served.* The words of the police officer came back to her. She reached over and picked up the envelope and tore it open.

Soon as she read the top few lines of the paper her rage soared out of control. The summons was clear and Emily's name was printed in bold letters. Certain words popped out at her in 3D.

Restraining Order.
Court Order.
1000 Feet.
Prosecuted.
Jail Time.

Down at the very bottom of the second sheet was Emily's name scrawled across in a beautiful penmanship. Sherry's vision began to blur and her breathing became erratic. Not being able to control her outburst, she began to slam her fist painfully into her thighs. Over and over again, she pounded down on her own flesh yelling obscenities. Even when the pain was unbearable, she continued.

Then instantly she stopped. Her head dropped forward and she drew in deep breaths through her mouth. Once the inside of the car stopped spinning and her vision cleared, she leaned back and stared out the window with a blank face seeing nothing.

It was him. He made her do this. He probably threatened her to do it. I know she wouldn't do this on her own, because Emily wouldn't violate our love like that.

But she signed it. She narrowed her eyes and shook her head in disappointed. *She needs to be taught a lesson. She needs to know that she has to respect me. And then I'll deal with him.*

"Don't worry, baby. I'll take care of him once and for all," said Sherry. A devilish crazed smile masked her lips.

Chapter Twenty

Seven

"You've got to be kidding me," said Daniel as he looked over the order sheet in his hand that read six thousand edible chocolate roses. An order that he'd never called in. Now he was stuck with six thousand chocolate roses and nowhere to store them. Since the orders that he'd actually called in earlier this week filled the freezers and refrigerators to capacity, there was literally no where to put them.

To put it plainly, Daniel was having a stressful week. Food that he'd ordered for the restaurant went missing and a customer's food was way too salty to be a mistake. Then the mirror in the men's room got smashed. Not to mention someone spray painted obscenities on the side of the building. Oh, and don't forget about the fuse box getting damaged and needing to be repaired, which caused them to close for nearly three hours before reopening. Now he has six thousand chocolate roses sitting in his office.

Then a smile crossed his face and he reached for the phone.

"I said come visit, not call me at all hours of the night."

Daniel laughed when he heard Veras' voice snapping at him on the other end.

"I will come just as soon as I get through this hellish week."

"Awww, poor baby. Tell Vera what she can do to help."

"You can take six thousand edible chocolate roses off my hands and I'll owe you one big time," he asked, hopefully.

Vera laughed. "Why the hell did you order so many?"

"Actually, I didn't order them at all."

"So send them back!"

"I tried that. The manager claimed it was a sale item with a no return, no exchanges and no credit pitch on it for a low price. Now I'm stuck with them because my food orders came in and the place is packed tight."

"That manager is pulling a fast one on you. He doesn't want to refund your money or credit? That's bullshit."

"I know, but right now I have a ton of these things sitting in my office packed in dry ice and in about half an hour, it'll be a pile of chocolate syrup. So what do you say? Can you help a brother out?"

"On one condition. I get to use some. I have two weddings I'm preparing for and I can use a few of them to help with deserts."

"Use as many as you like. Use them all if you want to. Just as long as you can get them out of my office."

"Deal! I'll send someone over to get them right away."

He sighed, knowing he had finally had a break this week. "Thanks Vera. I owe you one."

"You got that right. Now get off my line. I have to find Raul so he can get to you right away."

"Okay. Bye."

"Bye."

Daniel snatched up the phone again to let Anthony know someone from Vera's was coming to take all of the chocolate roses shipment. Usually, he'd stay to help close up, but he was exhausted and wanted to get home to Emily. He smiled. There was nothing like going home to see her waiting up for him.

When he felt himself sitting there smiling like a silly idiot, he hopped up and snatched his suit jacket. He closed his office door and locked it before heading down the hall. Anthony looked up from the Hostess stand when he saw him.

"Are you leaving sir?"

"Yup! Don't call me unless it's an emergency!" he called out as he breezed by him.

Anthony laughed. *I'd be happy to get home too if I had a woman like Emily waiting there for me. But my girl Tiffany is beautiful and one of a kind.*

The drive home was uneventful and the traffic moved quickly, allowing him to get home in about thirty minutes. He was super tired, but the moment he stepped through the door and saw Emily, he felt instantly better. There wasn't nothing that could compare to seeing her snuggled up on the couch reading a book.

When the door opened, Emily looked up to see Daniel and from the look on his face, she knew that he'd had another bad day. He looked dead tired and she stood to give him a tight hug.

"Do I need to ask?" asked Emily, already knowing the answer.

"Nope. I only want to take a hot shower, munch on that popcorn you got over there in that bowl, and hold you in my arms."

Emily smiled up at him. "I believe that can be arranged. Go take your shower. Have you eaten dinner?"

"Uhhh…"

"I'll take that as a no. Go on. I'll fix you a sandwich, then you can have your popcorn," she said, giving him a gentle shove towards his room.

Daniel smirked. "You want to join me?"

"Get your butt down the hall, Danny," she said, laughing.

Half an hour later, he returned to the living room to find a huge turkey sandwich on a plate and a tall glass of sparkling lemon water. Although he wasn't that hungry when he first got home, seeing the sandwich made him ravenous. He wasted no time brushing off his meal. Once he was finished, he glanced over at the two tall popcorn cups that were sitting on the table.

"Is one of those for me?"

"Yeah, greedy," she responded, smiling.

He picked up his cup and started popping fluffy pieces of popcorn into his mouth.

"What are we going to do now?" he asked while taking a peek at her bare legs. He popped another piece into his mouth.

"Not what you're thinking," said Emily, laughing. She picked up the remote and turned on the television. The large seventy five inch screen came to life and she searched through the movie files on Netflix for a movie to watch.

"How about Friday?" she asked, grinning.

"Really?" Daniel's tone was flat and lifeless.

"What'chu got on my forty fool?" Emily said, trying to imitate Deebo's voices from the movie.

He burst out laughing. He fell back against the couch holding his stomach. "You know what? Let's watch that, because I need to see you narrate all the characters."

Emily sucked her teeth, grinning. "You know you're going to be doing it too," she said as she pressed the button to start the movie.

"Come on over here with me," he said as he shifted his position making room for her.

Seeing him lying back on the couch in a pair of grey sweats and a white t-shirt had her imaging a lot of things to do other than watching television, but she decided to behave herself. Slowly she crawled across the couch and settle between his legs, her head resting on his chest. As soon as she was settled, he wrapped his arms around her and pulled the throw blanket down over them.

The movie was hilarious, but she didn't find out that she was watching it alone until she realized he wasn't laughing. Lifting her head, she saw that he was asleep. The soft sound of his breathing was soothing to her ears. Knowing he was dead tired, she hated the fact that she needed to wake him up and get him into bed.

Easing up from his chest, she removed the blanket and stood. First she took their dishes into the kitchen and placed them in the dishwasher. When she returned, she folded up the throw blanket and then turned off the TV.

Leaning over, she took one of his hands in hers and called to him quietly. "Danny." When he didn't respond, she called to him again. This time his eyes fluttered open and she could tell he was trying to get his bearings.

She gave his hand a gentle tug. "Come on, Baby. Let's get you into bed."

He sat up on the couch and glanced around. Another tug from Emily got him to his feet. Once he was steady, she led him to his bedroom and helped him beneath the blankets. He was out before she could turn down the lights.

She stood there watching him sleep, thinking about how complete she felt when she was with him. The moment they crossed over from friends to lover's her whole world changed. He was her sunrise and sunset. Her love for him had only grown stronger. There was nothing in the world that could match the love she felt for him. *And he's mine*, she thought with a slight smile on her lips. *All mine*. Stepping back quietly, she turned and left.

Back in her room, she decided to take a hot shower and get some sleep herself. She didn't take long in the shower. She only wanted the steaming water to relax her enough to drift into a peaceful sleep. Now dressed in a T-shirt only, she climbed beneath the cool sheets and turned on her side to stare through the patio glass doors.

The moon was high in the sky and the bright glow from its beams stretched across the bottom of her bed. She sighed in content as her eyes drifted shut.

Not knowing how long he'd slept, Daniel woke up feeling lonely. It was a horrible feeling that he'd been subjected to before Emily had come to his home. He hated it then and he hated it now. That feeling of waking up alone would lay heavy on his heart knowing he couldn't have what he wanted. But now things were different. He had what he wanted. Emily. And he wasn't planning on going a day without her.

Glancing around the room, he saw that she was nowhere to be found. He slid from his bed and headed towards her bedroom. Easing the door open quietly, he could see the outline of her body under the sheet.

Daniel removed his shirt and sweats and eased behind her in the bed. When she didn't stir, he pulled the sheet from her and tossed it to the foot of the bed. Seeing that her shirt had eased up to her waist, he let his eyes drift down across her hip and lower to her smooth legs. Knowing what he wanted and craved at that moment, he got out of the bed and scooped her up in his arms. He moved to the foot of the bed and placed her at the very edge.

Emily felt her body drifting and then being moved. She opened her eyes to find Daniel looming over her. "Baby, what's wrong?" she asked, concerned. It wasn't too long ago, she had helped him in bed.

"I'm hungry." His voice was husky and deep. She almost couldn't hear him.

"But you just ate," she said, confused.

"Yeah, but you didn't feed me the right meal," he said, and dropped to his knees between her thighs. Not wasting any time, he spread her legs wide, allowing the moonlight to beam down on her folds. With a deep groan, he used his tongue to part her lips, twirling and flicking. When he reached her clit, he twirled around it one last time before sucking it into his mouth.

"Ahhhhh!"

Emily arched her back and the muscles in her stomach clenched and trembled. She'd had her kitty licked by some damn good lovers, but not one of them knew how to trap her soul with desire. Daniel's head game was on point and she could tell he damn well knew it. He pulled her forward, gripping her hips firmly , making sure she couldn't get away from his assault until he drank his fill. The press and release game he threw at her, had her twisting and jerking. Then he would drive her mad with his relentless sucking and slurping.

"Ahhhh, Danny. Baby, please... shitttt. I can't... I'm— " That was the last word that formed on her lips before she lost focus and her body exploded filling his mouth with all her love juices.

"Mmmm." He lapped up every drop and only eased off when her whimpers turned into needy sighs. "I know what you need, baby. I got you."

Standing, he lifted her feet and placed them on the bed. Now she lay before him, knees bent, open and ready. The light from the moon caused the remaining juices on her pussy to glisten and shimmer.

"You're so beautiful." He stepped closer and lifted his shaft, rubbing the head all over her moistness.

Emily lifted her hips asking for more.

He delayed her pleasure a little longer. He leaned over her and sucked her nipple and grazed it lightly with his teeth. He loved it's twin with the same attention.

"Dammit, Danny!" she yelled out, reaching down between their bodies to grab his thickness. She stroked him with a firm grip and he sucked in air quickly as she caressed him.

Knowing he wouldn't last long with her jerking him like she was, he pulled back and stood up straight. Resting his hands on her knees, Daniel used his hips to guide his head where he wanted, then he pushed inside her slowly. The tightness of her wrapped around him was maddening. He always found himself having to work his way in, like it was her first time all over again.

There's always that thrilling feeling of amazement when you first enter a woman, but this… This was pure heaven. To put it plainly, she gave him something that he knew he'd never find in another woman.

The feeling of him invading her body, stretching her to accommodate his girth, was amazing. She felt her tunnel opening up and he began to press in deeper and deeper. When he hit bottom, he pressed further and hit her G'spot causing her to shatter in a million piece.

Daniel let her ride out the orgasm. He held perfectly still, watching as she jerked and shuddered in front of him. When the last of its affects passed through her, he leaned down and kissed her passionately.

"That was an amazing thing to watch," he whispered against her lips. "Now let's give you another," he said, and began to move inside her once again.

Pulling her legs up over his shoulders, he reached down with both hands and palmed her firm cheeks. One stroke after another he delivered the dick to her, slow and deep. Knowing she couldn't escape the position he had her in, he slowed down to an almost stop, easing in and then retreating. The slow rotation made her cravings increase, and her pussy flexed and clutched around him trying to obtain that orgasm she felt building inside her.

The excitement of what was to come, and the incessant time he was taking to get her there, had Emily moaning, nipping, and gripping his shoulder. She had lost all control and was now his for the taking. All she could do was lay there and enjoy the insufferable amount of pleasure she was given at his hands.

"Danny, baby, pleasseeee," she whined.

He kissed her behind her ear softly. "Is that a plea for more? It'll be my pleasure," he panted and that's when things really got hot.

He slow stroked her a few more times before picking up the pace. He knew she was enjoying it because she became wetter, slicker. Her moans turned into dirty words and the arms around his neck tensed up. The feel of her nails digging into his back drove him to push her further.

Biting her lip, Emily was holding on for dear life. The dick pounding she was receiving from Daniel was new to her and she was loving every minute of it. Having him on top of her, legs high over his shoulders, and trapped from moving, gave her a sense of raw sexuality that tipped her over the edge.

The Fourth of July had nothing on all the stars she saw blasting off behind her tightly squeezed eyes. Her body clenched up and trembled, as the explosion rocked her to the core. Every single cell began to tingle as the orgasmic current rushed through her. Almost to the point of being lightheaded, she allowed the intense waterfall to gush from her kitty while Daniel continued to thrust into her with his powerful plunges.

He felt it tingling across his back first, hot little pricks that traveled down his arms leaving small goose bumps. Suddenly, the tingling stopped and everything went numb. Then this unbelievable sensation filled his lower region. He couldn't focus on anything else except the part of him that was inside her. To him, nothing else existed besides that moment.

Knowing he was about to join her in orgasmic heaven, he buried his face into her hair and tightened his hold. His thrust seemed almost desperate and her hips lifted to match his rhythm. The loud sound of wet skin smacking together pushed him over the edge and he moaned a low guttural sound. His release was so great that it triggered another in Emily, and together they rode the wave until they both were sated.

Emily now lay sprawled like a rag doll on top of him. Their bodies were weak and limp as they lay quietly in the night touching and holding each other. All the tension and stress of the day had long been forgotten.

"Em, are you okay?" he whispered softly as he glanced down at her.

She met his concerned gaze and smiled. Unable to speak, she gave him a thumbs up signal, then drifted off to sleep.

Chapter Twenty Eight

Kimberly stepped into the restaurant and walked past the hostess desk like she owned the place. Her shades shielded her eyes and she flipped her hair over her shoulder, leaving the smell of her strong perfume behind her. Knowing that the three young business men that were waiting to be seated were watching her, she added a little more twist to her hips making her ass jiggle.

As she started down the long hall, Derrek caught sight of her and dropped the sack of onions he was hauling to the kitchen. He watched the sway of her hips and the way her hair bounced all around her. *She knows she wants me. I don't know why this bitch keeps playing.*

Closing in on Daniel's office, Kimberly was blocked from entering when Derrek stepped in front of her.

"The boss man is busy right now, but uh, I can give you what you need. You know you want me," he said with a sly grin.

Kimberly rolled her eyes. "Don't you have enough work around here to do?"

Derrek laughed. "I ain't got no problem doing a little overtime. Shit, looks to me like you need it."

"What I need is for you to get out of my way," she said stepping around him.

Laughing again, Derrek let her pass him by. He looked down at her fat ass and shook his head. "One day you gonna let me slide this dick to you. You can't say no forever."

"My ass is not a perk that comes with the job."

He chuckled as he watched her fix her hair and straighten her clothes before barging into Daniel's office.

Daniel looked up from his computer screen and frowned when he saw Kimberly rush into his office. She was sporting a blue dress that hugged her in all the right places and high strappy heels. Any other time he might have been interested in getting a round two with her, but now he found her lacking. He wasn't interested in the least.

Kimberly took off her shades and tossed them, and her bag, on one of the chairs in front of his desk.

"Kimberly, I asked you not to barge in my office like that. I'd like it if you'd do as I ask," he said, tossing his pen down on the stack of order forms.

"Yes, darling, I know, but I don't have a lot of time on my hands. I have a client waiting for me downtown. I only came to have you sign these permit forms for the inspection and I—"

"You can leave them, and when I get the time, I'll look them over."

"But if you sign them now, I can drop them off while I'm in the area," she said, speaking quickly.

Daniel shook his head. "Leave them, Kimberly," he said pointedly.

Seeing she wasn't going to get her way, she pulled the papers from her bag, and placed them on his desk.

"Fine. Please do so quickly," she said, giving him a tight smile.

"In due time," he said, letting her know he wouldn't be rushed. He still hadn't forgiven her for her rudeness to Emily, and answered her in a clipped tone.

Feeling snubbed, she picked up her bag and headed for the door. When she stepped out into the hallway, Derrek was still there stacking his trolley.

"So what's up, Ms. Thang? We gonna hang out or what?"

Upset from being slighted by Daniel, Kimberly lashed out. "Why don't you do what you're being paid to do," she snapped.

"Oh, it's like that? I'm not good enough for you, huh?" he asked with a sneer.

"Baby, you're not *man* enough for me. Now in there," she said, nodding towards Daniel's office door. "That's a man. A real man." She smiled wickedly at him. "You're small potatoes compared to him. Oh, and excuse the pun," she said, grinning when she saw he was now loading large bags of red skin potatoes. "Now do your fucking job," she hissed and walked off.

He watched her walk away. His eyes were narrowed and he was grinding his teeth together in anger. Then he began to smile. He glanced at Daniel's closed office door, then back down the hall where Kimberly had disappeared. *That bitch needs to be knocked down a peg or two.*

Just as he turned to finish with his work, Daniel came out of his office and headed towards the stock area. He passed by him and didn't even acknowledge that he was there. To him, Derrek was just another problem waiting to be fixed.

Derrek watched Daniel cut down another hallway and then out of his sight. He only waited a moment before grabbing the ice bucket and filling it. He then slipped inside Daniels' office undetected. Making haste, he sat down at his desk and grabbed the mouse to the computer. He found what he needed and his fingers began typing quickly on the keys. Satisfied with his message, he hit the send button and left.

***

No sale. Kimberly sat in her car pissed that she had been late to her meeting, which had caused the buyers to pull out of the deal. Her boss had given her a verbal lashing that left her feeling defeated. With another empty sale week looming ahead, she was depressed and anxious. She had to close some of these accounts or she would lose out on the promotion.

Bleep! Bleep!

Hearing her phone go off, she snatched it up hoping it was a client ready to make an offer. Her smile widened almost splitting her face when she read the email.

Kimberly
Don't ask questions, just follow the instructions.
Clear your schedule.
Come to my office.
Take off all your clothes.
Leave on your bra and panties.
Leave on the heels.
Lay on the couch with your legs open wide for me.
Don't speak.
Just feel.
Daniel

Kimberly squealed with excitement. Finally, Daniel had come to his senses about them being together. Checking her watch, she wasted no time in doing as he asked. The first thing she did was call the office where she worked and had her assistant clear her schedule for the rest of the day. Next, she pulled into an empty lane and rushed right back over to Sinful.

Now if I can only get him to hurry with this deal before he realizes the market value of that area has declined drastically and will soon be surrounded by nothing but Navy warehouses. There won't be any customers to sit down for a romantic meal within a five mile radius.

Remorse hit her for a split second, but she shook it off. *That was business. This is pleasure,* she thought, smiling as she hurried through the late afternoon traffic.

Anticipating the dick pounding she was about to receive had Kimberly floating down the hallway on cloud nine. She walked into his office without knocking again, knowing this time she had been invited in. Tossing her bag on the chair, she proceeded in following his instructions to the letter. Now she lay back on his leather couch, legs spread wide apart, still wearing her underwear and heels. Her sexy pose would cause a lesser man to dive right in.

Daniel was not that type of man. He was in his private bathroom, changing his shirt after having an accident with a can of tomato paste. When he came out, he stopped short at seeing Kimberly sprawled out on his couch, legs spread wide in her underwear, leaving nothing to the imagination.

"What the hell are you doing in here? I said there will be nothing more between us sexually, and I meant it. Now get up and put your damn clothes on!" He didn't mean to yell, but she was taking this too far.

"What?! What the hell is wrong with you? If you didn't want this, then why did you ask me to come?" Kimberly jumped up and began getting dressed. Her feelings had just gotten crushed and she turned away so he couldn't see the pain in her eyes.

He looked at her like she'd lost her mind. "I didn't ask you to come here. What are you talking about?"

Half dressed, she went to her bag and pulled out her cell phone. She tapped a few buttons to bring up the email she'd received and handed the phone over to him.

Suddenly, the door opened and in walked Emily with a smile on her face. A smile that instantly deteriorated once she saw Kimberly half naked, standing close to Daniel. Kimberly looked up and saw her first and gave her a cunning smile. She leaned closer to him and grazed her cheek against his shoulder.

Daniel looked up and froze. *Oh no.* The crushed look on Emily's face said it all. He had just been caught in a compromising situation, and he knew it was going to take God and a miracle to get him through it.

Emily's eyes filled with tears and she turned and ran from the room.

"Emily, wait!"

He shoved Kimberly's phone back at her. "Get dressed and get out," he ground out furiously.

Rushing from the office, he hauled ass through the hallway, but he was too late. Just as he reached the front entrance, she was pulling from the front of the building. He shoved his hands into his pocket for his car keys only to realize that he'd left them in his desk drawer. *Damn it!*

He hurried back to his office and almost knocked Kimberly off her feet as she was stepping out.

"I asked you to leave," he said, walking past her.

"I am leaving! Daniel, you can't be angry with me, because this is not my fault. I showed you the email that was clearly sent from your office. It may not have been sent by you, but I had every right to believe it was. Obviously someone sent it as a joke."

Daniel closed his eyes briefly and exhaled loudly. When he opened them, he tried to be as calm as he could. "I'll find out who sent the email later. Right now, all I need is for you to leave. Please," he said, strongly.

Kimberly rolled her eyes and stormed out the office.

After locking his office, Daniel left out the side door, putting him closer to his truck. He broke several speed limits driving back to his house trying to catch up to Emily. When he stepped off the elevator, the first thing he saw was one of her suitcases and his heartbeat went into overdrive.

Lord, please help me to fix this. Don't let her leave me. I can't lose her.

Walking slowly, he picked up the suitcase and hid it in the hall closet. He was coming through the living room when she came around the corner and stopped. Clearly, she had been crying and it made him feel like crap. When he looked down, she was carrying her other suitcase.

He swallowed hard.

"Em, please let me explain," he said, taking a step in her direction.

The anger in her eyes lit up and he took a step back. He had been on the receiving end of her wrath only once, and it was enough to last him a lifetime.

"Are you serious?" she asked calmly. "You can explain that?"

Her tone was calm, but it was making him uncomfortable. He'd prefer it if she was yelling or throwing something. This calmness was freaking him out. It was reminding him of the phrase, 'the quiet before the storm'.

Don't be a coward. You didn't do anything wrong. He was about to take another step closer, but thought better of it when her eyes narrowed.

"Yes, I can explain, if you allow me to." When she didn't move, only stood there, he went on. "It was all a misunderstanding."

"What!" she yelled. "You know what..." she brushed past him walking towards where she left her suitcase. When she saw that it was gone, she spent around. "Where's my bag?"

"Let me expl..."

"Where's my damn bag, Daniel!" she screamed, losing some of her control. She didn't want to cry in front of him. She didn't want to give him the pleasure of seeing her break down. *Don't cry. Don't cry.*

Her whole body shook with rage. The entire drive here, the scene of him making love to Kimberly the way he did to her, made her feel sick to her stomach. The shocked look on his face when he saw her standing there would be forever engraved in her mind. And when that bitch smiled. Emily shook her head.

Seeing things going South fast, Daniel threw caution to the wind and quickly walked up to her. Before she could mover, he wrapped his arms around her holding her tight.

"No! Let me go! Don't touch me!" she cried. "I don't want you to touch me," she bawled, her face buried in his chest.

Emily's wracking sobs tore at his soul. He held onto her as she struggled to get free. Knowing he was stronger, he didn't let go until she stood weak against him.

Feeling her relax against him, he took a chance by letting her go to pull his cell phone from his pocket. With one hand still holding her, he used his other hand to maneuver the phone. Once he had the message up, he placed it in her hand.

"Read it."

When she didn't take it, he tried again. "Take the damn phone Emily and read the message."

A few seconds went by before she lifted the phone and read the message. Fresh tears ran down her face and she tried to pull away.

"I didn't send this to her. Someone went into my office and sent that message to her. While I was in my bathroom, she was in the office doing what the email told her to do. When I came out, I saw her and I snapped. I told her to put her damn clothes back on and get out. She said I told her to come and I denied it. That's when she showed me the email. You came in while I was reading it."

Silence.

He became nervous. "I swear, Em. I never touched her. I haven't been with anyone but you. I promise."

More silence.

Emily reached down and picked up her suitcase. He freaked out.

"No!" He grabbed the other side of the suitcase handle. "Emily, I swear to you, I didn't touch her. I only deal with her for business. It's only been you. You have to believe me. I would never hurt you like that."

She looked up at him. "Let go." Those two words were said so flat and emotionless that Daniel did as she said.

When he let go, she turned and walked back down the hall to her room. Although it hurt like hell, she believed him. But she wasn't mentally ready to let it go. Believing you had been betrayed by the person you loved with your body and spirit, was enough to drain you for days.

As he watched her return to her room, he thanked God silently over and over that she believed him and would stay. He'd never experienced losing someone that he loved before and he never wanted to go through that again.

He returned to the closet and retrieved her suitcase. He carried it to her room and knocked lightly. Thinking she probably didn't want to see him right now, he left it for her to get when she was ready.

***

It was after midnight when Emily finally emerged from her room. Hunger was her enemy tonight and she quietly made her way to the kitchen. After raiding the refrigerator and eating some leftovers, she tidied up, and headed back to her room.

That's when she saw him. He was standing on the balcony, his head bowed low, and his hands gripped the railing. He didn't move a muscle. He was so still and she stood there watching him. She knew that her plans to leave had caused him pain. She wasn't insensitive or heartless. It had hurt her too. Yet, she didn't like knowing he was hurting because of her.

Stepping out onto the patio, she moved in front of him and wrapped her arms around his waist. Instantly, his arms snaked around her, pulling her closer. No words were spoken. They weren't needed. She placed her ear on his chest, listening to his strong heartbeat and sighed. They stood that way for a long time, just holding on to each other.

Tired of standing in one place, she took his hand and led him back to his room. They climbed into bed and sought each other out under the covers. They lay holding each other knowing just how close they'd come to losing what they had.

"So many things have been going wrong these past few days that it can't all be a coincident. I need to find out what's going on. But first I need to know who sent that email. I don't know who could've done it, because no one has access to my office except a few of my trusted staff members."

She snuggled closer and he nuzzled the top of her head.

"I almost lost you," he said with a ragged breath.

"Shhhh. Get some sleep, Danny. You can sort things out tomorrow."

Feeling drained, he held her quietly in his arms while listening to her snore softly.

Chapter Twenty Nine

It was almost the end of summer vacation and soon Emily would be making her way back to New York to begin a new year of teaching. But first, she had some unfinished business at Sherwood High School to attend to. She needed to deliver, in person, her choice for the scholarship to the principal.

She arrived close to nine o'clock and was happy that the door was unlocked. When she stepped inside, she noticed that the security guard was nowhere to be found. Not wanting to wait for an escort, she quickly made her was down the hall.

The principal wasn't in her office either, but she knew that she could leave it on her desk where she could find it. Pulling the scholarship folder from her bag, she leaned it against the computer screen where it wouldn't be overlooked. Now all she had to do was mail her hard copy to Julliard so the paperwork for their entrance of the new semester would be finalized.

As she passed the main office, she noticed the wire basket that was marked mail-in and mail-out on the desk, and headed for it. She figured that leaving the envelope here in the mail-out box would save her the task of finding a mailbox or having to go all the way to the post office.

Satisfied that her work with the scholarship was now complete, she left the building and headed back to her car.

***

The AC in the car was blaring as Sherry sat there watching Emily pull out of her parking spot in the school parking lot and drive off towards downtown. She had returned to Virginia a few days ago and had been watching her every move. She was focused on teaching Emily a lesson so she would know not to cross her again. After she dealt with her, she would then turn her full attention on Daniel.

Today she watched her walk into the school carrying envelopes and when she came out the building, she was empty handed. *What was so important that she had to come back here and drop it off personally?*

"Only one way to find out."

Sherry turned the car off and slid from behind the wheel. The blare of heat that she felt took her breath away and sweat instantly trickled down her back. Shaking off the uncomfortable feeling, she made her way over to the school.

Just like with Emily, the front desk where the security guard would usually sit was empty. She looked back and forth waiting for someone to pop out of a room or something, but no one came. She walked over and peeked into the first door she saw open and saw that it was the main office. She glanced around at the empty room and paused when she heard a low muffled voice from another room. No one came out to greet her, so she turned to leave. But something caught her eye and she stopped.

There, in a wire basket on the desk, she could easily see the name Julliard in bold letters. Picking up the letter she tore it open and read what was inside. Sherry was about to toss the letter back in the basket when an idea began to form. She looked over the counter and picked up a pen and a few sheets of printer paper.

Quickly, she scrawled out a note to the principal changing everything that Emily had said. She lied saying that she would not be choosing either student due to lack of talent. Walking around the front desk, she searched through the drawers until she found an envelope. She addressed the letter to Julliard and tossed it into the wire basket.

Needing to make sure her lie was concrete, she shuffled around on the desk until she found a school notice from last year. She scanned through it until she saw the principal's name. Now that she had what she needed, she picked up the schools phone and called Julliard.

"Good morning, thank you for calling Julliard. This is Lucy speaking. How may I direct your call?"

"Hello, Lucy. My name is Mrs. Vox and I'm the principal here at Sherwood High School, where Ms. Emily Bawler came to view a couple of our students for your scholarship fund."

"Oh, yes. That's correct. Is there anything you need help with regarding the forms?"

"No, that won't be necessary. Mrs. Bawler decided to pass on both students."

Surprised, the woman didn't know what to say. "I'm sorry about that, Mrs. Vox. I'm sure next year will be better."

"Actually, I'm sorry to say that I have a complaint against Ms.

Bawler," said Sherry. She was playing her part to the max.

"A complaint about Ms. Bawler?" Lucy asked shocked. She knew Emily personally and had never seen her act out of character or raise her voice.

"Yes. The woman had the audacity to come to the audition with a date. They sat right up front where they were seen by everyone showing inappropriate behavior in front of the students and our guests. I was appalled at her behavior and that someone like that was sent out to represent Julliard. I thought your school was prestigious and that you took pride in the type of staff you housed."

"I assure you, Mrs. Vox, that we are and we do. I don't understand why Ms. Bawler would do such a thing. She is held in high regard here at Julliard."

"Well, I can tell you this, next year I don't want that woman here prancing about in front of my students. She didn't give them the attention they required to fairly access their talent. You know, I would hate to put in a formal complaint with the state bored about this," Sherry threatened.

"That's not necessary. We will honor your wishes and send a different representative next year. I'm so sorry that this happened and I ask that you accept my apology on the school's behalf."

"Yes, well, I guess that's all that could be done now. You have a nice day Lucy." Sherry ended the call abruptly not giving the woman a chance to respond. She smiled, feeling that for once something had gone according to plan.

Lucy looked down at the note she had scrawled on the pink paper and sighed in anguish. Any other time she would have tossed a complaint like this into the trash, but the sound of Mrs. Vox's voice made her think that the woman would call back. Then Lucy would be in trouble for not passing the information on. In a disheartened mood, she moved towards the head mistress's office to deliver the bad news.

***

Four days later...

Thirteen. "Mmm." *Fourteen.* Emily popped another grape into her mouth. She was sitting in the center of her bed checking her email and enjoying a bowl of green grapes. Her hand was suspended in the air going for another grape when her cell phone rang.

"Hello?"

"Good afternoon, Emily. This is Mary over at Julliard."

"Oh, hello Mary. How are you?"

"Not so good. I'm calling to speak to you about an important matter."

Emily heard a sharpness in the woman's tone. "Okay, what can I do for you?"

"I'm trying to find out why you didn't choose one of the student's from Sherwood. When you left a message on my answering service, you spoke highly of the students' performance. I'd like to know what changed your mind?"

"But I didn't change my mind. I submitted my choice to Mrs. Vox and I mailed you a written note like you informed me to do. It was mailed out a few days ago."

Emily heard her shuffling through papers in the background.

"Yes, I received your letter and it plainly states that you wouldn't be choosing either of the students. With that being said, the funding went to another department."

Emily sat up straight and swung her legs off the side of the bed. She stood up and started pacing the floor.

"What?! That's impossible. I wrote in the letter that I chose Khandace Murphy. I also left the scholarship papers on Mrs. Vox desk."

Mary sucked her teeth and humped. It was something she did often with the students and Emily couldn't stand.

"Yes, speaking of Mrs. Vox, she called in a few days ago as well to leave an informal complaint about your conduct."

"My conduct?" Emily stopped pacing and began rubbing the tension she felt building between her eyebrows.

"That's correct. She said you arrived at the audition with an escort and that you were displaying unbecoming behavior in front of the students and guest. She also said that you never really showed any interest in the students or their performances."

"Mary, I don't know what's going on, but there has been an enormous mistake. I have no idea who or what Mrs. Vox is talking about. I would nev—"

"Maybe the mistake was my sending you out there."

Emily was taken aback. "Excuse me?"

"Maybe if you would have been doing your job properly, this mistake would not have happened. Your unsuitable behavior was probably the reason those students will now have to wait another year to attend Julliard or at all. And in lieu of your misconduct while on assignment, you will now have to be brought before the school board for review before the school year starts. Have a nice day, Mrs. Bawler."

Emily heard the click in her ear and shook her head in frustration. She put down the phone feeling confused as to how the mix up occurred. Had she written the letter wrongfully and hadn't noticed her mistake? Had she indeed caused Khandace to lose her chance at studying at Julliard? A deep sadness settled around her knowing it was true.

Chapter Thirty

Daniel looked up from his computer and realized he hadn't heard a peep from Emily in quite a while. He had decided to work from home today in order to spend more time with her. Now looking at the clock, it was well past the lunch hour, and he was sure that she would be just as hungry as he was.

After saving his work, he stood and left the office and went in search of her. He found her in the living room, staring out the glass doors to the patio. He was about to try and scare her, but her slumped shoulder's made him pause.

Easing up behind her, he slid his arms around her, pulling her back against him. "Em, you alright?"

She drew in a deep breath and released it with a sigh. "No."

He turned her around to face him and she wrapped her arms around his middle.

"Tell me what's wrong," he said, giving her a gentle squeeze.

Emily snuggled closer, drawing strength from his embrace.

"I think I messed up with the assignment I was given at work."

"What do you mean? Messed up how?"

She explained to him how she was supposed to make her choice for the scholarship, then mail it back to the school, but somehow things got mixed up.

"Mary called me about an hour ago complaining about it. She said in my letter I didn't choose either of the students, and the funding went to another department. The worst part is that Khandace won't be given the chance she deserves because I made a mistake." She stepped back and looked up. "I swear, Danny, I don't know what happened. I filled in everything for the funding and then I wrote the letter to Mary saying I chose Khandace. I then took the paperwork to Mrs. Vox at the school and personally put it on her desk."

"And the letter?"

"As I was leaving out, I saw their out-going mailbox and dropped in there. Obviously it was mailed out, because Mary received it. But what I don't understand is how everything I wrote got changed around. It's like someone purposely sabotaged that girls chance to go to Julliard."

Daniel looked down at her confused expression. He was thinking something totally different. "Or maybe someone done it to discredit you and your reputation. You got any enemies at the school?"

"Enemies?! No. I get along with all the staff, from the Principal all the way down to the janitors. I have no enemies," she said with conviction.

Taking her hand, he pulled her behind him into the house. "That may be the case, but someone changed your letter. Maybe you'll get better answers when you get back there next week."

Emily pulled up short. "Actually, I need to get back this weekend. Mary called a meeting with the board based on my conduct and it's on Monday."

Daniel's chest tighten painfully and his stomach knotted. "But you still have a whole week and a half before you had to leave," he said sounding miserable.

"I know and I believe that's why she called the meeting so soon. She knew I would have to cut my vacation short."

"Can she do that? I mean technically your on a vacation that's given legally through the company and state."

"Yes, I know. But, since I was also on assignment, which is based through the board, I have to report in person. She just made it sooner because of the incident."

Seeing the pitiful look on his face, she moved closer and took his face in her hands.

"Don't worry. I'll call you every day and every night. I promise."

"I'm not going to be satisfied with just hearing your voice, Em. I need to see you and touch you." He pulled her tightly against his chest and buried his face in her hair. "I'm not ready for you to leave." *And I never will be.*

"I know, Danny, but I have to go and see if I can find a way to fix the mess I've caused." She kissed him softly on the lips. "Please understand."

"Yeah, I understand. I don't like it, but I understand."

They stood like that for a while, holding on tightly as if trying to suck in as much of the other as possible.

"When do you have to leave?" he asked quietly.

"Sunday morning," she said, barely audibly. She didn't want to leave. She wanted to stay right there in his arms, safe, comfortable and loved.

He didn't say a word. He only held on.

***

Sunday came too soon and Emily was standing at Gate 3 in the airport, eyes full of tears as she said her goodbyes. People milled about, not knowing or caring, about the two strangers blocking the door kissing. When Daniel finally broke the kiss, he stepped back and picked up her carry case and handed it to her.

"Make sure you call me when your plane lands and after you get safely in the house," he said sounding worried.

"Okay," she said and nodded. "I'll call you. And don't forget I'll see you at Jordan's birthday party next week," she said, trying to boost his spirit, and her own.

"Yeah, that's right. Maybe afterwards I'll come by and spend some time with you." His statement sounded more like a question and he waited for her to approve it.

"There's no maybe about it. You're coming home with me." She stepped closer to him and leaned in. "I want you to make love to me in my bed." She kissed him deeply and sucked on his bottom lip.

He was happy that his shirt was hanging outside of his pants to cover the bulge of his semi-hard dick. He groaned when she stepped back, smiling.

"When I get there you're gonna pay for that," he said, returning her smile.

"Last call, Miss," said the blonde haired woman collecting boarding passes.

"Bye, Danny," she said, backing up.

"I'll see you later," he said not wanting to say goodbye.

She turned and boarded the plane, and he swore he felt his heart break.

Chapter Thirty One

Kids were everywhere. In the house, on the sun porch, on the patio, and in the backyard. There had to be at least twenty or more little one's running around. Some of the kids there belonged to family and friends, but most of them were Jordan's classmates. Rainy made sure to invite each and every one of them to come celebrate his sixth birthday. He was growing up so fast and she wanted to give him everything she'd missed out on at his age.

In the kitchen, Daniel was putting the finishing touches on his cake. Just like Rainy asked, he prepared the Teenage Mutant Ninja Turtle cake, and once it was complete, it would look exactly like the poster that hung from his wall. If only he could concentrate to get the job done.

There was a good reason for his being distracted and it sat out on the patio wearing a white tank top and blue jean shorts. To put it frankly, he couldn't keep his eyes off her. Although they've spoken daily, he missed her like crazy. *Every part of her*, he thought, as his eyes traveled across her smooth thighs, down over her lean calfs, dainty ankles, and clear polished toes. Feeling his mouth water, he swallowed hard.

Stepping into the kitchen, Miki was about to speak when he noticed how focused Daniel was. His focus wasn't on the cake he was practically destroying, it was on something outside. Leaning over a little, he smiled when he saw exactly what had him transfixed, Emily.

Thinking he was alone, Daniel's guard was down and he was wearing his emotions on his face for anyone to see.

"How many times are you going to put icing on that one spot?" asked Miki, laughing.

Daniel jumped and accidentally poked a large hole in the side of the cake. "Shit!" he said as he smoothed icing over the hole trying to cover it.

"Mind your language man. All the ears around here are rated PG," said Miki.

Pissed that Miki almost made him ruin the cake, and not to

mention the fact that he'd caught him staring at Emily, made him want a little payback.

"I heard about that striptease move you did in front of Mom. Smooth, man. Real smooth," he said, laughing.

"Yeah, well I saw your makeover photos. You'd make a beautiful woman," he said, resting his hand on Daniel's shoulder. Michael and Chase walked in just in time to hear Miki's come back and burst into laughter.

Daniel shoved Mikis' hand off his shoulder frowning. Soon his frown eased and he joined his brothers, laughing at the joke at his expense.

"Damn man. What did you do to the cake," asked Chase, as he frowned at the chunk missing on the side.

"Don't worry about it. I can fix it. It'll be as good as new," he said, smoothing more icing over the hole.

"He wasn't looking at what he was doing," piped in Miki, wanting to frustrate him a little more.

Michael looked from Daniel to Miki. "Is that right? So if you weren't looking at the cake, what were you looking at," he asked, looking around the kitchen for something out of the ordinary, but finding nothing.

"Yeah, Daniel. What were you looking at?" asked Miki with a devious smile on his face.

Daniel's head snapped up and he frowned. He stared at Miki trying to read his face. *Did he know?* Suddenly, Miki's smile widened. *Damn, he knows.*

***

The party went through without any problems. Even the cake was prepared and set out for Jordan, and he grinned as all his friends oohhed and ahhhed over the design. The food was great and spending time with his family was comforting. But he was still feeling like he was missing something and he knew exactly what it, or who it was.

He and Emily had made it through the day without accidentally saying anything that would show that they were seeing each other. They hadn't yet discussed how they would break it to their families, but by mutual agreement, they decided to put it off a little longer while they explored what they had together.

Now he stood near the side exit alone drinking a bottled water.

He watched her say her goodbyes like everyone else, smiling at the teasing from his brothers. When she made eye contact with him, she made kissy lips at him, and did a slight wiggle of her eyebrows telling him exactly what time it was.

Daniel went in search of his parents to say goodbye, before doing the same with his brothers. He found his mother in the kitchen directing the cleaning staff that catered the party. She was mumbling something to Stacey as he walked towards them. When he got closer, and she caught sight of him, she smiled.

"Ready to run are you?" she asked teasing.

He pulled her into a quick hug, but kept his arm around her shoulders. "Yeah. I have somewhere to be in a few."

"Mmm hmm. I know what that means," she said, shaking her head.

"I don't," he said, smiling. "What?" he asked, looking at Stacey.

"I didn't say anything," she said, holding up her hands.

"Good. Don't," he said, making a face at her.

Stacey sucked her teeth. "Whatever, boy."

"Shouldn't you be gone?" asked Chase. He walked into the kitchen, grabbed Stacey, and kissed her fully on the lips. "Whew! Just what the doctor ordered," he said, licking his lips.

Stacey blushed and buried her face in his chest.

"Gross. Now I'm definitely leaving. Mom, can you tell Dad I'll call him tomorrow. I saw him go into his office on his cell phone. It looked important, so I won't disturb him."

"No problem, baby. It's probably an office problem. I can't wait until he retires and be rid of the headache."

"You and me both. See you guys later," he said, hurrying towards the door.

"Have fun!" called out Stacey.

Daniel glanced back over his shoulder, and just like Miki, she was giving him a wide grin.

No way, he said to himself as he turned and left. *That was just a coincidence*, he said, rushing to his car. Thankful that his car wasn't blocked in, he quickly pulled out and headed to Emily's apartment.

It took him over an hour, but he was happy when he finally arrived in New York at her building. Although he knew where she lived, he'd never actually been inside her apartment. He found a parking space and rushed to her door. It only took a moment for her to open the door, and when she did, the tightness in his chest eased and he drew in a deep breath.

"Hi," he said, a soft smile on his lips.

"Hi," she said, shyly. "Come on in."

Emily stepped aside and let him enter. She didn't know why she was so nervous. She'd just spent the entire summer at his house and made love to him all through the day and night. So why would she be so nervous about him being here in her home? *Because this is all of me out in the open, exposed.*

Daniel walked in and looked around. The living room was decorated in white and a bright assortment of red, yellow, green and orange. There in the corner was a pile of huge pillows nestled against a tall shelf of books. Across the room, he saw several violins in a line, all different in color. Music sheets were placed neatly on pedestal stands at the ready.

The open design of the apartment allowed him to see into her kitchen and he was surprised to see how modern everything was.

"Nice kitchen." *Nice kitchen? Really?*

Emily glanced towards the kitchen trying to see it through his eyes. "Oh, thanks." She shoved her hands in her back pockets. "Do you want something to drink or eat? I noticed you didn't eat much at the party."

He smiled. "Were you checking me out?"

Smiling, she shook her head. "About as much as you were checking me out."

"Mmm hmm."

Just then his attention was caught by the chess board sitting on a small table. "You want to give it another try?" he asked, nodding towards the game.

I'd rather give you a try. "Are you sure you want to? The last time had you all dolled up looking your best," she said, referring to his makeover.

"How do you know I didn't let you win?" he said, walking over to the game. It was a nice set made of polished steel.

"Wow… You've reached a new low of sore loser," she said, laughing.

"Okay, laugh now, cry later. Let's make a wager."

Here we go again. Maybe I'll let him win so he'll feel better.

"Unless you're chicken because you know I'm going to win."

That's it! He's going down. And this time I'm going to do it fast to embarrass him.

"Sure, let's play. You move first," she said, taking a seat.

"The best *always* goes first," he said, taking his seat across from her.

Ten minutes later, Daniel was looking at the board confused.

"You study the board to see where you messed up. I'll be right back."

He was still staring down at the board when he felt something land on his shoulder. He pulled the material off and held it up. He glanced at her when he saw it was an apron.

"What's this for?" he asked grinning. *If she wants me to cook her dinner, then so be it. Talk about getting off easy.*

"It's for you to wear as you cook my dinner." When she saw him stand up smiling she dropped the bomb. "Naked."

His smile faded. "Come again."

Now it was Emily's turn to smile. "You're going to strip down naked right here, put on that pretty apron covered in cupcakes, and cook me dinner."

"Em, I…"

She crossed her arms over her chest. "Oh, so you're not going to honor the bet? Is your word not good, Danny?"

Knowing he wouldn't hear the end of it if he didn't follow through with it, he tossed the apron on the chair. When he reached for the bottom of his shirt, and lifted it over his head, Emily backed up and sat on the couch to enjoy the show.

Daniel pulled off every inch of his clothing, including his boxers and socks. When he stood there, tall, muscled, sexy, and completely naked, she allowed her eyes to roam freely over him. *Damn, this man knows he is some kind of gorgeous.*

"Your uniform," she said, pointing to the apron.

"Do you think you can help me put it on," he asked. His voice had dropped an octave and she knew what that needy look in his eyes was all about.

"Sure. I can do that."

Crossing the room, she picked up the apron and found the strings to tie around his neck. Daniel leaned over slightly so that she could tie the bow without straining. When that was done, he stared her in her eyes.

"Now the other."

"Turn around then."

He turned around giving her his back. And oh what a back it was. Strong, tight muscles formed his shoulders and blades, before tapering down to a slim waist. His ass was firm and smooth, and she wanted to touch it. Grabbing the strings, she tied them together, making sure it wasn't too tight. Stepping back in front of him, she took her hands and ran them down his chest, stomach, and lower, until she gripped his hardened staff beneath the apron.

She heard his breath catch. "What are you doing?"

"Smoothing out the wrinkles and the bumps," she said sounding distracted. Her hand was stroking him slowly through the apron and he had no desire to stop her. That didn't matter, because she suddenly released him abruptly. "Okay, all done. I'm going to take a shower. The kitchen is all yours," she said smiling. She slapped him hard on the ass and he tightened his cheeks.

"You know you're going to pay for that, right?"

"I hope so, Danny. I hope so," she said, smiling, and left the room.

I hope he can stay the night. Shoot, more like a few days the way my kitty's acting up.

Chapter Thirty Two

The weekend came and went, and so did Daniel. He left late last night so that he could make his meeting in the morning with his accountant. It was a good thing too, because if he would have stayed, Emily wouldn't have made it to her meeting with the board in the morning. She was now sitting in a large conference room with six board members. They were on one side of the long table and she was on the other. Mary sat in the middle looking down her nose at her.

Funny, it was only a few of months ago that she was showing me photo's of her grandson's Halloween costume. When did she become the Wicked Witch?

"Ms. Bawler, we want you to know that we've assessed all the information we have on the situation before we came to our conclusion," said Mary.

"Well, that's funny, because I'm not aware of what information that is, since I haven't seen it myself."

"Wait, are you saying you haven't been privy to the evidence that was brought forth against you?" asked Mr. Fletcher, one of the oldest school board members. Although Mary was seated as the headmaster, nothing really got done without his approval first. Rumor had it that it was his wife's family that started the school in 1905. He also was a huge fan of Emily's music.

"Yes, that's exactly what I'm saying."

Mr. Fletcher glanced over to Mary. "How come Ms. Bawler wasn't allowed to view the documents that you presented to us?"

Mary seemed flustered all of a sudden. "I just figured since she's the one who wrote it, then she wouldn't need to see it again." Her reason sounded lame to everyone, including herself.

"Ms. Bawler, if you will?" he said, and held out a folder containing the documents.

Emily took the folder and gave him a warm smile. "Thanks Mathew. I mean Mr. Fletcher." She quickly corrected herself. He had insisted that she call him Mathew and it was a little hard to remember not to do so at this formal meeting.

He leaned back and smiled, not bothered in the least.

Opening the folder, she saw the paperwork that she had delivered to Mrs. Vox and several other documents that she had emailed to Mary. When she came across the letter with a red marker tab on it, she stared at it strangely.

"Is something wrong?" asked Mrs. Andrews. She ran the registration department and she and Emily had become fast friends.

"Yes. I don't know who wrote this, but I didn't," she said, holding up the letter for them to see.

"It has your name on it," said Mary.

Emily looked at her pointedly. "Just because my name is on it, doesn't mean I wrote it. Besides, that's not my handwriting."

"What?" Mary uttered flatly.

"I said that's not my handwriting.

Mrs. Andrews pulled her copy of the letter from the folder and peered at it closely. "She's right. That's not how she signs her name. The penmanship is different and she never spells out her last name. It's always Emily B."

"Exactly. So it's plain to see that someone switched out my letter and sent this one."

Frustrated, Mary closed her folder. "Fine! It doesn't matter if you wrote the letter or not. It still stands that you were irresponsible with important paperwork and protocol, which caused a student to miss out on a much needed scholarship. Therefore, it still stands that this is your fault. So, our first intentions will continue."

"And that is?" Emily sat waiting patiently to hear their decision on her alleged mistake.

"We the board, have agreed to suspend you for the first semester of the coming school year without pay."

Emily could have sworn Mary wanted to smile, but she kept her composure. She didn't want to accept their judgement. She knew to accept it meant that she was agreeing to doing something wrong. However, she didn't have a choice but to follow procedure and deal with the suspension.

"So be it," said Emily. She pulled the document containing the suspension towards her and signed it. Her signature was exactly as Mrs. Andrews stated and didn't look nothing like the signature that was on their so called evidence.

Once she was done, she stood and collected her bag. "See you next semester," she said, and headed out the door quickly before they could see the tears in her eyes. *I won't give that fake friendly bitch the satisfaction.*

***

The apartment seemed too quiet now that Daniel wasn't there. She missed seeing him lounging on her couch or in her kitchen whipping them up something to eat. She missed his laughter, his smile and his smell. She plopped down on the pile of pillows remembering when they lay there together reading to each other. Closing her eyes, she tried pretending he was there holding her and consoling her, but it didn't work. She needed the real thing.

A song by *John Legend* blared from her pocket and she smiled. "Hello?"

"What's wrong?" asked Daniel. He was sitting in his office doing a taste test on a new recipe of hot chocolate when he thought of Emily and instantly felt miserable. He knew he wasn't unhappy after the weekend they'd spent together, so he picked up his cell and called her.

"How did you know I needed to hear your voice?" She rolled on her side and pulled one of the pillows to her and held it tight.

He got up from his desk and sat on the couch. "I don't know. I mean, I was working and then I thought about you. But as soon as I did, I felt sad. Tell me what's wrong?" he said gently.

Emily recalled everything that happened all the way up to the suspension. By the time she finished, she had shed a few tears and he was pissed off. He didn't know if it was because they suspended her knowing she hadn't been the direct cause of the mix-up, or because he wasn't there to console her and dry her tears.

"I'm sorry that happened to you, Em. If you want, I can make a few phone calls. I'm sure I can pull a few strings and…"

"No! Don't do that, Danny. I know you mean well, but this is something I have to accept and get through on my own. I may not have written the letter, but I should have dropped the letter in the mailbox myself. Instead, I was being lazy and left it up to the school staff to mail it. If I had mailed it myself this would never have happened. The letter wouldn't have gotten switched and Khandace would be starting school in September at Julliard. I dropped the ball and now I have to face the music."

Daniel sighed in defeat. "Alright. I won't interfere, but that doesn't mean I have to like it."

"I know, and I appreciate the fact that you wanted to do that for me," she said tenderly.

"I would do anything for you, Em. You know that, right?"

She smiled faintly. "I do now."

They chatted a little longer with Daniel telling her about his new hot chocolate flavors that he'll be adding to his kids menu at the restaurant. He asked her questions and got her input on things he didn't really need help with, all to take her mind off of her problems.

After their call ended, Emily called her mother, and then Stacey, to tell them about what happened. Her mother reacted the same way Daniel had. She wanted to get on the phone and make some calls to get the suspension retracted, but she wouldn't let her. Stacey's reaction was different. She wanted to come down to New York and get in Mary's face and beat the woman to a pulp. All in all, Stacey's shenanigans made her laugh hysterically. It was exactly what she needed.

The day dragged by and she was on the verge of nodding out on the couch when her doorbell rung. Glancing over at the clock, she saw that it was a little after six. She sighed in resignation and eased from her comfortable spot.

Making her way to the door, she happened to look in the hall mirror and cringed. *Damn, girl. Look at your hair*, she said to herself before using her fingers to rake through it. Satisfied that she looked halfway decent again, she opened the door.

"Damnnnn. I was about to call 911. What took you so long to open the door?" asked Laurie as she pushed past Emily into the house.

"Come on in. Kick your feet up," Emily said, sarcastically.

"Don't mind if I do," Laurie said as she sat down the violin she carried. "But first—"

She headed into the kitchen and returned with two wine glasses. She took the bottle Emily hadn't noticed she carried and poured them both a glass. She handed one to Emily and then took her hand, pulling her down to sit on the couch beside her.

"First, I returned your violin you left in the trunk of my car. It's been in there all summer. Secondly, I heard you were dating someone, but I couldn't find out who it was. So you'll need to spill your guts on that later. But right now, we're going to finish this bottle and get drunk, because I heard about that bullshit Mary pulled this morning. I swear, ever since her husband filed for a divorce, she's been prancing around the school breathing fire."

Emily sipped her wine and then opened her eyes wide. "Her husband left her?" *Wow, that explains her I hate everybody attitude.*

Laurie nodded. "Sure did. It happened over the summer. I worked the summer music program this year and he came right up to the school and told her in her office."

"Nooooo!" said Emily, shocked.

"Yup. She stayed in her office all day crying. I heard that he was seeing a woman at the school, although no name has come out as to who it is. I'm guessing that's why she's out to get every woman between the age of twenty five and forty. All I can say is you messed up at the wrong time. You need to stay clear of her ass. I know I will."

"Thanks for the heads up," said Emily. She couldn't believe her husband would do something so vile as to dump her at work. He could at least have waited until she got home. That was messy and petty.

"Okay!" said Lauried, rubbing her hands together. "Now that we've got that out of the way. What's her name? Where did you meet her? And are you in love, bitch?" she asked smiling.

Shaking her head, Emily smiled. "What are you talking about?"

"Don't play with me, heifer. I haven't heard from you all summer. The only time you go M.I.A. is when you're involved with someone. So spill your guts. Tell me everything. Let's start with something simple like her name."

Emily sat there grinning as Laurie took a long drink from her glass.

"The thing is it's not a woman. It's a man, and his name is Daniel."

The coughing and choking started, and the only thing Emily kept thinking was, *'Oh my God, I almost killed my friend.'*

Chapter Thirty Three

Daniel was in a good mood. Earlier today he'd heard from Emily and she sounded like she was feeling better. It had been a week since the suspension and she seemed to be getting back to her old self. Talking to her on speaker phone while he got dressed for work had him feeling relieved. He had been worried about her, and was about to catch a flight back up there, but her calling him this morning full of laughter stopped him.

Wanting to prolong her happiness, he decided to send her flowers. He reached for the phone on his desk and jumped when it rang. *That was weird.*

"Hello?"

"Oh, so you don't know how to call nobody?" the voice said in his Jerome voice from *Martin.*

Daniel laughed. "You're an asshole. What do you want Arnez?"

"Not a damn thing. I was checking up on you about that restaurant you said you were opening, and from the way you're dragging your feet, I don't think you ever will."

"Whatever, man. I slowed the process down to weigh my options on a few things."

Knock, knock.

"Arnez, hold up a second. I'm putting you on speaker. Someone's at my door."

"You want me to call you back?" asked Arnez.

Daniel pressed the button to electronically open the door. It was a new device he had installed and he was happy he did. "No, that won't be necessary," he said when he saw Derrek enter.

He hadn't had anymore problems out of him lately, which meant he finally got the point to stay in line or he would be fired.

"What can I do for you Derrek?" He noticed that he was holding a menu.

"Sorry to bother you, Mr. Tase, but the head chef made some changes to the menu and I need to know what to do. He left out the old menu and the new one. Which one am I supposed to follow?"

"Let me take a look at that," said Daniel. He was examining the menu's, and Derrek stood there quietly waiting.

"A man, you're still there?" Arnez asked after the line went quiet.

"Yeah, I'm still here."

"So how are things going between you and your mystery woman?"

Daniel smiled. "Things are going great. Now mind your business."

"Just asking." He paused only for a second. "Is she the reason you're holding off on making a decision about a new location?" asked Arnez, digging for answers.

"Nice try. But I have a good reason for the delay. I just need to work on a few personal issues first."

"Mmm hmm."

He laughed and shook his head. He then handed Derrek a menu and tossed the other in the trash can.

Knowing that was his cue to leave, Derrek left.

While waiting for Daniel to make a decision on the menu, he had the privilege to listen in on his phone call. He heard him talk about his mystery woman and about holding off on choosing a location for his next restaurant.

Derrek frowned and then smiled. *Once I'm finished with this place you'll be right back on the market looking. And this time, there won't be any dragging your feet.*

***

Sitting in the shadows near one of the many trees that covered the restaurant's landscape, Derrek sat as still as a statue. He waited patiently covered by darkness until the last employee left the building. He watched Daniel put on the alarm and the small group called out their goodnights and left.

Finally. He had waited for hours until the restaurant closed for the night and came back to set his plan in motion. He picked up his book bag and walked back over to the building like he hadn't a care in the world. Glancing around and not seeing anyone, he pulled out a large container of gasoline and began dousing the building and any surrounding bushes that were close by.

Once he was done, he pulled out his half finished blunt and lit it with a book of matches. He took a few long pulls, allowing the marijuana to mellow out his nerves. Feeling less stressed and more like he was ready for the world, he flicked the blunt into the bushes and watched as it ignited.

The bright orange flames flew up high and traveled along the ground until it reached the building. When the fire blazed higher, Derrek stumbled back and fell. Since he was high, it took him a minute to get to his feet. By then he was in awe of what he'd done and he stood there grinning.

From across the parking lot a young couple making out in the dark watched him in horror.

Chapter Thirty Four

Making it home in record time, Daniel entered his home and heading straight to his room and stripped. Going into the bathroom, he stepped beneath the sprays and allowed the hot water to loosen his muscles and take away any stress he ran into during his day. Thankfully, it wasn't much. The service crew, kitchen crew, and valet workers, all provided excellent service, which provided him an uneventful day. Life was good.

Finishing with his shower, he dressed in a pair of pajama bottoms, grabbed his cell phone, and made a beeline for the kitchen. He grabbed a bowl and spoon, then the Butter Pecan ice cream from the freezer. Scooping out a hefty sum into his bowl, he returned the carton and went to the living room. He sat on the couch, bowl in hand, cell phone on the table, and reached for the remote.

After I catch up on ESPN, I'll give Emily a call.

He clicked on the television and before he could change the channel, he saw 'breaking news' flashing across the screen. There, behind a smartly dressed woman, was his restaurant. Or what used to be his restaurant. Now, on one side, it was a charred mess. Hardly recognizable.

"My God!" he yelled and stood, shoving the bowl on the table. He couldn't believe his eyes. Sinful, his pride and joy. His baby, was a disaster.

In shock, he stood there listening to the woman saying something about it being a tragic accident. Out of the corner of his eye, he saw his phone lights flashing in the darkness. When he picked it up, he noticed that he had about thirty or so missed calls. Seeing that most of them were from his family, he called his parents first.

"Daniel! Oh God, baby, you're okay. We were calling you and when you didn't answer we thought that you were inside the restaurant working late. Your father and your brother's are on their way there."

He closed his eyes, hearing the pain in his mother's voice. "I'm alright, Mom. I was already home when it started. Actually, I'm just finding out from seeing it on the news."

"Oh no," she said in anguish. That must have been dreadful for him to see his life's work in flames on television. "Finding out that way must have been awful. I'm so sorry, Daniel."

That was an understatement. He felt physically sick to his stomach.

"I'll be alright, Mom. The place was insured. Listen can you do me a favor? Can you call everyone and tell them not to come down. I need to get dressed and get down there, and you know how they can get when they don't get what they want. I won't have time to be bailing anyone out."

"I understand, sweetheart. I'll let them know I finally reached you. Be safe, baby. I love you."

"I will, Mom, and I love you too."

He ended the call with his mother, turned off the TV and went to get dressed. Within minutes he was heading back in the direction of the restaurant. When he arrived, the first thing he saw was that the fire was out. He looked around at the crowd of people milling about, the police cars, ambulances, and fire trucks. The place was in total disarray.

He saw a fireman that looked like he was in charge and walked towards him.

"Excuse me, sir, but I'm gonna need you to stay over there with the rest of the bystanders. I don't want anyone to get hurt," said a young officer that stepped in his path.

"I need to talk to whomever is in charge?"

"Why is that?" the officer asked, looking at him suspiciously.

"Because I'm the owner of the building," he said sounding impatient.

The officer gave him a pained expression. "Oh! Alright then. Um, come with me."

He turned on his heels and Daniel followed him over to a group of men in uniform talking.

"Sir, this man says that he's the owner of the business," he called out, interrupting them.

The police Sergeant looked over at Daniel and nodded. "I'm Sergeant Jerrod and this is Chief Fire Inspector Mills. We're sorry for this incident happening to yah, Mr.?"

"Daniel Tase. Do you know what caused it?"

"Yeah, it definitely was arson," said the inspector.

"Arson?!" He wasn't expecting the inspector to say that. He figured it would be electric or a gas leak or something.

The inspector nodded. "That's right. Here, come with me."

He led Daniel over to the side of the building where he believed the fire initiated. "This is where the guy lit the match, and I mean that literally. He actually used a book of matches. Whomever did this was an amateur because they dropped the book right here. The police already have it as evidence. They're hoping they can get a print from it."

He then bent down and pulled a few leaves off of what was left of the bushes. "Smell this," he said, holding the leaves out to Daniel.

Daniel took the leaves and sniffed. The stench of gasoline was strong. "Gasoline."

"That's right. He soaked the place on this side with gasoline and stood right here and lit it. Arson."

Hearing loud voices behind them, Daniel and the inspector turned to see the same young officer raising his voice to a young couple.

"What the hell is that all about?" The inspector moved closer to hear better, and Daniel followed.

"Listen, all I'm saying is that I need to see your boss. I need to make a statement," the young man said, trying to keep his voice low. He didn't want to make a scene or cause anyone to look over at him, but the officer was being difficult.

"Look, kid. You need to get back, right now!"

"Jenkins! What the hell is going on?"

Hearing his Sergeant come up behind him made him nervous. "Nothing, sir." He grabbed the young boy by the arm. "Just someone making a nuisance of himself. I'll escort him back behind the lines."

"My boyfriend wasn't doing anything wrong. He just wanted to make a statement," the young girl said. She was also trying to keep her tone low. "We saw the hole thing."

Everyone froze.

"Jenkins, let him go."

Once they were released, Sergeant Jerrod moved them over between two police cars. Daniel and the inspector followed.

"Now talk," Jerrod said in a no nonsense tone.

"I picked my girlfriend Kate, up from work earlier as a surprise. She works as a service over at Donnie's Bar and Grill. Her mom's don't like me, so we couldn't go back to her house, and my mom's a drunk. So we decided to pull over and make out a bit in the lot over there. We were fooling around when we saw this guy hanging around over here. We smelled something funny and knew he was smoking weed. Then he shocked the shit out of us when he pulled a container from his bag and started splashing the bushes and the building with it. By the time we realized what he was gonna do, he tossed his blunt onto the tree and up she went. He must not of expected how fast it would light because he fell."

"So why were you whispering to my officer?" asked Jerrod.

"Alright, when I say this don't look or you'll be obvious. But, dude must of wanted to stick around to see his handy work, because he's still here."

"What?!" Daniel, the inspector, and the Sergeant, all blurted out together.

"Shhhh," said Kate. "He's right over there in the blue hoody, carrying the black and red book bag."

The Sergeant got on his radio. "Listen up. This is Sergeant Jerrod. Arson suspect has been spotted at three o'clock standing in the crowd. The suspect is wearing a dark blue hoodie, black pants and a red and black book bag. Close in and don't fuck this up. I want him with no fatalities."

"Copy that."

Daniel stood there with the Sergeant feeling the adrenaline rushing through his body. He wanted badly to turn around and see who it was, but he didn't want to tip him off. Everything needed to stay looking normal.

Suddenly, there was a slight commotion in the crowd and a few screams. When it all was said and done, they had the suspect in handcuffs and shoving him into a police vehicle. It was a clean arrest and no one got hurt.

"Mr. Tase can you come with me? I want you to take a peek at this guy and tell me if you've seen him hanging around before."

He followed the Sergeant over to the squad car where they had placed him. One of the officers saw them coming and pulled him from the car. When he yanked the hood from his head, he stared at him in anger. It was Derrek.

"From the look on your face I can tell you know him," said Jerrod.

Daniel had a bitter taste in his mouth from holding in his anger.

"Yes. He works for me. Well, he did."

"And I have to ask this, but are you pressing charges?"

"Hell yeah," he said between his teeth. "Please remove him from my sight," he ground out in rage.

"I was hoping you'd say that." He turned to the officer. "Read him his rights again and get him to the precinct."

"Yes, sir. Let's go!" he yelled, shoving Derrek back into the police car.

Once all the excitement was over, the crowd started to disperse. Soon, he was standing there alone assessing the damage. Thankfully the restaurant wasn't a total lost because the dampness from the rain earlier, and the state of the art sprinkler system he had put in last year, helped slow the fire from spreading. However, there was enough damage that would keep his doors closed for a few months until he got the insurance claim settled and had it renovated.

Returning to his car, he checked his phone and saw that Emily had called him several times. He pressed the button to call her back.

"Danny! Baby, are you okay. I couldn't get in touch with you so I called your mom. Please tell me that you're alright."

He felt comforted by her concern for him. Although he'd gotten the same call from his parents and brothers, it felt different coming from her. It filled his heart and calmed the fury he felt bubbling within him.

"I'm alright, Em. I'm better now that I hear your voice."

She could hear the tiredness in his flat tone. "I'm going to come down there to be with you."

"No. It's okay. I'm going to be tied up running around for the next few days. No need to have you down here sitting alone waiting for me."

"Are you sure, Danny?"

"Yes. Just… talk to me. I want to hear you." He wanted her to talk to him and keep him talking because he felt like he wanted to cry. Yeah, the insurance money will come through so he can rebuild, but it doesn't stop the outrage that's already there.

Emily knew what he needed from her. She had done it plenty of times for her brother Alexander. Every time he would have one of his nightmares about something he'd experienced in the service, he would call her and they'd talk all night.

"Was it a total loss?"

"No. Thank God. However, the damage is excessive enough to keep our doors closed for a long time. I'm not so concerned about me. It's my employees. A lot of them just had babies or are in college. Anthony just spent the money he had in his savings to buy his girlfriend an engagement ring. He was going to propose next month on her birthday." He sighed loudly. "This fire affected so many people's lives and he didn't even look like he regretted it."

"Wait a minute. He? Who is he?"

"Derrek. One of my employees. He's the one that started the fire. He was so high, that he stuck around to watch. He's in custody now."

"Wow. Why the hell would he want to do that?" she asked confused.

"I have no idea. But I'm going to the station tomorrow to make sure his ass don't walk."

"Danny?"

"Yeah?"

"Do you think he may have been behind all the problems you were having at the restaurant?"

He narrowed his eyes, thinking. It was then that he realized none of the problems occurred until he hired Derrek. "Damn, baby. I think you're right. Things didn't get out of control until he started working there."

"Then I'm glad he's gone. I just wish you'd found out before the fire."

"Yeah, me too."

Chapter Thirty Five

The rain was coming down in torrents causing it hard to drive. Visibility was almost impossible, but the driver of the car service Emily was using kept his cool and got her to her destination safely. As she hurried into the building, she briefly smiled and waved at the doorman.

"Hey, George. Has he come down yet?"

"Not yet, Ms. Bawler," he said with a smile.

"Great. Have a nice day," she said, stepping into the elevator.

"You too," said George, and continued to read his paper.

The doors opened to Daniel's penthouse, and Emily stepped off instantly feeling at home. She left her bag on the couch and went in search of him. She crossed the living room, and then down the hall, stopping at his office door.

Tap. Tap. Tap.

Daniel looked up and frowned when he heard the light tapping on his office door. His maid wasn't scheduled to come in until next week, so he was clueless as to who it was. Then he saw her step in and everything was alright in his world again.

"Hey you," said Emily as she made her way over to him.

He stood up just in time to take her in his arms. He inhaled her scent, loving the coconut smell. Closing his eyes, he held on to her tightly, grateful that she'd come.

"Em."

"I know you told me not to come, but I didn't want you to be alone. I wanted to be here for you, like you're always there for me."

"I'm glad you came," he said, giving her another squeeze.

Emily pulled back and looked up at him. "Did you eat breakfast yet?"

He sighed. "No. Not yet."

She narrowed her eyes. "And what about dinner?"

"I had a late lunch and was going to pig out on the couch eating ice cream, but that's when I saw the news."

"Come on," she said, taking his hand and pulling him behind her.

In the living room she gave him a gentle shove to make him sit on the couch. She then went into the kitchen and came back with two glasses of orange juice. When she sat next to him on the couch, she reached for her bag. Inside, she had three sausages, egg, and cheese McMuffins. Two for him, one for her.

"Eat."

Her instructions were clear and Daniel followed orders. He hadn't known just how hungry he was until he had finished off his second sandwich.

"Thank you."

"You don't have to thank me. I want to be here."

They sat there looking at each other until he heard his cell phone ring. Thinking it was the insurance people calling back, he stood up.

"I need to get that."

"Go ahead. I'll clean this up," she said, picking up their used napkins and sandwich wrappers.

Daniel returned to his office just in time to receive the call.

"Hello?"

"Good morning. This is detective Slaon from the 101 precinct. I'm heading up the arson case involving your restaurant. I had an interesting meeting with Derrek Miller and he had some interesting things to say."

He had Daniel's complete attention. "Things like what?"

"Well, once he heard how many years he would get, he figured he wouldn't be going down alone."

"You mean he was working with someone else?"

"Not *with* someone, *for* someone. We have his written statement and video confession saying that he was working for a woman that works at a real estate company. I believe you know her. Uh..." He moved some papers around on his desk. "Here we go. A Ms. Kimberly Reed."

"What the hell?" Shocked, he sat down hard in his chair.

"Yeah, Miller said that Reed had gotten afraid that you would back out of the deal and hired him to cause problems to persuade you to buy the property to relocate."

He felt his temper rising.

"He also said that the area she was showing you had a large property value decline and she had sold most of the surrounding property to the Navy for warehousing. Basically, your restaurant would be smack dab in the middle of a bunch of loud warehouses and Navy crewmen, with no customers due to most of the area becoming restricted. You would be out of your money, and she would walk away with a fat bonus, and a promotion for selling property with little to no value."

"I can't believe this," he said, rubbing his forehead. He could feel the beginnings of a headache coming.

"The good thing is that we caught this guy and you got warned about Reed before you signed on the bottom line. If I were you, I'd find a new real estate agency to do business with," said Sloan.

"What about Reed?" he asked gruffly.

"We've already got a warrant and I have a unit bringing her in right now. She'll be going down right along with Miller."

"Good. Listen, thank you for calling and letting me know all about this. I'm definitely going to find another agency to deal with."

"It's not a problem, Mr. Tase. I'll keep you posted if anything else pops up."

"Thanks."

Daniel ended the call and sat back, shaking his head. He couldn't believe that Kimberly would go through such extremes only to secure a sale. Feeling drained, he went in search of Emily.

He found her waiting for him in his bedroom. She was standing at the window watching the rain beat down on the city below them. When she heard him enter the room, she didn't say a word. Once again she took his hand, this time leading him over to the bed.

"Sit down," she instructed softly.

Doing as he was told, he sat on the side of the bed.

Emily kneeled down in from of him and started to remove his shoes.

"That was a detective Sloan on the phone. He said Derrek admitted to working for someone and they told him to sabotage my restaurant. Guess who he was working for?"

She began untying his other boot. "Who?" She pulled both boots off.

"Kimberley."

"Kimberly?!" She stood up, climbed onto the bed and reached for him.

He climbed onto the bed and they lay there face to face as the rain pummeled the windows. He repeated what the detective said to him leaving nothing out. Afterwards, he was so drained that he drifted off to sleep. Emily crawled closer and rested her head on his chest. Instinctively, his arms tightened around her.

***

They slept until the early afternoon hours. When they decided to get up, they sat on the floor in the living room talking. Emily brought up the incident about her job hoping to get his mind off of the restaurant.

"I wish I could find out who changed the letter I sent to Mary."

"Yeah, me too," said Daniel as he slowly ran his fingers through her short tufts of hair. Suddenly he stopped. "Hold up, baby. Let me run in my office real quick."

She sat up and watched him head down the hall, his jeans riding low on his hips. A naughty smile spread across her face.

"So much has been going on that I forgot to tell you Myka sent this to me."

"What is it?" she asked, eyeing the large white envelope.

"It's a file on Sherry."

She waited patiently as he pulled the stack of papers out. Together they poured over the information and was shocked at its contents.

Sherry's parents had divorced when she was six. Her father had remarried soon after. But that wasn't the shocking part. Her mother had been raped that same year and gotten pregnant.

Listening to her parents, she had kept the baby and had a boy. She named him Carl. She raised him up until he was five years old. However, the older he got, the more he started to look like the man who raped her and she couldn't bear to look at him. That's when she turned him over to child services. She never tried to keep in touch with the agency about him at all. She kept the paperwork only and that was for legal reason.

The file also said that Carl had two incidents with his foster parents. The first incident was that he attacked the foster parents' son for no apparent reason. But it also says that Carl stated that he was only defending himself.

The second incident had the foster parents returning him. They said he attacked the wife. Carl, who had shut down verbally, said that they made him touch them and watch them do things. He wouldn't say where he had to touch them or what they made him watch them do. That family was put under investigation. However, the damage had already been done. Carl was admitted, at first, to a children's hospital, and later to a psychiatric hospital where he still resides to this day.

Sherry never forgot that she had a brother. When she turned twenty one, she started searching for him. She found the hospital that he was admitted to and started visiting him. Based on the file, and the visiting chart, she went to see him at least once a week. However, her last visit was a few weeks ago.

"Did you know she had a brother?" asked Daniel.

Emily thought for a minute back to when they first met. "I think I recall her mentioning that she had a brother. Yeah, she said it was something we had in common."

Daniel was still scanning over the papers. The frown between his eyebrows told her that everything he was reading wasn't good.

"You know, even though he went through that trauma as a child, it doesn't mean that he's insane. Maybe we should go talk to him and see if he could tell us anything about Sherry."

Daniel's head popped up. "No," he said, shaking his head.

"Danny, think about it. This file was supposed to tell us everything about Sherry, but it told us nothing really. All we know is that her parents got divorced, her mother was raped and that she gave her son up for adoption. Then her son went through a traumatic childhood and ended up in a psychiatric hospital. That's it. There's nothing about Sherry."

"It's not a good idea, Em."

"Why not?" she asked, confused.

"Because it's not safe. He could be dangerous or doped up on medicine. The people in those types of places are put there because they are unstable. It's not a safe place for you to go."

"But you'll be with me," she said, looking at him with pleading eyes.

Damn.

***

Climbing out of the car, Daniel walked with Emily towards the tall white building. The gold letters on the sign that read Clairview Psychiatric Hospital, glittered in the morning sunlight. The place was immaculate with manicured hedges and wide open lawns. The beauty on the outside belied the mayhem hidden inside.

They were here because Myka pulled some strings so that they could get in to see Carl. Before seeing him, they had a brief conversation with his doctor and his nurse. That's how Daniel came to the conclusion that Emily was right. Although Carl had gone through trauma as a child, he wasn't psychotic. Yes, he was on medication for depression and he was constantly on suicide watch. They found out he became that way after a visit with Sherry.

Later, they were escorted to a room where he was sitting alone at a table putting together a puzzle.

"Carl, you have visitors," said the nurse.

Carl looked up to see Daniel and frowned. He wore a blank expression, but it was clear on his face that he didn't know Daniel and didn't want to see him. But then Emily stepped from behind him and he saw her. A big dimpled smile formed on his lips and he stood up.

Emily saw the resemblance between him and Sherry and was astounded at how strong it was. The height, hair color, and eyes, all were the same. The only difference was the dimples. She also noticed his instant acceptance of her. She figured she could use that to their advantage.

"Hi, Carl," she said, smiling back.

Carl lifted his hand, giving her a quick wave. "Hello. You can sit down if you like," he said, pulling out the chair closet to his.

When Emily moved to sit in the chair, Daniel held her back. He pulled out the next chair over and told her to sit there. He took the seat in the middle. There was no way he was going to let her sit right next to him when they didn't know just how unstable he could be.

Carl took his seat. He gave Daniel a dismissive glance and focused his attention on Emily.

"I'm glad you came to see me. I was hoping you would."

Emily looked at him sadly thinking he either thought her to be someone else, or he was fantasizing.

"Do you know me?" she asked out of curiosity.

"Yes. You're Emily," he said, grinning. "You'll soon be my sister in law."

Oh shit. Emily eased her hand into Daniel's and he squeezed it gently. It was clear that Carl's response unsettled her.

"How did you know what she looked like if this is her first time visiting you?" asked Daniel.

Carl frowned over at Daniel, but didn't answer his question. He turned back to Emily.

"Who is he?"

She knew that if she said Daniel was her boyfriend, that he would clam up. So she lied.

"He's my brother. I wanted you to meet him too. He will be your family as well."

That must have been enough for Carl, because he exhaled and smiled.

"Oh wow. Sherry never mentioned you, so I didn't know. Sorry about that."

"No problem," said Daniel. "Now can you answer the question I asked. I mean, if you want to." He threw that in, hoping to pacify him.

It worked. "Yeah, sure. Sherry showed me a picture of her."

"A picture?" asked Emily. Her voice trailed off and she began to feel sick to her stomach.

"Yup." Carl dug his hand in his pocket and pulled out two pictures of Emily. One was of her at the school in Virginia and the other was of her coming out of her apartment in New York.

Daniel began to get angry and had to dig deep to keep control of his temper. "So you're okay with Sherry dating a woman?" he asked.

"Oh yeah. I see that stuff all the time on the TV. Plus, Sherry said it's now legal for them to get married."

"Has Sherry always liked girls?" asked Emily, after getting herself together.

Carl shook his head and looked out the only window in the room. "No. She told me about a boy she dated before and he used her. She said he took her lady flower and then hurt her. Didn't even want to see her anymore. Men like that are bastards," he said in anger.

"You're right," said Daniel, wanting to calm him down. "But I bet she had a happy childhood though. Right?" he asked, smiling.

He shook his head. "Not all the time. Nope. She said her Daddy beat her. And she said his new wife and her son's beat her too. Grand Daddy only wanted the money. Yeah, that's what she said."

"Carl, why does Sherry want to marry a woman?" asked Emily.

"Because all men are evil. They lie, degrade you, and beat you. She said she won't let another man hurt or touch her again. Except me and now you," he said, looking at Daniel. "Because we're family."

"Yes, we're family," Daniel said, repeating his words.

"Alright now, Carl. It's time for dinner and then your medicine.

Your friends will have to come visit another time," said the same nurse that walked them in.

"They're not my friends, Nurse Burns. They're my family," he said, correcting her.

The nurse chuckled. "Well, I stand corrected. But the visit will still need to be rescheduled."

"It's alright Carl. I'll come back," said Emily as she and Daniel stood.

"Okay. I will make sure I'm here waiting," he said as he was ushered from the room.

The nurse held him by one arm as she escorted him down the hall.

"That was intense," said Emily.

"Yeah. Now let's get out of here. This place is giving me the creeps."

"I agree."

***

Sherry watched Emily and Daniel leave from her car. She had been about to visit her brother when she saw them go into the building. Unsure as to what to do, she decided to wait until they left. They were inside for about thirty minutes before coming out.

She sat and watched them from her car until they pulled off. Once they had left, she sat for another half an hour in the car knowing it was now Carl's dinner time. When she was sure he would be back to his room, she entered the building.

Carl had been placed inside his own room. It was filled with beautiful paintings and drawings that he'd done. Had he been in his right state of mind, he would have had an awesome career as an artist.

Sherry slipped past the guard that had a habit of staring down at his cell phone all day instead of watching the monitors. It bothered her that he was always slipping on his duties. Clareview had a strict policy on visitors and it was part of the reason why she moved him here. They kept their patients secure in their rooms, yet allowed them to have several hours to roam freely. It was perfect for Carl. She would have to see about having the guard removed.

When she reached Carl's room, she placed her head against the door listening. When she didn't hear any voices, she knew that he was alone. She opened the door quietly and slipped inside.

"Hey Carl. What'cha up to?" she asked, moving around the room.

He looked up from his painting and smiled. "Nothing much. Just painting. You want to see?"

Sherry moved closer to him and stood by his desk. He was working on a landscape that was almost completed the last time she'd seen him. But now he was adding more to it.

"What's that?" she asked, pointing to the dark color he was adding.

"That's my new sister, Emily and my new brother, Daniel."

Rage, hot and fierce, slammed Sherry in the gut.

"They were allowed to see you?" she asked, fighting hard to control her temper. Sherry had thought they had been in here all that time trying to get in because no one other than family was allowed access to patients. *How the hell did they pull that off*, she wondered.

"Yup. You missed them," he said, smiling.

Sherry nodded her head. She looked away briefly trying to collect herself.

"What did you guys talk about."

"Family stuff. Me. Oh, and you," he said, dipping his brush in the blue paint. "We talked a lot about you."

"What did you say about me, Carl?" she asked, slowly moving up behind him.

"All the stuff that you told me. It's okay because they're family and they won't hurt you."

Sherry's head dropped. "Yes, they will, Carl. And so have you. I'm sorry. I can't let you tell anyone else."

Carl didn't know that harm would come to him in the hands of his own sister. Sherry wrapped her strong arms around his neck and began to squeeze as tight as she could. The only sound in the room was the scratchy sound of him trying to speak as he fought to make Sherry release her hold. His fingers clawed at her arms to no avail.

All the while Sherry held on, tears rolled down her cheeks and fell into his hair. Only after his arms dropped, and she felt the last breath leave his body, did she let go and left him slumped in his chair.

Moving quickly, she snatched the sheet from his bed and tied it to the thin bar at the top of his small window. After it was secure, she proceeded in dragging his body over while he still sat in the chair. She turned it around until it was close to the wall. Then, she tied the other end of the sheet around his neck. Now that it was tied tightly, she eased the chair from beneath him, which allowed the sheet to support his body. It now looked as if he had somehow managed to commit suicide by hanging himself with his sheet at the window.

Sherry looked at him one last time. "You're just like the rest of them," she said, and left just as quietly as she'd come.

Chapter Thirty Six

Feeling the loss of her brother and the bitterness at being terminated from her job, Sherry headed to Virginia. She knew it was Daniel's fault. He was trying to turn Emily against her so he could have her for himself. She waited outside his building to confront him.

"Damn," mumbled Daniel as he started patting his pockets.

Emily stood there grinning. "You left them on the nightstand," she said, referring to his keys.

He looked at her sheepishly. "I'll be right back." Heading back upstairs, he left Emily in the lobby waiting for him.

"Mmm hmm." She shook her head and stood near the bench in the lobby. They were on their way to see a movie. It was a much needed distraction and she was glad she decided to return back to Virginia with him.

Sherry saw her through the glass standing by herself and made her move. She opened the large glass door and headed inside. The only guard at the desk was an old man, and she wasn't worried about him at all. She watched the younger guard leave a few minutes ago. He picked up a pack of cigarette's, so she knew he was on his break.

George looked up when he saw the woman. He had never seen her before, so he stood up. "Can I help you?"

Sherry ignored him and headed straight for Emily. When Emily saw her, she glanced over at the guard with a shadow of fear on her face. He saw her frightened look and pressed the panic button under the desk.

She swallowed hard, trying to be brave. She wasn't afraid of her. If she had to, she would fight back to stay safe. Remembering the TV shows she watched, and how they always talked softly to the criminals, she decided to do the same. *No use poking a mad bull.*

"Sherry… What are you doing here?" She tried to look surprised to see her. "I thought you were back in New York working."

Sherry stood staring at her for a long moment before she responded. "I don't work there anymore. Your little friend saw to that," she said calmly. It was a little too calm for Emily, especially for someone who just lost their career.

"I'm sorry about you losing your job."

"I don't care about losing my job," she ground out between clenched teeth. She began breathing heavily, her eyes narrowed in anger.

Okay, this is not going well. I must be asking the wrong questions. "Then what's got you so upset?" She figured if she got straight to the problem, maybe she could defuse the whole situation.

Sherry took a step closer to her. They still had several feet left between them, but Emily didn't like the fact that she kept coming closer, closing the distance.

"That man you've been parading around with got all up in my business," she said, and began to pace with short, slow steps. "Yeah, I saw him at the hospital. He went to see my brother. I saw you with him, but I know he forced you to go." She stated it as if it was the truth and she didn't need Emily to agree. In her eyes, it was only Daniel that was evil. Only he was at fault.

"Sherry, we only asked him a few questions," Emily said softly.

"He had no right!" she yelled violently. Tiny splatters of spit flew from her lips. "He stressed him. He made him uneasy and worried. He was turning him into a liar. I could see it. So I did the only thing I could to make it right again." The last sentence came out more like a whisper.

"Sherry, what did you do?" That look in Sherry's eyes didn't sit right with her. It wasn't clear or focused. It was blank and it sent a shiver of terror down Emily's spine.

Snapping back from her momentary lapse, instantly her face balled up in a sneer. "I didn't do anything. It was his fault,"she yelled out insinuating Daniel. "My brother killed himself because of him!"

The words were yelled out with hatred and had such an impact on Emily that she took a step back. Her hand covered her mouth to keep the small outcry from escaping.

"No, that can't be. He was fine when we left," Emily said feeling horrible.

"No. He wasn't. That friend of yours caused my brother to commit suicide." Her tone was flat and gritty. Then suddenly, she changed from being angry to worried. "That's why I'm here," she said softly. "He's not safe to be with Emily. I needed to make sure you were safe, baby."

Sherry was about to close the gap between her and Emily when the elevator doors opened and out stepped Daniel. If hate could be a costume, then Sherry would be the perfect model for it. Her body tensed up, and an ugly frown drew in her eyebrows, and her lip curled. She gave Daniel a hard stare and the burning hate radiating from her body caused the air in the lobby to thicken.

She approached Emily little by little all the while keeping her eyes on Daniel. When he took a step forward, Sherry pulled out a huge hunting knife, pointing it at him threateningly. He stopped moving. The old man at the front desk of the building was scared shitless. He didn't know what to do, so he only watched, but he made sure the cameras kept recording.

She looked at Daniel with disgust in her eyes. "He only wants one thing from you. They all do. He just wants to do filthy things to you. Then he'll beat you. They always beat you. Even when you don't fight them off, they still beat you. It makes them feel good," she said, staring at him with a weird look on her face as she flipped the knife around in her hand.

Daniel's body was tense with fury. He knew he wasn't going to let this lunatic hurt Emily. He was prepared to do everything in his power to keep her safe, even if it meant getting hurt himself.

"Sherry." Emily called her using a soft tone. When she didn't respond, she called to her again. "Sherry."

Sherry flicked her eyes to Emily and returned them to Daniel instantly. She intended to use all the training she received as a Customs Agent to take him down. Their training made sure they were prepared to handle women and men larger than themselves.

Emily started moving towards the small couch in the lobby. "Sherry, why don't you come sit with me so we can talk."

Sherry glanced at Emily, and this time held her gaze a little longer. Yet, it still wasn't long enough for Daniel to make his move.

"If you want to protect me Sherry you need to sit with me. Come on," Emily said, moving backwards in the direction of the small leather couch.

Emily started to back away, and just as he hoped, Sherry couldn't keep her eyes off Emily. *That's it. Take a look at her.*

When she turned to look at Emily, he moved quickly and launched his body at her sending them both flying to the floor. He didn't want to hurt her because she was a woman. Hell, she was almost his height and weight, but that didn't matter. She was still a female and he would do his best not to harm her.

Although Sherry was strong, he definitely was stronger. He watched her struggle to get free, yet he was finally able to force the knife from her hand. He rolled her over on her stomach and forced one of her arms behind her.

At that moment, the other guard on duty returned, and he ran over to help out. After that, sirens could be heard and the police filled the lobby. A few officers ran over and subdued Sherry, placing her in handcuffs.

"Get your fucking hands off me! Let me go, dammit!" Sherry continued to yell out obscenities as they dragged her kicking and screaming to the door. "Emily, he's going to hurt you. I was only trying to protect you."

Once they cleared the lobby, they watched as she struggled with the police kicking the vehicle doors and windows. Seeing the wild look on Emily's face, Daniel pulled her into his arms and held her tightly. He could feel her body trembling against his and he tightened his hold.

Two police officers walked up to them and took their statements. Almost an hour later, Emily's nerves were rattled, and Daniel was still trying to shake off the tension. He kept seeing Sherry and the huge knife she'd held pointed at the woman he loved. He'd damn near lost it.

With all of the excitement that happened, they didn't feel up to a movie. Instead, they decided to go for a walk on the beach hoping the cool breeze and the ocean sounds, would soothe their stress. They walked hand in hand across the sand in silence with nothing but the warm breeze cooling their skin.

"I'm sorry I left you alone down there. I should have thought better than to do that, especially after you told me about her following you."

Emily squeezed his hand and lifted it to her lips. "It's okay, Danny. It wasn't your fault. None of it was," she said strongly.

"I know," he said stopping. He touched her cheek and smiled faintly. "I got another call from Myka. That's what took me so long. He didn't like the fact nothing had come up on Sherry, so he had a buddy of his do some extra searching on her."

"What did he find out?" She could tell from the look on his face it was bad.

"Remember the boyfriend that dumped her?" When Emily nodded, he continued. "He was killed in a hit and run car accident a few months after their breakup."

"Oh my."

"Yeah, but it was turned into an unsolved murder, because they found that the driver hit him, and then put the car in reverse and backed over his body."

"And that was Sherry?"

Daniel nodded. "They believe so."

"Then why didn't the police arrest her?"

"They never had any witnesses. Plus, it was done in the ghetto, so they let it go."

Emily shook her head. "They didn't care to look."

"No, they didn't. But that was only the beginning. He also found out that she purchased a huge hunting knife some years ago from a pawn shop in Jersey City. It was expensive, so the store clerk required her to show ID for tax purposes. He cross referenced the dates that you gave him about the day she turned up following you, with murders in those areas, and got a hit."

"Murders! She killed more people?" she asked, surprised and curious.

"Several. The one's that were around you were at the club where you two met and at some beauty store in the area here."

"Oh, no. Who did she kill?" she asked, feeling a little sick to her stomach.

"Some guy she had words with inside and outside the club. Then a young cashier at the beauty store. They have it all on camera."

Emily dropped her head and rested it on his chest. She remembered the cashier locking the doors so she could get away from Sherry. He had paid with his life. *He died because of me.*

As if he could hear her thoughts, Daniel stepped back and lifted her chin. "None of this is because of you. It was all Sherry's fault. She's unstable and should've been getting help. She killed those people, not you."

There was more to tell her, but he was trying to decide if he should. Then he figured he might as well get it all out now instead of making this stretch out any longer. They needed to put this behind them and move on. He needed to get her back to smiling and laughing.

"There's something else, Em."

"What?"

"Carl is dead."

"Yes, I know. Sherry said he committed suicide. That's so sad."

Daniel shook his head. "No, baby. She lied. He was strangled to death and then she set it up to look like he hung himself."

"She killed her own brother?!" A tinge of infuriation could be heard in her tone.

"Yes. She killed an innocent man and she didn't care one bit. She did it for her own selfish reasons. So don't think that any of this is your fault, because it's not. It's all on her. You got that?"

Emily wrapped her arms around his waist and held on tightly. "Yes. I understand."

They stood there on the beach together, drawing strength from each other, and allowing all the upsetting circumstances to bring them even closer.

Chapter Thirty Seven

It was now September and the hot summer days began to turn cool. It had been a tough couple of weeks for Emily and Daniel. She had returned home to contemplate her next move, while Daniel was meeting with carpenters and insurance people about the restaurant. They missed each other like crazy and tried to keep in touch as much as possible.

Seeing that it was past noon, she got up from the couch and went out to check the mail. She sorted through several letters, but stopped when she came across a letter from the Country Wide Orchestra. They were a world renowned traveling orchestra that enlisted some of the greatest talent to perform, and they wanted her to join them.

It would require her to travel with them to France, Italy and Germany, for performances that would run for Four months, September through December. They quoted her an obscene amount as her pay for joining. She was excited about the offer and wanted to share her news with Daniel. When she grabbed her phone to call him, she came up with a better idea to catch a quick flight down to see him.

***

Taylor Mills finally returned from her extended business trip. She hadn't planned on being gone for so long, but her new designs were a hit in China and it was a smart move to stay as long as needed. Although her meetings and business dealings were a success, she was happy to be home and couldn't wait to see Daniel. She needed a little bit of his loving to help mellow her mood.

She made short work of unpacking, showering, and slipping into something sexy. She headed for his apartment in anticipation of him sending her on an orgasmic roller coaster over and over. Daniel's housekeeper who comes twice a month was leaving out just as she got there. She knew who Taylor was and greeted her with a smile.

"Welcome home, Ms. Mills."

"Thank you, dear. I had a wonderful time in China. It's a beautiful country. You should visit there someday."

"Oh, I couldn't afford a trip like that."

"Nonsense. It's not as expensive as you think. Just plan ahead, and look for discounts, and you'll be fine." Taylor pointed to a side entrance to Daniel's penthouse. She was the only one who ever used it. "Is he home yet?"

"No, but he's on his way." When Taylor started to go towards the still open door, the housekeeper stopped her. "Ms. Mills, maybe you should wait until he gets in. I don't want to get in trouble for letting you in without permission." Although it was something Daniel had asked her to do on many occasions, and she wouldn't think twice about doing, she felt things were different now. Emily was now in the picture.

"Oh, don't worry about anything. He knows I'm coming," she lied. "I already spoke to him earlier when my flight landed."

Relieved, and thinking Taylor was telling the truth, she stepped to the side. "Alright then. You have a nice day then."

"You too," said Taylor as she entered the living room.

It was a half an hour later when Daniel stepped into his apartment and saw Taylor heading in his direction with open arms. *Oh shit!* He quickly stepped behind the couch keeping it between them.

"Taylor! What are you doing here?" he asked, looking around for his housekeeper. "How did you get in?" he asked when he saw that the housekeeper was already gone for the day.

"Your housekeeper, silly. And is that any way to welcome me home?" she asked with her hands on her hips. When her hand went to the top button on her already low top, he began to panic.

"Listen, Taylor, we need to talk."

"Come here, sexy. We can talk later." Taylor was on button number two when his panic bubbled over.

"I'm seeing someone!" he blurted out.

Taylor didn't pause at all. "Okay. Why don't you take your shirt off. I want to see those muscles."

"No, Taylor. You don't understand. I'm in a relationship."

Her head tipped to the side and she watched him. "What?"

"I'm in love with her and one day I'm going to marry her."

Taylor was staring at him quietly. It was the way that he'd said it that let her know she had lost the fight in winning his heart. She was hurt, but she didn't want him to know it. Although they had an agreement of no strings attached, she still had fallen hard for her sexy landlord. It was hard not to.

"Oh." That one word held so much emotion in it that Daniel actually felt sorry for her and ashamed of himself. He knew that Taylor had been catching feelings for him, and he should have ended it a long time ago. However, he allowed it to go on pretending that he was wrong about it, and that she could handle the situation. He was wrong.

"I'm sorry, Taylor."

Her hands dropped from her blouse and she turned away. "There's no reason to be sorry. We never had any attachments other than sex. We agreed to keep it like that. We're still friends, Daniel. It's fine." She turned back around smiling. "I'm happy you found someone. Is she beautiful? Does she make you happy?"

Daniel smiled. "Look, let me go change and I'll come back and tell you all about her."

He dashed off to change and Taylor covered her mouth to keep the sob she held at bay from slipping past her lips. *I've lost him.*

***

Emily's flight landed and she took the same car service to Daniel's house that she always used. George waved to her as she took the elevator up to his apartment. When she walked in, she was shocked to see a woman standing in the kitchen filling two glasses with wine.

The two women sized each other up, and Taylor instantly knew she was the reason Daniel wanted to end their relationship. Even though Taylor wasn't a vindictive person, jealousy rushed forward, and just like any other envious, heartbroken woman, she wanted to invoke pain on the person that caused her to lose the one thing she loved the most.

"Hi," Emily said, adjusting the box she carried in her arms. She walked in and unbuttoned her coat. That's when she noticed how provocative the woman was dressed and that her top button was undone.

"Hello," Taylor said, smiling. "Who are you?"

"I'm Emily. Who are you?" *She better be a relative.*

"I'm Taylor. I live downstairs."

The tenant. Okay, but why is she here? "Where's Daniel?"

"Oh, he's getting dressed. We were about to have a glass of wine. Would you like to join us?"

Hot. Emily felt heat and nothing else. "What do you mean he's getting dressed?"

"Well, he was naked a moment ago, and now he's going to put something on so we can have some wine, play some music, and then…" She purposely let her sentence trail off unfinished leaving Emily to fill in the blanks.

Hurt and confused, Emily sat down the gift that she'd bought him. "Can you do me a favor and see that he gets this, please." She re-buttoned her coat and headed to the door. "Also, can you tell him I said I hoped he enjoys his evening."

Taylor smiled and nodded her head. "Sure, I can tell him that."

"Thanks," Emily said, trying to keep her cool as she turned and left.

It all happened within a few minutes, but the thought of him cheating on her would last a lifetime.

When Daniel returned from taking his shower wearing a sweater and some jeans, he was shocked to see that Taylor had dimmed the lights and had poured them some wine. *Did she not just hear what I said to her?*

"Taylor, I thought you understood what I said earlier. You and I can no longer see each other intimately. You do get that right?"

Taylor laughed, sounding almost high pitched. "Yes, baby. I understand. I only thought I would help you relax by dimming the lights and sipping on some wine. You know, just to kick back."

Her overly cheerful laugh let him see that Taylor was about to play games. That's when he decided it would be best if they parted ways without anything more between them.

"Look, maybe it's not a good idea for us to try and be friends. I think it will be awkward and uncomfortable for both of us."

Taylor's smile faded. "So now you don't want us to be friends either."

"I think it will be better that way."

He thought he saw a flicker of anger cross her face, but it was gone so quickly he figured he'd only imagined it. Taylor picked up her purse and headed slowly to the door. When she pulled it open she stopped and glanced back over her shoulder.

"You had a visitor while you were in the shower. She left that for you," she said, nodding towards the blue wrapped package.

Daniel walked over to the box and read the card that was attached to it. His face became tight and a sickening feeling took to his stomach. He looked over at Taylor with a gaze of steel.

"What did you do, Taylor?"

"Nothing," she said, trying to look innocent. "But she did tell me to tell you that she hoped we enjoyed our evening. Do you think she believed we were going to— . Oh, Daniel. I'm so sorry," she said with her hand covering her lips. Then she slowly removed her hand to reveal a cunning smile. "I guess we both lost tonight, huh?"

"Get the hell out of my house, Taylor," he said angrily.

"With pleasure," she purred and left.

He couldn't believe what just happened. *This shit can't be happening again.*

After Taylor left, Daniel rushed to get his cell phone. He called Emily several times, but she didn't answer. He left voice messages and text messages, but she never responded. In a panic, he grabbed his coat and headed for the door. He didn't pack a bag or anything. He just rushed to the airport as fast as he could and booked a flight to New York. He began to stress when his flight didn't leave for three hours, and then was delayed. Once he was finally in New York, he hurried to her apartment.

The incessant buzzing of the bell pissed Emily off and she yanked the door open without thinking. When she saw that it was Daniel, she tried to shut it in his face, but he stuck his foot in the door.

"Em, please give me a chance to explain," he pleaded through the crack his foot granted him in the door. When she kept trying to shove the door closed, he tried again. "I'll stand here all night with my foot in your door if I have to."

Sighing in defeat, she allowed him to come in only because she knew he wasn't going to leave. Wearing pajamas covered in little violins, she sat perched on the end of the couch. She would let him say what he had to say and then put him out.

Daniel talked slowly, explaining about Taylor and that ended things between them. "That's why she was there, Em. Nothing else. Whatever she insinuated was a lie. She was hurt because I ended it, and that was her way of hurting me. Of hurting you."

He noticed that she wasn't looking at him. She was avoiding eye contact, shutting him out. "Why did you wait until now to tell her it was over? Why not months ago?"

"Because she was away on business and I couldn't reach her. She was in China."

"Are there any more women that I'll have to worry about,

Daniel?"

The pain and anger was evident in her voice, and he was afraid that he'd messed up too bad to fix things. "I swear on my life Em, there's no one else. I promise you."

She sat there a minute gazing off into the distance. He could see the wheels turning in her head, and knew whatever she threw at him, he would accept it and deal with it.

"How did she get into your apartment?"

"I didn't let her in if that's what you're thinking. My housekeeper let her in."

"Why? Why would she let her in if you weren't there?" she asked, looking at him for the first time. The hurt that he saw made him wish she never looked up.

Just be honest. "Because before you and I started seeing each other, I told her to let her in, even if I wasn't home."

"And she lives there, in the building, right?"

"Em..."

"Doesn't she?" she asked in a clipped tone.

He nodded.

She looked away, shaking her head. "I don't trust that. I don't trust her."

"Em, you can trust me. I would never violate your trust in me."

Emily glanced up at him with tears flooding her eyes. "I want to believe you Danny, but you're making it really hard for me when I keep finding you alone with different women."

No. He could feel it coming. Doom. Heartache. Loneliness. "How can I prove it to you?"

"I don't know. I honestly don't know."

Grasping at straws, he comes up with an idea. "Okay, let's do this. Tomorrow we put an end to all this secrecy. I don't want to keep our relationship a secret anymore. I want to tell everyone, starting with our parents." He was hoping that once the women from his past saw that he was in a relationship, they would stop putting him in compromising positions.

She exhaled tired of the conversation. "I guess."

She didn't sound convinced, but it was a start.

Testing the water, he moved closer to her and then sat beside her. Taking her hand, he placed a kiss on her finger tips and then her wrist. He lifted her chin so she would look at him.

"I should have said this to you a long time ago. I love you, Em. I've never been so in love in my whole life."

The tears she had been holding finally won and began to trickle down her face. "I love you too, Danny. That's why this hurts so much. And you said you would never hurt me, but you keep doing it," she said, on a sob.

Ashamed beyond words, he pulled her into his lap and she buried her face into his neck and cried.

Chapter Thirty Eight

Staying true to his word, Daniel got Emily up and dressed early so they could go over to her parents house to tell them that they were seeing each other. It just so happened that his parents, Michael, Arnez, Jerome, Tara, and Alexander, were all there as well having brunch with Emily's parents. They were laughing and carrying on while discussing everything from movies to sports. No politics were allowed. Only fun topics.

"Sweety, I didn't know you were coming home. You're just in time to eat," Tasha said, giving Emily a big hug.

Since this was the first time seeing Daniel since they heard about the fire, his parents rushed him as soon as he entered the dinning hall.

"How are you holding up, baby?" Sabrina asked, touching his face tenderly.

"I'm fine, mom."

"Do you need assistance with anything," Morgan asked.

"No, Dad. The insurance will cover everything. It'll be fine."

"Good. Good," said Morgan, pulling Sabrina back. "Stop fussing, love. You're embarrassing him."

"No, I'm not," she said, smiling. She loved her boys with all of her heart and hated seeing them in any kind of pain.

"So Daniel, how did you know we were over here at the Bawler's?" asked Michael.

"Yeah, and how is it that you and Emily show at the same time?" asked Tara, knowing damn well Emily and Daniel were seeing each other.

Daniel and Emily looked at each other. When she smiled and he nodded, she took the floor.

"Guys, I have something to say." When all eyes were on her she went on. "I'm not gay. Well, not anymore."

Tasha eyes widened. "You're not?"

Emily laughed. "No, Mom. Actually, I'm seeing someone."

"Who?" her father chimed in. Joeseph was trying to figure things out.

When he asked who, she turned and looked at Daniel and smiled.

"Emily and I have been seeing each other for a couple of months now," he said, moving in her direction. His eyes were fixed on her and he didn't see the blow coming.

Alex punched Daniel, and since he wasn't expecting the blow, he fell on his ass.

Michael, Jerome and Arnez all started to laugh.

"I see you still have a soft jaw," said Michael, still laughing.

"Alex!" Emily yelled, giving him the evil eye.

"Get up, Daniel. I'm going to kick your ass for taking advantage of my little sister. I'm not going to stand by and watch you play games with her," yelled Alex. He was playing the big brother role to a tee.

"Actually, she took advantage of me," said Daniel, rubbing his jaw as he stood up. "And I'm not playing games with her. I love her, dammit!" He then retaliated by punching Alex, who stumbled and tripped over a chair. Again, everyone laughed.

"You do?" asked Joeseph.

"Yes," he said, still rubbing his jaw.

"Of course he does," said Michael, smirking. "He's been in love with her for quite some time now."

Emily looked at Michael, and then at Daniel in shock.

"How the hell do you know that?" asked Daniel.

Michael took a sip of his drink, drawing out the moment of having everyone's attention. "Because, two years ago you let me use your phone and I saw the photos you have of her. A lot of them are titled too. You want me to tell you some of the captions?"

"No!" Daniel ground out between his teeth.

Alex and Jerome laughed.

Emily moved over to him and touched his arm. "Can I see the photos?"

Embarrassed, he looked down and met her gaze. He could see that she was nervous about what she'd find, and he wanted to set her at ease. He pulled his phone from his inside pocket and unlocked the file that held the photos. He handed it to her, then leaned close to her ear and whispered. "This was the only way I could be with you."

Emily nodded and took the phone. She began moving through the photos sliding them to the side one by one. She smiled at some and laughed at others. When she came to the one with her playing her violin at the Shu Shen Festival in Boston, she glanced up at him.

"How did you get this?" she asked, curiously.

Daniel looked her right in her eyes. He needed her to understand just how deep his love for her ran. "I was at the concert."

"But this was my first professional concert. I was only twenty when I played there," she said in awe.

"I know," he said, smiling. "I've been to all of your concerts."

Emily's eyes began to water. "All of them?"

He nodded his head slowly. "Yes, all of them. I haven't missed one yet."

Emily flung her arms around his neck and kissed him fully right there in front of her parents, brother, and friends.

Alex cleared his throat. "You two want us to leave or..."

Instantly, Emily broke the kiss. Her cheeks were burning hot and they both were breathing heavy with excitement.

Laughter rang out around them.

"Can we get back to the food now," asked Jerome.

"You can't be that hungry," said Alex.

Jerome shrugged his shoulder's. "I'm just saying. We have the whole story now. Emily was the mystery girl he was getting advice about. They're in love, now let's eat."

"You know I can't believe I'm going to say this, but he's right," said Michael. "I'm starving. Come on man. Let's fill these plates."

Everyone sat around the table talking, laughing, and sharing things about their life. Michael shared a story about his neighbor struggling to keep her ranch. Jerome told them about his years in Russia.

Wanting to be involved with the conversation, Tasha looked over at Emily.

"Sweetie, have you made a decision about joining the Country Wide Orchestra? This will be a great opportunity for you, not to mention a great honor."

Daniel looked at Emily confused. "What opportunity?"

"I got an offer to play with a traveling orchestra. It's not a big deal," she said, trying to brush it off.

"Baby, don't be modest," said Tasha. "You deserve to be proud that they sought you out. They're the most prestigious and sought after orchestra in the world. To play with them for even one session will set your career for life. And just think, they want you for a few months."

Daniel sat quietly, pushing his food around on his plate. He no longer had an appetite. "When were you going to tell me about this?" he asked quietly.

"I came to tell you yesterday," she said, staring at him boldly. "But we both know how that ended, don't we?"

He looked at her with a weird expression, but he let the moment pass, because everyone started talking again.

Tara smiled over at Emily. "Emily, do you mind if I do a story on you? I'll come up with some questions and let you read over them to make sure you're comfortable with them. What do you say?"

"Sure. I'd like that. Just let me know when you're ready."

The rest of the day passed in a blur of conversation and laughter. However, Emily couldn't shake the feeling that something was wrong. She found out later that night.

Daniel brought up the orchestra subject again while they were relaxing in her living room. He was staring at the television, which was off, and she was staring at him. She knew sooner or later he would bring it up again.

"How long will you be gone?"

She didn't pretend she didn't know what he was talking about. "I never said I was going, Danny."

"Yeah, but if you decide to go, how long will you be gone?" He held his breath waiting for her to answer. Hoping she'd say for only a few weeks.

"*If* I go it will be for four months. I'd leave in September and be back late December. They said that if everything goes well, that it could become permanent. But, like I said, I haven't said yes."

Daniel heard a 'yet' hovering in the wind. "But you want to, Don't you?"

"I'd be lying if I said I haven't thought about it. It's definitely a great opportunity and it's something I've always wanted to do."

Daniel sat there quietly. "I'd miss you," he whispered softly.

All the hurt, humiliation and pain that she'd experienced after finding him in compromising situations with Kimberly and then Taylor, made her temper rise.

"Would you?" she asked in a tight voice.

He turned to her and frowned. "What the hell kind of question is that, Em? Of course I'd miss you."

Emily hopped up off the couch. She needed to put space between them.

"Well, how am I supposed to know that? You might have another woman that you forgot about ready to jump right in after I'm gone."

He stood up slowly. His body was tense from trying to hold back his temper.

"Emily, I told you that there isn't anyone else. I also explained to you the situation about Kimberly and Taylor, and you said you understood."

She crossed her arms tightly over her chest. "I know Danny, and I forgive you for it, but it's hard to forget. I keep seeing Kimberly barely dressed in your office and then Taylor looking quite comfortable with her shoes off prancing around your apartment like she belonged there. Hell, I felt so out of place and confused, I almost apologized to her for intruding!" Tears sprung to her eyes and rolled in torrents down her cheeks. "Do you have any idea how that made me feel?"

He stepped closer and reached for her, but she took a step back.

"No, Danny. I can't think straight when you're touching me," she cried. Her whole body shook with this new feeling of jealousy and mistrust.

"Em, please," he begged. He couldn't shake the feeling that he was losing her. "I would never do anything to hurt you. You got to believe that. You know you can trust me, right?"

A long moment passed between them in the quiet of the room and then she said the words that hurt him more than anything.

"No. I don't know if I can."

Her words were like a blow to his gut and he tightened his stomach trying to cope with the agony of its attack. He stood there and watched in horror as Emily began backing away from him before turning to run to her room. The sound of her door slamming made him flinch.

He felt his eyes fill with unshed tears as the reality of what just happened registered in his clouded mind. *It's was over.*

The Last First Kiss

Chapter Thirty Nine

The news was playing on the television turned down low. She made sure to keep the TV on all day to fill up the silence around her. The crisp September morning air that she breathed in did nothing to quell her thirst to be touched by Daniel. She pulled her robe tighter around her neck and glanced around at her view.

The sun beat down on the glass of the buildings surrounding her two bedroom, downtown apartment. She was smack dab in the center of Regensburg, Germany, where she was staying temporarily. While there, she would be performing at night at the Castle St. Emmeram and touring the beautiful city during the day. Or anything to take her mind off of missing Daniel.

She hadn't spoken to him after that dreadful night. She had forgiven him about the incidents with Kimberly and Taylor, but had found it difficult to get it out of her head. Even after they had declared their love for one another. It was crazy. All she could think about was him having sex with them. Touching them the same way that he touched her. It was mental torture.

"Uhhhhh!" she grumbled under her breath. It was hard craving his touch, his attention, and conversation, but at the same time feeling unsure and scared of being hurt. She missed him so much. But how can you get pass the pain? How do you deal with the fear of not knowing the outcome? Or if you can truly lay down your guard and trust someone?

This was all new to her. She'd never been in love before. She'd never been with a man before and had no idea how to read their moods, or tell if they were being honest. She was totally in the dark.

The sound of her cell phone ringing had her stepping back inside and closing the balcony doors. When she swiped the choice to answer, she didn't get a chance to say hello before the voice on the other end started in on her.

"So I went on this trip with my husband to one of his medical conventions and was bored out of my mind. However, he made it up to me by whisking me off to Tahiti for three weeks. By the way it was absolutely beautiful. Yet, imagine my surprise when I returned home only to find out that you and Daniel had broken up the same day you told everyone that you were together. I swear, it was the fastest love affair I'd heard of. What the hell happened?" asked Stacey, sounding frustrated.

Stacey was the one person she needed to hear from. Emily began bawling her eyes out while relaying everything that happened. She explained the whole ordeal that led up to her walking in on Daniel and Kimberly and then Taylor. She expressed feeling mortified, embarrassed, angry, and loads more of emotions that were alien to her until being him.

"I love him so much, but I don't know what to do?"

When she finally calmed down to just a sniffle here and there, Stacey spoke up.

"Okay, so do you want me to pacify you with a few hallow 'I'm here for you' statements, or do you want me to speak the brutal truth?"

Emily stopped pacing and blinked. She thought for a second and then sat down on the edge of the couch. She knew that whatever Stacey was about to say to her would be beneficial and not fake.

"I want the brutal truth."

"I want you to stop moping around like some coward ass bitch and put your big girl panties on, and go get your fucking man!"

Emily's mouth dropped open, but she listened. "Okay."

"How the hell you let those two Thot's run you out of your position, girl? Daniel loves you, not them. Yeah, he's an asshole for not ending those situations fully before getting involved with you, but he's your asshole. No man is perfect, Emily. I don't care how good he treats you, or who his mama is. When you get with someone, you have to train and mold them until they're the perfect fit for your needs. And yes, every now and then some trashy slut will try and take what's yours, and it's up to you to stand up and fight for it. You don't tuck tail and run. You got that?"

Emily nodded. "Yeah. I understand. But, Stacey, I was so messed up in the head I didn't know what to do. I understood that he hadn't purposely tried to hurt me, and was innocent in what happened, but at the same time I was so furious. I was fed up and sick of it. I mean, I actually asked him if there were any more women I should be worried about."

Stacey burst out laughing. "Damn. What did he say?"

Emily laughed. "He looked like I'd kicked him in the nuts, but he said there weren't any."

"And did you believe him?" asked Stacey.

"At the time, no I didn't. But now that I'vd time to calm down and get my head right, I believe him. I trust him not to hurt me."

"So when are you going to tell *him* that?"

Emily stared at the TV not really seeing it or hearing what the woman on the show was saying.

"I'll tell him when I get back in December. I don't want to do it over the phone."

"Good. And for future reference, when you're having problems and you don't know what to do, pick up the damn phone. Running only makes it worse."

"I know, and thanks for returning my calls."

"Well, did I have a choice? You left me about fifty messages. Hell, some of them I could barely understand, with you crying so hard."

Emily laughed. "Oh, be quiet. I remember someone boo-hooing over a certain doctor in the family."

Stacey smiled. "Girl, I don't know what you're talking about. I was a rock!" she said, and burst into laughter.

They talked a little more about Daniel and what she planned to say to him when she returned. Discussing it with Stacey helped Emily see things clearer and to soothe her homesick soul. If she could jump up and go home right now she would have. Unfortunately, she'd signed a contract with the orchestra and wouldn't be able to return until it was over. Yet, once she returned, she had a lot to think about.

When Julliard found out about the offer from the orchestra, they had given her an ultimatum. If she signed with them to go on tour, she would lose her teaching position. However, just a few days ago, the Orchestra had offered her a four year contract to tour with them six months out of the year. The salary and perks were ridiculously generous and they gave her until March to make a decision.

There was only one thing that held her back from saying yes... Daniel.

The Last First Kiss

Chapter Forty

Turkey, stuffing, ham, chicken, yams, macaroni and cheese, and cabbage. The list could go on and on, of all the delicious food that was prepared for Thanksgiving in the Tase home. Sabrina and all the brother's wives, had outdone themselves this year. They had come together to create a menu, then prepare the food for the men. Every person in the house was stuffed. Laugher, food and good times. It's what family was all about.

Now the grandparents were seated in the living room chatting about this and that, while keeping an eye on their grandchildren. However, in the game room, all the brothers had gathered to play a game of pool. Soon Stacey, Tara, Rainy and Kayla joined them.

Daniel was relaxing in near the stereo scrolling through CD's when he heard Miki call his name. When he looked up, everyone was staring at him.

"What was that?" he asked not hearing the question.

Miki leaned over the table, check the angle of the balls, and then took his shot. He missed.

"I said, how long are you going to be an asshole?"

Stacey was standing near him, going through a separate pile of CD's.

"I don't follow," he said, frowning.

Miki stood there looking at him holding his pool stick in front of him. "No? Well, let me help you understand then. It's been almost three months since you copped out and let Emily fly off to another country because you dropped the ball."

"Twice," said Michael.

"Damn. Twice?" asked Sydney, looking at Daniel. He shook his head. "She deserves better than that man."

"First off, I didn't cop out of anything. And yes, I dropped the ball. Twice," he said shooting daggers at Sydney. "But it was Emily's choice to leave. Not mine. I didn't force her to go. She left on her own free will."

"Because you hurt her," said Rainy, joining the conversation.

"I didn't intentionally set out to hurt her," Daniel said, heated. "I

276

had no control over what happened."

Stacey sucked her teeth and slapped him up beside the head.

"Ow! What was that for?" he said, looking behind him. He had forgotten that she was back there.

"For that lame ass excuse about not having control over what happened. All of that could have been avoided and you know it." Her eyes were narrowed and she was leaning over him in a threatening way.

"Uh, Chase, you wanna get your wife?" he said, leaning away from her.

"Not really," said Chase, grinning.

Daniel got up. "Alright, fine. Please tell me how I could have stopped Kimberly from stripping down in my office. Or how I could have stopped Taylor from showing up in my house when I wasn't even home. I didn't initiate any of those encounters. So how can I be held accountable?"

Everyone was shocked when Myka answered the question. He was standing near the window quietly listening with his back to them.

"You could've avoided all of this nonsense by correctly ending the affairs you were involved in. The moment you saw that Emily was approving your advances and returning your interest, you should have cut them off completely."

He turned around to face them. "You knew Kimberly wanted to continue your affair even after you cut her off. Yet, knowing this, you allowed her to remain working for you to find the property you needed. Hell, you even introduced them at one time. What you should have done after you ended the affair, was find another agency to buy from."

"And Taylor?" asked Chase.

"Taylor could have been handled with a phone call and an update to your staff that, she wasn't to be let into your apartment without you being there. No questions asked."

Daniel looked at him wide eyed. "You wanted me to break up with her over the phone?"

"Break up with her? You weren't in a relationship. So there wouldn't have been a break up,' Myka said sharply. "And as for the reference to the phone, isn't that how you two hooked up? Over the phone. Seems fitting."

Everyone's head turned in Daniel's direction. He was standing in the middle of the room looking thrown. He ran his hand over his face in frustration.

"Look, I love Emily. That hasn't changed. And yes, I want to be with her, but it's hard because of us living so far apart. We're flying back and forth several times a month just to spend time with each other. Then there's the two incidents that occurred. She said it made her feel like she couldn't trust me. Like I was playing games or something."

Miki placed his pool stick on the table and approached him. "All of that is easily fixable. If you really want to be with her then you'll need to prove it. Not by sex or gifts, but with something meaningful that will convince her that you're serious. Once you prove to her that you're willing to make the sacrifice and give her what she needs to trust you, the rest will fall back into place."

"But there are steps you'll need to take first," said Michael.

"Like what?" At this point Daniel was desperate and would take any advice he could to help get Emily back.

"Like getting rid of the center of your problems, Kimberly and Taylor," answered Michael.

"Kimberly is facing jail time, so that's definitely done. And I already ended it with Taylor."

"Then why hasn't Taylor moved out of the building," asked Tara. "It's going to be a problem for Emily to see her coming in and out, knowing that you've had intimate relations with her."

"There's nothing I can do about that. Taylor signed a two year lease and it isn't up until next year. She could sue me if I tried to get her out of the building sooner."

"Okay, she can't move out yet, but what's keeping you from moving?" asked Michael. "It's your building, so nothings keeping you from relocating. And don't act like you don't want to either. You've been holding off choosing a new location for your restaurant for months now and all of us here know the reason."

Daniel walked over to the window with his hands in his pockets. He knew Michael was right. He had been dragging his feet about choosing a spot because deep down he wanted Emily in his life, but he wasn't sure if she would be with him in Virginia or if he would move to New York. Suddenly an idea began to form in his head and he began to smile.

"Dear George, I think he's got it!" said Chase, and everyone laughed.

Chapter Forty One

The flight home to New York seemed endless with all the delays and the traffic was even more congested than normal. Even though it was three days after Christmas, the streets were still filled with holiday shoppers. The decorations were still up, and the lights were flashing festive colors, making rainbow patterns all across the snow.

After being home for hours, Emily made a call to her parents to let them know she'd arrived home safely. She called Stacey, but Chase answered her phone.

"Welcome home, shorty," said Chase as a greeting.

Emily laughed. "Thanks Chase. Where's the wife."

"Done with me already, huh," he said, laughing. "She's not here, but she accidentally left her cell phone. She flew to LA for some Gala she and Mom had to attend. They said it was business, but I'm starting to think it was a shopping trip. I'll see when I get my credit card statement in the mail."

"Wow." Emily laughed, even though she was upset that she missed her.

When she sat there quietly, he figured she wanted something else. "You still there?"

"Yeah."

"Did you need something else?"

She'd wanted to grill Stacey about Daniel, but Chase would have to do. "Yes. I called Daniel, but I wasn't able to reach him."

"That's because he's out of town on business. Something to do with his restaurant I believe. Been gone for a few days now."

"Oh. Okay, then," she said, sounding depressed. "I guess I'll let you get back to whatever you were doing. When you hear from Stacey, tell her to call me, please."

"Will do. Take care," he said before ending the call. Then he leaned back on the couch and smiled.

She sat alone in her apartment feeling sorry for herself. She knew she'd made a mistake letting him go and was ready to do anything to get him back. After the conversation she'd had with Stacey while she was in Russia, she'd come up with a plan on how she was going to make that happen, but how could she if he wasn't even here.

Chapter Forty Two

February 6

This weather was playing games with people. One day it was below four degrees and the next thing you know, it's in the high forties with the sun beating down on your face making you feel even warmer. Today was one of those weird warm days. It was beautiful outside and Daniel was grateful because it played right into his plans.

He'd arrived home two days ago and before he could get settled, Chase had called him to let him know Emily had been trying to contact him. The only reason she couldn't, was because he had changed his number. It was one of the many things he'd changed.

But she would know soon enough, because he was on his way to her house right now. He was determined to prove his love for her and that he would be faithful to her. He had made some drastic changes and he hoped that they would be enough to win her back. Hopefully, since she was trying to reach him, it was a sign that she wanted the same thing too.

After parking his truck, he hurried into her building and pressed her bell, then tapped the door lightly. Emily had just finished getting dressed. She was bored out of her mind and decided to go for a walk. Maybe the fresh air would do her some good. Or at least get her mind off Daniel.

Opening the door, the object of her sanity was standing there looking good enough to eat.

"Danny!" she called out, breathless. Her heart was beating a mile a minute and her kitty jumped reminding her of how long it's been since he'd been inside her.

Daniel smiled. "Hello, Em."

When she only stared at him, he reached out and let his fingers glide across her cheek.

"Can I come in for a minute?"

Embarrassed that she was standing there looking like an idiot, she opened the door wider. "Of course. Yes, come on in."

In the living room, he glanced around remembering the last time he was there. He shook the bad memory off and turned to her.

"You look good," he said, taking in her grey coat, jeans and grey snow boots. "If you need to be somewhere I can come back," he said when he realized she was dressed to leave.

"What? Oh, no. I was only going for a walk. Get some fresh air and stuff." *Wow, you sound lonely.*

He smiled. "Are you sure?"

She nodded. "Yeah. I'm sure."

"Good, because I wanted to talk to you about that night. About all of it, and I want to start by saying I'm sorry. I was a total idiot and I was wrong. I was wrong about how I handled everything and I was wrong for walking away from you. I shouldn't have let you leave without trying to fix this. To fix us. I shouldn't have given up on us."

"I hurt you twice by not handling my past better and letting it come between us. But, Emily," he closed the gap between them and took her hands in his. "If you give me another chance I will do everything in my power to show you that you can trust me. That it's okay to love me and let down your guard. I know I've messed up big time, but I won't again. That's a promise that I know I'll keep. I just need you to let me."

His apology, and everything he said, coupled with the pleading look in his eyes, was music to her ears. The funny thing is she was prepared to take him back months ago. His apology only made the make-up sweeter.

Eyes filled with tears, she threw herself into his arms and captured his lips in a heated kiss. Daniel's arms wrapped around her immediately and he held on to her closely. Their tongues met and passion between them flared to life once again.

The kiss ended amongst tears, heavy breathing and soft touches.

"I missed you so much, Em. So much," he repeated in a whisper, his forehead resting on hers.

"I missed you too, Danny. I don't want to fight anymore," she said sniffling.

"Me either, baby. I swear, everything will be alright from now on. As a matter fact." He took a step back from her. "I want to show you something."

Emily looked up at him, a slight smile on her face. "Show me what?"

He grinned with excitement. *I missed that smile.* "Come on," he said, taking her hand and pulling her towards the door. "Let's go for a ride."

I'd rather ride you. "Okay."

About twenty five minutes later he pulled over in a busy section of Manhattan. Manhattan is the heart of New York and was always busy. The area they were in was surrounded by an assortment of eateries and theaters. It was the number one stopping place for tourist.

He got out the truck first and came around to help Emily. After locking the truck doors, he took her hand and they walked about half a block before stopping in front of a building that was boarded up.

"Here we are," he said, nodding towards the boards."

Emily glanced at the boards and then back at him. "And what is this?" she asked, confused.

Daniel laughed. "Come with me." He unlocked the door and entered, pulling her right behind him.

First she had to adjust her eyes to the dim lighting, but once she was able to see, she gasped.

"Oh my goodness."

Inside, the place was huge and immaculate. There were high ceilings with large chandeliers showing off hundreds of lights. The floors were grey marble with great pillars throughout each room. The boards were covering the new glass in the vast windows. Although everything was beautiful, nothing would outshine the enormous fish tank built into the wall. It stretched the entire wall in the area. Beautiful fish were already inside swimming around. It was like nothing she'd even seen before.

"Do you like it?" asked Daniel.

The awe on her face gave a hint as to what her answer would be. "I love it, but wait..." she spun around to look at him. "Is this going to be your new restaurant?"

He smiled broadly. "Yeah. I wanted you to see it first."

"But how will you run it from Virginia? Isn't it crucial for you to be here at the beginning?"

"Yeah, you're right. Here, let me show you how."

Taking her hand, he left the building and locked it. Seconds later they were back in the truck heading out of the shopping area. She watched as he headed towards Lincoln Tunnel.

"Are we going to PA?" she asked, smiling.

"Nope. Califon, New Jersey."

"What's in Califon, New Jersey?" she asked, fishing for answers.

"You'll see. Why don't you put some music on and relax."

That's exactly what she did. The time passed by fast and they were close to their destination in a little over an hour. She was in awe of the neighborhood they were driving through. The houses there were as big as her parents, or bigger.

Daniel turned onto Indian Lane and pulled into the driveway of a lovely home. Emily eyes were wide as she stared at the enormous house that sat on a slight incline with acres of land around it. *I wonder who lives here.*

She was shocked when they got to the front porch and he pulled out a key and opened the door. When they walked in, the first thing she noticed was the curved staircase. It was jet black with intricate design work on the banister. It easily dominated the front hall entrance.

Looking to her left, she saw that there wasn't any furniture in the room. However, there was a gigantic Christmas tree in the corner near a black brick fireplace. Daniel walked towards the tree beckoning her to follow.

"Danny, should we be in here?" she asked, looking over her shoulder expecting someone to come out yelling for them to get out.

He saw that she was nervous and took her hand. "It's fine, Em. I brought you here to answer your question about how I would be able to get to be at the restaurant all the time to run it." He looked around the room and then back at her. "I bought this place not too long ago. That way I'll be closer to my business. But most importantly, I'll be closer to you."

"You bought this house?" she asked, looking around the room and then through the window that showed off an exceptional mountain view.

He was looking at her intently, trying to weigh her mood.

"It's gorgeous. And big," she said, smiling. *Now I can see him as much as I want. He'll only be an hour away.*

He laughed. *Big enough for a family.*

"You know I missed you for Christmas because you were in Russia, but I held on to your gift." He reached over onto the tree and pulled off a small, brightly wrapped box with a yellow bow.

Emily took the gift cheesing. When she opened it, she saw that it held a silver key. She looked at him curiously. "What's it for?"

"I'm glad you asked. Come on. I'll show you."

Daniel pulled her out of the house and helped her back into the truck. He then drove her right back to the same block his restaurant was on. Once there, he parked across the street in front of a smaller building. They were standing there at the door and he turned to her smiling.

"Now use the key."

With shaking hands, she unlocked the door and when she stepped in she stopped. Inside the building had bright white walls, circular windows and blue tiled floors. There were several doors leading off the room they stood in and they all were closed.

"Danny, what is this place?" she asked softly.

"It's your new music school."

She swung around to face him. "My what?"

"It's your dream, Em. It's your music school. It's for you to do what you love without anyone holding your future in their hands. Don't you like it?" He began to worry when she didn't respond.

Emily spun back around and gawked at the interior of the building. It was even more beautiful than she'd imagined in her dreams. Behind those doors could be classrooms, a small eating area, her office. *Oh wow. I'm going to have my own office.*

She spun back around with a big goofy smile on her face. "Oh my goodness, Danny. I love it," she said as she felt the first tear run down her cheek.

He took a step towards her. "Are you sure, because you're crying."

She laughed and threw her arms around his waist. "It's because I'm happy. These are happy tears, silly."

Feeling relieved, he tightened his hold around her. "Good. I plan on keeping you happy."

"Can I look around?"

"Go ahead. It's yours."

After touring the building and seeing her oohing and aahing over everything, he ended the tour and had her to lock the door. She was still smiling and he couldn't help but laugh.

"Come on woman. We have dinner reservations."

"Where, Vera's?" she asked grinning.

"No, greedy. It's a surprise. But it's in Virginia."

At the airport they boarded Miki's jet and sat back relaxing. Emily thanked him again for her Christmas gift. She wanted to say that it was too much, but she really loved it and wanted to keep it. During the flight, she talked about all the things she wanted to put in the school. Daniel just sat there smiling, loving the fact that he was the one who made her happy.

When they landed in Virginia, he arranged to have his car waiting for them. Happy that the weather held up, and it was still nice out, they hopped into the car and headed towards the dock.

Daniel planned ahead, hoping she would give him another chance. He called his staff to have dinner prepared and set up on his yacht. They would dine indoors and then he would take her to a spot he found where a swarm of baby sharks swam right up to your boat hoping you'd toss something out for them to eat.

Upon arriving at the dock, Emily started to grin.

"What are you smiling at?"

"Are we getting on one of those boats," she asked, looking at the small sailing ships.

He shook his head. "No. We're getting on that yacht over there," he said, pointing to the large black boat.

"Oh shoot," she said, staring at the boat. "It's huge."

"Don't worry. We're not going out too far. I want to show you the shark bay area. It's an area about a mile away where a bunch of sharks hang out at night to feed. We'll have dinner first, relax a bit, then check out the sharks. Unless you would rather eat at Vera's. I can call her and—"

"No! This is fine. I want to see the sharks," she said, excitedly.

"Okay. Let's go."

On the boat, everything was done in black and white. The living area consisted of a VIP stateroom, including living room, bedroom, bathroom and a large balcony. It also housed three large double staterooms, each with its own bathroom, luxury interior and LCD TV. There were two men standing inside the living room waiting to serve them. Saying the boat was fantastic was an understatement.

It was still early evening and the sky was still bright, so they sat down to enjoy their dinner that had been set up and kept warm by his staff who kept out of sight.

After dinner, Daniel and Emily were cuddled up on the couch. Suddenly, he got up and pulled out the Violin that he'd got her for her birthday. "You left this at the house in the closet. I thought I'd bring it along tonight. Maybe you'd play something for me?" he asked hesitantly.

She looked at him and then at the violin. Without saying a word, she stood and took the violin from his hands. Daniel pulled a wide foot stool over for her to sit on. She sat perched on the edge of the stool facing him as he slowly eased back down onto the couch.

All the times he'd heard her play, this would be the first time she'd play for him, and him alone.

Emily played for Daniel and he watched her speechless. He had seen her play many times, never missing one of her performances, but to have her here playing only for him was unreal. Dreamlike. She had her eyes half closed and was looking directly at him. He felt every note pass through him. It was a musical high and he was addicted.

Before she took the violin from his hands, she already knew what she would play for him. Emily played the song she wrote and had been having trouble with for months. She prayed that she wouldn't mess up in front of him. God must have been listening to her today, because the song played out beautifully. She paused and glided her bow over the violin creating a beautiful melody that hinted of deep emotional need and new found love.

It was by far the best day of his life. When she completed the song he sat staring at her, fascinated and captivated. He didn't move until he saw her place the violin on the stool and stand. He stood and closed the distance between them.

Daniel bent his head and took her lips in a kiss that held promises. The slight pressure of their lower bodies meeting was electrifying. It had been so long since he'd held her this close and his body was responding to it eagerly.

Emily urged him to move closer as she bunched her fingers in his shirt. He deepened the kiss and she moaned against his lips. With tongues dancing and hands exploring, it wasn't long before their clothes were removed, and they were lying on the fur covered bed in the other room.

Lying on his back, he made a move to change positions, but she stopped him. When her hands began to dip below his waist as she rained soft kisses on torso, his eyes closed enjoying her gentle teasing. However, when her fingers wrapped around his thickness he sucked in a quick breath. She steadily massaged him up and down, continuing with her kisses. When her lips softly touched the tip of his manhood, he looked down at her.

"Em, you don't have to do that," he said, knowing she'd never done it before.

"It's okay. I want to." She smiled up at him shyly. "I've been watching video's on what to do."

He let out a light chuckle, that turned into a burning moan when she opened her mouth and took him deeply into her mouth.

"Oh damnnnnn," he said, flexing his thigh muscles and curling his toes.

Emily took him in her mouth as deep as she could take him before sliding him out with a slow swirl of her tongue. When she heard him release the breath he was holding, she immediately took him in again. The rhythm she started with went from slow and curious, to intense and demanding. The jolt of ecstasy he felt when he received a strong suck or a quick jerk of her hands, was like touching heaven briefly.

His thoughts were racing all over the place. He had propped himself up with a pillow so he could watch Emily please him with her mouth, but now he wasn't sure if that was a good idea. Seeing her lick, flick, and suck him, was driving him insane. It was so erotic and sexy to see and he was having a hard time not ending things prematurely.

"Take your... ahhh. Take your time, baby. Shitttt," he croaked, when her tongue went lower and slid across his sac before covering it with her mouth. "Dammit, Em," he said, groaning.

He heard a little giggle and met her eyes. Shaking his head, he sat up and pulled her on his lap.

"I need to be inside you now," he said, and Emily lifted, then eased down slowly on his shaft.

"Mmmmm," she sighed, letting her head fall back, giving him a perfect view of her plump breast.

"That's it, baby. Take some more," he said as he rotated his hips, pressing up further.

Sucking in air through her teeth, she gripped his shoulders firmly. The feeling of him filling her was amazing. She'd missed the feeling of him invading her slick space and she wrapped her arms around his neck, nuzzling his ear. "I've missed having you inside me, Danny." She lifted and then slowly descended.

He moaned, then gritted his teeth. She was so tight. "Show me how much," he said, as he pulled her arms free of his neck, and lay back on the bed.

Emily sat on his lap with him buried deep inside her core. With a naughty smile and a quick squeezing of her vaginal muscles, she proceeded in showing him just how much.

***

Hours later they woke up together playful and fully satiated. After getting dressed, Daniel took her on deck to show her the sharks. She was so excited and he couldn't wait to share this experience with her.

"Stay right here, I'll go downstairs and turn on the lights so you can see them better."

"Okay."

Minutes later, the lights came on at the bottom of the boat creating a blue glow all around them. Daniel returned carrying a bucket filled with fish and Emily frowned.

"Yuck, that smells."

"I know, but they eat fish, woman," he said, laughing.

Grabbing a large plastic scooper, he began tossing out chunks of the fish into the water. She watched in amazement as the sharks appeared from every direction thrashing about trying to get the meat.

"Oh my goodness. This is so awesome. Look at them, Danny," she said excitedly.

He glanced over at her smiling, then back at the sharks.

"Hey baby."

Both, Emily and Daniel, turned around in disbelief at the sound of the voice they heard.

"Sherry!?"

"In the flesh!" Sherry said, stepping from the shadows.

Five days ago, Sherry was being held at the Virginia Beach Police Department. The facility had been informed via FBI, that a high profile prisoner was being transferred in temporarily, and required private accommodations, which meant a certain tier would need to be cleared for holding. A careless officer accidently added her name to the list of inmates to be moved from the tier, to the Virginia Beach Correctional Facitily.

During the transfer, a fight erupted causing confusion, and Sherry, along with two other women, managed to escape by means of the bathroom window. She slipped out of the guards eyesight and hid in the bathroom where she used the top of the toilet's tank to break the glass on the window and slipped out. She was long gone before anyone noticed she was missing.

Moving slowly, Daniel managed to maneuver himself in front of Emily.

"How are you out of jail? And what the hell are you doing on my boat?" asked Daniel. He looked Sherry up and down seeing she was still wearing the orange jumper.

"I got out early," she remarked snidely. "And I came to get what's mine," she said, glancing at Emily.

Emily ignored her last comment. "How did you know we were going to be here, on the boat?" she asked, peeking around Daniel.

Sherry nodded towards Daniel. "I've been watching this idiot for days. I didn't have a way to get back to New York, so I followed him around. When he came out here to this boat, I figured it would be a good place to lay low. Imagine my surprise when he came back today with you. Saved me the time and effort."

"I'm sorry you've wasted your time, but there's nothing here for you," said Daniel, his voice low and deadly. Emily could feel the tenseness in the muscles of his arm, and knew he was prepared for whatever Sherry would try.

Lifting the knife she carried, she turned it side to side in her hand staring down at it. "Oh, I haven't wasted my time. Emily knows who she wants. You've only been a distraction. Once I get rid of you, things will get back on track with us." Suddenly, her head snapped up and her eyes looked crazed. "I hope you said your goodbyes!" she yelled and then charged them.

Shoving Emily to the side, Daniel took the full force of her attack. His hand grabbed the wrist of the hand wielding the knife, while the other gripped the front of her jumper, yanking her to the side. Forgetting that the bucket was behind him, he tripped knocking it over, and they both fell to the deck floor. The blood from the fish was all over them, but it didn't stop them from struggling with each other.

Sherry landed several blows to Daniel and he only tried to subdue her. He wouldn't retaliate physically in any way. He was bleeding from a wide cut on his hand and leg, yet, she hadn't been harmed at all. To Emily, the fight was one sided and unfair.

She couldn't believe what she was seeing. Sherry was attacking him aggressively, and knowing he was holding back because she was a woman, she knew she had to help. Looking around for a weapon, her attention was caught by the open bottle of wine sitting on the table where they'd eaten dinner. Rushing over to get the bottle, she returned ready to use it to defend him.

Not paying attention to all the cut up fish and blood on the floor, she raised her hand to swing the bottle and slipped. Sherry had just kneed Daniel in his lower region, and turned in time to duck. She stood up and glowered at Emily. She advanced on her slowly, angry and hurt by her betrayal.

"You would choose him over me?" she asked, spit flying from her lips. "After everything I've given up for you?!" she screamed. "You made me kill my own brother!" she yelled, her whole body shaking with hostility.

Emily only stared at her, not sure what to do. She was only happy that she'd gotten her away from Daniel.

Seeing how she looked past her to Daniel with love and concern in her eyes broke Sherry's heart. In turn, it made her not want her anymore. Now she was just as much an enemy as he was.

"You were mine's first. And you know the rule, bitch," Sherry said, walking over to the speargun on the wall. "If I can't have you, no one can."

Sherry lifted the gun, aimed it at Emily, and pulled the trigger.

Daniel saw when Sherry pulled the speargun from the rack on the wall. He managed to get to his feet, and without slipping, ran in her direction. The spear tore through the flesh of his shoulder, but he didn't stop. He continued to run in her direction, knocking them both over the railing.

"Noooooo!"

Emily ran over to the railing peering over its side. She could see where they fell into the water, but didn't see either of them.

"Danny!" she continued to search. "Danny!"

No answer. And then she saw something that made her blood run cold. The sharks, tasting the blood in the water, had returned.

Oh my God! Lord, if you're listening right now, please don't let him die. Help me to find him, Lord, she prayed as her eyes continued to search the area. Moving to her right, her foot tripped over something and she fell. Scrambling to get back to her feet, she saw that she had tripped over a thin rope. The rope was attached to an electric winch that would reel in a fish. The other end of the rope was overboard attached to the spear that was in Daniel's shoulder.

Running over to the winch, she pressed the button to turn it on and then pushed the handle up to reel it in. When the rope started moving she ran back over to the railing. She grabbed the rope in her hands and started pulling with all her strength. Her hands were raw and bleeding, but she didn't stop.

She heard voices on the radio calling Daniel's name and then from out in the distance over the water, but she never stopped pulling the rope. When she finally saw his body emerge from the water, she began to cry. As he was brought up higher, she assisted the winch in getting him aboard. She then ran to hit the stop button.

Although he was now safe on the boat, he was barely breathing. She was holding him tightly, tears rolling freely down her face, dropping on his head. She said nothing. She only held him, rocking back and forth.

"Stop right there! Don't move!" yelled the Coast Guards.

Emily looked up briefly to see Sherry had emerged a little further away from the boat. When she began to swim towards them, shots rang out hitting her several times. Her body began to sink in the water and the sharks began their attack.

In a dream state, she remembered seeing Myka and Sydney climbing aboard the boat. It took some doing, but they finally convinced her to let Daniel go so he could receive medical attention. She let him go, but she was always close by. She watched the medics work on him, while one of them bandaged her hands.

It turns out that Myka had someone keeping an eye on Sherry, and when she escaped, he had come running knowing she would go for Emily. Sydney had already been in town helping Daniel out with the restaurant. It was pure luck that Sydney had been the one to help set up the boat, while he'd gone to New York to get her.

"Emily!" Daniel called out as soon as he gained consciousness. "Emily!"

Emily came barreling through the police and EMT's and almost knocked Myka into the water trying to get to his side.

"I'm here, Danny!" she called out. "I'm here," she said, leaning over to kiss him.

Daniel took her hand and held on to it for dear life.

"Stay close," he mumbled. The pain in his arm and hand was burning like hell.

"I'm not going anywhere. I promise."

Angel B

Epilogue

The dim lights in the apartment and the classic love songs playing on the stereo, set the mood just right as they danced together back at her apartment. They had only returned an hour ago from a Valentine's Day party at Arnez house. A few days had gone by since everything with Sherry had taken place. Her death was unfortunate, but Daniel would have done anything to keep Emily safe, even risking his own life.

Now he stood holding the woman he loved and felt nothing but peace. He sighed loudly near her ear, feeling relaxed and comfortable.

Emily was feeling the same way. Although she hated that Sherry had lost her life, the need to protect Daniel outweighed any choice in who was more important. There was no remorse. She was only saddened that her brother Carl had lost his life in her madness.

Wanting to shake off the gloominess she felt overcoming her, she excused herself and returned quickly. Daniel wondered what she'd been doing, but he shrugged his shoulders, not caring now that she'd come back.

"Em, can I ask you something?" he asked, pulling her back into his arms.

"Mmm hmm." She allowed him to hold her close as she inhaled his cologne and sighed. *Damn, he smells good.*

"Why did you become a lesbian?"

Emily burst out laughing against his chest.

"What? I'm curious. I'v always wanted to know," he said, smiling. He placed a warm kiss on her ear.

"It seemed like the right thing since I didn't have any attraction to any guys. Plus, I was always surrounded by women. I went to an all girls school where almost everyone was gay, so I kind of fell into step with everyone else. I've kissed women before, and I've had sex with a few. I just never went all the way, meaning I've never been penetrated. I wouldn't allow it."

"I knew about you being gay. I overheard you and Micheal talking about it a long time ago. I believe it was when you made a pass at Kayla at the dinner table."

"Really?" she asked, grinning. "You remember that?"

"Yup." They looked at each other and laughed.

"You know my Dad once told me that someday, someone would walk into my life and make me realize why it never worked out with anyone else. I believe that day came true for me when you came back from college and you were wearing that fitted white dress and high strappy heels. Your body looked damn good, and I wanted to run my hands all over you. Your hair was cut short, just like now, and it was shiny and soft."

"I was useless to every woman afterwards from that day. All because of you, Em." He pushed a soft curl behind her ear. "All because of you."

"How do you think I felt going out with women, yet dreaming of a man every night. It got so bad that I couldn't even concentrate at work. All I could think about was you. Your smile, your eyes..." her voice trailed off. "And when you danced with me at your mother's events, I could feel every part of you."

"Did you like what you felt?"

She moved in closer, pressing into the hardness she felt between them even now.

"Yes. It was incredible. It made me yearn for something I never knew I had a hunger for."

Daniel leaned down and kissed her.

"Am I the first man you've ever kissed?" he asked while looking into her eyes.

"Yes," she responded, breathlessly.

"Am I going to be the last man to do so?" he asked looking deeply into her eyes.

"Yes. This will definitely be my last first kiss. But there's only one way to make sure of that."

Reaching into her pocket, Emily pulled out a black velvet box and opened it, revealing a wide gold band with three sparkling diamonds. She took his hand in hers and slid the ring onto his finger. She smiled when she saw how well it fit.

She looked up into his dark eyes, smiling. "Daniel Christopher Tase, will you marry me?"

Daniel smiled and then shook his head. He reached into his own pocket and pulled out a white leather box, and when he opened it, inside was a beautifully cut diamond ring. He grabbed her hand and slid the ring onto her small finger.

"I was just about to ask you the same thing, but you beat me... Again."

Emily's smile broadened. "Well, you know I like to win," she said laughing. "And yes, I will definitely marry you, Danny."

Daniel pulled her tightly in his arms, burying his face in the side of her neck.

"I think we both win this time baby."

Angel B

SEND MONEY ORDER/CHECK TO:

DYNASTY VISIONARY
PUBLICATIONS

Dynasty Visionary Publication
4 S Pine LN - BLDG 9
Newark, NJ 07107

NAME		
ADDRESS		
CITY		
STATE	ZIP	
EMAIL		

BOOK TITLE	PRICE EACH	QUANTITY	TOTAL
LOVING RAINY DAYS: VOL 1	14.00		
MICHAEL'S HEAT: VOL 2	14.00		
UP FOR THE CHASE: VOL 3	14.00		
THE LAST FIRST KISS: VOL 4	14.00		
CHILD SUPPORT	14.00		
UNSTABLE CREATURE	14.00		
ACCUSATIONS	14.00		

FOR SHIPPING PLEASE ADD $3.00 PER BOOK TITLE	TOTAL	
	SHIPPING & HANDLING	
THANK YOU FOR YOUR BUSINESS	FINAL TOTAL	

298

www.ingramcontent.com/pod-product-compliance
Lightning Source LLC
Chambersburg PA
CBHW060534180626
46817CB00002B/561